TREASURE HUNT
A MAIDEN HARLOW MYSTERY – BOOK 5
CAMILLE SHARP

CONTENTS

Chapter One

It was a cold and blustery Saturday night in Golden Glen, Michigan. Maiden Harlow was sitting at a table for two in one of the nicer restaurants downtown. Soft music played in the background and a trio of candles sat on the table adding a romantic warmth to the intimate atmosphere.

She was there on her first date with Captain David McAlister, the head of the local police department. The months of flirtation, second-guessing and undeniably raw attraction had all culminated in this perfectly planned evening. And David had spent the last ten minutes of it standing in a corner talking on his phone.

Maiden smoothed her hands down over her silky skirt. She'd dressed very carefully for the date, determined to look her best. As far as she could tell it had worked; when David first saw her walk in his eyes widened and he almost dropped his waterglass. It had been a good start to the evening.

He'd pulled out her chair for her and ordered a bottle of wine. They'd exchanged a few smiling glances and had barely started chitchatting about what they'd both been doing that day when his phone rang. David ignored it at first, but then it rang again. And again. Even when he'd put it on silent it kept buzzing away on the table where he'd set it.

Maiden wasn't thrilled by the intrusion but she wasn't unreasonable either. He was the highest-ranking police officer in town and someone was trying very hard to get his attention. She'd finally relented and suggested that he just answer it. He'd murmured an apology and walked across the room to take the call.

She'd spent the next few minutes watching his body language subtly. His suddenly grim expression, combined with how long the discussion was lasting, told her that it wasn't good news.

Maiden sighed softly and tapped her nails on the menu that sat in front of her; she was growing increasingly certain that she wasn't going to be needing it tonight. While it was very disappointing, she was also curious about what had happened.

It had been a week or so since she'd helped expose another maniacal murderer. Although far from wrapped up, the case was solved. It seemed unlikely that anyone would bother their boss on a Saturday night over a killer that was already behind bars. This call had to be about something else. Something that must have been quite bad.

David slid his phone back into his pocket and pinched the bridge of his nose before glancing over at her. She saw the undeniable look of regret in his eyes and couldn't help smiling. That understanding expression seemed to give him the encouragement he needed to walk back to the table.

"I take it the evening's over?" she asked. "For us at least?"

"I'm so sorry, Maiden," he said quietly. "I have to go. They've found a body."

"Really?" She felt a little badly that she wasn't more surprised, but his demeanor was too serious for it to be much else. "Where?"

"In a parked car across town." He lifted his brows a fraction. "Raincheck? Again?"

"Yeah, I think I can manage that," she said with a faint smile.

***

David wasn't in the best of moods as he drove to the crime scene. He wasn't sure what sort of fanciful cosmic forces seemed to get twitchy whenever he and Maiden found a few minutes alone together, but he was getting very tired of the stupid interruptions.

He shook his head at his nonsensical grumblings. Obviously getting murdered was worse than having to call off a highly-anticipated date, but it didn't make it any less frustrating.

Sergeant Ramirez had reported that a man's body had been found in his car in the industrial corner of town known as the Eastern Quarter. The area was mostly populated with warehouses, along with a few derelict factories interspersed among one or two that were still operating. Golden Glen wasn't an industrial hub anymore, but some fragments of its past were still hanging around.

Once he'd turned onto the main street it wasn't hard to find what he was looking for. The flashing lights of a few patrol cars intermittently stained the brick exteriors of the surrounding warehouses with shades of red and blue. In the midst of all the commotion, a large black car was being carefully scrutinized.

By the time David had parked and approached the scene, Doc Jenkins had stood from where he'd been examining the backseat of the suspicious car. He wore his usual hazmat suit and his gloves were stained with blood. David gave him a nod of greeting as he neared.

"Good evening, David." Jenkins smiled faintly as he looked him over. "You're rather dapper this evening; I doubt it's out of consideration for any of us."

"As astute as ever, Doc," David replied. "Spare me, I'm not thrilled with life in general at the moment."

"You've got it far better than some," Jenkins retorted as he gestured towards the backseat of the big black car. "This unfortunate man, for instance."

David peered inside and saw a man's body slumped back against the seat. His head was tilted back and his lifeless eyes stared up at the roof. His hair brushed his shoulders and a scraggly beard obscured his chin and half of his throat. The man wore a cheap suit and a faded shirt that was utterly ruined by a massive bloodstain. The red pool had sprawled across his chest leaving little question of the cause of death.

"Shot?"

"Yes, and from close range," Jenkins confirmed. "I haven't finished prodding around yet, but I don't see any other signs of violence so far."

At that point Ramirez walked over and joined them. He gave David an apologetic look.

"Sorry to ruin your night, Captain," he said.

"Yeah," David didn't want to dwell on that and so moved the subject along quickly. He glanced around the rest of the backseat. "Who reported it?"

"A night watchman from the warehouse next door," Ramirez explained as he gestured towards a rather shaken man that was standing several yards away babbling to a few officers. "He said he'd noticed the car parked outside the warehouse he was patrolling and went to check it out. He said he shone his flashlight inside, saw the blood, and called the station immediately."

"Interesting...looks like whoever did it wasn't after money," David mused as he looked everything over.

The car had been searched; the glove compartment had been left open and its contents spilled out, the center console was the same.

Most telling, however, was that the victim's wallet and a fair bit of cash had been pulled out and dropped on the floor at his feet.

"So it would seem," Jenkins murmured. "He's got a fairly substantial gold chain still around his neck too."

"Any ID?" David asked, pointing at the wallet but refraining from touching it with ungloved hands.

"Yes, apparently his name is Charles Brown." Ramirez checked his notes. "Originally from the UK, Scotland specifically. We don't know too much more about him yet."

"Not the nicest welcome to the US he could've gotten," David sighed as he looked around the darkened rows of warehouses on either side of the street. They looked silent and empty. "All right, keep digging. Let's see if we can't find out what the killer was looking for."

***

Maiden's Saturday had finished on a definite low note and Sunday was just as quiet. Writing off the entire weekend after having looked forward to it eagerly wasn't a dream come true. By Monday afternoon, however, Maiden had accepted it and gotten on with her normal routine. Even now she was stationed behind the reception desk of the family's inn, Harlow House.

Apart from a few apologetic texts from David, she didn't hear anything more about the murderous incident that had ruined their date. She wondered who the victim was, so far nothing had made it into the newspaper. The Golden Glen Gazette wasn't exactly a beacon of journalistic grit or the dogged pursuit of unbiased truth, but they typically managed to at least get wind of murder.

Maiden had a feeling that the police had really clamped down on what got leaked to the press, particularly considering the local rag's tendency to praise her as an infamous amateur detective. She'd had plenty of attention lavished on her in recent months, it wasn't unearned but it did tend to ignore the efforts of the local police department.

David had never complained to her about it, and it really wasn't her fault, but it had to bother him at least a little. An untrained civilian kept being credited with solving his biggest cases, it would be embarrassing, it had to be. She assumed it would bother her a bit if she were in his shoes.

In any case, she hadn't heard anything more about this latest killing and that seemed strange. For all she knew it was a deer that had been hit by a car. The only thing that was certain was that, if it was an actual human murder, it couldn't stay hidden for long.

She was staring out the large front windows at the bare trees blowing in the late October wind and tried not to feel bored. It didn't help that it was a quiet day, the phone had barely rung and the guests all seemed content. There wasn't even a request for extra towels to break up the tedium.

She wondered what David was doing, probably something interesting that she wasn't allowed to know about. She was still toying with sending him a message when her mother wandered out of the dining room.

Gloria's bouncy blonde curls were pinned high on her head and her bright orange sweater nearly glowed amid the subdued tones of the room. She rested her hands on her wide hips and looked around at the quietly elegant foyer. Her warm brown eyes narrowed critically as she seemed to be searching for anything out of place.

Maiden watched her a tad uneasily. The older woman was looking for trouble and that was very unlike her. But both of her parents had been acting strangely for the last few days, even for them. Quirky eccentricities she was used to, it was part of Alfie and Gloria's charm, but this was different.

They were restless and twitchy. They'd become increasingly secretive too. Going out for hours and then slinking back in without saying much about where they'd been or what they were doing. It was strange behavior from the normally genial and chatty pair.

Maiden frowned as she considered the events of the past week. They'd all given their official statements regarding the grisly murders that had marred her Aunt Bella's recent wedding. Bella had gone back to Florida to deal with some legalities regarding her new family's estate and had welcomed the distraction. None of it was very pleasant but it seemed like the time for all of them to pull together, not act shifty.

Maiden pursed her lips and studied her mother with a quizzical scowl. Of course Gloria had been shaken up by her sister's brush with a maniacal killer and the law, but it was even before Bella had left that Alfie and Gloria went quiet and furtive.

Maiden wished she knew what was going on. Her parents had never made her feel so shut out before and she didn't like it. She forced her thoughts, or at least her expression, to calm as her mother approached the desk.

"Well," Gloria released a dissatisfied huff, "another slow day. That's fine, I suppose."

"We're almost fully booked," Maiden pointed out. "I wouldn't really say it's 'slow'."

"No, but everything's under control," Gloria said. "This place seems to run itself these days."

"It's not like I'm doing nothing!" Maiden protested even as she subtly hid the book she'd been reading. "What would you prefer? Complaints pouring in right and left? A gas leak in the kitchen?"

"I wasn't sayin' I didn't like it." Gloria waved a pudgy hand at her. "I was just thinkin' out loud."

"About what?" Maiden asked, doubting she'd actually tell her very much.

"This and that," she said evasively. "We could almost hire some reception staff at this rate. No need for all of us to be tied to the desk every day."

Maiden felt her dark brows climb her forehead. Her mother had never considered hiring additional staff before; she'd always shot down the suggestion on the rare occasions that it had come up. She'd always insisted that the family business was theirs to nurture and grow. According to her, no one else could ever love the place the way they did.

"It's never been an issue before," Maiden said cautiously. "Are you and Dad getting tired or something?"

"Of course not!" Gloria gasped and then scowled. "We're not a pair of old fogeys!"

"I'll say," she replied with a smile. "You've been out late for the last three nights. Are you staying in tonight, by any chance?"

"No, we got plans with an old friend tonight." Gloria abruptly turned towards the stairs.

"What old friend?" she asked loudly.

"Fred," Gloria said over her shoulder as she made her escape. "Don't wait up."

Maiden pulled a face and propped her chin in her hands. She noticed that her mother quietly assumed that she'd be home herself. She would be, but she didn't appreciate that it was being taken for granted. Her thoughts drifted to David again.

They'd met a few months ago when two murders had been committed in Harlow House. Since then they'd met up on several other murder cases and cultivated a very strong and very mutual attraction. That had made Saturday's disruption even more frustrating.

After all the tension, teasing and flirting, David had had to walk out before the night had really begun. She couldn't help feeling letdown.

In all fairness though, someone had apparently been murdered. A cancelled date really wasn't all that horrible in comparison.

She shook her head and looked around for some useful means of distracting herself. Gloria hadn't exaggerated; the inn had become quite efficient. There wasn't as much to do through the day as there used to be and, at times like this, it was a little annoying.

Maiden started rummaging through the desk, hoping she could organize some of the old forms and get rid of anything they didn't need anymore. She stopped and pulled a face when she opened a drawer and spied the top of a glossy, full color brochure tucked into yesterday's newspaper.

She pulled the items out and looked them over. What got her immediate attention was an article in the Golden Glen Gazette that had been circled in red ink.

What Have We Let Into Our Precious Town?

One of Golden Glen's most neglected historical treasures has fallen prey to greedy commercialism. The Old Chateau is the latest victim of the modern-day cash grab. Fred Eilers, the infamous owner and founder of the hotel chain Eilers' Arms has muscled his way into our sleepy little slice of small-town paradise.

The arrival of a bloodless, big-city conglomerate is chilling, but we have only ourselves to blame. The glory of the Old Chateau has long been taken for granted and now the lush and romantic historical wonder has been snapped up and comprehensively ruined. The charms we could barely be bothered to notice are lost forever because of our own neglect.

Maiden smiled faintly at the writer's dismal musings. The article droned on, lamenting that the beloved Old Chateau had been forgotten and abandoned to the point that it was sold for a pittance and left to the twisted clutches of some commercial and amoral megalomaniac.

Excerpts from an interview with Fred Eilers were quoted throughout and doubtless cherry-picked to portray him as a wealthy developer with no poetry in his heart and no appreciation for history or small towns.

"Fred?" Maiden wondered aloud as she lowered the paper.

Gloria had said that they were going to be out that evening with a friend named Fred. It was hardly an uncommon name, but the marked article made it seem like less of a coincidence.

She shifted her attention to the brochure. As she looked at the picture on the cover she gasped loudly. It said Eilers' Arms on the front, but it couldn't possibly be the same building that had once been the Old Chateau.

"Wow, that is...blue," she whispered to herself as she stared.

The Gazette's unflattering account, while perhaps harsh, wasn't exactly wrong. The site of the rundown and derelict Old Chateau was now an awkwardly glowing beacon complete with bright blue render and windows shaped like massive portholes.

Maiden turned the page but it didn't get any better. The photos of the interior were festooned—there was no other way to describe it—*festooned* with rusty anchors, waitresses dressed in mermaid costumes and walls draped in neon fishing nets tangled around plastic crabs.

Maiden pressed her lips together and tried to be kind. It occurred to her that this place was competition, there was a chance that the novelty would draw a lot of people in. She read through a bit of the blurb in hopes of gauging the threat.

Apparently Eilers Arms had 60 guestrooms and a world-class kitchen. There was a full restaurant and a separate bar with the promise of live music every weekend. Whether that meant a full band, an amateur solo performer with dreams of fame or a grade-school kid with a kazoo, it failed to specify.

Maiden shook her head and looked at the cover again. A banner at the top announced the grand opening, it was that coming Friday. She wondered why the brochure was in the drawer along with the scathing article.

Even if this Fred Eilers was the friend Gloria had referred to, it seemed odd that they'd collect and keep negative publicity about him. Unless they were a bit worried about a risk to their own business.

She turned to the computer and checked the forward bookings. They were reasonably full, there were a few vacancies but those would hopefully fill as the winter festivals drew closer.

Maiden glanced up as her sister stepped out of the office and joined her behind the desk. Vonny was smiling far more brightly than usual as she slid in beside her. In fact, Vonny had grown content to the point of blissfulness lately.

She was fortunate enough to be dating the man she'd had a crush on since elementary school, and they were almost sickeningly happy together. Tony Ferris was a long-time friend to them both, he was also the kindest and most patient guy Maiden had ever personally met.

She loved him like a big brother, but Vonny loved him rather differently. Despite the occasional, and steadfastly silent, concern that Tony was a little too gentle for someone as prone to stubbornness as Von, Maiden had always been very happy for them.

"There's my little sister!" Vonny said cheerfully, she'd been remarkably cheerful lately. "How are you?"

"I'm fine." Maiden turned back to the newspaper and skimmed through the article again. "You?"

"Great!" Vonny said happily. "Tony's taking me to a new restaurant downtown tonight. It's a sushi bar! I didn't know it was even there until he insisted that we check it out. What about you? What are you doing tonight?"

"I don't really have any plans," she replied with a patient smile. "But I hope you have a good time, I didn't realize you liked sushi."

"I've actually never tried it. But don't tell Tony that." Von gave her a quietly fearful look. "I don't want to make him feel bad, and I'm pretty sure I'm going to get sick on raw fish."

"I'm sure the chef knows what they're doing." Maiden chuckled.

"Yeah...probably." Vonny fidgeted uneasily. "Do you want to come?"

"And watch you two make kissy faces while you feed each other fish eggs?" Maiden pulled a face. "I'll pass, but thanks."

"Oh don't!" Vonny put a hand to her mouth and tried not to look as horrified as she probably felt. "I'm gonna die of fish poisoning!"

"At least you'll go adventurously." Maiden was laughing at her now.

"You're a riot." She rolled her eyes but then slid her a look. "Nothing from McAlister today?"

"No," she sighed and rested her elbows on the desk. "He'll be busy with this murder."

"You're not helping him?" she asked with a slight shake of her head. "Don't you always end up helping him with murder cases?"

"Due to circumstances, I was involved a few times...every time. But this is different, I don't even know who died." Maiden admitted. "It's got nothing to do with me this time around."

"Yeah but..." Von trailed off as she tried to come up with a valid reason for Maiden to get involved. She clearly had nothing, unfortunately she didn't give up easily. "You'd think he'd want you around as eye candy anyway!"

"Wow." Maiden just stared at her.

"Sorry, I'm still worried about the raw fish. It's affecting my judgement," Von said apologetically.

"Anyway," Maiden hurried to change the subject, "Mom said something about hiring staff to help run the desk. Has she said anything like that to you?"

"Staff?" Von blinked at her. "No! Since when do we need anyone else to help run this joint? We're not exactly rushed off our feet."

"No, we're not." Maiden chewed at her thumbnail. "Have you noticed that they've been acting weird for a few days?"

"A little, yeah," Von said in a quasi-bluffing tone that suggested she hadn't really been paying that much attention but didn't want to admit it. "What do you think is going on?"

"It might be nothing," Maiden said, although she didn't believe that for a second. "It was kind of odd, but she may have just been throwing some ideas around."

"Maybe. Hey, speaking of odd." Von nudged her with her elbow. "Have you heard about the new hotel downtown? Eilers' Arms?"

"Just now." Maiden held up the brochure. "It's not exactly subtle, is it?"

"We're going to find out," Von said dryly. "Did Mom tell you we're all invited to the grand opening?"

"What?" Maiden's eyes widened. "No, she certainly didn't! Since when do we go to parties celebrating the competition?"

"We're starting Friday, apparently." Vonny smiled and gave her a teasing look. "So, tell Captain Cutie-Pie he'd better be available."

"Hopefully before then..." Maiden slid her gaze away but didn't finish the thought.

The front door opened before Vonny could venture her own opinion. They both glanced over when Tony walked in and smiled at them.

"Good afternoon, ladies," he said nicely as he came and stood in front of them at the desk. "How are things?"

"We were talking about the grand opening of that new hotel, Eilers' Arms," Maiden said as she pushed the brochure towards him.

"And I was telling Mae that the captain had better get his butt in gear so he can take her," Vonny said happily as she leaned over the desk enough to plant a kiss on Tony's cheek.

"Ease up there, Von," Tony advised gently as he gave her chin an affectionate little pinch. "This murder sounds like a weird one. I was actually hoping to ask your opinion of it, Maiden."

"Mine?" She shook her head a little. "I don't have one, I don't even know anything about it."

"What?!" He gaped at her, both shocked and undeniably disappointed. "But Greg said you were with David when he got the call!"

"He didn't tell her anything." Von flicked him an unimpressed look. "He just dumped her and ran."

"Slight exaggeration," Maiden said but smiled at her sister's loyal annoyance on her behalf. She glanced back at Tony. "I take it *you* know all the news that's worth knowing?"

Tony had a knack for picking up the most interesting tidbits of gossip from all over town. He'd been a postal worker for years now and that had enabled him to construct a network of people that he saw often enough to form bonds with. They liked to talk and Tony liked to listen.

"The victim's name was Charles Brown. He was one of the touring managers for a Scottish folk band that's just arrived in Golden Glen." Tony held Maiden's gaze and lowered his voice a fraction as he leaned closer. "He was shot through the heart in the backseat of his own car and left there until someone came along and found him."

"Nobody heard the shot?" Vonny arched a brow dubiously.

"No one's come forward. But the killer could've used a silencer," Tony suggested. "Or if anyone did hear it they may have been afraid to get involved."

"Maybe...where was the car found?" Maiden asked as she pretended to read the brochure again.

"Parked outside a warehouse in the Eastern Quarter." Tony almost whispered, glancing around furtively.

"And on a Saturday night?" Maiden added and glanced briefly at Von. "There probably weren't a lot of people around to hear a shot."

"Well, someone found the body." She shrugged.

"That's true," Maiden agreed. "But he may have been there for a while before he was found. The police will have to check all of that stuff out. It takes time."

"Sounds like you're making excuses for David to turn you down." Von smirked.

"Oh, don't be mean, Vonny." Tony gave her a sad look that instantly shut her up. "I'm sure the captain will go if he can, he wasn't happy about the interruption to their date either. Greg said he was really cranky all day yesterday."

Maiden opted not to comment on that, although she was slightly heartened to hear it. And in spite of her genuinely realizing that she wasn't involved in this latest murder, she couldn't help wondering about it.

"So, did Greg say if they suspect anyone in particular yet?" Maiden asked as casually as she could.

"No, he couldn't talk too freely," Tony almost grumbled. "Officer Parker came into the lobby then and he clammed up. I think she's kinda strict with protocol and stuff."

"Yeah, I think she is," Maiden said.

"But that's not the really weird part." Tony braced his elbows on the desk, Maiden and Vonny did the same. "The guy was shot, his pockets rifled, but his wallet and all his money were just thrown on the floor. He even had a gold chain left around his neck. Whoever killed him was looking for something, and it wasn't money."

"That is weird," Maiden said quietly.

"Yeah," Tony nodded and then a smile lit his face. "Are you going to ask David about it?"

"I hadn't planned to, and I doubt he'd appreciate me prying." Maiden withheld a sigh. "Were you just hoping I'd scab more information for you?"

"No, of course not!" He stood up straight and waved it away lightly. "But if you *do* happen to find anything out, I'm here for you."

Maiden laughed at him and sat back. Tony was an incorrigible gossip, but he was such a sweet guy that it never seemed to annoy anyone, herself included. She gathered up the newspaper and brochure and was about to throw them back in the drawer when Tony pointed to them.

"That's trouble too, by the way," he said with certainty. "Mr. Eilers is ruffling some major feathers in some pretty stodgy circles."

"Great, the grand opening is sure to be a barrel of laughs," Maiden chuckled.

"It's going to be trouble," Tony said seriously. "Big trouble."

Chapter Two

David sighed loudly and finished pecking out another text to Maiden. He shut his eyes and shook his head as he sent it.

He'd realized an hour ago that he'd have to cancel their date again and had delayed telling her as long as he could. He was getting increasingly frustrated and he knew she was too. He'd already shifted their second attempt at a date from Sunday to Tuesday, then from Tuesday to Wednesday. But now that Wednesday had rolled around things had only gotten busier.

The discovery of Charles Brown's body had been bad enough unto itself, but the timing couldn't have been worse. The motive for the killing was still unclear, a lot of valuables had been looked through and simply discarded, and there weren't any fingerprints on them except those of the victim.

David shook his head as his eyes strayed to the stack of papers on his desk. Another unexpected hornet's nest that had been thrown at him.

He'd barely sat down at his desk that morning when his receptionist, Nancy, rather meekly brought the papers in. At his confused and unimpressed look, she explained that the abysmal slew of documents were structural reports from inspections he hadn't even known were scheduled.

They ranged from a leaking roof to a rotting floor in one of the public restrooms. They were apparently long-standing problems that had only gotten worse over the years and this was the first he'd heard of any of them. It was a mess and the last thing he needed with a new murder case on his hands.

His phone lit up as a message came in, he glanced at it, assuming it was Maiden's reply.

Maiden

I see. That's fine.

That was all she said. David flicked to his home screen and just looked at it for a moment. The picture he kept of her in that incredible red dress she wore to her aunt's wedding stared back at him. He hoped she wasn't too disappointed, or worse, annoyed with him.

He rubbed his weary eyes and thought about all the troubles that had been dumped on him without warning. The police station was old, he knew that when he applied to transfer there, but apparently it hadn't been properly maintained in years, if ever.

It was exasperating, but he couldn't help what his predecessors had ignored. The details, reports and quotes were quickly becoming overwhelming. He knew he'd have to notify his superior officer, Deputy Chief Boswell.

He'd spoken to the man a few times before and found him to be decent; he seemed fair at least. But this wouldn't go over well and wouldn't be easy to fix. The budget wasn't big enough as it was, it certainly wasn't enough to replace a roof or a rotted floor. And those weren't the only problems.

David glanced back at his phone and the photo of Maiden that reminded him of what he was missing out on because of other people's mistakes. He sank back in his chair a little, wishing that he was sitting on a tropical beach somewhere rubbing sunscreen on her back.

He glanced out the window as the chilly autumn wind tore through the trees. Then he thought about the steady approach of winter and the leaky roof over his head, then he decided to have another cup of coffee and think about the murder instead.

***

Maiden pushed her phone away and tried not to dwell on the prospect of another evening spent alone. In all fairness she could do worse than reading a book with her little black kitten, Ruffian, and a glass of wine. It was a far cry from a romantic dinner with a sexy detective though.

Maybe it was because she'd helped solve several murders already, but she couldn't see how one dead body could really be that time-consuming. She then reminded herself that she was being unfair. As a rank amateur, she wasn't lumbered by protocol or rules or any of the other time-consuming quagmires that went into proper investigative procedures.

I get results though, can't argue with that, she thought to herself with a wry twist to her lips that quickly faded. She was still left with a problem, not life or death, but a problem nonetheless.

What worried her more than anything at the moment was that David might cancel going to the grand opening of Eilers' Arms with her. Especially since she hadn't asked him to go yet. She'd been planning to do that tonight at dinner...but then he canceled dinner.

She had a sinking feeling that she was going to end up going alone while everyone else had a date. At least in the old days she and Von could hang out and talk, but Von had Tony now and she hardly blamed her sister for preferring his company. Her parents had each other and they'd been thick as thieves to the exclusion of all others lately.

She'd be the fifth wheel, alone and very obviously so. She couldn't even scramble to find someone else because David would almost certainly mind. By the time she'd resorted to thoughts of taking the kittens along in her handbag and sneaking them cocktail shrimp, Maiden was laughing at herself.

Don't be so pessimistic, she murmured internally. *People ask other people out all the time, just because you've never done it doesn't mean it's hard. Just go and see David and ask him to go with you. But he's busy today...ask him tomorrow. He'll have less opportunity to cancel it that way.*

She smiled at that last thought and shook her head a little. David would want to come, she was sure of it. It would be fine, she'd wear something extra cute and go to the station and ask him out. It would probably brighten up his day to have her make a move. Probably.

Deciding that she needed a distraction, she went back to the newspaper she'd been reading before David's text came through. She shook off the threatening feelings of rejection and found the article she'd barely started in the Golden Glen Gazette.

The Show Must Go On!

Beloved Scottish folk band, The Highland Hounds, has bravely announced that they will be fulfilling their scheduled appearance in Golden Glen.
The Highlanders were left reeling from the violent death of a member of their management team last

*Saturday. Charles Brown was shot dead a day after
arriving in our fair town and left in his car outside the
Mayfair Storage Center.*

*Police have declined to comment on the murder and the
investigation is ongoing. It is unknown at this point if
the victim was known to their assailant or if there is any
threat to the general public.*

Maiden pulled a face at the article. Apart from the appallingly inappropriate 'highland reeling' pun, there wasn't much information disclosed. But it was enough to make people feel generally uncomfortable, and that wasn't necessarily unjustified.

The article went on to discuss the band and quoted the surviving manager, a certain Sean Dowling, as he expressed his sorrow and dismay at the sudden and violent loss of his business partner. Regardless of the tragedy, Mr. Dowling expressed the band's determination to press forward and celebrate Charles' life through their music rather than wallow in the sadness of his death.

Maiden set the paper down and stared absently across the room as she sank into thought. What would the manager of a travelling band be doing parked outside a warehouse in a town he'd just arrived in? Who would shoot him, search him and then leave all his money thrown on the floor? Even if it wasn't a genuine robbery, it seemed the clever thing would be to try and make it look like one.

Maybe the killer was afraid of getting caught, maybe they heard someone coming and panicked. Or maybe they were so bold that they didn't care about hiding what they'd done.

It's none of your business, Maiden, she admonished herself. *It's not like David's invited you out for coffee and discussed what's going on in his life. Although that seems like a perfectly reasonable thing for people to do if they're actually interested in each other—don't get cranky!*

That last order was given a little too late to be completely effective. A tiny part of her found it offensive and finally admitted that to the rest. Deep down she felt like she was quite good at figuring things out, and it wouldn't hurt him to chat to her about the case. Especially if it meant they'd have time to actually see each other.

She didn't want to be presumptuous or grow resentful, however, so she tossed the paper aside and turned her attention to what she'd wear to the grand opening. At least that was something she could control.

***

Maiden found the rest of the day a tad boring but peaceful. Vonny, who'd survived her fishy ordeal at the new sushi restaurant with minimal whining, took over the desk for the afternoon.

Maiden headed upstairs to settle on a dress for Friday night, got distracted, and ended up spending a few hours organizing her closet instead. When she'd run out of excuses, she looked through her options for the grand opening. She finally made the obvious decision that had been the true heart of her procrastination. She was going to wear the same green dress she'd worn to her disastrous high school reunion.

She had never planned to wear the grim reminder again, but practicality and realism won out in the end. It was a beautiful dress and it had been way too expensive to justify wearing it once and then buying a new one. At least she was sure David liked it, he'd certainly checked her out a fair bit despite having been on duty that night. She decided to focus on that memory rather than the more disturbing ones that threatened to crowd in again.

With that decision made, Maiden threw out a few blouses she'd forgotten about and didn't really like and then ordered a few more online.

She heard the front door open and smiled. Stopping just long enough to prize Ruffy from the sleeve he'd tangled himself in, she headed down the hallway towards the kitchen. Her parents had been out all day again and she found herself really missing them.

She stepped into the kitchen just as Gloria and Alfie walked through the front door carrying bags of groceries. Maiden hurried over and helped her mother wrestle the heavy bags onto the table.

"Thanks, angel," Gloria puffed. "It's times like these I wish we had an elevator."

"Or a gym to improve our fitness," Alfie teased as he set his bags alongside the others.

"Don't you start, Mr. Harlow," Gloria smirked and dug him playfully in the ribs with her elbow.

"Wow, you guys really went all out," Maiden said as she started pulling the groceries from the nearest bag.

There were all the ingredients for one of Gloria's special dinners, the kind that were a lot of trouble and didn't get served up very often. Maiden glanced down at a rather pricey package of steak and some beautiful mushrooms and shallots. She immediately started to feel hungry.

"This looks like it's going to be great." She smiled as she turned to her parents. "What can I do to help?"

Gloria's gentle eyes widened minutely and Alfie glanced away and started pulling some lettuce and tomatoes from the bag he'd been carrying.

"Aren't you goin' out tonight?" Gloria asked awkwardly.

"Um, I hadn't planned to. David had to cancel again, he's got that murder to deal with." Maiden blinked at her. "But if you guys have something planned that's totally fine. I'm happy to do something else. I can easily eat downstairs, I love Kylie's cooking anyway."

Kylie was their shy but exceptionally talented cook. She and Gloria had never seen eye to eye and rarely spoke to each other if it could be politely avoided.

Gloria bristled at the mention of her culinary nemesis and Maiden immediately wished she hadn't mentioned her. She could see her mother's pride war with the desire to get on with whatever they'd had planned. But, ultimately, she could hardly tell her daughter that she wasn't welcome.

"Don't be silly, baby." Gloria smiled warmly. "I always cook plenty, you know that. You stay right here with us."

"No, I really don't mind. *Really!*" Maiden said quickly and even held her hands up and started backing away. "Just do whatever you had planned, it's totally okay."

"Nonsense!" Gloria said sternly. "We'll all have dinner together tonight! It's been a while since we did that anyway. It'll be nice, won't it Alfie?"

"Hmm?" Alfie glanced at her and then turned to Maiden and smiled way too broadly to be believable. "Yes! Of course it will! I can't wait!"

"Are you guys celebrating something?" She almost winced as she asked it. "I don't want to butt in."

"I said don't be silly!" Gloria almost snapped at her but immediately smiled again. Her accent was thick enough to choke on as she continued. "I can't remember the last time I so *badly* wanted to spend an evenin' with you, my little angel! Now stop arguin' with mama."

Maiden cringed and tried to excuse herself a few more times but each attempt only made Gloria more vehement about her staying. She finally gave up and quietly chopped onions while Gloria tossed a salad.

"So what's goin' on with that murder, anyhow?" Gloria shot her a curious look.

"I don't know." Maiden admitted, not sure why she was starting to feel embarrassed about it. "David hasn't discussed it with me."

"What?!" Gloria arched a finely penciled brow. "But you always work with him."

"I don't really." Maiden glanced away and tried not to feel like something was wrong in her barely begun romance. "We don't 'work' together. I got dragged into those cases by circumstance, that's all."

"But you solved 'em all!" Gloria dropped her salad spoons in the bowl and braced a hand on her hip as she gave her a worried look. "Have you two had a fight or somethin'?"

"No, don't be silly! We've barely spoken in days…but not in a fighting way!" Maiden smiled and shook her head. "He's just busy and I'm not a detective. I mean, it's not like I'm a total outsider but, well…he doesn't have to tell me about the case. I'm not an *actual* detective or anything…it's fine. Everything is perfectly fine, I promise."

Maiden watched her parents exchange a dubious look and then return silently to their tasks. She knew it was silly to let other people's perceptions convince her that something was wrong when it wasn't. She and David weren't arguing and he wasn't ignoring her. Murders were complicated and she wasn't a cop so why would he share his concerns with her?

He doesn't like it when you get involved, that's why, she told herself with an internal sigh. *How weird is that going to be when he won't discuss his work with you? What are you supposed to talk about when one of the biggest topics of mutual interest is off limits?*

She didn't realize that she was frowning until her mother noticed and turned to her again.

"Maiden?" Gloria gave her a worried look. "Are you all right, baby? Has somethin' happened?"

"No, everything's okay," she said with what she hoped was a convincing smile.

Dinner was a little quiet and uncomfortable. Maiden tried to be pleasant company but struggled to look at either of them. No one wanted her there, herself included, so she ate the delicious food as quickly as she could and then politely excused herself from the table. For perhaps only the third time in her entire life she said no to dessert.

She said a cheerful goodnight as she went to the wine cupboard and grabbed a bottle of white and a glass before retreating to her room. She spent the rest of the evening hidden away with a book, a couple of glasses of wine and her feisty kitten.

Ruffian was growing, but still on the smaller side. After tearing around the room chasing something that probably didn't exist outside of his little feline imagination, he sprawled on his belly across her left ankle and fell sound asleep.

Maiden smiled and looked up as the tiny cat started to snore. It was the first time she'd really felt herself relax all evening. She sipped her wine and let her book lay forgotten beside her.

Her thoughts drifted to dinner, the cozy dinner she'd had with her parents. They'd both been nice enough but she could tell they were a bit put out that she'd joined them. Not for the first time she wished she'd put her foot down and left the apartment, it's not like they would've dragged her back and force fed her.

Alfie and Gloria had sat and barely spoke as they ate, not even to each other. Maiden put a hand to her face as guilt assailed her; they'd gone to a lot of trouble and she'd just ruined their lovely evening.

Her dismal thoughts were closing in on her when she heard Vonny's door open and close down the hall. She glanced at the clock beside her bed, it was later than she thought. She felt a twinge of relief, at least she'd stayed out of everyone's hair for a while.

She sat up straight and pulled her legs up to her chest, sending Ruffian rolling across the soft quilt. She whispered an apology to the irate kitten and quickly climbed out of bed. She dashed to the bathroom long enough to brush her teeth, she then snuck straight back to her room without a word or a look at anyone.

Chapter Three

The following day Maiden put on her best jeans and a snug sweater that was cut a little lower than the cool weather advised. She drove to the police station and stepped into the doorway of David's office.

As she peered inside her courage faltered slightly; he looked very preoccupied and he wasn't alone. Greg and Sarah-Jane were standing nearby and seemed to be waiting while he read through something. Greg noticed her first and smiled.

"Hi, Mae," he said nicely. "How are you?"

"Good, thanks." She smiled back and edged a little further in. "You guys look busy."

"Yeah, that guy that got shot was—" Greg had barely started talking when David cut in.

"We're a bit busy, yes." He gave Greg a stern, silencing look but smiled when he turned to Maiden. "That's fine though, it's good to see you. Is everything okay?"

Maiden couldn't help noticing the way he deliberately stopped Greg from talking about the case. Greg looked a little confused by it and Sarah-Jane just glanced uncomfortably down at her highly polished shoes.

It was annoying and a little insulting. She was being shut out; that was happening a lot lately. She again told herself that it was nothing to do with her, but it still stung. That wasn't why she'd come there though, she gave herself a mental prod and got on with it.

"Yeah, everything's great, it's been a great week. Anyway, I won't keep you," she said, quietly impressed by how mild she sounded. "My family has been invited to the grand opening of a new hotel tomorrow night, I was wondering if you wanted to come with me?"

David stilled, she was pretty sure he held his breath. He slid his gaze away and shut his eyes briefly. Maiden felt some perverse blend of embarrassment and anger blossom inside her when it became obvious he was going to turn her down.

From the corner of her eye she saw Greg and Sarah-Jane exchange a look; her embarrassment grew. David sat a little straighter and pulled an apologetic face, probably wishing, as she was, that they had at least been alone for this exchange.

"I'd love to," he prefaced but quickly continued, "but there's so much going on at the moment. I'm so sorry, there's just no way I can get away right now."

Maiden felt her left eyebrow rise of its own accord. She thought of the men that had hit on her over the years, she wasn't vain but there had been a few, and suddenly had a lot more sympathy for the ones she'd turned down. It wasn't a nice feeling.

"Really?" she asked quietly but still managed to smile. "Still?"

"I'm sorry." He winced.

"Awesome," Maiden muttered under her breath and then turned to Greg and Sarah-Jane with a sardonic look. "Either of you want to come? It's bound to be stupid *and* boring."

"I gotta work too," Greg chuckled. "Sorry, Mae."

"Yeah, sorry." Sarah-Jane smiled.

"Suit yourselves." Maiden shrugged and turned to the door.

"I'll talk to you soon, Maiden," David said as she went.

She set her teeth but didn't reply or even glance back at him as she walked out and shut the door quite firmly behind her.

***

David looked at the closed door and felt his stomach sink a little. He hadn't expected the invitation and wished she'd asked to speak with him privately; he could see that she was upset. If it hadn't been tomorrow night he might've been able to make it work, but there just wasn't enough time.

Smith and Parker stood quietly in the awkward silence that had descended. David avoided looking at them as he waited for the uncomfortable heat in his cheeks to fade. Finally, Smith shifted a little and cleared his throat discreetly.

"Sir?"

"What is it, Smith?" David pinched the bridge of his nose.

"Um…I may be biased because she's my friend, but you do realize that Maiden's one of the hottest women you'll ever meet in your life, right?" He was watching him with a hint of genuine concern. "And she asked you out and…you actually said *no*. I'm just kind of wondering what that's about."

"It's not that straightforward, Smith," David said mildly enough. "Maiden knows that, she's been involved with enough murder cases by now."

"Yeah…" Smith looked skeptical and was now avoiding eye contact. "So, from what I've personally seen and heard, when Mae starts to cool off on a guy it happens pretty quick. All the ones I know of blew it when it was still early days…and you haven't technically been out with her even once yet. Just something to keep in mind maybe."

When she 'cools off on a guy'? David repeated internally and scowled at Smith.

"It hasn't even been a week," he said flatly.

"She's cheesed off, sir," Greg said with disturbing certainty. "I doubt Maiden's ever had to ask a guy out, but I think I can safely guarantee you that no one's shot her down before."

"It might have been nice if you'd at least pretended to think about it," Parker added as she studied the potted plant in the corner.

David shifted slightly in his chair as he considered their comments. He knew what he had in Maiden; as Smith had suggested, she was probably the sexiest woman he'd ever met. And she was smart and sweet, and rarely in a bad mood...and he'd just said he was too busy to go out with her. Again.

Not the smartest thing you've ever done, McAlister, he thought to himself.

"Right," David mumbled as he started pushing to his feet. "Maybe I should—"

"Yeah, you might want to go catch her!" Parker blurted and started to roll her eyes but quickly remembered who she was talking to. "Sir."

He slipped out into the hall and walked quickly to the lobby. Maybe it was his imagination but Nancy also seemed to be avoiding his eye as she stood at her post behind the front desk.

A sharp, icy wind hit him as he pushed the front door open and walked quickly outside. As he scanned the parking lot he spotted Maiden's dark green sedan as she reversed and turned towards the road.

David waved to get her attention. She glanced over and saw him, he was positive she did, and then proceeded to look away and continue on as though she hadn't. He felt his breath catch and his shoulders tense a little as she drove away.

***

Maiden spent the rest of the day, and the one following, deliberately not thinking about David, dates or relationships in general. What she did do was drink a lot of coffee, play with kittens and look up more information about the Highland Hounds.

She wondered why they'd gotten to Golden Glen last week. From what she could find they weren't actually performing until this week-end. Apparently they were playing Friday, Saturday and Sunday night.

She wasn't surprised to learn that the first two nights had already sold out. There would be a lot of curious snoops mixed in with the genuine music-lovers, all of them eager to get a closer look after the stories that had been in the paper.

The band appeared to be modestly successful, she hadn't personally heard of them before but that didn't mean much. They had already played a string of performances across the state but she noticed that they seemed to favor small, out-of-the-way venues. It seemed a tough way to make a living in an already tough industry.

She couldn't find very much information about their management team, apart from the relatively sparse articles about Charles Brown's murder. The story had been picked up by a few larger news sites but no one had shed any real light on anything.

Maiden glanced at the clock. It was Friday night and she had hidden in her room for as long as possible. She needed to get ready for the grand opening. She sat at her small desk and peered into the mirror above it as she started doing her makeup.

She still had no idea why they were all getting dressed up and heading across town to applaud the launching of more competition.

Her parents had barely mentioned it all week and they'd been out for the whole day.

Maiden had begun to entertain hopes that she might not be expected to actually go; she only knew of the party at all because Vonny had told her about it. But then Gloria had breezed in, fresh from getting her hair professionally styled, and urged Maiden to hurry and get ready.

Maiden wasn't in the mood to argue or make excuses; at least she'd be getting out for a change. She slipped into her green dress, refused to be creeped out by the memories of the last time she wore it, and pinned her hair back from her face in a graceful sweep.

Fresh out of ways to stall, she walked out to the kitchen and sank down into one of the chairs around the big table. She rested her chin in her hand and waited for her parents to assemble.

Vonny would be downstairs already waiting for Tony. He'd happily agreed to accompany her and they'd no doubt have a wonderful evening. Maiden certainly didn't begrudge them a single bit of happiness, but she did want a little something for herself.

Reminding herself that moping would only make things worse, she was gratefully distracted from her personal troubles when she heard Gloria approach. Her mother's powerful voice preceded her into the room.

"I can't believe I got a run in a brand-new pair of pantyhose!" she said with complete disgust. "Nothin's made to last anymore!"

Maiden smiled fondly when the boisterous southern broad sailed into the kitchen. She couldn't help noticing that her mother had gone to more trouble than usual with her appearance.

Gloria wore a tight black and pink polka dot dress with a shiny black patent leather belt and matching shoes. Her pale blonde hair was piled in bouncy curls on the top of her head and the powerful scent of her musky perfume was all-encompassing.

Alfie wore a smart charcoal gray suit and a dark red tie. He was fastening a pair of cufflinks at his wrists as he glanced at his wife with a smile. Maiden gave an approving nod as she looked him over; it wasn't often that she saw him wear anything that fancy.

"You look beautiful, my dear." Alfie said warmly as he slid his arm around his wife.

Gloria waved it away modestly but still preened under the praising words. Maiden smiled at them even as she glanced at her phone, knowing perfectly well that no messages would be waiting for her. Certainly nothing from a handsome police captain announcing that he'd decided he could spare her an evening after all.

"Are we ready to go?" she asked as she pushed to her feet.

Thanks in part to Gloria's ambitiously high heels, Maiden easily got downstairs first. She glanced at the front desk and saw Billie sitting there reading a magazine.

Billie was typically their housekeeper but, on rare occasions such as tonight, she was called upon to spread her wings a bit. She wasn't the most efficient of reception staff, and sometimes not the most tactful either, but she was honest, reliable and could answer the phones for a couple of hours.

"Hey Maiden," she gave her a smile and lowered her magazine. "Have fun scoping out the enemy. Be sure to look for any signs of weakness."

"I'm not exactly infiltrating behind enemy lines," Maiden chuckled.

"How do you figure that?" Billie challenged with a smirk.

Maiden considered it for a moment and gave a conceding nod. "I guess that's true. If I'm not back by tomorrow, promise you'll feed the cats."

"Deal." Billie gave her a wink and turned a fond look to Alfie and Gloria as they entered the foyer. "You guys look great!"

"Thank you, Billie," Gloria smiled as they filed past and on into the office. "We'll be late tonight, so see you tomorrow."

Maiden gave Billie a teasingly conspiratorial eyebrow waggle and then joined her parents out in the surprisingly cold evening air.

They climbed into Maiden's car and headed into the heart of Golden Glen's progressive downtown area. It paid homage to the nearby river and the fishing industry that used to thrive there. The now trendy area was known as The Docks.

The buildings throughout had mostly been restored and converted from industrial use to fashionable boutiques and restaurants over the past several years. The revitalization effort had been very successful and was a point of pride for Golden Glen's citizens. Most would have agreed that it was high time someone did something with the Old Chateau—until they saw the result, at least.

The Chateau had been a crumbling and derelict slice of history that most people never noticed. The building was large and sat on an ancient-looking stone foundation, nestled in the midst of its industrialized neighbors that had sprung up and faded away over the decades.

According to the Gazette, everyone that heard of Eilers' ambitious project was quite shocked that he had ignored the precedent of every other local business. He'd done nothing to capitalize on the history of the place, instead he'd elected to cover over every trace of the Old Chateau with a barrage of cartoonish sea-themed adornments. It was sacrilege, it was unthinkable.

In addition to this, Eilers had embarked on a lengthy and doubtless expensive advertising campaign, including radio ads, flyers and an entry to win a free car with every booking.

Garish and thoroughly over the top, Maiden had been hearing something, good or bad, about Eilers' Arms all week. She was incredibly curious to see the place for herself.

Out of consideration for her mother's feet, she parked in the closest spot she could find and they all piled out. Maiden shut her door and could only stare at the incredible sight before her. The building was large, imposing and unquestionably hideous.

The bright blue façade glowed in the movie premiere-style spotlights that swayed across it. There was a red carpet spread across the front steps, which were also framed with a massive balloon arch. It was almost surreal, she'd never seen a building like it.

She managed to tear her gaze away long enough to look at her parents. They were whispering to each other as they took in the view. As soon as they saw her looking at them, however, they fell silent and walked straight towards the door.

Maiden followed, half expecting to be scooped up and carried across the threshold by someone in a giant fish costume, but they were permitted to enter with relative quiet and dignity. The front doors glided open automatically and they were immersed in the remarkable lobby.

"Well, ain't this somethin'!" Gloria said brightly as she gave Maiden's hand a squeeze. "Why don't you have a look around and mingle a bit, angel. We'll see you later."

With that Gloria and Alfie hurried off through a doorway on the far right side of the expansive room, they moved with purpose, as though they knew right where they were going. Maiden now had no doubt that her parents had been here before.

As tempted as she was to dissect that strange revelation, she was too stunned by her surroundings to focus on much else. She walked to the center of the room and turned slowly, trying to take it all in.

Softly lilting music drifted out from one of the rooms, no doubt a taste of the live music that the brochure had promised. There was a medley of aromas in the air; fresh paint, cleaning solution and...fish. A definite waft of cooking fish. Maiden, whose favorite fish was chicken, wrinkled her nose and continued her study.

The walls were dark blue, very dark, and the ceiling was a mottled white and gray. She wondered if that was to simulate the effect of foaming waves, it didn't entirely work, but it was certainly eye-catching.

The reception desk was actually quite neat. It was made of highly polished wood and resembled the bow of a ship, complete with a ship's wheel mounted on the counter. It looked impractical but whimsical and very fun.

To the left were a couple of doorways, one led to the restaurant and the other looked like a bar. She didn't spare them too much notice as she swept her gaze to the right.

There she saw an incredibly wide staircase. The far side butted against a wall and the other was completely enclosed underneath. The closed in portion was also painted blue and disappeared subtly into the surrounding walls. She wondered if the staircase was original, she rather doubted that much of the place was though.

Between the stairs and the room her parents were in, a long hallway led off into inner reaches that she sort of wanted to explore. Maiden smiled faintly at her innate nosiness, she then decided to be more acceptably nosy and follow Alfie and Gloria rather than trespass.

She walked across a thick rug that featured ornate anchors and topless mermaids woven into a surprisingly pretty underwater scene.

She found the door they'd disappeared through and stepped into what turned out to be a large reception room.

This room was also painted blue but the shade wasn't quite as dark. There were three big chandeliers that were fashioned to look like clusters of seahorses. Maiden walked further in and admired the remarkable fixtures. As she did so, she searched her memory for the name given to groups of seahorses. Herds. She smiled at the aquatic herds and then glanced around at some of the other guests.

There were several groups of people scattered around mingling. Most were laughing and chatting happily as they sipped glasses of champagne and nibbled on canapes, but one group was a glaring exception.

Half a dozen men and women dressed in stolid corporate wear stood in a tight circle muttering to each other as they looked around contemptuously. Maiden wondered who they were, none of them seemed to be enjoying being there.

Shaking her head slightly, she tucked her little velvet purse under her arm and walked further into the room. She met her mother's smiling gaze and hid her surprise when she actually beckoned her over.

Alfie and Gloria were standing beside a stout man with short gray hair and an underbite that reminded her of a bulldog. She recalled seeing his picture in the papers almost every day, it was the notorious Fred Eilers.

"Maiden baby!" Gloria smiled as she grasped her daughter's arm. "I want you to meet our host and the owner of this hotel, Fred Eilers. He's also an old friend from your father's college days."

Maiden nodded slowly as the seemingly odd connection started to make sense.

"Hello, Mr. Eilers." Maiden smiled politely as she shook his sweaty hand. "This is quite a place you have here."

"Thanks, I'm quite proud of it." His expression reflected his claim. He looked her over with an appreciative smile. "Your mother told me you and your sister were knockouts, she wasn't kidding."

"Thanks." Maiden smiled faintly, quietly grateful for any words of admiration after being shot down only the day before. "So, you went to college with Dad? I didn't know that. He doesn't talk about those days much."

"He was probably afraid he'd bore you to tears! He was too studious for his own good!" Eilers chortled and clapped Alfie on the shoulder. "A fine and reliable man, your father."

"Yeah, I kinda figured that." Maiden slid Alfie a quietly fond look.

She watched as her father and Eilers started to banter back and forth. They really did appear to be old friends; she wondered why she'd never heard of Eilers before. She knew her father didn't often talk about his life before he met Gloria. Apparently he'd never been close to many of his own relatives.

In any case, she now understood why their entire family had gone to some trouble to spend a perfectly good evening congratulating another hotel on its opening. She still didn't know why they were so secretive about it, though. She glanced at her mother, Gloria was beaming at Eilers, and everything else, as she looked around at the décor. Maiden quickly banished a threatening frown and a feeling that something wasn't right.

She consoled herself that at least one mystery had been put to bed; she knew that her parents were friends with Eilers. As the older generation talked, Maiden let her gaze wander over the room.

She saw a series of pictures displayed on the far wall. It looked to be some sort of project timeline. She politely excused herself from the small group and wandered over to take a closer look at it.

As she drew nearer, she saw that she was right. It was a collage of pictures and drawings that depicted a three-stage progression of the hotel. She stepped a bit closer.

The first grouping of pictures began with the Old Chateau in its run-down state. A sign above them said *'Starting Point'*. The crumbling foundation and damaged roof, the crooked walls and broken windows. While clearly in the rough, it was still undeniably a diamond. Her heart almost broke when she saw a beautiful artist's rendition of how the original building had likely looked in its prime. It was so beautiful; ornate yet tasteful. It reeked of history and heritage rather than potpourri air freshener and fish.

She quickly pressed on to the next step in the chain. A small sign above this section described it as *'Concept Art'*. The Chateau was, of course, a classic French-styled estate. The concept art looked vastly different but still quite attractive. It looked like an old British pub. That also didn't fit the original history of the site, but it was still far preferable to what they were all standing in now.

In the artist's optimistic sketches, the exterior was tasteful brick and stained-glass windows, it had a gracefully pitched roof that boasted several chimneystacks. There was definitely a cozy, welcoming vibe.

The last sign read *'The Masterpiece'*. Unquestionably a very subjective definition of the final product. The display of the last stage of the exhibit was reminiscent of an attraction at a theme park. It was a startling, almost bizarre transition.

As well as images of the finished hotel, the exhibit featured bits and pieces of inspiration art. There were drawings of pirates and ships, photos of aquariums and even some pictures of blown-glass fish ornaments.

What had clearly been intended as a whimsical sea-faring theme had gone horribly awry and came across as tacky and cartoonish.

Maiden slid her gaze away from the startlingly honest display. She marveled that Eilers had chosen to make an art feature of a thought process that was probably better left ignored and, if necessary, openly denied. She walked back towards the door, pausing for an instant when her mother laughed shrilly and gave Eilers' arm a teasing swat, and then slipped out of the room.

CHAPTER FOUR

Back in the foyer, she looked around for some other means of killing a bit of time. She was tempted to sneak behind the front desk and check out what booking software they used, but she wasn't feeling that brazen. She did run her gaze over what she could see of the desktop, it was very tidy and the swivel chair that had been placed for the staff looked quite comfy.

Chiding herself sternly to mind her own business, she swung her gaze to the rest of the room. Her attention was quickly caught by a stuffed deep-sea diver suit stationed by the doorway of the restaurant, beckoning patrons to enter. She tsked loudly but managed not to roll her eyes when she saw the hand-painted sign over the doorway—The Peg-Leg Lounge.

She wandered a bit closer and peered inside only to be immediately met by a waiter with a ready smile and a tray filled with glasses of punch. Maiden accepted one with a quiet word of thanks. She had just taken a sip and turned back to the foyer when she heard chatter.

Several people had come from other rooms and were discussing the unique desk and the remarkable color scheme Eilers had settled on. Maiden was tired of being bored and wasn't standoffish by nature. She joined in and spent the next half hour or so mingling.

She had floated through a few rooms and was again wandering around the foyer. Sipping a second glass of punch, she wondered how many coats it had taken to thoroughly cover every wall in the dark ocean blue paint.

She walked on towards the long hallway, assuring herself that she was only looking at the pictures of old shipwrecks that hung randomly on the walls. But then she heard a low knocking sound. She stilled for a moment and listened until she heard it again. Maiden glanced around and headed back the way she came.

When she followed the noise and finally peeked around to the side of the staircase, she spotted a man tapping his knuckles down the wall that enclosed the area beneath.

He looked to be in his fifties, he was reasonably tall and had wide shoulders. Maiden calmly drank her punch and simply watched him for a moment until he glanced back over his shoulder and spotted her.

He was visibly startled but quickly recovered. He immediately straightened, adjusted his smart suitcoat and ran a hand over his thick, snow-white hair. He sauntered towards her with impossible aplomb all things considered.

"Good evening." He smiled, showing a mouth full of gleaming teeth, as he inclined his head a fraction. "I thought I'd seen the most beautiful women this shindig had to offer. You must've arrived late, I know I couldn't have missed you. The name's Ulysses Mercier."

Yikes! I bet you got teased a lot as a kid, she giggled to herself but managed not to venture the comment aloud.

"Nice to meet you," she said mildly, deliberately refrained from introducing herself, and glanced at the stairwell. "Why are you knocking on walls?"

"Hm? Oh, that! Yes, it's a bit odd, but don't mind me," he chuckled. "I used to work for a construction company, doing inspections and things. I sometimes slip into old habits and test for quality. Usually only when I see something that looks substandard. I'm afraid this place definitely qualifies."

"Interesting." It was a lame excuse but she decided to let it go. "So, do you work for Mr. Eilers now?"

"Not exactly. I'm more of a freelance agent," Mercier smiled artfully. "Please excuse me, my dear, I'd best get back to the party."

Maiden watched the strange man walk away and then glanced around at the walls, they didn't look particularly 'substandard' to her. Reminding herself that it really wasn't her business, she strolled towards the warmly lit room that she was confident was the bar.

As she entered, Maiden nearly skidded to a halt when she saw the yards of neon fishnets and plastic sea-life replicas that peppered every wall. She quickly recovered and tried to look sophisticated as she strode further inside. As sophistication wasn't her strong suit, she was happily distracted when she saw the grumpy group of suits again. She sidled in a bit closer and overheard a few of them muttering critically.

"This whole place is a travesty!" One man said tightly.

"It looks nothing like he said it would," another complained bitterly. "It would've cost a fortune!"

Maiden wondered if they were from the corporate office, or maybe they were investors. In either case, she couldn't blame them for being upset. If she'd been expecting the concept art and ended up with a giant turquoise brick, she'd be disappointed too. She wondered what the fallout would be.

Less than a minute later, Ulysses Mercier approached the group and started schmoozing. Maiden toyed with her glass and pretended to be looking at the glossy advertising flyers while she shamelessly eavesdropped. Mercier was laying it on pretty thick.

"Investor input is the most valuable asset a company like this could ask for," he sighed and shook his head sadly even as he flashed a stern-looking woman a winning smile.

"I certainly agree, Mr. Mercier. We all expected better from Fred," the lady's frosty demeanor thawed noticeably as she replied to him. She smiled and smoothed back her deeply brown, tightly permed locks.

"I don't blame you for that." Mercier folded his arms over his broad chest. "It's an absolute *necessity* to have everyone in agreement when this much money is involved!"

"You're right," another man muttered. "Where does he get off making these sorts of decisions without our input."

"Well, if you all feel that strongly about it—" Mercier began with a small shrug and a pensive stroking of his chin when he was loudly interrupted.

"*Mercier!*"

The group turned sharply at Eilers' irate approach. Maiden saw the man's face flush angrily as he stormed in and physically nudged everyone apart. The two men were of similar height but Mercier's build was a little more formidable, that didn't seem to slow Eilers down though.

Maiden fiddled with her glass and watched subtly as Eilers boldly confronted a startled Mercier and pointed to the door. The ensuing discussion was largely indecipherable but it was clear that Eilers was the only one that was angry.

Maiden wandered over to join the small group, evidently investors in Eilers' company, and watched as the man of the moment glared and jabbed an accusing finger at Mercier as he maneuvered him out of the room. For his part, Mercier held up his hands innocently and shook his head, frowning in consternation.

Maiden edged closer to the doorway of the bar and watched. The strange encounter came to an equally dramatic finish with Eilers actually shoving Mercier towards the front door.

"Can you imagine?!" the woman with the perm gasped in shocked disgust from somewhere behind her.

Mercier threw up his hands with an exasperated exclamation as he backed away. But as he turned to go, Maiden saw a smirk slip into view before he walked out the door. It glided firmly closed behind him.

At that point everyone in the room had noticed the fracas. Maiden stepped back subtly as Eilers returned to the barroom. He glanced around and found himself the center of some very unwanted attention. He was still grumbling under his breath but he had to have realized the need to try and salvage the situation.

"Serve the food!" he called with remarkable aplomb as he cleared his throat and straightened his jacket.

A slew of waitstaff strewn with fronds of fake seaweed appeared with trays of appetizers and more punch. Maiden was ready for something stronger than punch. She set her empty glass on a passing tray and deftly avoided the offerings of pale shrimp sticking out of an unknown and oddly gelatinous sauce.

Her efforts thus rewarded, she glanced around and noticed a cozy pair tucked away at the bar. A woman was looking with an irate glare towards the doorway where Eilers still stood. She had her hair in an attractively careless bun and wore a dark purple cocktail dress that showed off long legs encased in black stockings.

Beside her sat a tall, gaunt man with thick glasses, a pale brown combover and a tan corduroy leisure suit that looked like it came from 1972. Paired with a burnt orange paisley shirt and a brown tie, it was weirdly awesome.

The man murmured something to his companion and she instantly cleared her expression and turned back to him with a docile smile. They thereafter talked quietly as they sipped fluorescent cocktails and looked surreptitiously from Eilers to the unimpressed suits that now sat at a table in the corner. The grim group had tucked themselves in and talked in low, intent voices.

The sounds of conversation resumed as everyone else tried to carry on as though nothing had happened. Maiden raised her dark brows and shook her head; whatever was brewing certainly didn't look good. She was glad that her family didn't have investors or shareholders to cater to.

She was distracted by the sound of Vonny's delighted laughter. She glanced over to see her and Tony snuggled up at the other end of the bar enjoying a conversation with a rotund older woman with over-teased pink hair. The sight of them made Maiden smile but also sigh wistfully. She pulled out her phone to see if David had tried to call or at least sent her a message to see how she was doing. There was nothing.

He'd sent her a text yesterday after she left the station and another one this morning. Both were apologizing for him being so preoccupied with work but neither expressed a real desire to be with her or held out any promise of an actual date on the horizon.

She found it all a bit tepid and unsatisfying and hadn't gotten around to replying to him yet. She kind of doubted he had time to notice so she didn't feel too badly about it.

Maiden shoved her phone back in her purse and distracted herself by looking for her parents. She quickly spotted Gloria's magnificent blonde curls and headed towards them like a shining beacon.

She and Alfie were talking to Eilers again, they seemed the only ones inclined to talk to him after his bullish outburst. He was dabbing at his sweaty forehead and neck with a handkerchief while Gloria fussed.

"Now Fred, don't you let it worry you," she said as she patted his arm.

"She's right," Alfie said firmly. "The old dog is just sniffing around looking for trouble, nothing new. Don't let it spoil the evening."

"You're both right," Eilers sighed loudly. "I know you are."

Maiden listened as they tried to keep the talk light and cheerful whilst neatly avoiding any mention of Eilers having just physically confronted a guest. She wondered who that Mercier guy actually was and why he was really there.

***

The peculiar evening came to a close when Gloria's feet were too sore to withstand another moment in her shiny new high heels. Maiden obligingly got the car and pulled it up to the door for her.

Her parents huddled together in the backseat and almost whispered to each other about the fine weather and the last time they'd had shrimp cocktail. Maiden cleared her throat and glanced at them briefly in the rearview mirror.

"So, who's Ulysses Mercier?" she asked. "You talked about him like you know him."

"He's another guy that went to college with me and Fred," Alfie replied, a touch hesitantly. "We all graduated around the same time."

"Nice," she murmured. "Why did Mr. Eilers throw him out like that? He didn't exactly make the greatest impression on his opening night."

"Oh, yeah that. I'm not completely sure. They never got along terribly well." Alfie turned to the window and didn't look away again for the rest of the drive.

"I'm sure it wasn't nothin'," Gloria batted it away like a stray balloon. "You know how competitive boys can get."

"'Competitive'?" Maiden asked mildly. "That's what we're calling that behavior? Interesting. What if he'd put him in a headlock and spit in his hair?"

"Don't be childish, angel," Gloria murmured.

"*That's* the word!" Maiden snapped her fingers and grinned. She also succeeded in killing any trace of conversation for the rest of the drive.

They pulled into the parking lot of Harlow House and Maiden slid into her usual spot. As they all climbed out and walked towards the door to the office she decided to try and get her parents talking again before they slipped upstairs and locked themselves away in their room.

"Well, what did you both think of Eilers' Arms?" she asked mildly as Alfie fumbled with his keys.

"It was nice," he said as he finally got the door open and stood back so that she and Gloria could enter first.

"Yes." Gloria nodded. "Very bold of Fred to go in such a different direction. His building really pops. But he's always been a real forward thinker, hasn't he, Alfie?"

"Sure has," he quickly assented.

"That's one way of putting it," Maiden said quietly as she followed them past the reception desk and around the corner to the stairs.

It struck Maiden that her parents were being unusually diplomatic. She would have expected her mother in particular to complain that the whole place looked like it'd been hosed down with toilet bowl cleaner.

"What did you think of the food?" she tried again.

"Pretty good," Gloria said simply and left it at that.

"I'm not so sure about all the stuff on the walls," Maiden said dubiously.

"Now don't be negative, baby." Gloria held up a long pink fingernail and wagged it in a gently scolding manner. "Sometimes we gotta give people the benefit of the doubt."

"How does that apply when we're talking about candleholders made from rusty fishhooks lining the bar?" Maiden chuckled. "Does he offer a free Tetanus shot with every drink?"

Gloria gave her a chiding look and opted not to reply. Maiden stared at the tactful and benevolent creature that had somehow managed to take over her mother's body. Usually Gloria was the first one to start cracking jokes in situations like these, but she was being so polite about the whole evening, she and Alfie both were.

The instant they set foot inside the apartment her parents said goodnight and shut themselves inside their suite. Maiden looked at the closed door and then around the seemingly empty apartment. Everything was quiet. She wasn't sure if Vonny was home yet, she and Tony had left before them.

She walked in further and slipped out of her shoes. Setting her purse on the table as she walked past, Maiden approached the couch and saw the kittens fast asleep in the middle of it.

Rowdy and Ruffian were sprawled across each other and snoring contentedly. She smiled at the soothing sight but glanced over her shoulder to her purse when she heard her phone cheep as a message came in. She walked back to the table and pulled out her phone; she frowned for a heartbeat as she looked at the screen.

David

> Hey beautiful. Sorry I couldn't go tonight.
> Hope you had a great time.

"I don't think I'd go as far as to say 'great'," she said under her breath and smiled wryly. "It was certainly interesting."

Maiden debated whether or not to send a reply, but she really didn't feel like starting a conversation with him tonight. It was late, she was tired, and he'd left her on her own all evening again. With a faint smile, and no genuine malice, she decided to return the favor. She put her phone on silent and tucked it back into her purse.

Chapter Five

David sat at his desk the following morning and looked at his phone for at least the tenth time. Maiden still hadn't replied to any of the messages he'd sent her yesterday.

He knew she'd been annoyed with him for not going to that hotel thing with her, but he couldn't believe she was actually ignoring him over it. It wasn't as if he'd rather be at work; she had to know that he'd be glued to her side if he could.

His evening hadn't been fun but it had been productive. They'd started digging deeper into Charles Brown's past and found a few promising leads. This hadn't been the man's first foray into America, he visited every year, ostensibly on business. Brown didn't appear to have been a hardened criminal but there was a bit of petty larceny and an assault charge on his record.

Doc Jenkin's report on the body had been interesting too. There were no signs of bruising or any other trauma, only the wound that killed him. There were no indications of a struggle and he hadn't been moved, he'd been sitting in the backseat of his car when he was shot. They'd even found the bullet embedded in the seat behind him.

It wasn't inconceivable, but David couldn't recall the last time he'd sat in the back seat of his own car. The whole thing felt odd. So did the location of the murder. There wasn't much in that street, a few warehouses and an old textile factory. Everything else was closed up and had appeared undisturbed.

As peculiar as that was, David's focus didn't stay on work for long. His attention was again dragged to thoughts of Maiden and unwelcome recollections of Officer Smith's warning.

When Mae starts to cool off on a guy it happens pretty quick.

Shut up, Smith, David grumbled internally. *There's no way she could kiss me the way she has and then get tired of waiting so quickly...But I have cancelled a lot, and I said no when she tried to arrange something. And we don't have anything planned at the moment, and she's definitely ignoring me.*

He exhaled shakily and rubbed his eyes. This was the first relationship in his life that he was actually quite serious about. The last few times he'd dated someone it had felt different, kind of flat, he was never fully invested. He'd tried but he'd never been able to see himself spending the rest of his life with any of those women. But he didn't feel the old doubts and uncertainties with Maiden.

He knew that they hadn't officially been together for very long, they hadn't even succeeded in having a date yet. But the rapport between them had started early on and had been building for months, it wasn't as if there was no history there at all. It was different with her, it was special.

He sat up straight and picked up his phone again. He dialed her number before he could think it over too much and possibly lose his nerve. She answered after a couple of rings.

"Hey, David." She didn't sound angry, that was a good start.

"Good morning." He kept his tone light and refused to ask her if she really thought it necessary to ignore him. "I thought I'd call...I sent a few messages, they must not have gone through."

"Oh, they did," she replied a little quietly, he could almost hear her shifting uncomfortably. "I put my phone on silent, sorry."

"That's okay. I'm really sorry about last night—" he began when Vonny's caustic voice chimed in from the background.

"Let me guess, there's a cat stuck in a tree so he can't see you for another couple of weeks?" she asked dryly.

"Knock it off, Vonny, *please!*" Maiden's exasperated voice was slightly muffled as she put her hand over the phone, but he still heard every word. When she came back on the line she sounded harassed and a little grumpy. "Look, its fine, you don't have to keep apologizing. I know you're very busy, just go take care of whatever you're doing. I'm sorry, I've gotta go."

She hung up before he could say anything else. David sat for a moment and really considered what he was doing. He cared about Maiden, a lot, but he wasn't showing her that. And he hadn't considered that she would be getting pressure from other directions.

She was surrounded by family and friends that had been expecting something to happen between them and, as Vonny had just demonstrated, weren't shy about expressing their views. He started to understand a bit more of her frustration.

David looked at the ever-growing stack of failed inspection reports and witness statements and came to a decision. He wasn't going to throw away an incredible woman like Maiden to keep picking up someone else's slack. He was taking her out tonight no matter what. Assuming she would agree to go.

***

Maiden gave Vonny an irate look until her sister got up and skulked self-consciously towards the dining room.

"I'll get us both a coffee," she said as she made her escape.

Maiden took a deep breath and slid her phone away. She felt badly for being a bit sharp with David, but she couldn't help it.

He wouldn't take her out, wouldn't agree when she asked him out and wouldn't even talk about the case in front of her. It was a triple threat of rejection.

Maiden was tired of feeling stressed and unwanted, she certainly didn't want to feel guilty for snapping at David. She pushed those concerns away and turned to the computer, eager for any distraction.

One person had called that morning and booked in but another two had canceled their reservations. She couldn't help wondering if they'd decided to stay at Eilers' Arms instead.

It was a very different kind of hotel. All flash and gimmick with no real charm or substance, they weren't going to attract the same sort of customer. But it was new and unique and had had no shortage of publicity over the past couple of weeks.

Maiden took a deep breath, she knew better than to overreact. Harlow House had an excellent reputation; they'd be fine.

She heard Gloria's noisy tread on the stairs a moment before the lady walked around the corner, pecking at her phone as she went. Her long acrylic nails tapped the screen loudly as she came and stood beside Maiden at the desk.

Maiden studied her subtly from the corner of her eye as her mother checked her phone. She was wearing a rather cute rose-print satin dress, a lot of mascara and even more perfume. Gloria muttered indecipherably under her breath before setting the phone down and flouncing off into the office.

Maiden said nothing as Gloria slipped on her long black coat before grabbing her purse and rummaging through it. Maiden's eyes slid to her mother's phone when it dinged as a reminder popped up. She couldn't help noticing what it said:

> *Lunch with Fred @12:30.*

Why are you meeting another man for lunch? Maiden frowned and looked over in time to see the other woman layering on more dark red lipstick. Gloria breezed past, snagging her phone as she went, and gave Maiden's shoulders a squeeze.

"I got some errands to run," she said as she hurried to the door. "See you later, baby."

Maiden scowled at the door as it fell shut. Gloria had been inexplicably polite about Fred Eilers' debacle of a grand opening last night and now she was meeting him for lunch without telling anyone about it? That couldn't be right.

She took a deep breath and assured herself that her mother wasn't silly enough to put a date with an illicit lover in her calendar. There must be some innocent explanation. There had to be.

She concluded that she was just looking for drama because she had nothing interesting of her own to dwell on since her relationship with David seemed to have been put perpetually on hold.

Until Aunt Bella's wedding had brought their simmering tension to the surface she'd only known David as a cop. He was around a lot because he was working and she was involved in his cases. She'd gotten used to seeing him, but it was quite different when she wasn't allowed in the case. That was a concern that she hadn't anticipated.

Vonny came back with the promised coffee, shaking Maiden from her worried thoughts. She thanked her as she accepted her cup and groped for something neutral to discuss.

"What did you make of the grand opening?" she asked as soon as it occurred to her.

"It was all right." Vonny said slowly and then pulled a face. "Until Mr. Eilers threw that other guy out, that was kind of uncomfortable."

"Yeah, it was weird," Maiden said. "I saw Ulysses Mercier poking around in the foyer not long before that."

"Ulysses?" Vonny gave her a startled look. "Is that the guy's name?"

"Well, that's how he introduced himself," she said.

"Nobody would make up a handle like that," Von laughed. "So, what do you mean he was poking around? What was he doing?"

"Knocking on walls." Maiden pulled a face and shook her head. "I know, it's weird. But then he started talking to those people in the suits and Eilers lost it."

"Those were a few of the bigger shareholders," Von informed her. "I was talking to that lady with the pink hair, she's a shareholder too, but she wasn't so grumpy. She loved the décor."

"Mm." Maiden chose not to venture an opinion on that. "But the finished project *was* lightyears away from the pictures they'd probably signed off on. Imagine sinking a lot of money into something for it to come out totally different from what you wanted."

"The pink-haired lady—Margaret, I think." Vonny tapped her chin thoughtfully. "Yeah, Margaret said the Old Chateau actually came pretty cheap. Someone helped negotiate a good price since it needed a lot of work."

"I guess that's fair." Maiden said slowly. "But it really is a shame they changed the place so much. It's not like we have an endless supply of ancient relics."

"Yeah, maybe." Von said with little concern. "But at least someone finally did something with the place, it was just rotting away anyway."

What she said was true, but Maiden didn't fully agree with it. Even the ruins of the Old Chateau had an air of dignified grace to them, but maybe she was biased. It didn't help when she picked up the newspaper and saw Eilers' Arms mentioned on the front page yet again.

Local Historical Association Labels Fred Eilers A Public Menace!

Golden Glen's newest tourist hotspot is now officially open. Mr. Eilers cut the ribbon on his latest hotel yesterday and has reportedly been inundated with phone calls from people desperate to see what all the fuss is about. Mr. Eilers claims that they are heavily booked for the next three months and that's a trend he fully expects to continue.

But not everyone in town is so enamored of the hotel's unique style. The Golden Glen Historical Association has sent a letter formally complaining that Mr. Eilers was permitted to structurally alter a building that's reputed to date back to the late 1700s.

When asked to comment on the complaints, Mr. Eilers replied that nothing in the building had been "significantly structurally altered". We're expected to believe, it seems, that adding an additional floor and building on an expansive kitchen isn't "significant".

"Maybe if you stopped plastering his hotel all over the front page," Maiden sighed under her breath, "he might not be so richly rewarded for ignoring everyone else and doing whatever he wants. With *whoever* he wants."

"What was that?" Von glanced at her with a faint scowl.

She debated whether or not to say anything about Gloria's lunch date and ultimately decided not to. Not yet. All she had to go on was a calendar reminder and that was too flimsy to justify the fit Vonny was capable of throwing if she knew about it.

"Nothing." Maiden replied mildly and even managed a smile. "Just thinking out loud."

About fifteen minutes passed before Vonny remembered she had a hair appointment and rushed out the door. Maiden didn't mind the resulting solitude. She was tired of thinking about Fred Eilers but couldn't stop herself. She was in a conflicted state as a result, but a few more people rang up and booked reservations, which bolstered her mood a bit.

She glanced up as Billie, back on cleaning duty, wandered into the lobby and started polishing the woodwork. The small table that sat between a pair of wingback chairs gleamed as she wiped her cloth over it. She looked over at Maiden and smiled faintly.

"How's it going?" she asked.

"Okay. Kinda quiet." Maiden shrugged nonchalantly. "How about you?"

"Fine thanks." Billie trailed off but looked like she was working up to saying something.

Maiden braced for whatever Billie might be thinking. She *really* didn't want to talk about Eilers' hotel and what it might mean for their own business or chitchat about her non-existent plans for the evening. Casual conversation was the enemy at present.

Billie glanced around the foyer to ensure they were alone before taking a few cautious steps closer to the desk. Maiden fought an exaggerated and needless urge to run away and hide.

"Are your mom and dad okay?!" she finally blurted.

"Huh?" Maiden stared at her.

"I-I heard Alfie whispering to someone on the phone earlier," Billie bit her lip and wrung her polishing cloth uneasily. "I think he was talking to a woman. Then Gloria came along and he ended the call really quick."

"Did you hear what he was saying?" Maiden tried not to look as worried as she was starting to feel.

"No, I hid by the stairs but he was keeping an eye out so I couldn't get too close," she said openly, clearly feeling no qualms about spying on her employer. "They're not breaking up, are they?"

"What?! No!" Maiden gasped. "Why would you ask that?"

"Secrets between couples are bad news, Maiden," she said. "That's where it starts. Secrets, then lies and then everything gets blown to crap. That's how marriages die."

"That's ridiculous!" Maiden said firmly. "Especially if you're talking about Mom and Dad. They have a great marriage."

"Maybe we only think they do." Billie's pale eyes were round and quietly horrified. "Some couples bluff, they stay together for the kids' sake. Now that you and Vonny have both found someone, maybe the charade is just too much to maintain. I'm sorry, Maiden. This must be so difficult for you."

"They're not splitting up!" Maiden managed not to yell or laugh at the woman's absurdly serious expression. "It was one phone call and we don't know what it was about, just relax."

"They're acting weird," Billie whispered intently. "They're both out all the time and looking over their shoulders when they are here. It's more than a phone call, Maiden. Something's not right."

Billie noted Maiden's anxious look and gave a satisfied nod. She backed away slowly, pausing long enough to point her cloth at her for emphasis, and then turned and disappeared upstairs.

Maiden took a deep breath. Despite her flare for the dramatic, Billie was at least partly correct. Something with her parents wasn't right and now she knew she wasn't imagining things, others had noticed too.

It was unfathomable. Her parents weren't splitting up, they couldn't be. They weren't even fighting...but Alfie had apparently hidden a phone call from Gloria...who was out having lunch with his old college buddy. Maiden reminded herself to breathe.

She was still trying to get her head around her growing fears when she heard the front door open. She looked over and shut her eyes briefly when she saw David walking inside. Maiden really didn't feel up to any sort of confrontation and she didn't like the watchful look on his face.

She quickly tried to bolster herself up with reminders that she was a strong, sexy and vital woman that didn't need to feel swayed by any man. Even if he was gorgeous and clever and absolutely perfect for her except for being surprisingly clueless and inattentive.

David approached with a sense of wary determination. Maiden clasped her hands together tightly on the desktop and cursed her indecisiveness. She'd been moping about not seeing him all week and now that he was standing across the desk from her, she wanted to bolt.

"Hi, David," she said lamely and with a forced smile. "I thought you'd be busy today."

"I am, but whatever." He waved it away and locked his eyes with hers, probably because she looked anxious and shifty. "Is everything okay, Maiden?"

"...Yeah. As far as I know." She glanced away from his piercing gaze because lying made her uncomfortable. "H-have you been well?"

"What?" he sounded confused.

"I don't think repeating it will help," she murmured more to herself than to him.

"Right, listen, I can't help feeling like you've been ignoring me," he said candidly.

Maiden felt her eyes widen and her mouth drop open at that unbelievably ironic statement. She'd been given the brush off repeatedly and *he* felt ignored?!

"I came to see you the other day," she reminded him grimly, not appreciating him taking offense at anything at this point. 'I realize that you're *always* busy, but if you try hard you might remember."

She would almost have preferred that he rankled at that rather grumpy statement, it would make it easier to be angry with him. He didn't rankle though, he didn't even scowl, he lifted his brows with a hint of regret.

Maiden felt her heart thump a bit harder as he walked around the desk. She knew she wasn't terribly strong where he was concerned, and she was already lonely and missing him.

"I do remember. I tried to catch you, but you kept driving—which is okay! I know you were upset with me," David quickly added when she shot him an irate look. He studied her carefully as he came and stood beside her. "But you haven't replied to any of my messages since. So, what's up?"

"Nothing," she said after way too long of a pause.

He frowned faintly and carefully turned her chair until she was facing him. Maiden glanced up at him and forced herself not to stare at his broad shoulders or be swayed by his cologne.

"Please talk to me," he said gently and touched his fingertips to her arm.

"It's…it's just really frustrating," she finally admitted, very quietly. "Is this what it's always like when you're working on a case?"

"No! Absolutely not, I swear." A look of understanding, and possibly fear, passed over his face as he shook his head very definitely. "The last few weeks have been unusually busy; things have been happening that definitely aren't typical. Please remember that I only moved here a few months ago. I haven't even finished unpacking yet, but that doesn't mean I'll always have cardboard boxes stacked in the kitchen."

"Maybe. But I wonder if we should step back until you've got yourself better organized," she suggested softly.

"What?" he almost whispered and stared at her with widened eyes. "Are you breaking up with me?!"

"No, we'd have to be dating first," she said dryly but then met his troubled gaze and felt herself soften. "Oh, David, no I'm not. I just want to be with you but, to be honest, it's getting really hard to keep being told that you're too busy for me."

"Baby, I'm not!" He grasped her by the arms and pulled her gently to her feet, hugging her to his chest. He looked so anxious. "Please don't think that!"

You actually just called me 'baby', that is so much sexier than when Mom says it. Maiden stared up into his richly brown eyes and knew she was going to crumble. He looked hurt and worried. She managed not to throw her arms around him and apologize for feeling neglected, she did manage to stay that strong at least.

"It's been such a weird week," he whispered as he cupped her cheek in his big hand and kissed her. "Not only the case, but there are major structural faults all through the station and the roof's ruined. But I never meant for it to affect you. I'm so sorry, Maiden."

Don't say it's okay, Maiden! she sternly ordered herself. *It's not okay to ignore you for days, there's no way he's been working until midnight every night. I know he smells amazing and his hand is warm, that's not the point. Don't be pathetic!*

"It's okay, David," she said softly. *Pathetic.*

"No, it isn't. You deserve better," he whispered and kissed her again. "Look, dinner tonight, definitely. Please?"

"I don't know," she said reluctantly. "I really don't think I can deal with another disappointment right now."

"You won't need to, I promise," he assured her and pulled her a little tighter against his chest. "Please, Maiden."

"Okay," she said quietly.

Chapter Six

As evening approached, Maiden was feeling a bit nervous but was looking forward to their date.

After their earlier discussion, she had to believe that David wouldn't dare cancel again. If she meant anything to him at all, he wouldn't even think of rescheduling.

She had pulled out one of her best dresses, it wasn't new but she hadn't worn it yet. She'd found it on sale and loved it so much that she bought it without any specific plans to use it, she knew the opportunity would arise someday. It was black and fitted and fell gracefully just to the knee. It was sexy but still ladylike and she adored it. She even put her hair up and took a little extra time on her makeup.

David had chosen her favorite restaurant, an Italian place called Martinelli's. They had agreed to meet there at 7 pm sharp. The 'sharp' had been David's playful addition.

She smiled to herself as she slipped out of the apartment unnoticed. This was easy since Alfie and Gloria had left a while ago. She had no idea where they'd gone this time but she took some comfort in knowing that they had at least left together.

She headed downstairs and walked to the reception desk where Vonny would be sitting for another half hour or so.

Von glanced up from the magazine she'd been thumbing through and let out a wolf whistle as she looked her over. Maiden chuckled and twirled, sending her filmy skirt out in a graceful flutter.

"You look great." Von smiled slyly. "Are you giving him a real second chance or showing him what he's missed?"

"Both, hopefully." She rolled her eyes but still smiled. "What about you? Are you and Tony going out tonight?"

"No, he's helping his mom rearrange furniture or something." She shrugged. "I can't complain, I get most of his evenings."

"A generous sentiment," Maiden said approvingly and gave her a dainty waggle of her fingers as she slipped past into the office. "I'll see you later."

"Have fun, Mae."

It was a cool and clear evening. The sky was growing steadily darker as countless stars began to appear and twinkle down at her. The short drive to Martinelli's was quiet and peaceful. Maiden felt a happy fluttering in her stomach at the prospect of an evening with David's attention on her and not work.

She parked outside and looked around for his car. She didn't see it but that didn't surprise her, she was a few minutes early. She stepped out into the brisk evening air and strolled inside gracefully, just in case he drove up in time to see her. Maiden smiled at her own silliness but enjoyed it anyway.

She approached the young guy at the desk inside the door and gave him David's name. She was quickly shown to a table in the far corner that had been reserved for them.

She took in the rustic but elegant atmosphere, ignored the admiring stares of a few men she walked past, and took up the seat the waiter pulled out for her. The room was large and cheerfully noisy with almost every table occupied. The walls were decorated in warm shades of yellow, with earthy paintings of buxom peasant girls and baskets of fruit hanging in gilded frames.

The waiter returned with a loaf of crusty bread and a plate of roasted garlic doused in olive oil. He set these and two small plates in front of her and the vacant chair to her left before lighting the candle in the center of the table and asking her if she'd like something to drink while she waited. She requested water as her companion would be joining her soon.

She checked her watch, she was still five minutes early, she wondered if David was there but waiting for the stroke of seven to step inside, she smiled at the thought.

Her eyes scanned the room; the nearby tables were clearly set aside for couples. Like her own table, these were on the smaller side and only allowed for two seats. The lights were slightly dimmer above them too.

She had been there many times of course; it was the only dedicated Italian restaurant in town and that was her favorite cuisine. She sometimes came for lunch with her mother or Vonny, occasionally the whole family came for dinner, but this was the first time she'd come for a date. The thought made her smile, but then she glanced at the empty chair opposite her and her smile faded slightly.

Another glance at her watch told her that David was now a minute late. She quirked a brow and pulled out her phone. There were no messages and no missed calls, he had to be on his way. He might have got caught up in a bit of traffic. It hadn't occurred to her until now that she didn't actually know where he lived, he might have a longer drive.

Fifteen minutes passed and the waiter had returned twice to offer her a drink or an appetizer while she, *ahem*, waited. She opted to keep waiting even as a gnawing suspicion began to blossom inside her.

When the kindly man returned at nearly 7:30 with a reluctant expression, Maiden propped her chin in her hand and smiled serenely at him.

"How long do you think a woman should wait before she finally admits that she's been stood up?" she asked.

"I think you've been patient enough," he said politely but then gestured to indicate her entire person. "But I'll tell you one thing, I'd have to be dead in a ditch before I'd stand up a stunning woman like you. He must be crazy."

"If he thinks I'll ever speak to him again he certainly is," she said rather tightly as she stood and gathered up her jacket and purse. "What do I owe you for the bread?"

"Nothing at all." He smiled nicely. "Just come back with someone who knows what he's got next time."

Maiden gave him a crooked smile and walked out with as much dignity as she could muster. It was all fake, of course, she'd never felt so humiliated and couldn't recall the last time she was so angry. She was sure the people at the tables around her were watching her disgraced exit. They'd sat alongside her enjoying their evening while she'd been alone with her phone.

Tears of anger and hurt stung her eyes as she climbed into her car and slammed the door shut. She grasped the wheel with one hand and shoved the key angrily into the ignition with the other. Knowing that she needed to calm down before trying to drive anywhere, Maiden took a deep breath and shut her eyes. They popped open when she heard the cheep of a message sound on her phone.

"Really?" she demanded as she pulled it out of her purse and glared at the screen. "Let me guess."

David

Maiden, I'm so sorry.

She scowled bitterly as she started typing.

Maiden

I don't care.

David

I need to talk to you.

Maiden

Not a good idea. Find someone else to talk to.

There was a moment's pause before he replied.

David

There's been another murder.

"A murder?" Maiden whispered aloud as she frowned down at the glowing screen, she started typing again.

Maiden

Who was it?

David

Come to Eilers' Arms. Your parents are here, you'd better hurry.

***

Maiden's stomach was in knots by the time she reached The Docks. The flashing lights of several police cars threw eerie shadows over the front of Eilers' hotel. She parked and hurried towards the garish building.

She looked around, frantically trying to find her parents, but quickly spotted Sarah-Jane and Greg when they glanced over at her. Greg looked placid enough which made her hope that her parents were at least safe.

"Hi, Mae. I wondered if you'd get a call." Greg waved as he and Sarah-Jane started towards her. "Are you looking for Captain McAlister?"

"No!" she said a little too vehemently. "I was told my parents are here."

"They are, yeah." Sarah-Jane pointed towards the hotel with her thumb. "They're still inside, you can't go in yet, but they're okay."

Maiden gave a relieved sigh and ran a hand over her carefully styled hair. She couldn't believe she'd gone to the trouble of putting it up into an elegant twist for the occasion, it was just one more thing that made her feel like an idiot now. Her only hope was that David's underlings weren't privy to *every* whim of his personal life.

Seemingly reading her mind, Sarah-Jane looked her over when the breeze pushed her jacket back off her shoulders.

"You look really nice," she said companionably, but then pulled an apologetic face. "Were you and the captain called away from a date again?"

"Something like that." Maiden rolled her eyes and then nodded towards the hotel. "Who died?"

"A Mr. Ulysses Mercier, if you can believe that's a real name." Greg smiled faintly as he checked his notes.

"Mr. Mercier?" Maiden frowned as she took that in. "Really? How did it happen?"

"Hi, Maiden."

They all glanced over at the sound of David's deep voice. Maiden's blood turned to ice when her eyes settled on him.

He was still in his usual daily look of brown trousers, off-white shirt and a dark tie that always hung loose around his neck. Although he'd slipped on a long trench-coat against the chilly evening breeze. He definitely didn't look as though he'd been called away from a hot date at the last minute.

He'd clearly been on the scene for a while. In that moment, she knew with a furiously burning certainty that he'd forgotten about her. She wondered if she'd have felt less angry and pathetic if she weren't the only one overdressed for the occasion.

"Miss Harlow was only asking about her parents, sir," Sarah-Jane quickly spoke up, perhaps to distract from Maiden's question about the murder.

The tomboyish young officer's attitude towards Maiden had certainly mellowed since Gloria and Bella had worked their magic on her appearance. Sarah-Jane looked to be doing her best to maintain the makeover and mostly succeeded.

David barely acknowledged her or Greg, his attention was on Maiden. He glanced away long enough to dismiss them. The pair looked uncertainly at her and then each other before quickly walking away.

When they were alone, David edged closer and gave her a very careful look. She distantly wondered if that's what people who disarmed explosives looked like.

"I swear I can explain," he said quietly.

"I'll bet you can, but I'm in no mood to hear it," she replied coolly. "You said my parents are here and you know that's the only reason I came. Where are they?"

"They're inside, I'll take you there in a minute. I promise you they're fine." He raised a hand in a soothing gesture. "I'm so sorry about tonight."

"You've been sorry every time." She did her best to sound disinterested rather than enraged, it wasn't easy. "*I'm* sorry I wasted yet another evening waiting around like a fool."

"You can't seriously blame me for this one." He took her arm and led her a discreet distance from the quietly interested officers that were trying to look like they weren't watching.

"Why not?" She gave him a sardonic look. "You *may* have killed the man, I certainly don't know where you were all evening."

"I was home and about to get ready when the call came through about a body being found." He looked frustrated and frazzled. "I had to come straight here. What was I supposed to do?"

"Oh, I don't know, maybe remember me sooner than half an hour after you promised to meet me?" she suggested, in no way moved by his explanation. "Possibly take thirty seconds out of your busy day to tell me not to bother sitting around by myself looking like some pathetic loser while you're off taking care of things you find more important?"

"That's not fair!" he muttered, trying his best to argue without raising his voice. "I'm as frustrated by this as you are!"

"You didn't even think about me until you sent that text, did you?" She held his gaze mercilessly. "You've probably been here for hours and were too caught up to remember that I was waiting for you."

His grim and unhappy silence told her she was right. It was both gratifying and disappointing, but it was also time to get moving.

"So, Mom and Dad are where?" she asked, folding her arms.

David exhaled through his nose and gestured for her to follow as he stalked towards the hotel. Maiden walked along with as much cool dignity as she could muster.

She was obviously dressed up and David just as obviously wasn't. It wouldn't be hard for a group of people that investigated for a living to work out what had happened. She hid behind the anger to hold off the embarrassment; she could cry over that later and privately.

All she wanted for now was to collect her parents and get them safely home. Once she knew everyone was safe and back where they belonged, she could decide what she would do about the phantom captain. Her first notion was to block his number in her phone and never speak to him again.

He led her through the dark blue foyer, past the big staircase and the paintings of wrecked ships to a small private lounge.

She peered inside and saw Alfie and Gloria sitting anxiously at a small table. It was spread with enough food and dishes to betray where her parents had gone for dinner. They glanced up in surprise and then obvious relief when they saw her walk in.

"Maiden!" Gloria hurried over and hugged her tightly. "How'd you know we were here?"

"It doesn't matter," she said and shook her head. "Are you both okay?"

"*We* are," Alfie said quietly, "but Fred isn't. He's been arrested."

"He's just been taken to another room for questioning, Mr. Harlow." David's steady voice reminded them he was there watching and listening. "No charges have been laid yet."

Alfie pulled a face and rubbed his weary eyes. Maiden noticed and felt her stomach tighten with concern. She took his arm gently and glanced at David with a decidedly cooler expression.

"Are my parents free to leave?" she asked.

"Yes," he almost sighed, "just stay in town."

"Fine." She turned to her father. "Did you drive here?"

"No, Fred sent a car," he mumbled.

"All right, let's go," she said gently. "You can come home with me."

She herded them towards the door. They both looked stunned and worried. As she passed by David he reached out and touched her shoulder; she glanced over just enough to give him a look.

"Good night, Captain," she said flatly.

He closed his eyes briefly and let his hand drop.

***

David watched them go with the same gut-twisting uneasiness he'd felt since he realized he'd missed his date with Maiden. He couldn't remember the last time he'd felt so horrible.

He really had been about to get ready for their date, it had been on his mind all afternoon. He'd been determined to leave in plenty of time to get to the restaurant first and maybe even grab some flowers on the way. He was just climbing into the shower when he got the phone call.

A body had been found in an upstairs office at the Eilers' Arms hotel. He'd quickly dressed and rushed across town to oversee the initial foray and meet with forensics. Time flew by while he was deeply immersed in examining the crime scene.

When he'd been told that the owner of the hotel had been having dinner with Alfie and Gloria and had apparently had a public argument with the victim the night before, David realized that it had probably been the party Maiden had invited him to. And then it hit him. He checked the time and realized he was half an hour late to meet Maiden. It was a complete disaster.

She'd already started to break up with him once, she'd barely agreed to dinner, and he actually stood her up. It was a horrifying moment that had felt frozen in time.

Ultimately, he played the only card he had, he told her that her parents were there. He'd then hovered around the foyer waiting for her to turn up, and then she did, and he'd almost lost the nerve to face her.

He could see that she'd put a lot of effort in, she looked incredible; the date had still been important to her. It had been important to him too, but she'd probably never believe that and he really had no decent excuse. Missing the date was one thing, but forgetting it was colossally stupid.

David felt a bit sick and more than a little scared as he stared at the door she'd closed behind her. She was so coldly angry with him, and he couldn't blame her; he'd blown it big time.

Apart from his personal disasters, he still had another murder to solve. The first thing he needed to do was deal with Eilers; he could try calling Maiden after that.

David used the time it took to return to the lobby and climb the large stairs to get his head together. He knew that Eilers had already been questioned by Ramirez, but it was a surface skim and the answers hadn't been especially clear.

He went straight to a private office on the third floor where Eilers was being detained. Officer Briggs was standing nearby with an emotionless expression. Briggs was a hard-core introvert; unrevealing looks were one of his specialties.

David nodded in acknowledgement to the younger officer as he walked in and then turned his attention to the suspect.

Eilers was of average height and quite barrel-chested. He wore a suit that probably fit him when he bought it, but the fabric over his stomach was stretched taut and the buttons were strained. His pale eyes were watchful, and he was dabbing at his sweaty brow with a handkerchief.

"Mr. Eilers," David said as he pulled out his notebook and pen from his top pocket. "I'm told that you found the body."

"Yeah, I did," he admitted quietly. "I already talked to one of your people."

"I'm aware of that." He flicked to a new page and started writing. "You saw the body when you entered your office?"

"Yes, I went to get some papers from the filing cabinet and," Eilers stopped to wet his lips, "there he was. Laying on his stomach in front of the fireplace."

"Tell me your exact movements for the evening," David said impassively.

"I finished up a bit of work in my office—it was empty when I left." He glanced up for emphasis on that last point. "Then I went downstairs to one of the private dining rooms to meet up with the Harlows. We were having dinner and got around to talking business, that's a bad habit of mine. Anyway, I went to grab some papers and found a dead body instead."

"What did you do then?" he prompted.

"I-I was in a daze. I stumbled out of the room and back downstairs." Eilers shook his head and dragged the handkerchief over his forehead. "I mumbled something to Alfie and Gloria, and she started telling me to call the police, so I did."

"You didn't think to call us on your own?" David quirked a brow.

"I was barely thinking at all!" he protested, raising his palms in a gesture of helplessness. "I've never seen a dead body before! There was blood on his head and all over the rug—I panicked and ran out of there!"

"Were you acquainted with the victim?" He watched Eilers closely, curious to see if he'd try to lie about the argument they'd allegedly had the previous evening.

"Yeah, I was," Eilers said resignedly. "We went way back. Ulysses and Alfie and me, we were best friends through college."

"You were observed having an altercation with the deceased last night," David advised him. "Are you sure you were 'best' friends?"

"Back then we were pretty tight, not as much these days," he conceded. "Ulysses hadn't turned out to be the nicest guy in the world, but we lost touch, so it didn't overly matter to me."

"Why would he have been in your office then?"

"I have no idea," Eilers said. He failed to hide his annoyance at the mention of it. "I certainly didn't invite him, and he had no right to be there."

"Hmm." David turned back a few pages in his notes to his discussion with the Harlows. "How long were you out of the room when you went upstairs?"

"What do you mean?" Eilers frowned.

"You said you left the dining room to go and get some papers from your office," he reminded him. "How long were you gone?"

"Oh, not very long." Eilers wet his lips again. "I saw Ulysses lying there and headed straight back."

"You were reportedly gone for over ten minutes," David murmured. "I've seen your office; it doesn't take ten minutes to get there and back. Particularly if you ran out in a panic. What else were you doing?"

"Oh..." Eilers blinked widened eyes and seemed to be searching his memory. "I-I um...Oh! Sorry, I got mixed up. I didn't see the body straight away. I went to my desk to look for those papers first. Then I looked up and, yeah, there he was. I would've sat there for a few minutes digging around. My brain is scrambled eggs at the moment, sorry."

"Perfectly understandable, Mr. Eilers." David's smile was cool and didn't reach his eyes. "Where are those papers now?"

"I never found them." He shook his head.

"What did they pertain to?"

"Just some stocks, my investment portfolio." Eilers waved it away.

"Had you searched the filing cabinet?" David asked.

"No." He shook his head. "I didn't get past the desk. That's when I saw Ulysses on the floor. Look, if you don't believe me, I'll show you. I'm a bit shaken up, but I'll bring them to the station tomorrow."

"Your office is a crime scene, Mr. Eilers," David informed him. "You aren't permitted to enter or remove anything until I give the word."

"What?!" Eilers' face flushed irately. "You can't bar me from my own office! I have work to do!"

"Not in there you don't," David replied. "Not yet."

"I won't be bullied or harassed, McAlister!" he said through his teeth. "I'm not some backwater hick that doesn't know their rights!"

"You're a suspect in a murder that took place in your office, potentially during a window of time when no one can vouch for your whereabouts," David said with chilling calm. "I suggest you keep that in mind. I also suggest you remember that tampering with a crime scene is a serious offense. Understood?"

Eilers' countenance changed immediately. His angry snarl softened into a look of contrition. He held up his hands and leaned back a fraction.

"Of course, I'm sorry," he said far more politely. "I'm still in shock and I overreacted. I'm perfectly willing to cooperate."

"Excellent." David flicked his notebook closed and put it away. "Stay in town. We'll be in touch."

CHAPTER SEVEN

M aiden followed her parents up the stairs to their apartment. She was watching them uneasily as they walked wearily towards the front door. They'd all been quiet on the way home, each being preoccupied with their own particular worries.

They walked inside and saw Vonny sitting on the couch reading, her shoulders wreathed in sleeping kittens. She glanced back at them in obvious surprise. She ditched her book and then gently shifted the cats onto the cushion beside her.

"You're all home early," she informed them as she came to join them at the table. "And at exactly the same time. What's going on?"

"That Mercier guy was killed tonight," Maiden said as she slid down into her usual chair.

"The great and mythical Ulysses?" Von stared at her.

"Not mythical," Maiden sighed. "But definitely murdered."

"In Fred's office," Alfie added as he sat down across from her.

"Whoa!" Vonny's pale blue eyes widened. "I'll make hot cocoa. Tell me everything!"

Gloria kicked off her shoes and winced and waddled her way into the kitchen to help. As the pair made cocoa Gloria exhaled loudly and started talking.

"We were eating dinner with Fred when he, uh, went to make a phone call." She patted her blonde curls absently. "Then he came back, white as a sheet, and said he'd found Ulysses' dead on his office floor."

"How'd he die?" Von's tone was full of macabre wonder.

"That young detective said he'd been struck on the head." Alfie nodded his thanks as Gloria set his mug in front of him before taking up the seat on his right.

"With a fireplace poker. That's what they reckon anyway." Gloria shuddered and sipped her cocoa.

"It's a shame. To be honest, the guy looked like trouble, but still..." Maiden said and fell silent.

She knew her father's reference to the 'young detective' meant David and the thought of him still hurt. She was getting lost in thought when she noticed her mother lean towards her.

"You'll help Fred," Gloria's soft brown eyes were pleading as they locked on Maiden, "won't you, baby?"

"I guess I can try." Maiden submerged many conflicting feelings as she met her mother's gaze.

She wasn't overly interested in anything that would bring her in contact with the police or a certain police captain, and she wasn't sure how she felt about Fred Eilers or Gloria's obvious concern for him. But she did want to know what her parents were up to and this seemed like a promising excuse to snoop around in their personal business.

"Thank you, sweetheart," Gloria said shakily and rubbed her forehead. "We already told him you would."

"Thanks for the heads up then," Maiden said under her breath before continuing. "So, what's the real story with Eilers and Mercier?"

"I told you before. We all sort of knew each other back in our college days." Alfie glanced at her. "Fred and Ulysses were always competing with one another, always trying to come out on top."

"Why?" Vonny pulled a face as she plonked down next to Maiden and set a bag of marshmallows in the middle of the table.

"They were both always determined to be the best." He shrugged it off. "But Fred wasn't as nasty about it. He was stubborn, sure, he still is. But Ulysses was a heartless snake in the grass. He didn't care who he hurt as long as he won."

"Okay. But Eilers threw him out publicly at the grand opening of his hotel. So why was he in Eilers office?" Maiden asked carefully. "Was he supposed to be meeting him tonight?"

"That's the funny thing." Gloria tapped her long acrylics against the side of her cup. "Fred was havin' dinner with us. He wouldn't have had an appointment with Ulysses as well. But Fred went to his office and found him lyin' on the floor."

"What time was that?" Maiden asked.

"About 5:30, or thereabouts." Alfie absently patted Rowdy when the speckled kitten hopped up on his knee.

"How long was he out of the room?" Maiden's eyes narrowed slightly.

"Ten minutes, maybe more," Alfie sounded like he was guessing.

"Didn't he have his phone on him?" Vonny asked as she packed as many marshmallows as she could in the top of her mug.

"I think he may have forgot it in his office." Alfie didn't sound concerned.

"It took him ten minutes to get to his office, find the body, and come straight back?" Maiden frowned a little. "That's kind of a long time. Is it that far away?"

"Oh, um, not really," Gloria admitted and glanced away. "Maybe he stopped to use the bathroom before he got there."

"I guess that's...possible." Maiden knew she sounded dubious. "Okay, let me get this straight, Eilers had a public fight with Mercier.

And then Mercier was murdered in his office while Eilers was on site and out of the room so you didn't actually see him. Anything else I should know?"

"I think Fred might be havin' some financial troubles," Gloria murmured after a long pause. "He didn't go into too many details but he'll be able to tell you more about it."

"All right." Maiden said. "I'll see if there's anything I can do."

"Thanks, baby." Gloria smiled quietly. "And thanks for comin' to our rescue tonight."

"Yeah, that reminds me. How did you get there so fast, Mae? I thought you were going out to dinner." Vonny frowned at her. "Wasn't this your big 'he wouldn't dare cancel this one' date with McAlister? Did he get the call while you were out again?"

"No…" Maiden let her gaze drop to the marshmallows melting in her cup, feeling embarrassed all over again. "He never showed up."

Gloria's brows rose sharply but she clamped her mouth shut to keep from blurting out whatever she was thinking. A qualm that never seemed to occur to Vonny.

"He stood you up?!" Von demanded angrily. "After begging you to go out with him, he actually *stood you up?*"

"Yes. It was disappointing and mortifying so feel free not to lean on it," Maiden mumbled and propped her chin in her hand. "I wish he hadn't chosen Martinelli's; it was my favorite restaurant and now I can't show my face there again."

"Is that really what's botherin' you, angel?" Gloria asked gently.

Maiden felt tears sting her eyes. She didn't know what to say so she took a shaky breath and sipped her cocoa. Alfie shifted uncomfortably as he tried to figure out how to comfort his daughter while not knowing most of the details of the situation.

Gloria and Von looked more sympathetic and understanding. Vonny reached over and grasped her hand, she met her tearful gaze with a kind smile.

"Dump him," she said.

Maiden gave her a look and pulled her hand away.

"Now Vonny, don't pressure your sister!" Gloria patted her arm. "Don't you pay any attention to anyone else, angel, you take your time and make up your own mind what you want to do. But maybe leave it alone for tonight."

Maiden sniffled as she considered that. Her mother was right, she was in no condition to think deeply on any future plans tonight. The disappointment and anger were enough on their own without the complication of another murder case thrown in. She needed to sleep on it.

She opened her mouth to speak when her phone buzzed with an incoming call. She pulled it out and stared down at David's name on the display. Taking a shaky breath she glanced up and met her mother's kind and loving gaze.

Maiden smiled a little and dredged up the strength to press the button and refuse the call.

"I'm going to bed," she said mildly as she pushed to her feet. "Don't worry, I'll think about Mr. Eilers in the morning and see what I can do to help him."

***

Maiden wasn't at all surprised when David walked into the foyer early the next morning. He looked her in the eye and gave her a wincing, apologetic smile as he came and stood before the desk. The sight of his handsome face immediately made her grumpy.

"Hey," David said gently. "Are you guys okay? How are Alfie and Gloria?"

"Tired," she said. "We're all tired, it was an awful night for everyone."

"Yeah, it was." He glanced away briefly before facing her again. "Um, can we go and get a coffee?"

"I'm working, sorry," she said sardonically, privately amused to throw his own excuse back in his face.

"I'll come back later, then. Whenever you want, I'll make it happen," David said patiently. "We really need to talk."

"No, we really don't." She arched a brow.

"I know I messed up." He leaned a bit closer.

"Good." She nodded once. "I'm glad you've realized that."

"Maiden, please." He reached for her hand but she pulled it away. "I'm incredibly sorry."

"David," she sighed loudly, "I know that. That's not really the point and it's obviously not the solution to the problem. You can't even give me one evening. I need more from you than your spare time and I'm certainly not going to settle for nothing."

"I'm not asking you to," he assured her. "Maiden, we have something special. We get along great, we think alike, we have chemistry. I get that you're angry and feeling neglected; I *have* neglected you, but never deliberately."

"I asked you, David, I asked you to leave it alone until you had yourself organized. You didn't even consider it. You didn't think about what this is doing to me," she told him grimly. "Do you have any idea what it feels like to be tossed aside repeatedly and then be completely forgotten? Last night was humiliating! I told you, you don't have time for me!"

"Maiden, I understand how you feel, I swear to you—"

His phone rang. She held his gaze intently, daring him to look at his screen. David's jaw was tight, his brows drawn together in an earnest frown. Maiden draped her hands on her hips and gave him an expectant look. He shook his head and pulled his phone from his pocket.

"There really are two murder investigations unfolding right now," he said seriously.

"I wouldn't know about that since speaking of it in front of me is apparently forbidden," she said dryly. "So why are you wasting your breath on me, Captain? You don't have time for anything but work after all."

He shut his eyes briefly. She knew she was drawing a hard line but she didn't like the excuses and didn't want to give the impression that she'd always be the one to fit around his other priorities. She could see herself going to parties alone and perpetually explaining that David was stuck at work while she sat by herself and watched as others built actual relationships.

"It's Doc Jenkins, I have to take this," he muttered at the phone and then looked at her.

"You *have* to? Right this second? He's a coroner, he's calling with details or some report, he's not breaking news of a bank robbery in progress! It could've waited five minutes while you finished lying about not putting work ahead of me," she said angrily and turned to the office. "Goodbye, David."

Maiden kept her shoulders rolled back and her head held high until she shut the door and leaned against it. She covered her face with her hands and tried not to shake. She absolutely hated fighting, and fighting with David was even worse.

She pushed away from the door and went to the coffee pot in the corner. After she poured herself a cup that she really didn't want, she sat down and tried to calm her nerves. The adrenaline of the conversation was still coursing through her, making her heart pound.

How do people do this on a regular basis? she wondered to herself as she thought about all the sniping, squabbling couples she'd seen come through the inn over the years. She could always tell the ones that fought often. They were cold and indifferent even in their milder moments, there was rarely affection or kind words exchanged. It was terrifying.

Maiden took a deep breath and tried not to get too upset. She knew she had to look at the situation with brutal honesty or it would never get any better.

David was right, when they were together they did get along extremely well. And they certainly had chemistry. She was strongly drawn to him physically and knew it was mutual; she still had his stupid necktie in her underwear drawer. But he didn't want her badly enough to make anything happen. He needed to look at his priorities and actually do something about them.

"This stinks," she mumbled down into her coffee.

She glanced to the door when she heard the knob rattle. Maiden looked at her sister expectantly when Vonny slipped into the office and shut the door behind her.

"Did he leave?" Maiden asked quietly.

"Yes, finally." Von rolled her eyes. "How a guy can be so persistent and yet never around when you need him, I simply don't know."

Maiden didn't reply, she just stared glumly down into her cup. Vonny edged closer and rested a hand on her shoulder.

"Are you okay?"

"Fantastic, thanks."

"Oh, Maiden. Enough sitting around feeling awful, okay?" Von said gently and came to sit next to her. "You need to get out and do something. Tell you what, Tony and I are going to the Addison Theater tonight, why don't you come too?"

"I really don't feel like it," she said sullenly. "I can't imagine being around people tonight."

"Maiden, stop it!" Von grasped her shoulders and gave her a worried look. "You never do anything anymore! You just sit and mope. Go out and actually enjoy yourself without David! Like you *used* to do all the time!"

"I know but...I feel like garbage." She let out a weary groan. "I don't know if he really listened to what I said or if he's angry now. It's all such a mess."

"No, it isn't! It's a stupid spat! He can either treat you better or get lost." Vonny was settling into one of her stubborn moods and fisted her hands in her lap. "You're coming tonight. You have to! Are you gonna sit home and cry all night or do something fun? C'mon!"

Maiden considered that. It was true, she and Von used to do things all the time. She hadn't had a truly fun evening in a while, not since Aunt Bella's wedding and even that had ended in murder.

She needed to lighten up and clear her head. Maybe David would think about what she'd told him and decide what he really wanted. In the meantime, life still went on and if her options were sitting home with her cat again or going to the theater with her friends it wasn't such a hard choice.

Apart from that, she knew exactly who was playing at the Addison tonight. She'd be lying if she claimed that getting a closer look at the recently, and suspiciously, bereaved Highland Hounds didn't stir her curiosity.

"What time do we need to be there?" she asked.

Vonny grinned happily and hugged her.

Chapter Eight

A cold rain was lightly falling as Maiden, Vonny and Tony arrived at the Addison Theater that evening. It sat nestled in the heart of the bustling downtown area. It was three stories high and in its long life had been everything from a school house to a fire station before finally finding its niche in the arts.

The eclectic building was decades old and full of character. It had played host to countless travelling musicians, acting troupes, motivational speakers and even the occasional magic show. It was a well-loved local landmark and was usually quite busy whenever a show was in town. Tonight was no exception.

Maiden was pleasantly surprised that any tickets were available after the band's first two performances sold out. Apparently enough of the gawkers had gotten their eyeful and generously left some seats for everyone else.

She, Vonny and Tony laughed and dashed quickly through the steadily falling rain. When they reached the meager protection of the red and white striped awning that lined the front of the building, Maiden chanced a peek at the large advertising posters that featured the current act.

The Highland Hounds, the band whose manager was murdered a week ago, were soldiering on in their multi-city tour. She paused in front of the poster nearest the door, ignored the cold raindrops that slid down her collar, and looked them over curiously.

Long hair and beards of various sizes adorned the four men that posed with their favored instruments. She looked from one colorful, well-travelled man to the next and distantly wondered if one of them was capable of murder.

"Hurry up or you'll catch a cold!" Tony laughed as he grasped her hand and tugged her gently towards the door behind them.

Maiden obligingly followed as the wind picked up and howled around them. They stepped inside along with dozens of other happy, chattering music-lovers and brushed the rain from their sleeves.

The foyer was done up in rich shades of red and heavy black and gold brocade fabrics. The lights were dim enough to provide a warm and welcoming glow. Maiden closed her eyes briefly and inhaled; it had that special theater smell that she couldn't quite decipher. It was a blend of velvet curtains, traces of countless perfumes and a hint of buttery popcorn.

She smiled and opened her eyes to survey the crowd; she was relieved to see that she wasn't the most casually dressed among them. She'd worn her favorite jeans and a dark red top under a black leather jacket, despite Vonny opting for a knee-length velvet dress. Maiden hadn't been worried about being under dressed when she'd gotten ready, it was cold and rainy and she didn't want to be shivering all evening. It wasn't as though she had anyone there to keep her warm.

Maiden quickly ordered herself not to sulk. She turned her thoughts to the show and tried to get more excited about it. She'd always loved Celtic music and culture; it was so full of emotion, romance and rich history.

It hadn't been easy to keep her word and come along, despite her interest in the band's murdered manager. As the afternoon had propelled her relentlessly towards the evening she had fought a powerful urge to hide in her room and refuse to leave it.

She let Von drag her along as she and Tony forged a path through the crowd. They found three seats together and waited another ten minutes before the house lights dimmed and the spotlights flickered to life, illuminating the stage. The heavy burgundy curtains were drawn back even as the slow, mournful sound of a fiddle wafted gently through the air.

Maiden released a soft whisper of a breath at the sad and beautiful sound. The spotlights revealed a tall and slender man with a glossy blue fiddle tucked under his chin. His eyes were closed as he swayed with the music.

Bright blue eyes popped open a second later as he began to play a rousing tune with ever increasing vigor. The crowd clapped along and several let out appreciative whistles as more lights hit the stage, revealing the rest of the band. A man with a ponytail that emphasized his receding hairline banged away at a few small drums while a broad shouldered and quite handsome man stepped forward with a tin whistle.

The last to join them was a tall man with blonde hair and a full, bushy beard. He was playing a guitar but stepped up to a microphone that was set up at the front of the stage and began to sing.

Maiden had never heard the song before but it was bright and lively. The man's accent was so thick that it sounded like he was switching between English and Gaelic, but she couldn't be sure. She was smiling and clapping along with the rest of the audience by the end of the song.

The room was filled with applause and more whistles as the group finished the tune and took a bow. The lead singer greeted everyone and introduced himself and the rest of the band. His name was Arran, the fiddler was Harris, the piper Ewan and the drummer Braden. Maiden's unusually sharp memory assured her that she'd keep that straight, along with countless other bits of information that rarely came in handy ever again.

The music started up again and song after song filled the room and captivated the attention of the enthralled listeners. The band was very talented and charismatic; throughout the show they smiled at each other and at people in the crowd as if they were all old friends.

Maiden felt herself brighten up a bit. The concert was intimate but lively, and a welcome escape from her various troubles. For a couple of hours she stopped thinking about her forgetful boyfriend, her secretive parents and a murder she'd recklessly promised to help solve.

After the show, the crowd started shuffling out of the auditorium. Maiden followed the flow of foot traffic into a reception room where the band was already mingling. At the side of the room there was a table set up with CDs and t-shirts featuring a picture of the band. A smiling young blonde woman in a navy-blue tunic with 'Addison Theater' embroidered on it was sitting there collecting the money and chatting with the customers.

Maiden, Von and Tony looked the table over and each bought a CD. Maiden handed the lady her money and noticed a name tag that said 'Stacey' pinned to her shirt.

"Thanks, Stacey," she said nicely and turned to the far end of the room as she stepped out of the way of the next person.

The band was stationed at another long table signing autographs but there was already a long line of people trying to meet and get pictures with them. Maiden grimaced and glanced at Vonny and Tony, quietly hoping they'd decide they didn't want to stand in line all night.

"Forget that." Von pulled a face as she looked at the tittering women hanging shamelessly on the hunky piper, posing for photos.

"Yeah," Tony chuckled. "How about a drink instead?"

They slipped out of the reception room and down the hall to the restaurant. This was also pretty full but Tony managed to find them seats at one of several tall tables in the middle of the room. He got them settled and then bravely made the trek to the noisy bar.

The room was buzzing. A large portion of the audience opted to stay back and meet members of the band and then have appetizers and drinks.

Maiden glanced around at the vintage posters that were framed and hung on every wall. Most were signed by the artists they portrayed. Maiden had never heard of most of them but it still made for an interesting display.

She saw Vonny watching her surreptitiously from the corner of her eye. Suppressing a groan, she tried to look completely engrossed in studying the chandelier above them. It was massive and looked like an intricate candelabra with each fake candle crowned by a different colored lampshade.

"Having fun?" Vonny, failing to take the hint, asked brightly.

"Yeah." Maiden turned to her and managed a smile. "It's nice to get out of the house for a bit."

"Mm." Von clearly noticed her little sister's preoccupation and tried to keep her talking. "We should do something again soon. What about the corn maze? Do you want to try that again? It's still open for a couple of weeks."

"Not really," Maiden said dryly. "You yelled at me for months after we went the last time."

"You memorized the whole thing!" Von pointed a finger at her. "It was over in five minutes!"

"Yeah, so I'd rather not." Maiden smirked. "Thanks though."

"Fine. Apple picking?" she tried instead. "Then Mom can bake a cobbler."

"Why don't you learn how to cook?" Maiden asked rather than agree to any more outings.

"I can make salad...and cereal." Von scrunched her face up thoughtfully. "And coffee. What more do I need?"

"You could be a chef with a repertoire like that," she laughed.

Vonny mercifully gave up, they both fell silent and people-watched while they waited for Tony. Maiden was grateful for the moment of peace. She was holding it together but, as nice as the concert was, the handful of love songs they'd played only made her think of David.

She glanced up as Tony came back carrying a beer and two glasses of white wine. Maiden thanked him as she accepted her glass and took a sip. Tony sidled in close to Vonny and gave her a kiss.

Maiden, feeling awkward and suddenly very much on her own, started studying the cover of her CD. She half-listened to Von and Tony chitchat about the concert and which songs had been their favorites but didn't join in.

The cover of her chosen CD was a shot of the four band members standing in front of an ancient castle. She sipped her wine as she admired the lush green landscape beyond them and then turned the case over to peruse the back. She was reading over the full names of each member and marveling at how many instruments some of them played when a man approached the table.

"Good evening! Did you lovely folks enjoy the show?" he asked. He had a heavy Scottish accent but he hadn't been on stage with the band.

"Absolutely!" Tony said cheerfully. "Best live concert I've been to in a long time."

"Excellent!" The man grinned. "The name's Sean Dowling. I'm the touring manager for the Highland Hounds. Always glad to talk to music lovers."

Maiden glanced up sharply at that and made herself smile when Tony introduced them to Sean. He had a friendly smile, bright green eyes and a long, slim face. His jaw was roughly stubbled but lacked the luxuriant beard of the band in his charge.

She tried not to squirm as Sean looked at her with a long, slow smile and started asking them about themselves. She let Vonny and Tony do most of the talking; the guy was checking her out rather obviously and she didn't want to seem encouraging. She was, however, interested in his role with the band.

She politely waited while Von told him about the family's inn, all the while biding her time to bring up the subject that really interested her. When there was finally a pause, she pounced.

"So, Mr. Dowling," she began ingenuously, "you said you're the band's touring manager?"

"That I am, lass." He turned to her and smiled warmly. "I'd love it if you called me Sean, incidentally."

"Oh, thank you. Um...forgive my asking," she fingered the stem of her glass idly, "but the papers said Charles Brown was the manager, did you change roles after...what happened?"

"Alas, poor Charles," Sean sighed dramatically and ran a hand through his sandy blonde hair. "No lass, he and I were business partners. We used to share the load. It was a good arrangement, two heads are better than one as they say."

"That's so sad." Maiden let her gaze drift sorrowfully to her glass and then back to his. "Have the police figured out what happened to him yet?"

"No, I'm afraid not."

"How terrible not to know. I'll bet you were friends for years, weren't you?" She shook her head when he nodded stoically. "Well, I do hope you won't think less of Golden Glen. It's an unusual thing to happen here."

She distantly wondered if that could be considered a lie. She'd personally found enough corpses in the last few months to render the statement iffy.

"Don't be silly, lass." Sean flashed her another smile and a wink. "There's more good than bad in this town, that's a certainty. In any case, Charles could be a bit reckless. It's gotten him into some tight scrapes before. Nothing like this though...I'll miss that fool, to be honest."

They were all quiet for a moment while Sean stared down into his whiskey. Maiden was observing him but affected a sympathetic smile when he glanced up again.

"At least no one was caught up in it with him." She kept her tone solemn. "You or any of the band, I mean."

"No, he went off on his own to 'sightsee'." Sean rolled his eyes and sighed again. "He did that often in a town he'd never visited before. Why he went to that grubby little corner of the place I truly don't know."

"Well," Tony piped up when another silence descended. "What will you do from here? Keep managing the Highland Hounds?"

"Yes, of course. I love music and I love travel," he said as his charming smile returned. "It's a bit of a whirlwind life, but it's exciting in its own way. The lads are great and very talented, and I guess I enjoy being able to help share a bit of our history with anyone who wants to listen."

"It sounds so cool!" Von breathed.

"It is, it certainly is," he smiled and gave a conceding shrug as his gaze stole back to Maiden and drifted down over her bust. "It gets a bit lonely at times, but so it is."

Maiden felt her left eyebrow lurch but quickly reined it in. She reminded herself that Sean had no reason to assume she wasn't single, and she wanted to keep him talking. It was time for a more subtle plan. She gave Tony's leg a discreet kick and he quickly started talking again.

"How long have you been touring in America?" he asked.

"We're about a month in to this latest trip," Sean replied but his gaze soon wandered back to Maiden and his tone grew slightly distracted. "The Hounds do an American tour every couple of years."

Maiden glanced away and pulled her jacket closed. She and David may have been fighting, but she wasn't available and didn't feel like being ogled. She wasn't sure if Sean finally picked up on her disinterest, but he sipped his drink casually and glanced at the CDs they had sitting on the table.

"Ah, you've snaffled some souvenirs!" He smiled again. "Did you get the lads to sign them?"

"No." Von shook her head. "The line was massive, that's okay though."

"Oh nonsense, lass!" Sean gave her a look of mock horror. "Give them here, I'll get it sorted for you. Won't take a moment."

Maiden was about to politely refuse when Tony spoke up.

"That's so kind, thank you! You're sure it isn't too much trouble?" he asked even as he gathered up the CDs and handed them over.

"Nothing of the sort." Sean smiled and waved his concerns away as he quickly downed the rest of his drink. "I'll be back soon."

With that he turned and slipped out into the foyer. Tony smiled happily and gave Vonny a playful nudge with his elbow.

"You're adorable." She shook her head fondly at his excited expression.

"Thanks," he said with feigned modesty but then turned to Maiden and his smile grew. "I've never seen you at work before! That was great!"

"What are you talking about?" Maiden frowned questioningly and sipped her wine.

"Oh, come on!" he whispered and smirked at her. "The way you got him talking about Charles Brown, checking his relationship with the victim, prodding for his alibi? And he just told you, it's incredible! If I were prettier I'd know every secret in town!"

Maiden and Vonny both laughed at his teasingly devious expression. Von grasped his chin and pressed a kiss to his lips.

"You *are* pretty," she said affectionately.

They all chuckled but Maiden's thoughts didn't stray far from what Sean had said about his former business partner. It seemed strange that Charles Brown would go off to sightsee and end up parked in front of an old warehouse.

Golden Glen was a beautiful little town with no shortage of adorable shops, picturesque streets, orchards and vineyards. There were much better things to see than the industrial district.

It was possible that he'd gotten lost and someone attacked him, but then why wasn't his money taken? Something else was going on. And David wouldn't even let Greg mention the case in front of her. It wasn't as though she wouldn't find out eventually anyway.

It took Sean about fifteen minutes to come back with the promised signatures. By that time Maiden had made a mental list of possible motives and suspects, but she had very little by way of reliable information to go on. She did her best to banish another niggle of annoyance at David's tightlipped approach.

"Sorry for the wait." Sean smiled apologetically as he handed Tony and Vonny their CDs.

"Don't apologize." Tony waved it away. "We're very grateful."

Sean inclined his head graciously. He turned to Maiden and stepped a bit closer.

"There you are, bonnie lass." He smiled warmly as he held out the CD. "Thank you for coming tonight, you really brightened the place up. If you—all of you, of course—are available tomorrow, the lads are playing in Westfield. I'd be happy to leave word at the door to let you in as my guests."

"Oh, that's very nice of you." Maiden smiled politely but took a tiny step back. "I won't be able to, but thanks anyway, it's very kind."

"Fair enough." He took the refusal quite gracefully. "But the offer stands if you change your mind."

Vonny noticed the exchange and grinned at Sean, making a point of shaking his hand and thanking him again for the autographs. Maiden just avoided further eye contact and shoved her CD deep into her purse.

She murmured a quiet goodnight to the overly friendly manager and led the way through the remaining crowd to the exit, only assuming her companions were following. She noticed, rather gratefully, that the rain had stopped as they all stepped outside and headed for Tony's car.

She tiptoed around a few puddles and smiled at the cheerful conversations of a few other groups of friends that were walking out as well. Despite the air of happy excitement that had permeated the theater, Maiden was grateful to slide into Tony's nice, quiet car.

As they drove back to Harlow House Maiden curled up in the backseat and closed her eyes. She was exhausted after the long and emotional day and just wanted to wash off her makeup and crawl into bed.

Sean Dowling's attention had been flattering but she wasn't interested. She checked her phone for anything from David but there was nothing, no text, no missed call. Maiden sank deeper into the seat and hoped he wasn't going to get huffy. She knew she'd been cranky with him but it was his fault for forgetting her.

"That Sean guy was really nice, wasn't he?" Vonny glanced back with a sly smile.

"I guess," she said mildly. "So what?"

"It just might be nice to remind Captain Better-things-to-do that he's not the only guy in the world," she said with a smirk.

"I don't play those games, Vonny," Maiden said very seriously.

Chapter Nine

Maiden was still a bit tired the next morning. Going out had been a novelty and she'd enjoyed some of it, even though she was still lonely and concerned over her relationship with David. But she'd enjoyed the music and she'd even been admired, that helped her pride to float back to the surface like a dead, bloated fish.

The smell of coffee greeted her as she walked out of her room. She could hear Vonny's voice coming from the kitchen, talking about the concert. Maiden realized she must have lingered in bed for longer than she thought if Von was already up and about.

She peered around the corner and out into the main room. Her parents and Vonny were sitting at the table drinking coffee and eating what looked like eggs and toast.

Any hope that Von hadn't also blabbed about her argument with David vanished when Gloria looked over with obvious concern and got immediately to her feet.

"Good mornin', sweet baby." She smiled and bustled into the kitchen. "Sit down and rest, angel, I'll bring you somethin' to eat."

"Thanks," Maiden replied quietly and did as she was told.

She slid into her seat and gave Vonny a warning look. Her sister smiled innocently and poured a cup of coffee for her. Maiden didn't trust her for a second, but she rarely turned down coffee at any hour of the morning.

She took a tiny sip and let her eyes drift closed as Vonny told their parents more about the concert and the size of the crowd that had turned up for it.

Gloria set a plate of food in front of Maiden and gave her a worried look or two when Vonny mentioned Sean Dowling's attentions. Maiden met her gaze and wrinkled her nose as she shook her head. Gloria smiled with some relief.

"Be careful there, my dear," Alfie intoned ominously as Maiden started to eat. "Musicians are a different sort of trouble. Always chasing women, they're a lot of lascivious cads!"

Maiden laughed at that, mostly because he was serious, and took a few more bites. She was just reaching for her coffee and reflecting on how nice it was to have a casual, albeit silly, conversation with her parents again when they heard a knock on the front door.

They all turned towards it with startled frowns. It was very early and they rarely received unexpected visitors to their apartment door. If guests had questions or complaints they were always instructed to only call downstairs.

"I hope that's not that pair of cackling hens staying down the hall," Alfie grumbled as he walked over and looked through the peephole. "Oh."

He opened the door immediately and stepped back. It was Greg and Sarah-Jane, and they were clearly there on official business. Apart from being in full uniform, they both looked watchful and serious.

They looked past Alfie and settled their collective attention on Maiden and Vonny. Gloria shifted slightly and set her coffee aside as she too turned to her daughters.

"Hey guys," Maiden said a little tentatively.

"Hey," Greg managed weakly. "Um, Billie let us in. Sorry for the early visit."

"That's okay." Maiden attempted a smile. They both looked un-comfortable; that wasn't good. "What's up?"

"Good morning, Miss Harlow." Sarah-Jane was all business as she took a step ahead of an apologetically uneasy Greg. "I regret to inform you that a certain Mr. Sean Dowling was found dead in the early hours of this morning."

"Really? Whoa." Maiden shook her head slightly. "That's a shame."

Sarah-Jane frowned briefly at the tepid reaction. She shifted her tawny gaze to Vonny and found her similarly nonplussed.

"I...was under the impression that you knew the victim," she tried again.

"No, we only met him last night." Maiden shook her head and frowned. "Terrible that he's dead though. You said 'victim', I take it his death wasn't an accident?"

"No...it wasn't." She glanced at Greg and gave a confused shrug.

"Mae, Von." Greg edged forward and smiled nicely at his old friends. "It's okay to be upset, especially if it's someone you liked. These things are difficult."

"What the heck are you talking about, Greg?" Von scowled at him. "Like Maiden said, we met the guy once. Why are you even here telling us about it?"

"Gregory," Alfie gave him a stern look, "my daughters were both home last night, I saw them come in. They certainly weren't out murdering some travelling showman!"

"Oh no, Mr. H!" Greg shook his head vehemently. "No one thinks they...*killed* the guy. Look we sort of have to take your statements ladies, could you come to the station? Please?"

"Don't beg people to give statements, Smith!" Sarah-Jane whis-pered a little too loudly as she rolled her eyes, she then faced them all boldly. "Let's go ladies. The sooner we get this done, the sooner you can get home again."

"Okay." Maiden gave them a wary look as she pushed to her feet; she glanced at her sister. "C'mon, Von."

They all filed through the door. Maiden paused long enough to give her anxious parents a bemused shake of her head before following the others down the hall. As they walked she and Von looked at each other nervously. Greg glanced back and, seeing their unease, smiled feebly.

"Just relax," he said with forced lightness. "This won't take long...Tony's already on his way."

They were given a ride in the patrol car, which would have been exciting if she were eight. Since she wasn't, Maiden tried not to feel like she and her sister were being arrested. She and Von ducked down into the seat and tried to hide their faces as they drove past a few people they knew.

Maiden assured herself that everything was fine, she was fairly confident that the police couldn't arrest someone without at least telling them about it. But it was still an embarrassing feeling to be taken to the police station in the back of a cop car, and it didn't help that neither of the officers in the front seat spoke a word on the journey.

It felt like forever by the time they arrived at the station. Maiden felt a hint of relief when she spotted Tony walking inside as well.

Maiden hugged herself as they were led through the foyer, past a quietly watchful Nancy, and on into David's office. It was empty except for the captain himself and he didn't even look up from his computer screen as they walked in.

Maiden wasn't sure what to expect from him today; it was weird that he'd sent officers to bring them in rather than contact her personally. It was also strange that he'd willingly involve her in a case, whatever had happened to Sean must have been very suspicious.

They settled into the row of hard wooden chairs in front of his desk and waited for him to say something, or at least look up and acknowledge that they were there. Maiden looked at David as they sat still and solemn.

He looked well enough, certainly as handsome as ever, but there were faint shadows under his eyes like he hadn't slept much and his mouth was set in a firm and displeased line. He exhaled slowly and finally looked over.

It was immediately obvious that the man wasn't about to ask her out again. His expression was cold and distant and he wouldn't look at Maiden at all. He ran a coolly assessing gaze over Tony and Vonny, ignored Maiden, and turned back to his laptop.

After typing out a few lines of text he sat back and looked at Tony and Vonny again. Maiden felt herself start to frown; he was acting so different today. She started to wonder if they were under suspicion after all, despite what Greg said earlier.

"Right. A man named Sean Dowling was found dead in the alley behind the Addison Theater around 4 am this morning." David's tone was detached. "Witnesses have indicated that you three were among the last people to be seen with him. I want a detailed account of *all* your dealings with this person. We'll start with you."

He'd flicked his ice-cold gaze at Vonny with that last remark. She swallowed hard and sat a bit straighter in the uncomfortable wooden chair. She fumbled nervously at first but was able to describe the evening reasonably clearly. David typed loudly and then pointed at Tony, who proceeded to tell a similar story.

Maiden stared as David uttered brief, to-the-point questions as if he'd never met any of them and suspected them of everything. It was eerie and she was getting increasingly nervous; did he actually think they'd killed Sean Dowling?

Tony and Von answered everything he asked as mildly as could be expected under the circumstances. Vonny started getting hostile when David asked her to repeat herself several times but Tony grasped her hand and she settled enough to respond. Tony never ruffled and never betrayed a hint of anger or resentment at the captain's harsh demeanor.

Finally, David ran out of questions for the others and had to deal with Maiden. It was obvious that he had put this part of the process off as long as he could.

He took a deep breath and released it with deliberate slowness. He still wouldn't look at her. She frowned anxiously, her stomach twisted and she wished she'd skipped breakfast.

"All right," he said grimly and stared at his computer screen even as he spoke to her. "What were your movements from the time you entered the Addison Theater until 4 am this morning?"

Maiden wet her lips and recounted a very similar story to the one Vonny and Tony had given. She detailed their arrival, the show and then stopping in the bar afterward. It was hard to tell if David was listening or not, he glanced in her direction once or twice from the corner of his eye but he wasn't typing anything.

When she finished, he tilted his head to the side until his neck cracked, the sound was loud in the self-conscious silence of the room.

"How long have you known Sean Dowling?" he finally asked in a flat, emotionless tone as he tapped furiously at his keyboard.

"I didn't know him." Maiden shook her head, starting to get frustrated by how he was acting. "I spoke with him for about ten minutes last night, that was it."

"Witnesses say you were *quite* friendly to each other." He still wouldn't look at her.

"What does that mean?" She blinked at him. "I didn't throw my drink in his face but that's about as 'friendly' as I was. Who even told you that?"

"Confidential," he said flatly. "Mr. Dowling got into town a week ago, around the same time that your behavior started to become noticeably altered. Then you're seen in a bar having a drink and an intimate conversation with him. You expect me to believe there's no connection at all?"

"What?!" Maiden stared at him and shook her head. "No, there isn't! I only met the man last night! We barely spoke at all! There was nothing *intimate*!"

"Dav—Captain McAlister, honestly." Tony, after abruptly deciding against trying to be too familiar with the surly cop, leaned forward and rested a hand protectively on Maiden's arm. "Von and I were there when he introduced himself; none of us had met him before."

"You *know* that?" He flicked him an icy look. "Have you spent the entire week with Miss Harlow?"

"Well, no but—" Tony began, startled by the harsh reaction, when David continued.

"Eye witnesses said that Mr. Dowling was very obviously flirtatious towards Miss Harlow." His eyes narrowed on his prey, he was in cop mode. "Is that what you observed?"

"Um...he was, sort of. Yes." Tony gave her a brief apologetic look. "But Maiden wasn't."

David took a deep, shaky breath and closed his eyes. Maiden could see him struggling to stay professional but it wasn't working, that familiar stab of nausea was coming back with a vengeance. Finally he pushed to his feet and walked swiftly to the door.

"Excuse me," he muttered tightly and stepped outside.

Maiden shielded her face with her hand and turned away as she felt tears sting her eyes. He was crushed, she'd crushed him. He wouldn't have walked out if he was just angry. A moment later she heard Vonny stand up; she came and sat on her other side, hugging her gently.

"I'm so sorry, Maiden!" Her voice was low and quavering. "I should have stayed right out of it the whole time. I'm sorry."

That tearful admission somehow made everything worse; if even Vonny felt badly for David then it was obvious that he was as devastated as she feared. Maiden couldn't begin to understand why or how anyone could have misconstrued her brief discussion with Sean Dowling so completely.

She remembered Vonny was still hovering when she laid her head on her shoulder and squeezed her tighter.

"It's not your fault," Maiden whispered. "I just don't understand how going out once with friends has turned into this. I should've never left the house."

"It'll be okay, ladies," Tony said softly as he tried to hug them both from his perch beside Maiden. "None of us have done anything wrong. Maiden didn't know that guy; it'll get sorted out. Okay? We'll tell David again when he comes back, he just needs a minute to cool down."

A few painfully long and anxious minutes passed before the door opened again. Maiden stiffened and didn't dare look up, but her eyes flew to the desk when she heard Greg's voice as he sat down.

"Hey guys," he said with a weak smile. "How's it going?"

"Where's David?" Maiden asked with widened eyes.

"Oh, the Captain had to step out for a bit...said he had an appointment." Greg cleared his throat uncomfortably and met her gaze. "So what's actually happening? He told me to take over and then he left."

Maiden closed her eyes and sank down in her chair as Tony recounted the whole horrible story all over again. As he reached the part about David's reaction to her statement she had to rush out of the room herself or risk getting sick all over his desk.

They left soon after and Tony drove them home. Maiden didn't once turn from the window and Vonny felt so badly that she said nothing for the entire drive.

***

As soon as they got home, Maiden ran to her room and locked herself inside. Only the kittens dared enter and that was through the cat flap she and Vonny had both had installed at the bottom of their doors.

Maiden laid in bed trying to stop her stomach from aching and her head from spinning. She was sure that Von would tell their parents what had happened. She was fine with that; she couldn't bring herself to dredge it all up again.

She couldn't recall ever being so miserable in her life. David was so clearly hurt and that knowledge forced her to realize how deeply she felt about him.

She rolled onto her side as Rowdy and Ruffian curled around her neck and purred as hard as they could. She cuddled them but the tears didn't stop until she finally fell into troubled sleep.

She woke up soon after but stayed in her room for the rest of the day. By the time it was dark outside she was a little calmer and found herself wanting some advice. Specifically, she wanted to talk to her mother.

Maiden sat up slowly and slid off the bed, taking care not to wake Ruffian, who had stayed loyally at her side. She slipped out of her room and shuffled down the hallway towards the kitchen.

She peeked out cautiously and was relieved to see Gloria sitting alone at the kitchen table. The sight of her pale hair and flouncy pink housedress gave Maiden a hint of nostalgic comfort; she almost smiled as she stepped into the kitchen.

They hadn't spoken very much in the last week or so; both her parents had been distant and secretive. But Gloria was suddenly there and alone and she doubted that was a coincidence.

Maiden came and sat down a few seats away, she still felt fragile and didn't want to deal with too much eye contact or hugs, not yet.

Gloria smiled at her and then stood and got them both a glass of wine without a word. After setting Maiden's glass in front of her, she took up her former seat and patiently waited.

For a long moment they sat in silence. Maiden knew that she would have to broach the subject. For all her well-intentioned nosiness, Gloria sometimes knew when it was best to keep quiet. Maiden stared down at the table and braced herself.

"Mom?" she said quietly.

"Yes, angel?" Gloria glanced over at her.

"I...I think David really cares about me, and I think I hurt him," she whispered down into her untouched wine.

"What about you, baby?" she asked kindly. "Are you hurt too?"

"Yeah." Her voice was barely audible.

She heard Gloria stand and walk over; a moment later she was sitting beside her and slipping an arm around her. Maiden felt a strong urge to weep again but fought it back. She waited and hoped her mother would tell her what she should do.

"I can't tell you what to do, baby," Gloria said gently.

"You must have an opinion." Her shoulders drooped.

"I do, but I'm not gonna tell you what it is, because it's *my* opinion." There was a fond smile in Gloria's voice as she stroked her daughter's dark hair. "What do you want to do?"

"I want everything to be straightforward and just work out without all this stupid fuss," she grumbled.

"I know, but that ain't what I asked," Gloria chuckled.

"I feel badly that he's hurt. But I didn't do what he thinks I did," she explained softly. "It's frustrating, but I miss him."

"Then do what you think is best." Gloria kissed the top of her head. "I'm sure it'll work out just fine."

Chapter Ten

The following morning was cold and gray. Maiden had woken up at daybreak and sat in bed for a while trying to dredge up the courage to go and talk to David.

She put on one of her nicer and lower cut sweaters and took care with her makeup. Maybe it was petty, but she wanted every advantage she could get. Having learned her lesson yesterday, she only had coffee for breakfast and drove straight to the police station.

She made herself park and go inside before she could change her mind. She walked in slowly, feeling ridiculously skittish, but rallied when she saw Nancy at the desk. The lady looked cautious but not unfriendly.

"Good morning...is Captain McAlister in?" Maiden asked quietly, sounding as pale and uneasy as she looked.

"No, Miss Harlow," Nancy replied watchfully. "He's off today."

"He's what?!" Maiden's mouth fell open. The sheer irony that he had time off *now* was staggering.

"I'm afraid so." Nancy glanced around at the empty foyer and then grabbed a scrap of paper and started scribbling. "He's due to be in tomorrow, you can always try to see him then. You can even call to make certain he's available if you don't want to risk another wasted trip."

Nancy had barely finished murmuring the politely professional suggestion when she slid the paper subtly across the desk to her. Maiden frowned gently and took it, a cursory look confirmed that it was David's home address. She glanced at Nancy and smiled faintly.

"Thanks," she said quietly.

"I hope you have a pleasant day, Miss Harlow." Her expression held all the sincere worry that her placid tone lacked.

Maiden inclined her head in silent gratitude and left. She knew Nancy was very fond of David, she was heartened that the quietly observant woman seemed disposed to help rather than discourage her.

As she drove the short distance to the address Nancy had given her, she spent the time trying to bolster herself up. She really wasn't sure what sort of reception she was going to get or if he was even home.

He might be out, she cautioned herself as she parked outside the handsome house. *What do I do then? Try later? Leave a note? Maybe I should have just called...no, don't be a coward. You can do this, you can set the record straight, it's going to be fine.*

As she climbed out and made her way up the concrete path to his front door, she tried to ease her nerves by taking in the details of his house. It was white with old-fashioned shutters in duck-egg blue. It was cute, not huge but probably big enough for three bedrooms. The front yard was tidy and the front step was swept clean. She noticed the birdhouse her father had gifted him a couple of months ago sitting cozily in a large oak tree.

She took a deep breath and rang the doorbell. A moment later she heard footsteps on the other side and resisted the urge to run back to her car when she saw a curtain pushed back from the corner of her eye. Maiden kept her expression serene and pretended not to have seen him there.

A frown chased over her features when a long, tense silence passed. He wouldn't actually refuse to come to the door? A hint of irritation leapt within her; she hadn't done anything wrong, he was overreacting.

She quickly reminded herself that she came there to clear things up, not to win an argument. With renewed poise she started reaching for the doorbell again when she heard the bolt on the other side slide back.

The door finally opened and David stood there with a coolly distant look on his face. He wore a faded pair of jeans, probably a favorite, they looked worn and comfortable and fit rather nicely. His dark blue shirt was long-sleeved but pushed up to his elbows. Maiden focused on these incidental observations since he was looking at her like she was there to try and sell him a set of encyclopedias.

"Hi," she said quietly, he said nothing. "Look, you left before I could finish explaining what happened."

"I read your statement," he said simply.

"Okay..." She frowned faintly and shook her head. "Then I don't understand why you're still upset."

David glanced away and took a deep breath. He folded his arms over his chest and leaned against the doorjamb in a casual stance that was clearly fake.

"Anyone can claim what they want," he said in an unreadable tone. "Especially when they're caught doing something or they're afraid they're in trouble."

"What?" she demanded loudly and felt her urge to reconcile start to weaken. "Are you accusing me of lying in my statement?"

"I'm not willing to conjecture about what you might do or why," he said implacably but his eyes drifted to his feet.

"Are you serious?!" she demanded incredulously. "After everything we've been through together you honestly believe I'd prance off with someone else and then lie about it? That's what you think of me?!"

His jaw was tight and he still wouldn't look at her. She was surprised by how standoffish he was acting, but she absolutely couldn't believe he was so unwilling to listen.

"I've been incredibly snowed under but still trying to make something work for us, but you just gave up," he said grimly. "You think you can do anything you want and then just turn up on my doorstep and it'll be like it never happened?"

Maiden quirked a brow and tucked her hands into the snug back pockets of her jeans.

"Yes."

David looked at her again, startled by that frank admission, but she meant it and wasn't ashamed. As far as she was concerned she'd put up with far worse and was at least willing to swallow her pride and make an effort.

"Nice," he said and stood back, obviously done with the discussion. "I really can't trust you anymore."

"*You can't trust me?!*" Her large eyes widened and she felt a swift rush of anger that hit so quickly she had to glance away to regain her composure. She took a deep breath and then shot him a cold look. "So, just to be clear, I put up with one embarrassing disappointment after another and was supposed to be understanding; which I *was*. You get upset once over an assumption and that's it? I'm dead to you? Really fair, David. I don't know why I was expecting as much from you as *I* was willing to give."

"I didn't go out with someone else behind your back!" he muttered through clenched teeth.

"Neither did I!" she said angrily and stalked away, hearing his door slam behind her.

***

David leaned his back against the door and shut his eyes as he listened to her walk away. His stomach was in knots and his hands were shaking. Since shortly after he met Maiden he'd never seriously doubted her honesty, but she was lying to him now, he was sure of it.

An eyewitness claimed to have seen her and Dowling flirting heavily and openly, they swore to it and signed their name to it. That had been almost as devastating as listening to her deny it. He'd tried to keep it together but it was too much; his only option had been to walk out before he broke down.

It wasn't as if he had time to spare at the moment, but it didn't matter anymore. He couldn't focus; everything made him angry, everything hurt.

While Maiden had been off with some other man, he'd spent that night at home alone thinking about her. It had been his first real night off in ages and the one person he'd wanted to spend it with wouldn't even speak to him.

He'd spent the time reading through their text messages from the past few months. Reliving the gradual progression of their relationship and kicking himself for not putting his foot down and refusing to drop everything to fix someone else's mistakes.

He thought about the conversation they'd had after he forgot to meet her. She'd been so cold and just walked away from him like what they had meant nothing. He knew he should have followed her; he should have thrown his damn phone out the window. But, as it turned out, it was probably already too late for that.

David pushed his sleeves down and rubbed his arms but he still felt cold.

She'd already drifted, just like Smith said she would, he thought somberly. *Why else would she walk away from what we could've had? You wasted every chance and she found someone else.*

He slid down to sit on the rug as he heard her car start and drive away. He sat there and stared down at the floor for a long time.

***

Maiden's stomach churned the entire drive home. She hated fighting, she hated it so much, and she couldn't stand it when people spread lies about her. It used to happen in high school when other girls started rumors that she was sleeping with every boy they could think of. This was annoyingly similar, as was the effect on her physically.

She ran back into Harlow House and straight into the nearest restroom. After giving herself a moment to be sick, she stumbled back into the foyer. Maiden took a shaky breath, she felt a bit woozy now and shut her eyes tightly.

"Maiden? Are you okay?"

Maiden tensed at the sound of Kylie's uneasy voice. Anxiety always affected her physically, and that had always embarrassed her. Kylie was standing in the doorway of the dining room peering at her. Maiden pressed a hand to her stomach and forced a weak little smile as she met the shy chef's worried look.

"Yeah, I'm fine," she replied quietly.

"Are you sick?" Kylie leaned back almost imperceptibly.

"No," Maiden whispered, further embarrassed when tears blurred her vision.

"Oh," Kylie's eyes widened a little as she started to understand the situation. She glanced around furtively. "Well, come in the kitchen until you settle down a bit. I always hate it when people see me upset."

Maiden didn't have the heart to argue with anything at that point and shuffled along behind her. Fortunately, the dining room was empty. What she really wanted was to curl up in her bed and wait for the hurt and anger to ebb, but there was too much chance that she'd be intercepted by a well-meaning family member. There was no way that Gloria or Vonny would be as quiet and non-intrusive as Kylie.

Maiden wandered into the pristine kitchen and noticed that the shades on the windows were open today. Kylie tended to keep them closed but today the cloudy gray sky was clear to be seen through the spotless glass. Kylie followed her gaze and smiled quietly.

"I love this time of year," she confided. "Rain and snow are my favorites. It feels like everything in the whole outdoors wants to be snuggled up and left to enjoy some peace and quiet."

"I guess that's true." Maiden settled into one of the rarely used seats in front of Kylie's work station. "It's easier to feel hidden away."

"Exactly!" Kylie's eyes widened a fraction. "A lot of people don't understand that...they don't understand anyone with a different viewpoint from theirs."

Maiden met her gaze as she considered that. Kylie quickly busied herself with switching on an electric kettle. As she pulled out two cups and a box of peppermint tea, Maiden felt an urge to focus on someone else's issues.

"You've been picked on a lot in your life, haven't you?" Maiden asked kindly. Kylie met her gaze very briefly but didn't say anything. Maiden smiled. "It's okay, I get it. I got picked on a lot too."

"Yeah, I've heard about that." Kylie admitted. She eyed her curiously. "So, how do you manage to still be comfortable around people?"

"I guess...because not everyone is mean," Maiden said with a shrug. "We need friends, it's how we're wired. My friends remind me that there are people that love me...even if some people hate me."

"How do you know who you can trust to be a friend though?" Kylie asked softly as she turned off the heat under the kettle.

"Sometimes you just have to test people out and see. If they aren't nice or if they lie to you, well, it's a safe bet they won't be a good friend. But if they treat you well and are actually interested in you...assuming it's not a lie or an act." Maiden felt tears well up again. "Or that they actually don't trust you even though you've never given them a reason not to...I'm sorry."

Kylie dropped a teabag into one of the cups and filled it with boiling water before setting it in front of her. Maiden let out a shaky breath and nodded her thanks. She could almost feel Kylie mustering all her nerve.

"What happened?" the quiet chef finally asked.

"Someone lied about me..." Maiden stared down into her cup as the dried leaves slowly tinted the water. "And he believes them."

"You mean Captain McAlister?" Kylie frowned. "That's weird, he seemed pretty sharp."

"Well, at the moment, he's about as sharp as a fist," Maiden sniffled.

Kylie smiled, she almost chuckled but it didn't quite emerge. "What are you going to do?"

"The only thing I can do," Maiden replied as she sipped her tea. "Clear my name."

***

By the time Maiden had finished her tea she felt a bit steadier. She thanked Kylie for her kindness and slipped back out into the foyer. Gloria was sitting at the reception desk now and looked over at her. The hopefulness in her eyes promptly withered, only to be replaced by a wince when she saw her daughter's stoic expression.

"What happened?" she asked gently.

"Oh, yeah, apparently I'm not trustworthy, and he's a *complete* jerk." Maiden smiled tightly as she breezed past. "But at least I don't feel guilty anymore."

"Well, I guess that's somethin'," Gloria sighed and rolled her eyes.

Maiden hurried upstairs and into the family apartment. Grateful that she didn't see Vonny anywhere, she hurried to her room and locked herself inside. Ruffian, who had been dozing on her bed, blinked sleepy eyes at her and meowed in polite inquiry. Maiden gave him a look and then a tiny smile.

"Don't ask," she whispered and scratched his fuzzy chin.

Despite the chilly nip in the air she walked out onto her balcony and curled up in her favorite peacock chair. She shut her eyes and took a deep breath, but it did little to ease her growing irritation.

It was infuriating to be slandered, it always had been, and she found David's reaction to the mess incredibly hypocritical. She was also a bit annoyed with herself for sticking her neck out by going to see him. She could have left it alone and spared herself the sting of being dumped, but she'd take anger over guilt any day.

Her thoughts shifted to Sean Dowling, debatably the source of her latest romantic woes. Was it strange that he went out of his way to meet her and her friends and then ended up dead the next day? Or was it just coincidence?

Vonny and Tony had chalked his actions up to general schmoozing and an attempt to flirt with her, but Maiden wasn't so sure. He had flirted a bit, certainly, but he'd spent just as much time talking to Tony and Von.

There was something strange about the Highland Hounds. There had to be, both their managers had now been murdered. She wondered if Sean had also been shot but knew she would have to work around a cranky and fickle Captain McAlister if she wanted to find out.

David simply wasn't being rational. He wouldn't hear her out and since when did he take a day off right after a body was discovered? This was the same man who couldn't spare a single evening to take her to dinner. How was he going to solve two murders and clear up her reputation if this was his approach? It was even more hopeless because he actually believed the ridiculous lies.

"Focus, Maiden. You have to do this alone. David's not going to help you this time," she whispered to herself and grabbed the fluffy throw that was draped across the other chair.

She tucked her feet up under her and snuggled into the soft blanket. She had a few problems now and she'd already been neglecting one of them. Fred Eilers' potential involvement in Ulysses Mercier's death.

Mercier had been snooping around Eilers' Arms on the night of the grand opening, an event he likely hadn't been invited to considering Eilers' angry reaction to him. The next night Mercier was back in the hotel and ended up murdered in Eilers' private office.

The most obvious suspect was Eilers himself. According to her father the men were old college rivals, perhaps holding old grudges, but there could be more to it. And now she had to wonder if there was a connection between Mercier's death and the others.

Why would there be? She shook her head. *Why would a high-flying American businessman have even met the touring managers of a Scottish folk band? But for that matter, why wouldn't he have? Who's to say what connections are likely or not? They were all murdered within the same week in the same small town; it could be connected.*

The trouble was that Maiden didn't know enough about any of the victims to really form a clear picture of them. She needed more information if she was going to keep her promise to help Eilers. That was also the easiest place to start; he must have some information to share about the long-time rival that ended up dead in his office.

CHAPTER ELEVEN

Maiden asked her mother to call and make an appointment with Fred Eilers; he agreed to see her that same morning. Determined to make good use of her day, Maiden braved the cold wind and the darkening sky and drove back to Eiler's Arms.

The building looked as garish as she remembered set against its clever and quirky neighbors. On one side there was a bakery that used to be a blacksmith and on the other a brewery that was once a grain mill. Both establishments, like most others in the area, kept as much of the original equipment and features as possible. Anything that couldn't be repurposed was treated as artwork.

Maiden walked into the hotel and was again visually attacked by the hideously overdone décor. There was even more deep-sea paraphernalia scattered around now. She glanced around and shook her head.

Wow, this place looks like a dockside brothel. Oh stop it, Maiden! she chided herself sternly and headed for the reception desk. *Someone thought this looked good. Yes, it looks like a drunken sailor vomited in a fish bowl, but that's not your problem.*

After stopping at the reception desk to ask the girl on duty for directions, she made her way up to Fred Eilers' temporary office on the third floor. His usual office was, of course, still a crime scene.

While it had occurred to her that there might be police on site, she knew for a certainty that David wasn't on duty today. It was a perfect opportunity. If she was careful she could do some looking around without risking him finding out about it.

A legacy that showed the building's age, despite the attempts to update it, was the lack of an elevator. Maiden climbed the richly polished stairs to the top floor, noting that the under-the-sea theme ran throughout. The walls were papered in a starfish motif and picture frames shaped like portholes hung between every door.

The long corridor was cozily lit and almost achieved a level of ambiance that made her wish she was actually on a ship at sea. Maybe a tropical cruise in a fantasy world where David wasn't a jerk that practically ignored her for a week and then accused her of cheating for no good reason.

Suck it up, loser. She smiled at herself. *You're a vibrant, successful woman, lots of men would be happy to have you. You've got options...you can always get more cats, for instance.*

Fortunately, she soon reached the office. The door was ajar and she heard voices as she approached. It was a man and a woman; they weren't yelling but they didn't sound happy either. Maiden quickly identified the man's voice as Fred Eilers, she didn't recognize the woman though.

She stopped and leaned a bit closer as she tried to decipher what the irate pair were saying. They were both too muffled and far away from the door. She quickly gave up and knocked loud enough to be heard over the argument. A self-conscious silence descended heavily before Eilers spoke up.

"Come in." He sounded far too cheerful.

Maiden walked inside and took in the scene. Fred Eilers' stocky frame was tucked behind a smallish desk as he puffed away at a cigar. His dark suit looked expensive, as did the gold ring that glinted on his stout pinky finger.

The woman with him was the same lady she'd seen sitting at the bar at the grand opening. She again wore her dark auburn hair pulled into a messy bun on the top of her head. She wore a snug pencil skirt and a flowy white blouse. A pair of glasses perched at the end of her nose, along with a pencil tucked carelessly behind her ear, gave her a sexy-secretary look.

A single look from sharply intelligent eyes quickly dispelled such superficial conclusions, however. Those dark eyes locked onto Maiden in a shrewd and assessing manner.

"Good morning." Maiden turned politely to Eilers. "I'm Maiden Harlow, we met briefly the other night."

"Yes, I could hardly forget a woman like you," he chortled. "Come in, dear lady, have a seat. Gloria said you'd be coming by today."

"Thanks," Maiden said placidly and perched on one of the chairs by the desk, she looked expectantly at the lady that was standing there watching them.

"Sorry, I forgot my manners," Eilers shook his head at himself and gestured towards her. "This is Maddie Norris, the hotel manager here at Eiler's Arms."

"How interesting." Maiden looked her over more carefully. "How long have you worked for Mr. Eilers?"

"Two years or so," Maddie replied, her expression was guarded.

"Oh, then you were here during the renovations." Maiden deliberately lightened her tone and tried to sound companionably interested. "It must've been very exciting to see the changes."

"Yes, I suppose it was." Maddie forced a smile. "More challenging than exciting, I'd say."

"Oh nonsense!" Eilers laughed and puffed on his cigar. "And I wouldn't say 'renovations', it's an understatement of what we've done here. This place has been transformed! What used to be a hollowed-out shell is now a thriving business enterprise. That's cause for celebration!"

"Except for the dead man in the corner," Maiden pointed out, only slightly dryly.

"Yeah, that's kind of put a damper on things," Eilers admitted and then flicked a glance at Maddie. "Leave us for a bit, would you?"

"Certainly." She turned and walked to the door. "It was nice to meet you, Miss Harlow."

Once the door had shut behind Maddie, Eilers turned to her and shifted slightly in his chair. Maiden could see that he was uncomfortable, maybe even nervous, that struck her as odd. His air of confidence and bombastic pride in the hotel wavered and then settled into something a little more subdued.

"You know why I'm here." She liked the confidential importance that remark leant to her visit.

"Yeah, well kind of." He shrugged and set his cigar in a large glass ashtray that was shaped like an octopus. "Gloria insisted that you could figure out who really killed Ulysses. I've been in and out of town for a while, heading up this project, I've seen your name in the papers and read about some of the cases you solved. So, if you can help me at all, I'd be incredibly grateful."

"I'll see what I can do, Mr. Eilers," she said in a non-committal tone. She distantly wondered how long he'd been in contact with her parents, and specifically with her mother. "It would help if you could give me a little more information."

"Of course, anything I can do," he said and sat back in his chair.

"Were you actually friends with Ulysses Mercier?" she asked calmly.

"Oh sure." He smiled easily. "We went way back, all the way to our college days. We were good friends."

"Bearing in mind that I was at the grand opening and saw you throw him out," she replied tactfully.

"Ah, yes. I did, didn't I?" Eilers grumbled under his breath and scowled at her. "Why'd you ask if you already knew?"

"I was curious if I could trust you to be honest with me," she said frankly. "This isn't an encouraging start. Do you actually want my help or what?"

"You're a tough cookie, aren't you?" He rested his chin in his hand. "All right, we weren't exactly friends, but the rivalry was never quite this dirty."

"Why did you get so angry with him at the party?" she asked. "What was he saying to those people that upset you so much?"

"*Those people* are some of the biggest shareholders in my company," he clarified. "And good old Ulysses was right in there trying to butter them up. He was an old-fashioned flim-flam man; always had been."

"What exactly was he trying to do?" she murmured.

"He was trying to barge his way into joining the company." Eilers rolled his eyes. "Typical of him, if he saw something he wanted that was it, it was his and nobody was gonna talk him out of it. That's how he ended up divorced three times; one woman was never enough for him. Anyway, I told him to get lost so he tried to weasel in behind my back. Tried to convince the investors that he'd look out for their interests, be their man on the ground so to speak. I can understand the temptation I guess, this place is a gold mine."

"Business is good so far?" She tried to keep her tone indifferent.

"It's great!" he scoffed. "It might not show this early in the day, but the place will be hopping by this evening. We're packed every night!"

"So, you believe that Mercier saw you had a potentially successful enterprise here and wanted in on it?" she asked.

"Yeah, basically." He picked up his cigar and took a few puffs. "I don't know where he came from and why he started fixating on me now; we hadn't spoken in years. Next thing I know he drops in, starts asking about the Old Chateau and tells me he wants a piece of the action. A *big* piece; he wanted to be partners!"

"Which you refused?"

"Absolutely!" He pulled a face. "The guy was a snake; I wouldn't let him put a toe in the door! No, I told him that the Eilers hotel chain was a family business and always would be. Well, he doesn't have a family so that didn't get through his thick skull."

"Not like the fireplace poker, that did the trick," Maiden said sardonically.

Eilers actually chortled. Maiden hadn't meant it to be funny, more of a stark reminder of the situation. In any case, she suspected that Eilers was sugar-coating the truth.

"Don't think of me as a terrible man, Maiden." He held up his hands innocently. "Honestly, it's hard to miss a guy that tried to stab me in the back. Sure, we always competed. Test scores, sports, women, you name it we tried to one-up each other. But that finished when we graduated. For me it did, anyway."

"So, what could have made him come around now?" Maiden pressed. "You must have a suspicion at least."

"Well...I suspect that he'd fallen on hard times," Eilers said after a somber pause. "He was a high-flyer, Ulysses. When your parents saddle you with a name like that, they obviously expect big things from you. Last I'd heard he was doing all right but, like I said, he had three divorces behind him and that ain't cheap. So he came here trying to cozy his way into some easy money, at my expense!"

"And then he ended up dead in your office," she said simply but continued before he could rankle. "Anyone you can think of that might want to get Mercier out of the way and then frame you for it?"

"Oh sure," he almost laughed. "Anyone who'd ever done business with Ulysses would've hated him. Not to mention his ex-wives, old girlfriends, everyone. I'm just the scapegoat who was in the wrong place at the wrong time."

"Can you please be more specific?" Maiden managed to suppress a sigh. "It would really be more helpful to your case if we could narrow down the suspects to fewer than everyone he'd ever met."

"That's true," he laughed again and looked thoughtful. "Tell you who does come to mind, Graham Harper. He's my accountant, but he's been off his game for a while now."

"You think that *your* accountant would have a reason to kill Ulysses Mercier?" she asked carefully.

"I think it's highly likely." He sounded confident despite the abject stupidness he was suggesting. "Graham isn't exactly earning his keep, and he's exactly the sort of guy that Ulysses would sniff out and try to use against me. But Graham has no leverage; he's on thin ice and he knows it."

"But how does that give him a motive for killing Mercier?" she endeavored to sound patient.

"Maybe Ulysses started nosing around and he got nervous," Eilers suggested. "I don't know. But I do know that Graham hates me and he'd be happy to see me take the blame for this murder."

"Okay," she said as she considered the peculiar theory. "Can I talk to him?"

"Yeah, his office is on the ground floor, down the hall next to the restaurant," Eilers replied. "Just be careful what you believe, the guy's a natural liar. I've also instructed Maddie to cooperate with you."

"Thanks." Maiden stood, eager to get away from the foul-smelling cigar smoke. "Anything I ought to know about her?"

"She can be a little cold," he mused as he thought that over. "I get the impression that she's been kicked around pretty bad; she went through a nasty divorce from some creep. I think she said he was a doctor or something. She's good at what she does though, keeps the place running when I'm too busy to do it myself."

"I'll keep that in mind." She nodded. "Where's her office?"

"Second floor," he pointed towards the carpet. "Next door to where I'm *supposed* to be right now."

"Thanks."

Maiden slipped out into the hall and relished the fresher air. She made her way downstairs and glanced at the reception desk, the girl that was there before was nowhere to be seen.

She was looking around the foyer for the hallway Eilers mentioned when a tall, slim man approached her. He was friendly-looking, with black hair that was graying at the temples and smiling blue eyes.

"Good morning, can I help you?" he asked kindly.

"Possibly," Maiden replied in a similar tone. "Do you know where I could find Graham Harper?"

"Oh, he's not in at the moment, sorry." He made an apologetic face. "Anything I can help with? I'm Cooper Henderson, I do a bit of everything around here."

"Really?" Maiden kept her expression polite. "What does that mean exactly?"

"Jack of all trades," he smiled and tucked his hands in his pockets. "I've been here since the days when this place was the Chateau, before old man Eilers ruined it by trying to make it look like a mermaid's brassier."

Maiden failed to hide an amused snort but quickly put a hand to her mouth and glanced at the stairs to make sure Eilers hadn't followed her. She turned back to a grinning Cooper and decided to try and learn from a potentially more honest source.

"I remember this place before the...transformation," she said tactfully. "But I'm afraid I didn't really pay much attention to it."

"A sadly typical sentiment around here," Cooper sighed. "This town didn't know what it had when it had it."

"You obviously did." She smiled again.

"Yeah, I'm one of those boring old guys that likes history," he admitted with a shrug and then gave her an assessing look. "Do you like history?"

"Yes, I do actually."

"Do you like coffee?" He narrowed his eyes a fraction.

"Yes." She felt herself smiling again; she knew what was coming.

"Good, I'm buying." He waved her towards the bar. "Step this way."

Maiden obligingly followed him into the dimly lit room. It was late morning and the place was empty. She took up one of the aqua colored velvet stools in front of the bar. Cooper walked behind it and flicked on an enormous monstrosity of pipes and valves. At his enquiring look, she requested a cappuccino and waited while the over-grown pipe organ went to work.

When he returned with two large cups he set one in front of her and started wiping down the bar. Maiden watched him subtly as she picked up her cup and took a sip. He finally glanced at her and instantly smiled again. She didn't get the impression that he was flirting with her; he seemed more bored and maybe lonely than interested.

"You clearly don't share Mr. Eilers' vision for this place." She studied him quietly. "Why are you still here?"

"I don't really know sometimes. Too lazy to look for another job and too fond of the Chateau to really leave her, I guess," he mused, but he frowned unhappily as he looked at the dark blue walls and the nautical paraphernalia that cluttered them. "She's still here, underneath all this, the old bones are still intact."

"That's something," she said in what she hoped was an encouraging tone.

"It's everything! This place has quite a history, you know." Cooper smiled proudly as he glanced around. "Even if you can't see it under the garbage."

"What kind of history, Mr. Henderson?" Maiden smiled at his grumbling and propped her chin in her hand.

"Would you believe pirates?" His cheerful demeanor resurfaced. "A family of brazen, seafaring bandits that left a trail of terror, seductions and stolen treasure in their wake?"

"In Michigan?" she asked tactfully. "I know we have the Great Lakes but that's a far cry from the open sea."

"They didn't do their pilfering here, sweetie," he chuckled and pretended to be polishing a glass when someone walked past the doorway. "This was generations back. The Arnaud family, according to legend, came from some village in rural France. Three brothers named Gabriel, Jean and Phillipe and a sister, Claudia, were notorious and highly successful.

"They came from a desperately poor family and made a pact that they would one day be rich and never have another worry for the rest of their lives. They stole a ship, convinced the crew to turn rogue, and spent the next decade or so seeking their fortunes on the high seas collecting huge amounts of gold and whatever else they fancied."

"And then they retired to live out their days freezing their butts off in Golden Glen?" she enquired with a smile.

"There used to be a lot of French settlements across North America, including in Michigan," he pointed out.

"I know, I learned a little about it in school," she laughed softly. "I was just being a brat."

"If you're going to mock me, I won't finish the story," he said with a teasing wag of his finger, she held up her hands in apology so he continued. "Near the end of the so-called golden age of piracy, the Arnauds decided to retire. They'd agreed to divide their spoil evenly amongst them and part ways. None of them would ever speak of how they gained their fortune. They would all reinvent themselves in the life of their choosing.

"But by the time they decided to quit the family business, their way of life had twisted them far from the loyal siblings they used to be. Gabriel was the oldest, he'd also married a cruelly ambitious woman, Marie, who encouraged him that he deserved the captain's share of the fortune. This escalated to distrust of the other three siblings and finally a plot to kill them and keep everything."

"Oh, that's sad. Even though they made that pact when they were young?" Maiden leaned forward slightly. "So what happened?"

"Gabriel, at his wife's urging, murdered Jean and Phillipe, but Claudia escaped. Gabriel and Marie had the vast fortune and were satisfied with that. They moved to Louisiana and built a palatial house for themselves. They lived in appalling luxury and thought they had everything they could ever want." Cooper held up a finger. "But Claudia didn't give up. Apart from leaving her penniless again, she hated Gabriel for betraying them and killing their brothers. She knew that Marie would have had a hand in the scheme and hated her too. She followed them to America and found their beautiful home. Just imagine how she felt, how she seethed, when she saw the decadent life they were living off the money that she and her brothers had risked their lives to get."

Maiden did imagine it for a moment and it didn't feel good. Cooper had paused to let his words soak in and then continued in a dramatically ominous tone.

"She used her wiles to infiltrate the household and found where Gabriel hid their fortune. She stole back the most expensive treasures, taking all she could carry. But before she left, she strangled Marie and left her body for Gabriel to find. Then she escaped into the night."

"Whoa." Maiden wrapped her fingers around her warm cup when she felt goosebumps raise on her arms. "What happened to Claudia?"

"By the time Gabriel found his wife and realized what had happened, he was too late to catch her. Claudia avoided his attempts to hunt her down and made her way north." He leaned slightly closer and lowered his voice. "She settled in a little fishing village not far from Lake Michigan. Right here in what would eventually be called Golden Glen. She built this house in the style of her homeland and hid her treasures somewhere inside it. They were never found."

Maiden held his gaze for a long moment. The anchor-shaped clock on the wall ticked loudly in the resounding silence. She pulled a face and gave him a sideways look.

"Is any of that true?" she asked skeptically.

"No. Of course not," he said in the same intense voice but then a smile broke over his face again. "It's a fun old tale though, isn't it?"

"It's a great story," Maiden said. "So, who did build this place if it wasn't Claudia?"

"Don't get me wrong, when I say the old tale isn't true I just mean that it isn't proven," Cooper explained. "For all we know, this was originally a pirate's nest of sorts. There used to be plenty of them, usually in port towns, but who's going to tell a ruthless pirate queen where she can or can't live?"

"I can't believe no one's capitalized on that backstory," Maiden shook her head. "Maybe this place wouldn't have ended up so neglected."

"We'll never know, unfortunately," Cooper said. "I did suggest to Eilers that he could take advantage of the legend but he wasn't interested. Imagine having wine tastings in the Claudia Arnaud Cellar. It would be great, he'd sell more wine and cheese than he could keep up with."

"It would certainly be a more elegant alternative to what he's got now," Maiden acknowledged wryly. "He could've called this place the Pirate's Arms."

"Perfect!" Cooper gave her an approving nod. "That's not even the only tale attached to this place. Saucy old Claudia seemed to have set the tone. It was abandoned for years but it wasn't exactly empty, or so they say."

"Don't tell me some other daring pirate took up residence?" Maiden smiled faintly.

"Not far off," he laughed. "It was a scary looking old house next to a few abandoned factories and old stores, easily accessible and no one paying much attention to it. It became a hideout for some pretty serious crooks over the years. Anything could be hidden here."

"But wouldn't they have found it when they renovated?" She raised her cup to her lips again.

"Not necessarily." He held up a finger. "Pirates knew how to hide things so they wouldn't be easily found. Big time crooks do too. It's not like a chest full of pirate swag was shoved in a corner behind an umbrella stand."

"It would be sadly anti-climactic if it had been," she acknowledged with a smile. "Does this place have a cellar or a basement?"

"Not that I've ever found," he said with a hint of regret. "But she's not my only lady. I've had a hand in researching a lot of the county's historical buildings. I've hunted around a few times over the years, but it's not like I lived here."

"So, you really do love history." She regarded him with a smile. "It's more than just a hobby to you, isn't it?"

"It is." His cheerful eyes narrowed minutely. "That's why I hate what Eilers has done to this place, it shouldn't have been allowed. I would've never helped him if I'd known what he planned to do."

"What do you mean 'helped him'?" She shook her head a little.

"I was his first contact when he started looking at buying the place," he explained quietly. "I introduced him to the right people, told him what the condition of the building was, helped him negotiate the price. Lots of things I now regret."

"Oh...well," she trailed off awkwardly.

She quickly realized that Cooper had to be the person that pink-haired Margaret had told Von about. The contact that helped Eilers buy the Old Chateau cheaply. As she looked at Cooper now she could clearly see his disappointment and searched for some words of comfort.

"You couldn't have known that it would turn out like this," she said gently.

"I certainly couldn't. He lied to me, said he wanted to preserve the Old Chateau, protect it from rotting away any further. I never would've gone along with it; I'd have done what I could to block him!" Cooper betrayed a hint of anger. "But my name was linked to his because I *did* go along with it. So, I share a measure of responsibility for what's been done. And that hasn't gone unnoticed by everyone that used to respect me in my professional circles."

"You mean the Golden Glen Historical Association?" She lifted her fine brows a fraction. "I read in the paper that they were pretty upset about Eilers' changes."

"To put it mildly," he said dryly. "I assume they still are, but I haven't shown my face at a meeting in months, and I'm not game to try anytime soon."

"What can they do, though?" She shook her head a little.

"Oh they can cause a few headaches if they really want to," he said confidently. "There were some guidelines attached to the sale of this place and Eilers didn't do a great job of honoring them. But I couldn't honestly tell you whether any of my old cronies would actually try to give him a slap on the wrists or not."

Maiden didn't know what to say to any of that, any words of reassurance would be hollow at best. The historical grace and character of the Old Chateau had been changed into a gaudy themed motel. For a historian, however casual, being held partly responsible for that would be an infuriating embarrassment.

Cooper looked angry and somber, it seemed so unlike the man that had been gleefully telling pirate tales only a few minutes before. She shifted her eyes to his and smiled kindly. He instantly cleared his expression and folded his hands on the bar.

"Well, for what it's worth, I'm glad you stayed on to share the stories of the real Chateau," she said as she slid from the stool and stood before him. "You're still working to preserve the place, I think that's really cool."

"Thanks, sweetie." He smiled faintly. "I don't think I got your name."

"Maiden," she told him. "Thanks for the story and the coffee. I'll see you around, Cooper."

Chapter Twelve

M aiden was still thinking of pirates and hidden treasure as she climbed back into her car and considered her next move. It was Tuesday and she had a rare opportunity to do some investigating without the risk of David catching her. She needed to use the time wisely.

She drove to the Addison and parked a few spots down on the opposite side of the street. Unsurprisingly, the alleyway on either side of the building was blocked off with police tape. The theater itself was dark and quiet but there was an OPEN sign on the door.

Maiden chewed at her lip as she considered the best way to get a peek inside without looking too obvious. She removed one of her earrings and tucked it in her pocket before climbing out of the car and dashing across the street.

She glanced subtly at the alley as she walked past. It was dark and dismal with a whiff of garbage clinging to the damp air. She didn't see much beyond a few empty crates and a couple of trash cans. There didn't seem to be any police on the scene, so she doubted there was much that had been left behind to look at anyway. Her real hunting grounds lay in the theater itself; she reached the front door and slipped inside.

The Addison had a different sort of vibe when it was empty but the rich furnishings and that elusive smell still lent it an air of drama.

Most of the lights were off, particularly the ones that pointed upwards to highlight the posters on the walls. The place felt abandoned but the door had been unlocked, someone had to be there. Maiden walked across the carpeted foyer and looked around for any sign of life.

Everything was quiet and she'd reached the restaurant by the time she finally found someone. A blonde in an Addison uniform was standing behind the bar refilling salt shakers. Maiden immediately recognized her as the lady that had been collecting the money the night of the concert. The name tag was nowhere to be seen but she remembered her easily.

"Stacey, right?" she asked nicely as she approached.

"Oh!" Stacey gasped and jumped, flinging salt into the air like confetti, before turning to her with a laugh. "Dang, you walk quietly! Yeah, I'm Stacey; what can I do for you, doll?"

Maiden smiled at the old-fashioned greeting and pointed to her bare ear.

"I may have lost an earring here the other night," she said. It *was* something that *may* have happened, it wasn't technically lying. "Just wondering if there was any chance that someone found it and turned it in?"

"Um, that's not very likely." Stacey grimaced and set her half-empty shaker aside. "But we can have a look anyway."

"Thanks, I really appreciate it." Maiden followed at a polite distance as she walked to the far end of the bar and pulled out an old cardboard box.

It was dusty and someone had written *Lost and Found* on the side in black crayon. Maiden highly doubted that any of the items in there had seen the light of day in years. Stacey carried it over and set it on the bar.

"You're welcome to have a dig through." She gestured towards the grungy box with a dubious look.

"Okay, thank you." Maiden reached in and tentatively pawed at the grimy contents. She pushed aside an oddly sticky sweater and was quietly relieved that no vermin were hiding beneath waiting to leap on her face. "None of this looks like anything I'd own, if I'm completely honest."

"Yeah, I kinda didn't think so," Stacey said with a laugh. "Sorry."

"It's all right," Maiden sighed and pretended to take a look at the carpet around the bar stools. "I guess you guys have had bigger problems than lost jewelry anyway."

"I'll say," Stacey grumbled. "It's been such a huge mess, and for no good reason."

"What do you mean?" Maiden gave her a curious look. "A guy did die here, didn't he?"

"Yeah, he did, and it was awful. But it was just a fluke of a thing." Stacey leaned her elbows on the bar. "Sean and the other boys stayed in here and drank for a while that night. They tended to do that a lot."

"You mean they got drunk every night?" Maiden smiled curiously.

"Well, maybe not drunk," Stacey allowed, "but not too far from it. And they really knocked them back Saturday night. I was working behind the bar by then; they all talked and drank until after midnight. Sean was looking really pickled. But it was nothing bad and there were no arguments or anything, just a bunch of musicians hanging out together."

"What actually happened then?" Maiden asked with a perplexed frown.

"I'm not entirely sure. I didn't hear anything, none of us even knew that something was up until a couple of the boys started shouting for help." She rubbed her arms as though they were cold.

"You must have been here late." Maiden blinked owlishly and left it to Stacey to elaborate if she wanted to.

"I sometimes stay back on performance nights," she shrugged. "Especially when the bar closes late and I'm scheduled on the next day. There's a couple of small rooms backstage, the manager lets us use them."

"That's nice," Maiden gave an impressed nod. "But you didn't see or hear anything strange that night?"

"No, not really," Stacey admitted. "But one of the boys was staying next door to Sean and heard a loud crash. Apparently Sean's body landed on the garbage cans and made quite a racket. They all started to panic; we called the police straight away."

"So, it was an accident?" Maiden asked, despite knowing for a fact that his death was being treated as suspicious.

"I think so," Stacey said mildly. "He probably tried to open the window and was too drunk to keep on the right side of it. It's awful, but it's also pretty obvious that's what happened. But the police were really serious about the whole thing."

"That sounds kinda scary. Any idea why?" she asked mildly.

"No, they didn't tell us *anything*," she grumbled. "And the band isn't allowed to leave town; they had to cancel their next gig. Fortunately we have spare rooms until the next act arrives this weekend, but it's tough for them if they can't earn money."

"It must be so difficult," Maiden tsked sympathetically. "Especially since they've lost *both* their managers now. How awful."

Stacey nodded sadly but then she glanced beyond Maiden's shoulder and instantly smiled. Maiden followed her gaze and saw a brawny man with a short beard approach. His hair was long and dark, it brushed the collar of his yellow shirt and the brown leather vest he wore over it. His snug-fitting jeans were tucked into a quirky pair of medieval-looking boots.

"Good afternoon, beautiful ladies!" His thick accent made his lascivious look seem charming rather than sleazy. "This can't be real, but it's too early to be dreaming."

Maiden recognized Ewan Fraser, he played the bagpipes along with a few flutes and tin whistles for the Highland Hounds. She'd seen him smoothly transfer from one instrument to another depending on the song they played. It had been impressive. He was obviously talented, and he was quite handsome; a fact she could see wasn't lost on Stacey.

"Hi, Ewan," Stacey said with a flirty smile. "How are you today?"

"Better for the view I've been treated to, that's for sure." He grinned and leaned casually on the bar. He turned to Maiden and looked her over. "*Please* tell me you're single and love music."

"Subtle. I am and yes, I do. But I'm not here for either reason." She smiled at him even as she eased back a step and touched her earlobe. "I don't suppose you've come across a stray earring?"

"It's not this one is it?" he teased as he turned to show her the small gold hoop that hung from his left ear.

"Unfortunately not," she laughed. "Ah well, it was a long shot. I could've lost it outside, I guess."

"Family heirloom?" Ewan shifted a tiny bit closer.

"No, but they were a gift from my mother." That much was true. "I'll just have to hope she doesn't notice."

"You were at the show Sunday night." He snapped his fingers as though remembering something. "I thought I'd seen you before."

"You wouldn't have seen enough to remember me." She pulled a face and he grinned again.

"You're memorable, lass. Trust me," he chuckled as he flitted his gaze over her again.

"I'm standing here too, by the way," Stacey said dryly, but there was a trace of genuine annoyance in her gaze.

"Oh, don't be jealous, my love." Ewan clutched at his heart and gazed longingly at her. "I could never care for anyone but you!"

"You're an idiot." Stacey rolled her eyes but smiled again.

"Stacey was just telling me about the accident Sunday night." Maiden kept her expression sympathetic. "It's terrible."

"It is that, lass, yes," he sighed loudly and shook his head.

"What will you do now?" she asked gently.

"Depends on if the local coppers let us leave or not," he said with a humorless smile. "We have several gigs already booked. We'll play those, then see if we can get any help from a few of our old contacts...if not, we'll head home early, I suppose."

"Can't you get another manager?" she asked ingenuously.

"Are you volunteering?" he asked mischievously but quickly relented. "It's not like they grow on trees, bonnie lass, and it's probably not worth the bother at this point anyway."

"Fair enough," she acknowledged and then slid him a doubtful look. "Are the police *really* not letting you leave? I heard he got drunk and fell out the window."

"Who told you that?" he asked quietly.

"Stacey," Maiden replied, pointing at her with her thumb.

Ewan laughed with genuine amusement and shook his head at them.

"It sounds wrong to say it, but I hope he did. And I hope the police reach that conclusion quickly," he admitted as he hooked his thumbs in his studded belt.

"Well, maybe they will," she said mildly. "They have to be thorough, I guess. Was Mr. Dowling alone in his room?"

"As far as I know," he murmured. "I was down the hall in my own room, fast asleep."

"So you didn't hear him fall?" She shook her head a little.

"No." His expression was a little more circumspect now. "Not that I noticed."

"Well, then hopefully the police will have no real cause to detain you," she concluded, hoping to make her nosiness sound more like friendly concern. "Assuming the rest of the band didn't see or hear anything either. It's not like you could help them figure it out, is it?"

"Arran heard it; he's the lead singer," Stacey volunteered. "He's the one that called the police."

"Oh, I see," Maiden murmured but noticed that Ewan was eyeing them both watchfully. She decided she'd pushed as much as was wise for the moment and stepped away. "I'm sure that such a cooperative attitude will help. In any case, all the best. I'm sorry for *both* of your losses."

"Kind of you, lass." He inclined his head cordially.

"Thanks for the help," Maiden said as she headed towards the door. "If you do ever find that earring, enjoy it with my compliments."

"That I will." There was a smile in his voice.

Maiden felt eyes on her as she walked away but it didn't overly worry her. Ewan had started to get defensive but, judging by the way he started the conversation, it was just as likely that he was simply checking her out. She didn't think her father's sweeping statement about over-sexed musicians was fair, but she definitely got the impression that Ewan quite happily fed the stereotype.

She stepped out into brisk, drizzly weather and smiled. She thought about what Kylie had said about this kind of weather, it was definitely cozy and she felt like curling up and hiding herself away. It had been a productive day that had given her plenty of ways to distract from a rather bruised heart.

Maiden climbed into her car and headed home in a much better mood than she'd left it with. Between Cooper's charming kindness and Ewan's appreciative staring, she felt nicely boosted. All she had to do was avoid thinking about David and she'd be fine.

She stepped into the foyer of Harlow House and glanced over to find Gloria and Alfie in the office talking quietly. She also spotted Vonny and Billie trying to read their lips from across the lobby.

Feeling a smidgeon of mischievous amusement, Maiden shut the door deliberately loudly, causing Von and Billie to jump and her parents to come rushing to the doorway of the office.

"How is everyone?" Maiden asked sweetly as she met their uncertain looks.

"We're fine, angel, just fine." Gloria said with a hint of concern in her voice. "You okay? How was your meetin' with Fred?"

"I'm not sure yet," she murmured and headed towards the stairs. "But don't worry, everything's fine."

Billie watched her dubiously, there was little chance she hadn't heard about the breakup with David by now. The lady showed unusual discretion and kept quiet as Maiden neared, but Vonny exhaled loudly and folded her arms stubbornly.

"Mae, you need to listen to me," she said firmly. "You're putting yourself under too much stress. I think you should just—"

"Vonny." Maiden stopped and turned to face her, holding up a warning finger. "If you try to push one more piece of advice down my throat, I'll grab Billie by the ankles and beat you over the head with her."

Von stilled at that absurd and serenely spoken caution, but then smirked and nodded. "All right. That sounds fair."

Maiden smiled and winked at a startled Billie as she pulled her earring out of her pocket and slipped it back in her ear. She headed upstairs feeling hungry for the first time in days.

She'd learned some interesting things today and it was time to recharge. There was a sandwich and a nap calling to her and she wasn't about to ignore either one of them.

CHAPTER THIRTEEN

The entire Harlow household was home for dinner that night and acting refreshingly normal. No one mentioned anything of a particularly serious nature and the more sensitive topics of wilted romances and inscrutable murderers were steadfastly avoided.

Maiden and her family talked and laughed for a couple of hours without anyone really saying anything of note. It was a veneer and she knew it, but that still suited her fine. She went to bed early, worn out from a taxing but successful day, and snuggled under the blankets with a softly purring Ruffian.

Maiden slept remarkably well through most of the night. But somewhere in the darkest depths of the early hours she started to dream. She dreamed that she and David were on opposing pirate ships, locked in battle.

The wind howled around her and icy rain poured down on the deck. Bleak skies and endless murky waters surrounded the warring vessels. Maiden looked around frantically but there was no one there, no trace of a crew to assist her.

David, on the other hand, had countless minions scurrying around him like ants. He was shouting orders and lighting the fuses of a row of cannons. Loud explosions split the air and chunks of wood went flying as a cannonball crashed into the deck beside her.

Maiden gasped and tried to run to her own cannons where they laid in a formidable lineup at the edge of the deck, but her fingers felt feeble, like jelly, and her legs didn't want to work. The waves pushed and pulled at her ship as another loud bang jostled her. An instant later a cannonball smashed through the hull.

Maiden gaped at the resulting hole and then glared at a stone-faced David.

"You creep!" she shouted indignantly. He didn't reply.

The ship took on water and started to pitch and sway. It was going to sink; she didn't have a chance. Maiden felt panic well up within her and started dumping chests full of gold and jewels overboard as the frigid water rushed towards her. The world was spinning, she struggled to run towards the rail but her movements were slow and groggy.

The next thing she knew she was wearing a kilt and holding a bottle of whiskey. Celtic music blared all around her along with a renewed chorus of cannon fire. It wasn't until Ruffian started dancing across the deck on his hind legs while playing the bagpipes that she finally woke up.

Maiden sat up in bed and felt the kitten roll off her stomach and into her lap with a startled grunt. She looked anxiously around her room, pleased that it wasn't the sinking ship she'd half expected to see, and noticed a few rays of moonlight streaming in the balcony doors.

"Dang," she whispered to herself as she flopped onto her back and shook with silent laughter. "If I were Claudia Arnaud, I'd have settled that jerk's hash."

She'd never been dumped before and her subconscious clearly wasn't taking it well. She stared up at the ceiling and waited for her giggles to subside. A moment later she felt Ruffian scamper across her stomach and stand on her chest. He looked quite unimpressed as he studied her through half-closed eyes.

"Sorry, Ruffy," she murmured as she stroked his fuzzy neck in apology for waking him. "I am officially losing it."

The kitten purred but still punished her with a swat of his tiny paw; she respected that. She sighed and sat up slowly, carefully setting him on the quilt beside her this time.

She climbed out of bed and slipped on her robe as she walked over to the French doors. She pushed back the curtains and looked outside at their quiet street. She wasn't sure what time it was but it was still a bit dark out and there was no one to be seen.

She stood there for a while watching the first rays of sunlight slowly stretch up from the horizon. The weather was getting steadily colder, in a month or so there would be snow. Staring out at gray skies and ominous but pillowy clouds, Maiden felt herself calm.

The past few days had taken a toll, but she felt more clear-headed; at least the uncertainty was gone. Some of it anyway.

Her romance with David was kaput but there were still three murders that she was now involved in. She couldn't deny her interest in Sean Dowling's death, that choice had been made for her when someone decided to lie about a connection between them.

That murder was undoubtably linked to the first, Charles Brown, the business partner. What sort of business? Maiden couldn't help but wonder what was actually going on there. It seemed unlikely to her that both the men would be murdered, and only a week apart, if they weren't involved in something unsavory. And then there was the puzzle of Ulysses Mercier. Where did he fit in?

Her visit with Fred Eilers had been interesting. Despite his insistence that his hotel was packed every night, there hadn't been too many cars in the parking lot when she'd gone there. And she hadn't seen anyone except staff members inside. He was definitely lying to her, or at least holding back.

He didn't mention that his investors were unhappy with what he'd done to the Old Chateau. He also didn't explain why he was employing an accountant that he neither liked nor trusted. It was weird, the whole place was weird. She needed to try and get a fuller picture of what was really going on.

Thinking of Eilers also made her think about her parents. They were still being a bit furtive but they'd settled down a bit. Soon after Ulysses Mercier was found dead. Her mother's lunch date with Eilers flitted through her mind. There was something happening there; both Gloria and Alfie were connected to Eilers more deeply than they admitted. But she had no idea what that connection was.

She narrowed her eyes pensively. She'd planned to go straight to Eilers' Arms to try and speak with his accountant, Graham Harper, but she quickly decided that could wait until later in the day. Yes, this morning would be perfect for a little reconnaissance.

***

Maiden enlisted Vonny and Billie to keep an eye on her parents and report back to her. Through a series of texts, she learned that Gloria had left a couple of hours ago and no one seemed to know where she went. Alfie was going out for lunch alone and wouldn't say where or why beyond 'meeting up with an old friend'.

So Maiden waited until he walked out the door, whistling cheerfully, and gave him a moment before slipping out after him. She ducked behind her car and glanced at Alfie, he was struggling with his seatbelt.

She took the opportunity to climb in her car and waited until he got settled and drove out of the parking lot.

Feeling only a little funny about doing it, Maiden started her car and followed her father downtown. The sky was still darkened and it looked like it might rain any time, somehow that made her feel even sneakier. Everything was gloomy and mysterious; she half expected a thick fog to roll in.

Alfie drove his old station wagon to the business district, where Town Hall and most of the more prominent office buildings were. She followed slowly and kept back far enough that he hopefully wouldn't see her.

Maiden pulled into a parking spot along the street and watched him park outside a familiar building; it was his lawyer's office. As he climbed out and walked inside she took a deep breath and tried to reassure herself that there was no way her parents were getting a divorce.

They loved each other, they got along so well. She rarely heard them bicker, and when they did disagree or even argue they never stayed upset for long. What could possibly come between them?

Fred Eilers. Her temper flared up so fast she nearly strangled the steering wheel. *Is that why Mom wanted me to help him? If they think I'd lift a finger to protect some home-wrecking gigolo—stop it, Maiden! You're letting Billie get in your head. Collect facts, not hysterical theories.*

Maiden forced her hands to unclench and sank back in her seat. She waited over half an hour before Alfie walked out carrying a thick folder under his arm. She watched curiously as he climbed back into the old station wagon and started the engine.

Knowing that her father would recognize her car, she gave him plenty of space as he pulled out and headed off down the street. Giving him time to become focused on his destination, and distracted by the mix of Motown and 80's girl bands that he typically listened to when driving, she started her car and again followed at a distance.

He parked next to one of the larger Chinese restaurants in town and clutched the folder tightly as he walked inside. Maiden parked a discreet distance away and contemplated just walking in as well. She wondered what Alfie would actually do if she joined him and his 'old friend' for lunch.

It was tempting, but she decided not to tip her hand and reveal her suspicions too early. Not that she knew exactly what she was suspicious of, but there was definitely something strange going on.

She dashed out and got a sandwich to go from a café across the street. She sat and ate in her car as she watched the front door of the Golden Emperor Family Restaurant. She glanced at her phone when it lit up and cheeped as a message came through.

Vonny

> What's happening?

Maiden

> Dad's at the Golden Emperor. I'm not sure who he met there, though.

Vonny

> Just walk in and look. If Dad sees you tell him you're getting me some eggrolls. And while you're at it, get me some eggrolls. I'm hungry and it's the perfect cover.

Maiden grinned down at the screen and quickly started typing.

Maiden

> Walk across the foyer and get your own lunch, and stop distracting me, I have to watch for Dad.

About ten minutes later Alfie emerged...with Gloria. Maiden could only stare as the pair trundled down the sidewalk holding hands and chatting. They continued down the street and into a little boutique. Her father didn't like shopping but he'd just willingly, and with a smile, escorted his wife into a shop that had more lace in the windows than an old lady's blouse.

"What the heck?" she whispered with genuine bewilderment.

A little while later they emerged holding what looked to be books of fabric swatches. They waved to someone inside, walked back and climbed into the station wagon and were off again.

Maiden spent the next couple of hours following them as they fluffed around town doing what appeared to be nothing in particular. They went into several furniture stores, a paint shop and an expensive boutique that specialized in overpriced curtains.

She started to wonder if they were planning to redecorate the inn. She hoped not, none of the existing furnishings were all that old, it would be a huge waste of money. At least they weren't having a screaming fight in a lawyer's office or meeting with illicit lovers, though. Not today anyway.

Maiden shook her head and glanced at the time, it was already after 4 pm. The day was gone and she'd only succeeded in confusing herself more. Deciding she'd had enough, she gave up the hunt and headed back to the inn.

She was just pulling up outside Harlow House when she saw a man in a mask climb over her balcony railing and drop into the bushes. Her heart started pounding and she froze for an instant. She then swerved over to the curb and threw the car into park. She jumped out and shut the door loudly.

"Hey!" she shouted angrily as he stood and brushed himself off.

The man looked at her sharply and then took off across the street. She knew it would be stupid to chase him so she pulled her phone out of her purse and fumbled to get to her camera. By that time the man had ducked into a waiting car and drove off. She couldn't get a clear look at the license plate either.

Maiden silently fumed but quickly thought of her sister. She ran in through the front door and found Vonny at the desk staring at her in surprise.

"What's going on?" she asked.

"Are you all right?" Maiden demanded even as she ran across the foyer.

"I think so." Von shook her head. "Why? What's wrong?"

"Someone just climbed out of my bedroom window!" she muttered as she hurried past and headed for the apartment.

"What?!" Von shrieked and ran after her. "Don't go in alone, you idiot!"

They ran up the stairs together and found the front door open. She and Von stood staring at it for a moment before edging closer. Maiden took a deep breath and pushed it wide, peering cautiously through the doorway. Everything was quiet and looked undisturbed.

A moment later the kittens came scampering out from under the couch to meet them. Vonny bent to scoop them both up and cuddled them protectively to her chest. Maiden motioned for her to stay near the door and crept in further.

Vonny started to speak, probably to order her to come back, but quickly recalled the need for silence. She clamped her mouth shut and hopped nervously from one foot to the other like a child that desperately needed a pee.

Maiden looked around carefully in every room, deliberately leaving hers until last. There was no one hiding in the rest of the apartment and nothing seemed out of place. She finally started down the hall to her bedroom but stilled and looked back sharply when she heard quiet steps behind her.

It was Vonny; she'd swapped the kittens out for Gloria's biggest rolling pin and held it ready to swing.

Maiden stared at her for an instant but then gave a conceding shrug and resumed tiptoeing down the hallway. Her bedroom door was ajar, she took a deep breath and pushed it open. She and Vonny gasped loudly.

The room was empty, but it was also trashed. Her drawers had all been pulled out and their contents rifled. The bookshelf on the side wall had been spilled across the floor and even the shoes under her bed had been thrown across the room.

Maiden let out a shaky breath as feelings of shock, anger and violation washed over her. Von laid a hand on her shoulder and gave her a serious look.

"Call the cops, Mae," she said quietly.

She was right, of course, that was the smartest thing to do at this point. Maiden nodded and, very reluctantly, pulled out her phone and dialed the police station. Nancy answered after two rings, her tranquil and familiar voice was oddly comforting.

"Hey, it's Maiden Harlow," she knew she sounded quiet and wary but she couldn't help it. "Um, someone broke into my room and searched it. I saw them climb over the balcony and drive off."

"I see," Nancy answered steadily. "Where are you now, Miss Harlow?"

"I'm in the apartment," she mumbled. "It's okay, it's empty."

"It's probably safer to wait outside anyway." There was a tinge of worried disapproval in her tone.

"Yeah, thank you." Maiden rolled her eyes but kept her tone polite. "Can you ask someone to come check it out please? I can just call Greg if it's easier."

"Miss Harlow, that's not necessary or wise," Nancy said rather tightly. "Someone will be over very soon; find a safe place to wait and sit tight."

"Okay, thanks," she murmured.

"Certainly," Nancy said as she pulled the phone from her ear. "Captain—"

Maiden tensed even as the line went dead. The first thing Nancy did was turn to David. She reminded herself that it didn't matter. He was the head of the department and would hear about most things regardless. He was probably just passing by when she called; he wouldn't particularly care. That was done now, they were done, he'd dropped her.

She stared down at her phone and desperately hoped that he wouldn't come personally. There was no way, he didn't have time and hated her guts, he wouldn't come. He was the last thing she needed to deal with at the moment. She swallowed her concerns, along with another urge to be sick, and glanced at Von.

"They're sending someone over," she said unsteadily. "You'd probably better go back and watch the desk."

"Okay," Vonny agreed after giving her quiet sister a worried look. "I'm right downstairs if you need me. Leave the door open just in case."

After Von left, Maiden walked to the couch and sank down into the cushions. The kittens hopped up and climbed into her lap as though they could sense her unsettled mood. They circled a few times before curling up and infusing her with purring warmth. Maiden smiled faintly and stroked their fuzzy heads.

Think straight, Maiden, don't get overwhelmed, she urged herself. *This is all happening for a reason. You need to figure out what it is. Once the cops check everything out and make sure the apartment is safe, you can regroup and go from there. It's going to be okay.*

Chapter Fourteen

About ten minutes later Greg and Sarah-Jane knocked lightly on the open door as they walked in. Maiden glanced back and smiled with relief to see them, and only them.

"Hey guys," she said quietly as she carefully shifted the kittens and stood. "Thanks for getting here so fast."

"All good." Greg cleared his throat and nodded towards the door at the back of the kitchen that led to her room. "Just through here?"

"Yeah." She frowned faintly, noticing that they both looked stiff and uncomfortable again. Something was wrong.

Maiden gave them both a wary look but quietly led the way to her room. She stood to the side and pointed at her door. Greg and Sarah-Jane stepped into her room and looked around. Maiden wondered why they were being so distant; she was starting to fear that David had somehow turned the entire police department against her, but then Greg turned to her and finally smiled.

"You sure you're okay?" he asked nicely. She shrugged but stayed silent. "We'll have a look around; everything's going to be all right."

Maiden didn't believe that reassurance but still appreciated it. She obligingly waited in the hall while the two officers poked around the disheveled room. They spoke quietly to each other a few times but she couldn't make out their words. Finally, Sarah-Jane snapped a few pictures and then they both turned slowly to face her.

Uh-oh, I know that look. You have to deal with me and you don't want to…something's up. Something bad.

"What's going on?" Maiden said aloud, tucking her more paranoid thoughts away. "You guys are acting weird."

"Um…" Greg glanced at Sarah-Jane and motioned for her to proceed.

"Under the circumstances, Miss Harlow," Sarah-Jane stood tall and looked her in the eye, "we've been instructed to bring you in for questioning."

"What?!" Maiden's worry instantly dissolved into simmering anger.

"It's all kind of strange, Mae." Greg eyed her anxiously. "I'm so sorry."

"You're arresting me because someone broke in and searched my room?" she demanded. "Are you crazy?!"

"You're not under arrest!" Greg hurried to assure her. "But the Captain—I'm so sorry, Mae!"

"Did David tell you to bring me in?" She stared at them incredulously and then looked away and pulled in a deep breath. "Whatever. I don't even care. Let's just go."

"Thank you for cooperating," Sarah-Jane said placidly. "Rest assured we'll be sending someone over soon to dust for prints."

"The guy wore gloves but whatever," Maiden said tightly. "Why should I be the only one that gets to waste her afternoon?"

She didn't bother grabbing her purse, she just shoved her phone in her back pocket and gestured for them to get on with it. They walked silently downstairs and out through the foyer.

Greg was pale, Sarah-Jane was quietly determined and Maiden was seething. She followed behind them with her arms folded over her chest and a thunderous expression on her face.

Vonny stared at them as they filed past but Maiden just met her gaze and shook her head irately. She walked outside and sucked in a deep breath of the chilly afternoon air, hoping it might cool her temper a little. It wasn't working, she was still ready to scream or kick something.

She forced herself to stalk to the patrol car with a measure of grace and civility but stiffened and pulled away when Sarah-Jane opened the rear door and instinctively started to push her inside. The young officer immediately caught herself and backed off.

"Force of habit," Sarah-Jane mumbled sheepishly.

Maiden gave her a warning look as she climbed in unassisted and again submitted to being driven to the police station like a criminal.

She refused to speak to either of them on the way. Greg apologized repeatedly but she just stared out the window and said nothing. She was too angry and felt too betrayed to speak mildly and she really didn't want to snap at Greg.

Maiden wasn't feeling any better by the time they reached the station. She stalked into the lobby after Greg and Sarah-Jane, refused to even look at Nancy, and followed them down the hallway to the left and into what turned out to be an interrogation room.

It was a blank, sterile and thoroughly miserable place to be. She told herself that it made no difference, she would put up with whatever nonsense they threw her way and then she'd go home and not talk to any of them ever again. It was a valuable lesson learned, they'd all sided with David, and David had obviously lost his damn mind.

Greg gave her a wincing smile and shut the door behind him as he escaped into the hall. Only Sarah-Jane remained in the little room with her and pointed her to a hard plastic chair in front of a bare and depressing little table that was bolted to the floor.

Maiden dropped into the chair without a word and kept her irate gaze lowered. Sarah-Jane sat opposite her and opened up a small laptop. As the stone-faced officer typed away, Maiden flicked an unimpressed glance around the room.

It was all done in shades of lifeless beige. Dull lights flickered occasionally as they hummed overhead. The wall to their left bore a large mirror that she knew would be two-way glass; she had little doubt that David was there sitting and observing everything from the room on the other side.

"All right, Miss Harlow," Sarah-Jane said as she looked her in the eye. "I want you to explain exactly what happened this afternoon."

"I drove home and saw someone dressed in black, with gloves and a mask, climbing over the balcony from my room. They got into a car and drove off," she obliged in a flat, emotionless monotone. "I went inside and checked the apartment, found my room ransacked, and followed Vonny's brilliant advice to call the police."

"You checked the apartment before calling us?" Sarah-Jane demanded with a disapproving look.

"Yes, I did," Maiden replied easily.

"You should have called us first and waited outside," she grumbled.

"Are you suggesting that calling you sooner would have been more advantageous to me?" Maiden was a bit startled by her own sarcasm but was powerless to rein it in. "Is that because things are going so well for me *now*?"

"The attitude is not necessary, Miss Harlow," Sarah-Jane advised.

"None of this feels particularly necessary, Officer Parker," she retorted and then fell frostily silent.

Sarah-Jane exhaled tolerantly and consulted her notes.

"So," she mused. "You're claiming that you saw someone climb down from your room and jump into a waiting car. You subsequently called the police after also finding that your bedroom had been searched?"

"Correct," Maiden said simply.

"Any idea who it might've been?" Sarah-Jane gave her a speaking look.

"No." She sat back in the hard plastic chair with her arms folded over her chest. "As I mentioned, he wore a mask."

"So you think it was a man?"

"Yes."

"Why?"

"Is that an actual question?" Maiden frowned at her.

"It is."

"Could you repeat it?" She shook her head slightly.

Sarah-Jane rolled her eyes and sighed. "Do you believe the person that broke into your room was a male? And, if so, why?"

"You've caught me out there, you cunning devil," Maiden grinned in spite of herself, "I suppose it *could've* been a woman with unusually broad shoulders and a sock down her pants."

Sarah-Jane pressed her lips together and turned slightly pink as she took a moment to type some more. She cleared her throat and looked to be trying to fight a fit of giggles.

"I find it unlikely that you have no idea who this person could be." Sarah-Jane quirked a luscious brow as she dared to face her again. "You've been connected to a recent murder victim and now your bedroom's been searched. You can't offer any reason why?"

"I am not connected with Sean Dowling," she said slowly and clearly. "I met him once and that was it."

"We've been told otherwise," Sarah-Jane murmured.

"You've been lied to," Maiden felt her scowl resurface. She detested being lied about and it was so much worse when no one would believe her. "Who's saying it, anyway?"

"Let's leave that for a moment," she held up a placating hand. "Are you in danger?"

"What?" Maiden gasped softly and glanced reflexively over her shoulder. "Why would I be in danger?"

"You've claimed your room was searched," she said.

"You saw my room, you know it was searched." Maiden shook her head uncertainly.

"Yeah," the officer frowned at her, "so, do you feel that you're in danger?"

"I reported a break-in and your response has been to bring *me* in for questioning," Maiden knew she was looking at her like she was a twit but she was honestly starting to wonder. "It would be fair to say that I've felt safer."

"So, do you know who the threat is coming from?" Sarah-Jane tried again.

"Why on earth would I know that?" Maiden asked.

"Because you're involved," she strove for patience.

"Not by choice," Maiden said. "In any case, I certainly won't be bothering any of you with my problems again, so no need to get too worked up about it."

"I do understand your frustration, Miss Harlow. Did you disturb anything before the officers arrived at your apartment?" Sarah-Jane gave her an unrevealing look.

"Before *you* got there, you mean?" she replied acerbically. "I didn't touch anything."

"So no idea if anything in particular was missing?"

"Not without having looked yet." She knew she sounded incredibly annoyed; she was fine with that.

"Okay, Miss Harlow, settle down." Sarah-Jane smiled so briefly it almost escaped notice. "Now, let's go back to Saturday."

"Why?" Maiden demanded flatly.

"Because I'm nosy." The young officer leveled a steely glare in return. "Is that a problem? Good. Now, you were with a Mr. Sean Dowling at approximately 9:30 pm in the bar at the Addison Theater, is that correct?"

"Yes." Maiden was grateful the table was bolted to the floor as a sudden urge to fling it around the room took hold of her.

"Tell me exactly what happened that day and what led up to your conversation with him."

"I've done that," Maiden said through clenched teeth.

"Well not with me, so you can do it again!" Sarah-Jane said sharply. "And start from the beginning."

Maiden shut her eyes and took a deep breath. She could almost hear her mother's voice telling her not to lose her temper and never to argue with cranky police officers; it wasn't worth the potential consequences.

"I had a...difficult discussion with someone that morning, my sister found me soon after and started pestering me to get out of the house for an evening. She told me she and her boyfriend were going to see the Highland Hounds play at the Addison and insisted that I go too," Maiden said as she stared straight into Sarah-Jane's obnoxiously stern eyes. "Tony drove us to the theater around 7 o'clock. After the show, we bought some souvenirs and went to the bar for a drink. Sean Dowling approached us and introduced himself as the Hound's touring manager. He sat with us and had a drink, then he offered to get our CDs signed by the band, then we said goodnight and left."

"That's it?" A full brow arched dubiously once more.

"Yeah."

"What led him to introduce himself to you?" she watched her expression closely.

"I didn't ask him that," Maiden replied.

"A witness claims to have seen you and Mr. Dowling behaving in a manner that denotes," she looked up for emphasis, "closeness."

"They're lying," Maiden said again.

"Really?" Sarah-Jane's tone was impassive.

"Yeah, we all talked to him for about ten minutes, that was it. I was never even alone with him," Maiden murmured. "Who was this 'witness' anyway?"

"I can't really say."

"Oh stuff it!" Maiden glared at her. "If you can accuse me of something I never did, you can at least tell me who's slandering my name and reputation! Was it another patron?"

"No," Sarah-Jane allowed.

"The staff?" Maiden tried again but Sarah-Jane wouldn't look at her. "It couldn't have been a member of the band."

The young officer stilled and looked up at her with slightly widened eyes. Maiden just stared at her in mild disbelief.

"None of them were even in the room," she said quietly.

"It doesn't take long to observe an exchange," Sarah-Jane mused. "And I never said it was a band member."

"You didn't have to, poker-face," Maiden grumbled. "They were all in the reception room down the hall signing autographs, they didn't come into the bar while we were there. Sean had to go to them to get our CDs signed; he was gone for kind of a while."

"Why would they lie about seeing you together?" Sarah-Jane asked.

"I don't know! You're the police, you figure it out," she replied with a scoff. "Why would I lie about knowing the guy?"

"It's been suggested that certain other 'relationships' might have led you to keep any dealings secret," she said tactfully.

"I don't cheat. I have *never* cheated. And I'm not a good liar," Maiden said angrily. "Quite frankly, if I was mad enough to chase after some other man, I'd have told him to his face and told him to choke on it."

"But you did break up with your boyfriend that morning," Sarah-Jane reminded her.

"No I didn't." Maiden frowned slightly. Sarah-Jane looked confused so she reluctantly explained. "I didn't break up with him; we had a fight."

"Okay...is, um, is he aware of that distinction?" she asked delicately and slid her gaze very briefly to the mirror.

"I have *no* idea. I've given up trying to follow his thinking process, it was giving me a headache," Maiden said dryly. "It doesn't matter anyway, we're definitely broken up now, but that was his doing not mine."

"So what did *you* do?" Sarah-Jane shook her head a fraction.

"I tried to use reason and grown-up communication, and when that failed I went home and threw up," she muttered. She wasn't about to tell them that she went to confer with Eilers after that.

Sarah-Jane bit her lip and started typing. Maiden watched her for a moment and waited for her to say something else. She could almost feel the eyes on her from the other side of the glass and it was getting to her. The silence stretched on until she couldn't stand it any longer.

"So, despite *never* having done anything seriously wrong or irresponsible, my name's worse than mud because a bunch of strangers claimed to have seen me do something I'd never have done?!" Maiden eyed her furiously. "One guy you don't know from a bar of soap breezes into town and makes a nasty claim about me and that's it? You all just take his word for it?!"

"Not *all* of us do, Miss Harlow," Sarah-Jane replied, flicking another uncomfortable glance towards the two-way glass.

Maiden followed her gaze and then faced her again. She folded her arms and sank back into her chair.

"So, not all of you?" she demanded calmly enough. "Just the petty, self-absorbed jackass that's heading up the case? Awesome! My reputation's safe."

"Settle down, Miss Harlow. Let me finish this note." Sarah-Jane twisted her mouth to the side to hide her threatening smirk. "Is 'jackass' one word or two?"

"One," Maiden sighed and turned her face up to the ceiling. "Unless maybe the guy's name is Jack, which it isn't in this instance."

A subtle tapping on the other side of the glass was enough to sober Sarah-Jane, but it didn't bother Maiden one bit.

"Back to the night in question." Sarah-Jane cleared her throat. "Did Mr. Dowling actually flirt with you?"

"Yes, he did," she exhaled loudly. "I've been hit on once or twice before, it's not all that suspiciously incredible."

"And did you flirt in return?"

"No, I did not." Maiden glared at her again.

"Did he ask you out?"

"No. Oh, well...sort of, I guess he did, yeah." Maiden frowned briefly as she considered the question. "He offered us free entry to the next show. It doesn't matter, I said no anyway."

"Did you exchange phone numbers?"

"No, we did *not*. I thought I was still in a relationship at the time." Maiden shook her head at her own naivete. "In any case, I'm very careful about men."

"And why is that?" Sarah-Jane asked.

"Because every man I've ever been involved with has ended up treating me badly," she said and rubbed her eyes as though they were sore. "All of them."

Sarah-Jane fell silent and started typing again. Maiden felt herself start to calm at last. She opened her eyes to see Sarah-Jane watching her with less of the tough-cop bravado. She turned back to her notes and scrolled through them with a stony expression.

"So, basically what you're telling me," she drummed her fingers loudly on the tabletop, "is that you sat in a crowded room at the same table with Mr. Dowling and two other people and had a drink that you would've had even if you'd never set eyes on him? You then parted ways with no plans to ever speak to each other again?"

"That's exactly right, officer," Maiden said wearily.

"And the only person who claims otherwise was unlikely to have seen enough to make a definite claim to the contrary." She gave her an assessing look.

"Correct."

"It doesn't really sound like that big of a deal," Sarah-Jane said loudly as she looked with some irritation towards the mirror.

"Which pretty much sums up every relationship I've ever had." Maiden smiled a little too sweetly before her stoney expression returned. "Can I go now?"

"Yes, Miss Harlow." Sarah-Jane closed the laptop and stood. "Thank you for your cooperation, I'll walk you out."

Maiden wasn't sure what the point of that whole farce had been, she was just hopeful that it was over. Surely no one else in town ended up at the police station as often as she did? She scowled and shook her head to herself as Sarah-Jane ushered her out and shut the heavy door behind them.

"You did great, Maiden!" She smiled at her and gave her a pat on the back. "C'mon, I'll buy you dinner."

"What?" Maiden blinked at her and gestured towards the door. "What was all that nonsense?"

"Hopefully, it was a means of clearing the air." She rolled her eyes and urged her down the long corridor. "I'm sick of the moping and the tension, it's impeding the case and putting the rest of us on edge. He took a day off right after we found a body! It's ridiculous!"

"I don't care if the air's clear or not, I'm not talking to him!" she said resolutely even as Sarah-Jane propelled her down the hall. "He's a hypocritical jerk."

"That's fine," she glanced over her shoulder, "but if you don't want to see him you need to walk faster."

They both stiffened as they heard a door behind them open, they sped up their pace and neither looked back.

CHAPTER FIFTEEN

Maiden was too confused to be annoyed anymore. She sat quietly in the passenger seat as Sarah-Jane drove them to her apartment a few blocks away from the station. They ducked inside long enough for Sarah-Jane to change out of her uniform and into jeans and a sweater.

It was a cute little place. There looked to be only one bedroom and the combined kitchen/dining room/lounge was tiny, but it was nice. Maiden glanced around at the surprisingly colorful décor. It was very much in contrast to the tomboyish officer's usually plain and unadorned style.

"Are you part Spanish?" she asked mildly as she looked at the brightly patterned cushions on the sofa and a large painting of a quaint looking village on the wall.

"Yeah, on Mom's side." Sarah-Jane nodded as she dragged a brush through her dense curls a few more times before giving up and letting them spring back where they wanted to.

Maiden was about to ask her about it when her phone cheeped at her. She pulled it out and gasped when she read her sister's frantic message.

"Oh!" she quickly started typing. "I forgot to let Vonny know I'm okay, she'll think I was arrested!"

"You don't get arrested for being vandalized," Sarah-Jane shook her head and smirked.

"Not the impression I was given," Maiden gave her a testy look. "Was hauling me into that dingy little room David's bright idea?"

"Yeah, but only because he can't look at you without falling to pieces," she chuckled. "Cut him a little slack if you can bear to, he's been a quiet, cranky mess these last few days."

Maiden glanced up at that unexpected insight but then became very involved in putting her phone back in her pocket. Sarah-Jane must have noticed and took pity.

"So, where do we want to go for dinner?" she asked lightly.

"Eiler's Arms has a restaurant I've been meaning to check out." Maiden tried to sound nonchalant but doubted her friend would fall for it.

"Sweet." Sarah-Jane grinned sneakily and threw her hairbrush carelessly into the half-empty fruit bowl on her small table. "Exactly what I was thinking."

"I know why I want to go, but what's your angle?" Maiden gave her a curious look.

"Something always happens when you're around." Sarah-Jane said rather deviously. "I'd like to be in on it for once."

"Thanks a lot," Maiden laughed. "I feel like a science experiment. Let's go."

They took a taxi, as they both planned on having a drink or two. It wasn't a long drive but Maiden spent it thinking about her next move. Bringing Sarah-Jane along was a potential risk, but it also gave her an opportunity to look around a little with someone she could trust to be discreet. Whereas Von would talk at full volume and say whatever she was thinking.

Maiden wasn't sure if the person that searched her room had gone after her because she'd come to see Eilers yesterday, but it was a possibility that had to be considered.

She was also very interested in finding out why a member of the Highland Hounds would try to fabricate some sort of relationship between her and one of their deceased tour managers. As far as she knew she'd never had anything to do with any of them.

That question would have to wait, however. She could only follow one lead at a time. For the moment, she was more concerned with Eilers and how involved he really was in the murder of Ulysses Mercier.

They arrived at the Docks and stepped out into the breezy evening air. Maiden paid the driver and then joined Sarah-Jane in gazing up at the expensively refurbished exterior of Eilers' Arms.

"Wow!" Sarah-Jane breathed as she looked it over with widened eyes. "I've never seen anything like this place. It's incredible."

"I would have to agree with that," Maiden said and then headed for the door. "Wait until you see the inside."

***

David sat in his car outside Eiler's Arms. He'd already checked in with Ramirez, who was in an unmarked car watching the front door along with Briggs. From where he was parked, David could see both the front door and the right side of the building.

He'd done his share of stakeouts in his time, but he was struggling to stay focused at the moment. It was dark and cold outside, he hadn't slept well in days and now he felt sick.

It had been barely an hour since Maiden had effectively ripped his heart out again. The first time was bad enough, hearing some creep laugh as he talked about her being intimately familiar with another man was among the worst moments of his life.

The witness had sworn it was true, he'd described her, he'd known her name, he'd signed the statement without qualm. It was a kind of pain David had never felt before and it had hurt like hell. But now Maiden had cut him even deeper, and not because she'd done a thing wrong, it was because he was starting to understand the scope of his mistake.

Why did I believe that guy? David asked himself for at least the fiftieth time. Everything Maiden said in her interview with Parker was true. She'd never really lied to him, and he'd never seen her flirt with anyone else. She was honest and she was decent.

But he'd been certain that she'd dumped him. That last conversation with her had seemed so firm and final; she'd been so angry with him. It had all seemed to fit into place when he'd been told that she was halfway in bed with someone else. He knew that he'd put her off too many times and then he'd completely forgotten the date he'd practically begged her for.

Settle down, David, falling apart isn't going to help anyone, he told himself. He really had no idea where to go from here, but he knew that he needed to be focusing on finding a killer, not trying to put his personal life back together.

David shifted in his seat and took a deep breath. He was just rubbing his sore eyes when he heard Ramirez' voice come over the radio.

"Are you seeing this, sir?" he asked quietly.

David glanced back at the front of the hotel and froze. Maiden and Parker were standing there looking up at the building. There was absolutely no legitimate reason for Maiden to be visiting a rival hotel on the heels of a dead body being found there. He watched with a hint of incredulous disbelief as they walked inside. The sheer gall of that woman was staggering, and somehow she'd roped Parker in.

"You've got to be kidding me," he whispered to himself and grabbed the radio to reply to Ramirez. "I see it. I'll check it out, stay put and keep watching."

"Yes, sir."

He was just opening his door when he saw another familiar person walk inside rather furtively. Anger poured through David as his eyes narrowed on the man that had calmly and casually blown a massive hole in his life.

***

Maiden and Sarah-Jane walked inside the Peg-Leg Lounge and looked around at the nautical paraphernalia that swathed every wall. It had been cheesy enough before but was worse now that it was combined with the softly playing sea shanties in the background.

"This is neat." Sarah-Jane smiled as she looked around admiringly at the glow-in-the-dark fishing nets and the plastic crustaceans that were hopelessly tangled in them.

Maiden glanced at her sharply and then looked around at the room again. She had to admit that the place was kind of fun, especially if you ignored the history that it had obliterated. Perhaps she was viewing it from the perspective of someone that ran a similar business while Sarah-Jane was able to just enjoy the show without taking it too seriously.

The smell of garlic and deep-fried seafood reached out to embrace them as they walked further inside. Maiden quietly hoped that there would be a chicken-based option, but dinner itself was the least of her worries.

They were shown to a table by a smiling but distracted waitress wearing a sailor's hat and left to look at the menu. Maiden quickly found the Chicken Parmesan and then started studying their surroundings more closely.

There were a few dozen tables scattered throughout the large room. Each one was spread with a checkered tablecloth and held an old-fashioned lantern that was burning cozily. The lights were fairly dim and the atmosphere was intimate. Maiden ran a calculating eye over the room.

There were other diners at a few of the other tables but the place was far from packed. Eilers had claimed that business was booming, but she wasn't so sure. In her experience with her family's inn if the rooms were full the dining room often reflected that. She noted that she still needed to talk to Eilers' accountant; he might have more insight to share.

Noting that the waitress was filing her nails and still hadn't returned to offer them a drink or appetizers, Maiden glanced over when she saw movement in the doorway. A man was standing there and she recognized him instantly; she raised her menu to hide her face.

It was Braden Blair, the drummer for the Highland Hounds. He was skulking around studying the room cautiously. She glanced subtly at Sarah-Jane, who was engrossed in the drink menu.

"Hey, is that the guy that said I was all cozy with Sean Dowling?" she whispered, nodding subtly towards the doorway.

Sarah-Jane glanced over from the corner of her eye and held her breath; she inclined her head almost imperceptibly. Maiden exhaled slowly, trying to control her thundering heartbeat. She watched, still hiding behind her menu, until he finally ducked out of sight.

"I think I need to use the lady's room," she murmured and stood.

"I'll go too," Sarah-Jane whispered back, "for moral support."

They dodged the slow and inattentive waitress and slipped out into the foyer in time to see Braden duck upstairs and into one of the nearest doors. They exchanged a look and were about to investigate when strong hands grabbed them both by the arm and pulled them into the bar.

Maiden gasped and Sarah-Jane instinctively reached for her gun before remembering that she didn't bring it. They both whirled around to see David watching them irately. Maiden's breath caught and she looked around quickly, fortunately, the bar was empty.

"Captain McAlister!" Sarah-Jane whispered anyway. "What are you doing here?"

"I was checking in with the stakeout until I saw you traipsing in," he said tightly. "What are you pair up to?"

"We were about to order dinner when we saw one of the guys from that Scottish band." Sarah-Jane quickly explained and straightened her sleeve when David released them. "He was acting suspiciously so I was going to check it out. I wasn't aware there was a stakeout, sir. I'm sorry."

"No one knows about the stakeout. I don't want Eilers to realize we're still watching him." He gave Maiden a brief, displeased look. "Anyway, why take Miss Harlow along?"

"I didn't think it was safe to leave her on her own, not after the break-in." If Sarah-Jane was making this up as she went along she managed to sound incredibly convincing. "I was only going to observe the suspect, sir, not confront him."

"Great." David rolled his eyes. "Well, I don't have time to argue. Get out of here, will you?"

"No, take me with you!" Maiden met his angrily incredulous look and held up a silencing hand. "I'm the only one who has the hope of a reasonable excuse for being here. I know Mr. Eilers. Do you want to be discreet or not?"

"She's got a point, sir." Sarah-Jane said cautiously.

"And how do you plan to explain us if we get caught?" He turned to Maiden with a look of challenge.

"I might not have to if you stop glaring at me and keep your mouth shut!" she replied.

"Good," Sarah-Jane interrupted smoothly. "We have a solid plan. Maybe we can actually go before he gets away?"

David muttered under his breath as he walked out first. They all strolled calmly towards the stairs as if they belonged there. It didn't overly matter, no one was at the desk and the foyer was empty. He motioned for Sarah-Jane to lead the way and gave Maiden a look as he pushed her to the safety of the rear.

They climbed to the second floor and Sarah-Jane pointed towards the door they'd seen Braden sneak through. David just nodded once and gestured for her to step aside, he slid a hand inside his jacket, ready to draw his gun, and opened the door. Maiden chewed at her lip as she peered over his shoulder; the room was empty.

They all walked inside cautiously and Maiden shut the door softly behind them. It looked to be some sort of lounge or casual meeting room; there were a couple of tables as well as a few armchairs and couches scattered around.

Right in front of them was a long wooden table that held a huge flower arrangement and some pamphlets for the hotel and some nearby points of interest. As they started looking around Sarah-Jane went straight to the window and peeked carefully outside.

"Fire escape, sir. And the window's unlocked," she murmured. "Do you want me to check it?"

"In civvies and without a gun?" he asked with a sigh. "I'll go."

Before he could take a step they heard voices outside the door. Maiden's eyes widened when she realized they were trapped. She wasn't honestly as confident that she could explain their presence there as she'd claimed; if Eilers recognized David he might suspect a double-cross. But there weren't many places to hide and they'd never all reach the fire escape in time.

David clearly wasn't banking on Maiden's improvisational skills either. He signaled to Sarah-Jane who quickly ducked down behind a chair.

Without a word he grabbed Maiden by the waist and lifted her onto the table. She was too frightened of their imminent discovery and startled by his strength to say anything. As the doorknob rattled David wrapped his hand around her right knee, pulling her hard against him, and kissed her.

Her heart was pounding. She had to clutch at his shoulders to steady herself when he sank his other hand into her hair and held her in place. Not that she was struggling. *Mostly* because she quickly realized what his plan was.

Maiden pressed herself against him and slid her arms around his neck, assuring herself that it was in an attempt to further the ruse. He responded by holding her closer and deepening the kiss. She felt her heart beat even faster, marveling at how good they both were at acting the part. She knew she was being an idiot but ignored it when he pressed his hand against her back.

The startled gasp and awkward apologies that preceded the hasty closing of the door told them that the tactic had worked. David lifted his head and their eyes met for a breathless instant.

And there's the chemistry, Maiden thought as he loosened his hold and carefully pulled his hand free of her long hair. She slid her hands down over his shoulders, letting her fingertips brush along his chest a little longer than was necessary, before resting them at her sides. He eased back half a step and looked behind them; they were alone again.

She wondered who had opened the door and who they had expected to find there. By then Sarah-Jane had stood again and was politely pretending to have seen nothing.

"Um, maybe we should all avail ourselves of the fire escape before someone comes back?" she suggested quietly.

"Yeah, let's go," David said quietly.

He grasped Maiden around her waist and set her carefully on her feet again. She didn't need the help but felt it might sound ungrateful to make an issue of it. Fully aware that she was being weak and quietly at peace with that knowledge, Maiden did at least have the presence of mind to know that they weren't out of danger yet.

Chapter Sixteen

They headed over to the window as quickly and silently as they could. Maiden felt flushed from the kiss and embarrassed that Sarah-Jane had doubtless seen it, but there was no time to dither. She followed them outside and felt the brisk night air hit her face and cool her cheeks. David and Sarah-Jane were surveying the area; she also looked around but nothing stood out to her.

As they descended the metal steps to the alleyway below, Maiden was sure she could feel sinister eyes watching them. She tried not to shudder but she was certain she looked as terrified as she felt.

Braden Blair had snuck off somewhere and he hadn't had time to get far. He also evidently knew who she was and had tried to involve her in his manager's murder for some reason. She wasn't happy about walking into a dark alley where he might be hiding.

Her feet touched the cold ground last and she hurried to keep up with her watchful companions. A loud scuttling sound behind a row of garbage cans made her jump. David glanced over and touched her shoulder; he put a finger to his lips.

He then motioned for her to follow, rather pointlessly since he grasped her hand and pulled her along anyway. Maiden didn't care; she would have ridden him piggyback if it meant getting out of that creepy alley sooner.

He led the way to his car, which he'd parked discreetly next door. Sarah-Jane took the back seat without a word and Maiden rather nervously slid in the front beside David. She said nothing and slumped down in the seat a little as he reached for the radio.

"Blair slipped out, no sign of him now, but keep an eye out," David said quietly as he scanned the area. "I've got cargo now so I won't be back, call me if anything happens."

"Yes sir." Ramirez managed to sound impassive. "Have a good night."

Maiden wasn't sure how she felt about being described as 'cargo', but she'd certainly been called worse. She stopped worrying about it as David started the car and pulled away slowly. No one spoke for a few minutes as they put a little distance between them and the hotel.

"Do you think anyone will follow us?" Maiden asked as she sat up straight and looked out the back window for suspicious cars.

"Not honestly, no." David glanced in the rearview mirror and then at her. "It's okay, Maiden, you're safe."

Maiden just looked at him and then settled deep into the seat. She doubted he'd tell her otherwise so his reassurance was hollow at best. She then recalled the stakeout. Sergeant Ramirez was still there watching the hotel, that made her feel a little better.

Her mind quickly shifted back to their near-miss upstairs; her lips were still tingling from David's kiss. It had been forceful and unapologetic and, as it turned out, she quite liked that. Sarah-Jane spoke up, intruding on her wandering thoughts.

"Why would a member of the band managed by two of the victims be skulking around the hotel where we found a third one?" Sarah-Jane mused. "It looks like Eilers' Arms is being suspiciously misused."

"Shut up!" Maiden looked back sharply and gave her an irate glare.

"I wasn't talking about you two!" she started laughing.

Maiden felt herself blush as she realized that Sarah-Jane wouldn't be as preoccupied by the encounter as she was. It didn't help when she saw David shaking with silent laughter from the corner of her eye. She flopped back into the seat but felt a smile threaten to break free.

"You both suck."

They all laughed as the tension that had been simmering for days finally broke. Maiden was still a little embarrassed but the relief was profoundly welcome. Sarah-Jane had fallen over in the back seat; she wiped at her eyes and pushed herself back up, hugging her sides as though they ached.

"Sorry, Maiden!" she snickered. "I dragged you into another misadventure, and before we could even order drinks."

"And no dinner. Again." She gave David a look. "Do cops not eat or what?"

"You are *brutal!*" he laughed and shook his head.

He turned into one of the rows of stores that filled the side streets. After pulling into a space in front of a small pizzeria, he stopped the car and glanced towards the back seat.

"Parker," he said mildly. "Get us a couple of pizzas. We'll eat at the station while we discuss your curious choice of restaurant this evening."

His tone was just stern enough that Sarah-Jane took the card he'd pulled from his wallet and climbed out without argument.

"Pepperoni and mushroom," Maiden said right before she shut the door.

She and David sat in silence for a moment as they gazed through the front window and watched Sarah-Jane line up. There were three people ahead of her plus however long it would take to prepare their order; they had time. Maiden shifted awkwardly, she could feel David looking over at her. She wondered what he was thinking but didn't dare ask him. As it turned out, she didn't have to.

"Hey, I'm sorry about...back at the hotel," he said at last.

"What?" She chanced a glance at him. "Getting mad at me for being there? You should be sorry; it wasn't just my idea."

"No." He picked at some non-existent speck of dirt on the steering wheel. "For grabbing you like that. I was completely out of line, but it was the first thing I thought of...That came out wrong. Sorry."

Maiden was just giving him a sideways look, trying not to smile at his embarrassed expression and failing completely.

"*Are* you sorry?" she asked, her smirk was in her voice. "I don't claim to have endless experience in that sort of thing, but you seemed to be enjoying yourself."

David grinned and rubbed his hands over his face as he let out a rueful groan.

"You weren't exactly squirming to get away," he pointed out.

"I also didn't apologize for it," she retorted.

He smiled down at the steering wheel. When he spoke again it was in a quiet and very genuine tone.

"I don't want to be one of the men that treats you badly."

She knew, of course, that he'd heard her interview with Sarah-Jane. It was heartening to know that he'd actually listened and felt something about what she'd said.

"Thank you." Was all she could think to say. He was quiet for a long moment but she knew he was thinking.

"I thought you'd broken up with me that morning," he said cautiously.

"No." She glanced out the passenger window so he wouldn't see her roll her eyes. "I didn't."

"You were really angry," he reminded her.

"Were you surprised by that, all things considered?" she asked patiently.

"No, not at all." He was quiet for a minute but then slid his gaze back to her. "Did you really throw up after we argued yesterday?"

"Yeah." She smiled faintly and let her gaze drift down to her lap. "*And* after you walked out in the middle of my statement…it's been a really bad couple of days."

She heard him let out an unsteady breath and saw from the corner of her eye as he rubbed his face with his hands and shook his head.

"I'm so sorry, Maiden, about everything. All the times when I wasn't there for you, and the way I handled the Sean Dowling thing," he said softly. "I won't make excuses and I won't lie to you. I just made decisions that I wish I could change."

Maiden felt her heart beat a bit faster as she watched the line at the counter gradually progress without really noticing it. This was actually happening, after all the disappointment and the infuriating argument, he was apologizing.

She truly appreciated that, it would be hard to admit those mistakes, but she wasn't going to be mollified too easily after what he'd put them both through.

"Why wouldn't you listen to me when I tried to tell you what happened?" she asked as mildly as she could.

"I was hurt," he admitted quietly. "*Really* bad, and angry…kinda scared."

"Were you jealous?" She frowned faintly, still not looking at him.

"Yes." He sounded ashamed of himself.

"You should know that I don't use men like that," she said, confident that she'd never given him any reason to distrust her. "I'm not mean."

"I know." He shut his eyes briefly. "But I honestly thought you were done with me."

"After only a week and a single stupid mistake? You think I'm that demanding?" she slid him a look and then shook her head with a faint smile. "I only went to that concert at all because Von was bugging me about being home every night. And talking to the cats too much."

"I really do believe you," he sighed softly. "What can I do?"

She considered that for a moment. In her heart she knew that she didn't want to simply walk away from him; they had too much going for them that they wouldn't find with anyone else. She was fairly confident that she loved him, but she wasn't going to tell him that, not yet anyway.

"Don't ever stand me up again." She flicked him a look. "If I don't like anything else you do, I'll try to let you know."

"You're incredible." He let out a shaky breath and smiled but he didn't seem to have the nerve to look at her now.

"In a good way or a bad way?" she joined him in watching Sarah-Jane approach the counter and place their order.

"Good...really good." He rubbed his chest absently. "I've never been in this deep before, to be honest."

"You mean a few months in and still no first date?" she teased.

"Yeah," he chuckled. "And still interested enough to keep trying."

"Well, assuming we actually get any pizza," she pulled a face when Sarah-Jane looked at them and shrugged before going to sit in a chair, "let's call this our first date. Get it over with."

"You romantic fool!" David laughed at her bluntness.

"Do you have a better suggestion?" She gave him a challenging look.

"No!" He was laughing too hard to elaborate.

They both went fairly quiet after that as they let it all sink in. It wasn't exactly a warm and amorous moment; they'd been snapping at each other less than an hour ago. Sitting right in front of the little take-out place in the glow of its big neon sign wasn't the most conducive setting either.

It was a relief when Sarah-Jane returned with three large pizza boxes balanced on her hip. She squeezed back into the car and set them on the seat beside her.

"Are you sure there'll be enough?" David gave the stack a wry look.

"I'm active, I eat a lot," she told him without apology and handed him back his card. "Are we really having dinner at the station?"

"There's wine at my place." Maiden said mildly. "Just saying."

"I vote for Harlow House!" Sarah-Jane raised her hand and bounced in her seat.

Maiden was distantly amused that their first date would now include her parents as well as Sarah-Jane. The fact wouldn't have been lost on David either, but he evidently decided that it was worth it. He didn't take much convincing; he just started the car and they were off.

CHAPTER SEVENTEEN

Maiden led them through the side door in the office and on past the empty reception desk. David and Sarah-Jane were veering towards the dining room where a few of the guests were already gathered for dinner but Maiden just motioned for them to follow as she headed for the staircase.

"We'll eat upstairs," she told them and led the way to her family's apartment.

She unlocked the door and held it open for her companions who filed in after her. The lights were on but the whole space was quiet.

"Mom! Dad! We're home!" she said loudly.

They walked into the big open room and David set the pizzas on the long table that sat near the kitchen. The dining space was warm, cozy and empty. Maiden glanced around and considered that her family might be out again, but then she heard shuffling steps from the far side of the room.

Gloria appeared through the doorway that led to the master suite. She peered out with a cautious expression but smiled delightedly when she saw them.

"Well, hello, darlins'!" she said happily and with obvious relief. "Vonny told us what happened today, I'm so glad to see you here!"

"Hi, Mrs. H. Yeah, everything's fine now." Sarah-Jane smiled back and pointed to the boxes on the table. "Join us for dinner? There's lots."

Maiden wasn't sure that 'everything's fine' was an accurate update on the situation but Gloria seemed mollified.

"Aren't you babies sweet." She beamed at them and then glanced over her shoulder. "Alfie! The kids brought dinner; put some pants on!"

Maiden just smiled and shook her head as she went to a cupboard and pulled out some plates. She saw from the corner of her eye, but pretended not to notice, as Gloria put an arm around David and whispered something that made him smile at her.

She tried not to worry or be embarrassed about whatever her mother might be saying to him. Maiden was soon distracted by a new kind of dread when she heard her sister's bedroom door open. A moment later Vonny appeared, heralded by her kitten entourage.

"Oh!" She froze when she walked out and spotted their guests. "Hey guys. What's happening?"

"Pizza," Sarah-Jane said by way of explanation and took a seat as she flicked open the nearest box.

"I'm in," Vonny replied. She'd started towards the table when Gloria pointed a hot pink acrylic nail at her.

"Make a salad first," she said.

"Why me?" Vonny pulled a face but went straight to the fridge anyway.

"Because you've just been sitting around all afternoon," Gloria said as she grabbed a bottle of wine.

She set it down on the table and then went back for glasses. She'd just started filling them when she glanced up and smiled at her husband. Alfie was strolling over to join them, graciously wearing his pants.

"Detectives in the house!" Alfie intoned ominously. "How goes the case?"

"It's going," David replied vaguely and helped pass the wine around the table.

"Any idea who broke into Maiden's room?" Vonny asked as she threw together a large bowl of salad. "Or who killed Mr. Dowling?"

"It's too soon to say," David replied.

"Are they likely to come back here?" Alfie arched a grizzled brow as he pulled up a seat. "I don't like people breaking into my daughter's bedroom."

"I wasn't thrilled with it either," Maiden said and then gave him a teasing smile. "You can help me clean up the mess if it'll make you feel better."

Alfie smiled back but he still looked worried. Maiden was a little worried too, but she was trying not to show it. The whole day had been such a strange muddle, but at least she didn't feel like the entire police force was against her now.

"I'm sure it'll be all right, Alfie," Gloria said gently, perhaps seeing the need to keep the mood light. "Anyway, it ain't nice to talk about crime and killin' at the dinner table."

"We could always talk about that toddler that threw a tantrum in the lobby this afternoon." Vonny smirked as she set the hastily assembled salad on the table and flopped into a chair. Rowdy and Ruffian curled up against her feet and started purring.

"That wasn't his fault," Gloria clicked her tongue, "he saw Kylie skulkin' around in the dinin' room and got scared."

Maiden nearly choked on her wine. David glanced at her with a smile and patted her on the back as she quickly set her glass aside. She cleared her throat and gave her mother a look, which was completely ignored. Gloria glanced away innocently and started passing plates around. Maiden decided the best option at this point was a change of subject.

"Where's Tony tonight?" She glanced at Vonny as everyone started to eat.

"He drove his mom to visit a friend in hospital," she sighed. "I probably should have gone too but hospitals creep me out. Tony didn't need the added stress of me fainting, so I volunteered to stay out of the way."

"Can't take the sight of blood, eh?" Sarah-Jane smiled smugly at her.

"No. Or the sight of needles, or intubations...or bedpans." Vonny rolled her eyes at herself and bit into a slice of pepperoni pizza.

Maiden was halfway through her wine and starting to relax a bit. Everyone was talking and laughing, it was nice, it was a far cry from the internal turmoil she'd been dealing with only a few hours ago. She felt a light impact on her knee and then tiny paws moving around as Ruffian pounced into her lap and poked his fuzzy head up over the table.

David glanced down at him and smiled, holding his hand out for the kitten to sniff. Ruffy's little nose twitched as he leaned closer, he started to purr and then tentatively rested a paw on his arm. David waited patiently, holding his hand still, until Ruffian scaled his arm and then hopped onto his leg.

Maiden tried not to smile too much as the kitten started snuffling David's shirt. He purred louder as he inhaled David's scent.

Yup, you're my cat all right, Maiden thought to herself, realizing with some amusement that they were both suckers for David's cologne. She also pretended not to notice as David glanced around and then snuck the kitten a piece of Italian sausage from his plate.

They all ate and talked and laughed for a couple of hours. Gloria served more wine to those that wanted it and then discreetly, by her standards anyway, withdrew along with Alfie. They said goodnight and closed themselves up in their suite.

"I'll finish my wine and call a cab," Sarah-Jane said with a yawn. "No sense taking you out of your way, Captain."

"I'll drive you. I could use the fresh air," Von volunteered. "Mom wasn't kidding, I've been sitting around all day."

David and Maiden said nothing. It was kind of awkward but Maiden wasn't in a huge hurry for him to leave, not until they had a chance to talk alone. She peeked at his glass and was happy to see that he had a lot more wine left than Sarah-Jane did, he wasn't rushing through it either.

Ruffian, who'd wandered off to play with Rowdy after scoring a few more illicit treats, seemed conscious of Maiden's wishes. He scampered under the table and hopped up on David's knee again. He uttered a determined meow as he started climbing the front of his shirt. David smiled faintly at the kitten and scooped him up in one hand, supporting him gently while also rescuing himself from the surprisingly sharp little claws.

Ruffian shut his clear blue eyes and purred loudly as he leaned into his chest, effectively pinning the handsome cop in place. Maiden smiled and opted not to comment.

A collective silence stretched on until Vonny got squirmy. She cleared her throat and absently patted Rowdy as she cuddled the cat that was now sleeping in her lap.

"Um...at the risk of being nosy," she began carefully, "were you guys working tonight? All I know is that someone broke in and then Mae got hauled away and now, hours later, you're all together. So, what's actually going on?"

"It's weird and kind of complicated." Maiden propped her chin in her hand. "It was one of the Highland Hounds that claimed they saw me flirting with Sean Dowling. Braden Blair; he's the drummer."

"What? They weren't even in the room!" Vonny said angrily. "What a tool bag! And why did he pick on *you*? I was there too!"

"Weren't you sitting with Tony?" David asked.

"He sat between us; he usually does," Von admitted. "Mae and I argue less that way."

"Anyway, I was the lucky duck that got picked, for whatever reason," Maiden sighed. "And then we saw the same guy sneaking around Eiler's Arms tonight."

"He *was* sneaking." Sarah-Jane nodded in agreement. "And he must have slipped out through that window. I wonder why."

"He wasn't supposed to be there." Maiden and David said in almost perfect unison.

They looked at each other and then away again as Vonny and Sarah-Jane sniggered at them.

"You guys are really great when you're together. It must annoy the heck out of you when you fight." Sarah-Jane grinned and then added sardonically. "I know it annoys the rest of us."

"Can it, Parker," David murmured as he scratched Ruffian behind the ear.

"Sorry, sir." Her smile didn't look terribly repentant.

"You too, Vonny." Maiden gave her smirking sister a warning look.

"Sorry, sir," Von chuckled.

Sarah-Jane still looked quite amused but self-preservation won out; she knocked back the remainder of her wine and stood. Vonny set Rowdy on the chair beside her and also pushed to her feet. They chit-chatted constantly and slipped out quickly, presumably to make it less obvious if David wanted to stay.

As the door shut behind them Ruffian apparently felt his work was done. He leapt to the floor and went in search of kibbles while David quietly brushed the cat hair from his shirt. Maiden glanced at him and wet her lips.

"Would you like another?" she asked as she pointed towards the wine bottle.

"Maybe half a glass; I still have to drive," he said.

She poured a bit into both their glasses. After setting the bottle aside, she turned her glass distractedly in her hands and decided to let him say something more if he wanted to. Now that the opportunity arose, she wasn't sure how much discussion she was actually up for.

"Are you feeling all right now?" he asked.

"How do you mean?" she replied a little cautiously.

"You've been through a lot." He held her gaze steadily.

"I guess we both have." She raised her glass to her lips because she needed something to do with her hands. "But yeah, I'm okay."

"Good...Could I see your bedroom?" he asked.

"What?" She stared at him.

"The break-in," he reminded her with a smile.

"Oh yeah," she laughed softly at herself and stood. "Sorry, it's been a weird day."

"Tell me about it," he said under his breath as he pushed to his feet and followed.

She led him through the doorway at the back of the kitchen and down the hall to the left. She opened the door to her bedroom and stepped inside, flicking on the light as she walked in.

David followed and ran his gaze over the ransacked room. He walked around carefully, probably taking in minute details that she wouldn't think to check.

In spite of that, Maiden also studied the room again. She still hadn't had a chance to see if anything was missing. As much as the trespass made her angry, it also stirred her curiosity. From what she could see everything appeared to be there, just flung around carelessly. She shook her head at the random approach the intruder seemed to have taken.

"Closet?" David asked as he pointed to a door beside the balcony.

She nodded so he walked over and opened it. She peered past him enough to see that it had been rifled as well, but maybe not as thoroughly. He frowned and exhaled thoughtfully as he shut the door again.

"Any idea what this person might have been looking for?" he asked as he headed back towards her.

"None," she said honestly. "I don't even know if it happened because of my connection to Eilers or the invented connection to Sean Dowling."

"Yeah." He sounded thoughtful as he glanced back over the mess. "What does your gut tell you?"

"That it's actually both." She noticed his pleased grin even though he wasn't looking at her.

"What about the Highland Hounds? Did anyone in the band stand out to you?" David asked as he stepped briefly onto the balcony and subtly looked down to survey the street.

"Not especially." Maiden replied carefully. She wasn't sure she wanted to tell him about her visit to the Addison or her chat with Ewan and ultimately decided not to mention it. "They all had a sort of eccentric and well-traveled look about them."

"What about Dowling?"

"Is this a set-up question?" She gave him a watchful look.

"No," he smiled faintly, "I promise it's not."

"He seemed nice," she admitted. "He tried to flirt with me but he talked to all of us. It was just chatter though. He didn't really say anything, if you know what I mean."

"Yeah, I think I do," he said and then glanced at his watch and sighed. "I should probably go and let you get some sleep. You're not staying in here tonight, are you?"

"No, I'll bunk in with Vonny." She rolled her eyes. "According to her I kick her in the back all night. So that's something to look forward to."

***

David chuckled at her joke but it was subdued. He followed slowly and at a slight distance as Maiden led the way out again. He watched the gentle sway of her hips as she walked towards the front door; he wondered what she was thinking and how she was feeling about him now.

He wished he'd acted more rationally when she came to his house yesterday. It wouldn't have been easy for her to make that move and he made it worse. He'd been too hurt to hear her out. The thought of her turning to someone else despite what they had between them was more than he could deal with.

You shouldn't have believed the lies and you know that. How can you ask her to trust you if this is the best you can give her in return? he chided himself and shook his head as he drew closer. *I really hope you're willing to be more reasonable than I was, baby.*

His fears and doubts were mostly settled. He did trust her, and all he wanted to do now was make sure he never gave her a reason to wander.

That desire was becoming more motivating as the prospect of leaving for the night grew inexorably closer.

Please let me kiss you, give me even the tiniest sign that you want me to kiss you, he pleaded silently as she stood by the door and turned to him with a small, unreadable smile. *I can't just go home and sleep after what's happened. I need to hold you, I have to kiss you. Grabbing you at the hotel doesn't count, it was incredible and I'd do it again in a heartbeat, but it doesn't count. You have to be with me on this. Please! This has been the longest and most frustrating week of my life!*

"Well, it's been quite a day." Maiden shifted slightly and glanced away shyly. "It feels like everything's been turned upside down again...I'm not sure exactly where we go from here."

"Where do you want us to go?" he asked without hesitation as he stood close.

"Um..." She blinked widened eyes up at him as he loomed closer. "Well..."

"Hm?" he prompted gently as he reached up and brushed a lock of her dark hair behind her ear and ran his forefinger along her jaw.

David realized that he was coming on a bit strong, all things considered, but he couldn't talk himself into reining it in. Not that he tried terribly hard. While they hadn't been apart for long, and had barely been together before that, he'd lost her completely and he wasn't fully confident that he had her back now. He couldn't even articulate in his own head how badly he wanted her back.

He was still stroking her cheek but braced his other hand against the wall behind her and leaned in even more. She didn't look unhappy about it, she was maintaining eye contact and she hadn't tried to sidle away.

"You run a bit hot and cold, don't you?" She let out a tiny, uncertain laugh.

"No, I typically run hot." The corner of his mouth tilted up slightly. "I just wound a bit easily. Sorry, I never realized that, I'll work on it."

"Do you—" she held her breath and touched a hand to his chest to hold him back as he moved closer, "do you think we're moving too fast?"

"No," he said simply as he leaned in.

"But you don't trust me," she said cautiously.

"Yes I do, I lied yesterday," he admitted. "I do that when I'm crushed. That's not an excuse, just fair warning. I'm completely out of my depth here."

Maiden smiled up at him, her cheeks were flushed and her breath was coming a little faster now. She spread both hands against his chest as she subtly raised her face to his.

Good enough. I'll take that as a yes. He wrapped his arms around her and kissed her before he could caution himself out of it.

***

Maiden felt a fluttering in her stomach, she slid her hands up his chest and throat before running her fingers through his thick hair. She tried to assure herself that she wasn't dreaming again.

David had gone so far from his cold anger of yesterday that she could almost wonder if she was dealing with the same man. She knew his incredible scent, however, and despite only a little experience with it, she knew his kiss as well.

Her heart pounded in her chest, she wondered if he could feel it so close to his. David's hands splayed on her back as he pressed her closer against him and kissed her urgently, as if they'd been forced apart for years.

I think you might have missed me a little, Captain McAlister. She smiled against his mouth and gently caressed his cheek.

He broke the kiss but didn't raise his head. Maiden tried to keep breathing as he lifted her against him and shifted his attention to her pale throat. She found herself standing on tiptoe and squeezed her eyes shut when she felt his lips and then his teeth on her sensitive flesh.

She clutched at his shoulders and was sure her legs were about to buckle when they both heard loud, tipsy laughter outside the door. David froze and raised his head abruptly, letting her slide slowly back to her feet. Maiden locked her eyes on him as she grasped his waist and held him close.

Their uneven breathing was the only sound as they both stood still and listened. Then it came again, the sound of happy conversation and then hasty, giggling shushing as a few guests made their way past and on to their rooms.

Maiden couldn't think who the people were, she didn't care, she just needed David to look at her again instead of scowling like he was. He was staring at the door but she doubted he was thinking about it, or the noisy people that had interrupted them. He finally pulled in a shaky breath and shifted his warm, chocolatey brown gaze back to her and smiled.

"I'm sorry," he leaned down and touched another kiss to her forehead, "I didn't mean to get carried away like that."

"I don't mind," she said softly and pressed her hands more firmly against his back.

His smile was so fond and pleased that she couldn't think of anything else to say. He didn't look worried by her silence, he just cupped her cheek in his palm and lifted his eyebrows slightly.

"If I call you tomorrow," he whispered, "will you answer?"

She managed to nod once. "Yeah, I will."

"Thank you." He smiled again.

"So," she felt silly asking but she wanted to know where she stood, "are we...together again? Are we actually dating?"

"Would you be happy with that?" He tipped her head back gently so she'd have to meet his gaze.

"As long as we treat each other well," she made herself be strong enough to voice that concern, "yes. What about you?"

"Yeah, I'd be really happy." David's entire body relaxed, she hadn't noticed how tense he'd been until then. "I...yeah."

"Okay." She smiled up at him but felt oddly shy now. "Good."

"I'll call you in the morning, if that's okay." He lingered, still standing so close to her.

"That would be nice," she said softly and realized she still had her arms around his waist.

I should probably let go, she mused. *I don't want to though...but I also don't want him to pull away first. No, I need to let go. I'm overthinking this. He smells incredible and he's really warm. Hot. He said he runs hot. Stop thinking about that. Let go now.*

She slid her hands from his narrow waist and noticed the way he shut his eyes briefly.

If Mom was out here we'd be engaged already. The thought made her smile, it nearly made her laugh but she held it in.

"Are you laughing at me?" David asked quietly and with a smile of his own.

"No, I'm laughing at myself," she chuckled and sighed. "You'll drive carefully, won't you?"

"I promise." He stole another quick kiss and then stepped back, giving her some space. "Good night, Maiden."

"Good night, David."

***

"Rise and shine, little princess."

Maiden frowned at her sister's wryly amused voice and rolled stubbornly onto her side. A moment later she felt tiny paws scaling her back and emerging triumphantly on her shoulder. Warm fuzz pressed against her cheek and a loud purring reverberated in her ear. Maiden smiled and looked over to see Ruffian snuffling at her hair. She reached up and scratched the kitten behind his soft ear and reluctantly sat up.

Sunlight poured through the glass doors. Vonny's room, like all the rooms in the inn, enjoyed a private balcony. She'd pulled back the curtains and let the cool morning light fill the room; sleeping in obviously wasn't going to be an option.

"Why are you up early? You're *never* up early." Maiden gave her sister a cranky look. "I don't even know what time you got in."

"I passed Captain Cutie-pie on his way out. He certainly looked a lot more...cheerful." She murmured suggestively and looked Maiden over with a smirk. "Funny that you were already asleep when I got up here, you must've been exhausted."

"I was. So what?" Maiden asked in a warning tone and cuddled Ruffian to her chest.

"Nothing." Von shrugged innocently. "So, you two made up?"

"We've reached an understanding," Maiden allowed, rather demurely, and noticed Vonny's barely concealed laughter. "Why is that funny?"

"No reason. But were you planning to cover all that up before sitting down to breakfast?" She was shaking with amusement now.

"It's up to you of course, but I think you might spoil Dad's morning if you don't."

Maiden just shook her head in silent enquiry, Vonny pointed towards her throat. Maiden's eyes widened and she jumped out of bed, stopping just long enough to carefully dump the kitten onto the soft mattress, which earned her a disgruntled mew.

She rushed over to the long mirror on the back of Vonny's closet door and gasped. He'd left marks, big ones.

Her skin was pale and had always bruised comparatively easily but this was a first. Maiden's mouth was still hanging open as she studied her reddened flesh.

Hickeys?! she thought frantically. *Seriously? Hasn't this week been strange enough?*

"No, no, no!" she breathed. "You've got to be joking!"

She turned her head to the side, there was no way no one would notice. She couldn't possibly walk around all day splotched with evidence of exactly where David had been. Warmth stained her cheeks and made the stupid bruises stand out even more. She pressed a hand over them and turned to Vonny, wide-eyed and shaking her head, looking for any sort of sisterly advice.

Vonny was clutching her pillow, doing her best to muffle her laughter in it. Maiden stared at her for a moment before she felt her own mirth bubble up inside her.

A giggle finally escaped. She buried her face in her hands and dropped to her knees on the softly carpeted floor.

Chapter Eighteen

When Maiden finally got hold of herself she pushed to her feet and scowled ineffectually at her unhelpful sister. She put a finger to her lips, silently demanding secrecy, and then slipped out into the hall with Ruffian close behind.

They tiptoed to her room and shut themselves inside. Maiden stood there for a moment and considered her options. She could try covering the tell-tale marks with makeup but she didn't have anything heavy enough to fully disguise them.

She shook her head, she needed something more reliable. She went to her dresser and dug through one of the rifled drawers. After a bit of searching she found a dark purple turtleneck. It would do the job nicely.

She pulled on the snug, knitted shirt and carefully arranged the high collar over her discolored flesh. A glance in the mirror assured her that she looked perfectly normal. She may have felt like a naughty teenager but she looked like a grown woman that hadn't gotten up to anything exciting last night.

She had just brushed and pinned back the top and sides of her hair when her phone rang. Maiden glanced over at it and held her breath, it was David.

"Good morning." His deep voice made her smile.

"Hi, David." She bit her bottom lip. "How are you?"

"I'm a lot better than I was yesterday morning," he chuckled. "Are you free for lunch?"

"Yes." She felt like a teenager again but couldn't help it.

"Good, can you meet me at O'Neil's at 12:30?" He was smiling, she could hear it in his voice.

"I'll be there," she promised.

Yes! I officially have a boyfriend! She grinned to herself after he said goodbye and hung up. She put on a little extra mascara to celebrate and then braced herself to face her parents without giggling like an idiot.

She stepped into the kitchen and saw only her mother standing at the counter and Vonny sitting at the table. Gloria was cutting up some fruit but smiled knowingly at her when she spotted her.

"Hey, angel," she said slyly.

One look at Vonny's clumsy attempt to appear absorbed in the newspaper confirmed that she'd already blabbed at least a little. That was annoying but Maiden didn't overly mind. It saved having to answer too many well-meaning but nosy questions.

She was becoming increasingly self-conscious about her turtleneck though. She could only hope Von had been somewhat discreet.

"Good morning, Mom." Maiden smiled faintly and sat at the table, giving Vonny a chiding look that her sister neatly avoided.

"Now then," Gloria said happily as she placed a plate of sliced fruit on the table between them and sat down, "I get the impression that you and David have sorted things out?"

"Looks that way," Maiden allowed as she snagged a few apple slices from the plate.

"Excellent." She rubbed her hands together. "Now, how are you going with helpin' Fred?"

Maiden frowned vacantly before recalling that she was supposed to be conducting a clandestine investigation. She hid her lapse masterfully by cramming more apple into her mouth.

"Oh, yeah. I'm working on it," she assured her after she swallowed. "The third murder has complicated things a bit. Hopefully Eilers has a better alibi for that one."

"Fred wouldn't kill some random musician!" Gloria scowled at her.

"I didn't say he would. I said I hope he has a good alibi." Maiden studied her suspiciously. "So, what's the real story with Eilers anyway? You and Dad are both acting weird about him. But especially you."

"No, I'm not. He's an old college friend of your father's." Gloria waved it away. "He's nothin' special to me, but Alfie's real worried."

"Yeah, maybe he is." Vonny finally looked up from the financial pages that she wasn't possibly trying to read. "But something's going on. You've both been acting strange for a while, what's the deal?"

"Nothin'," Gloria said after a long pause.

Maiden and Vonny looked at each other, exchanged a subtle nod, and then slowly turned back to her. Gloria shifted but tried to look casual as she started eating a chunk of pear. Maiden decided to try a little deductive reasoning.

"Let's look at what we know so far. Eilers' Arms opened for business a little over a week ago—" she began when Von snorted loudly.

"Eilers opened his Arms!" she sniggered. "What a doofus!"

Maiden had no idea if the childish remark was aimed at Eilers or herself. Either way, it was incredibly unhelpful so she gave Von a withering look and continued.

"And, supposedly, is doing a roaring trade." Maiden watched Gloria closely. "I found a flyer for his hotel in the drawer at reception and then we actually turned up to support his grand opening. Despite him being in direct competition with us. Finally, you and Dad have suddenly become secretive and sneaky."

Gloria glanced down at her hands and pulled an unhappy face. Vonny, who had gotten over her tittering, pinned the older woman with a stern stare. Maiden kept her tone steady as she continued.

"You've had dinner with Fred Eilers a few times already, and it would possibly have been more if his chief rival in life hadn't been found dead right in his office," she mused. "Since then, you've settled down noticeably, but you're *very* concerned with getting his name cleared. So what's actually going on?"

"It's nothin' weird or dishonest, babies," Gloria promised and sipped her coffee. "We really are just worried about Fred."

"That's not all," Maiden said. "You've also talked about hiring in staff to free up your time, you've never done that before. Are you two getting tired of running the inn? Are you thinking about selling?"

"What?" Vonny's eyes rounded and flew from Gloria to Maiden and then back again. "How could you? We helped build this place. We live and work here too! You'd pull everything out from under us?!"

"No, of course not." Gloria rolled her eyes. "Look, Fred did ask us to buy in to his hotel and we said we'd think about it. We did, but then we talked it over and decided against it."

Maiden was genuinely shocked that this was the first they'd heard of such a big potential change to the family's financial matters. She did her best not to get angry, but it wasn't easy.

She didn't expect their parents to check with them before making every little decision, but this was major. Potentially buying into another business would have huge financial repercussions on them all. She and Vonny had done a lot to lift Harlow House from a pokey little family motel to a beautiful inn with a reputation for elegance and charm. Surely they had a right to at least be consulted.

"How interesting," Maiden said tightly. "So you're saying that Eilers is nothing more than a friend and maybe you feel guilty for not investing in his business?...Is that everything?"

"It's all I have to say at the moment. Yes," Gloria said firmly. "You girls settle down, all right? Harlow House ain't goin' no place, so just relax. Now I'm gonna go get dressed."

With that she stood and swanned out of the room. Maiden and Vonny watched her go and then turned uneasily to each other. Maiden shook her head and tried not to assume the very worst.

"Wow. Very strange," she murmured.

"I can't believe they were thinking about investing in another hotel and never even told us!" Vonny breathed.

"I'm sure they would have if they'd decided that they were really interested. Maybe," Maiden ventured as she popped a strawberry in her mouth. "Ultimately, they don't really have to check with us about how they spend their money...we should talk to them about what we can and can't count on in the future, as far as the business goes."

"Yeah." Vonny chewed at her thumbnail. "I guess I just trusted that we had a share...we've poured a lot of time and effort into making this place successful. I thought that meant we had some say in things."

"So did I. But let's not jump to conclusions yet," Maiden said more steadily. "I'm sure Mom and Dad wouldn't leave us with nothing."

***

With the jarring knowledge of her parents' fickle whims hanging over her head, Maiden did her best to shoo them away and went to meet David for lunch.

O'Neil's was a cute little café just down the road from the police station. It was a family business that had been there for years. The large front windows opened onto the scenic park where she and Von sometimes went walking. They'd stopped in for coffee a few times.

Maiden parked down the street and walked inside; she was quietly pleased to see that David was already there. He was seated at a small table in the corner looking through his notebook. He glanced up at her and she felt her mood lighten. At least something was going as planned today.

He stood and waved to get her attention, he also quickly tucked his notebook back into his pocket. Maiden smiled as he slid a hand to her cheek and kissed her before gesturing for her to take up the seat next to his.

"How are you?" she asked nicely as she slipped out of her coat and draped it across the back of her chair.

"Good, it's been a productive morning." He smiled warmly at her. "And the afternoon is off to a great start. How about you?"

"I'm happier now, put it that way," she murmured but returned his smile.

"What's up?" he quirked a brow.

"Mom's acting weird, even by her standards." She sat back and blinked at the waitress as she set a cappuccino in front of her and said she'd come back after they'd looked at the menu. She gave David a questioning look.

"I'm a detective, Maiden," he smiled at her. "I've studied you enough to have noticed that half the time I see you you're drinking cappuccino."

"So much for my aura of mystery," she said playfully as she took a sip. "Thank you."

"What's wrong with Gloria?" He returned to her previous comment. "She seemed fine last night."

"She and Dad have been really secretive lately. Going out constantly and deliberately not talking about it," Maiden said uneasily. "And today she told us that Eilers had asked them to buy into his hotel."

"Yeah." David said without even a hint of surprise.

"You knew about it?" She sat up straighter. "You never told me!"

"I assumed you already knew," he said. "I only found out because I asked why they were with Eilers the night Ulysses Mercier died."

"Reasonable." Maiden considered him through half lowered lids. "Annoyingly so."

"Besides, I didn't get the chance. I'd been avoiding seeing you for a week," he said with a perfectly serious expression.

Maiden's eyes widened incredulously.

"That's a pretty gutsy joke considering that we've only been back together for about twelve hours." She couldn't help laughing.

"It's closer to fourteen." He grinned shamelessly. "We're good."

"Cute," she chuckled and ran a hand through her hair.

"Be fair. Your amusing little 'jackass' remarks made it into the official record." He sipped his own coffee. "Parker's notes were obnoxiously thorough."

"At least I didn't identify you by name." She was struggling not to laugh again.

"She put my name in brackets," he informed her mildly enough. "Right after 'petty, self-absorbed jackass'."

Maiden closed her eyes and glanced away as she struggled to maintain her composure. A part of her felt badly for what had to be a professional embarrassment for him, but the rest of her was amused enough to bludgeon her sympathy into submission.

"I'm guessing that didn't go unpunished?" She only laughed a little.

"No. It certainly didn't," he replied with a placid smile. "Let's just say she's going to have a very long week doing every job she hates."

"Sounds fair." She smirked but then maturity reared its stalwart head and she decided to change the subject. "So, Eilers wanted Mom and Dad to invest. Any idea why?"

"Mercier had his sights on the company. It looks like he was orchestrating a hostile takeover." He watched her curiously and noticed the obvious surprise in her eyes. "Didn't you know that?"

"No," she silently kicked herself for not talking to Eilers' accountant already; then a worse thought occurred to her. "Did Mom and Dad know?"

"Very possibly," he said as diplomatically as he could.

Maiden just stared at him for a moment as her fury at her parents flared up and then settled into a simmering background crankiness.

She noted his watchful, wary and distantly amused expression and decided she wasn't going to waste a lovely lunch date on anger and uncertainty. She'd deal with her parents later.

"That's rather interesting," she said with a forced lightness that made him smile at her. "So Eilers was likely trying to lure my parents into investing in his tacky aquarium-themed nightmare to get more shareholders on his side and prevent the takeover?"

"Looks that way," he chuckled. "Mercier had been targeting the existing investors pretty aggressively. We're still looking into the details but apparently Eilers had sold off a lot of shares over the years, too many to maintain control if enough of the others disagreed with how he was running things."

"So business probably isn't as good as he claims." She rubbed her forehead, pleased that her earlier suspicions were correct but worried about the implications for Eilers' innocence. "Awesome."

"We don't always have to talk about cases, you know," David said quietly after a moment.

"I didn't intend to, sorry." She turned to him with a sweet smile. "I was only trying to complain about my parents. Change the subject."

"Right," he laughed and looked her over. "I've never seen you wear a turtleneck before. It looks really nice."

"Thank you," she sniggered like a child and stared down into her coffee.

"What's so funny?" he asked a tad cautiously.

"Nothing." She smiled broadly.

"C'mon, Harlow, don't give me that." He drummed his fingers expectantly.

Maiden finally sighed and somehow didn't laugh as she pulled the edge of her high collar down a bit. David stilled when he saw the marks on her throat; he lifted his brows a fraction and glanced away as casually as a man could in such a circumstance.

"Oh...right," he said mildly and fingered his coffee mug absently.

"Yeah, that's what I thought." She sipped her cappuccino.

"I'm, um..." he started awkwardly but trailed off.

"Sorry?" she suggested helpfully.

"No." He made a thoughtful face and shook his head. "Not really. I hope they don't hurt, though."

Maiden smiled down into her cup, aware that her cheeks had gone pink again.

"Good, we'll leave it as my attempt to revitalize the turtleneck. Maybe I'll start a trend." She pushed the fabric carefully back into place and picked up the menu as she tried to ignore his quietly pleased expression. "What are you thinking of having?"

"Are you trying to elicit a naughty joke?" He barely managed not to laugh. "Because I've apparently got all the maturity and finesse of an overheated eighteen-year-old."

"Dad was right about you, then," she teased but kept her gaze stubbornly on the menu.

They spent the rest of the meal talking about everything they could think of that wasn't related to murder. He told her more about his family, particularly his aimless little brother and his mischievous but sweet twin sisters. Apparently his father was a cop, that was one of the reasons he was drawn to the profession himself. He said very little about his mother; Maiden noticed but didn't press him on it.

She watched him with a quiet smile as he told her a few stories of him and his brother, James, getting into mischief when they were much younger. They were both laughing by the time he'd finished regaling her with a tale of him trying to rescue James from the roof of their house—after the younger boy's failed attempt to rescue a cat from the same fate. The cat had climbed down without trouble and sauntered off home while James panicked and refused to climb down their rickety ladder again.

By the time Maiden had told him about Vonny's youthful insistence that squirrels could grant wishes, and the subsequent afternoons they'd spent trying to catch one, it was time to go. When they left he walked her to her car. It was cold out so they sat inside.

"Okay," David murmured and turned to face her once he'd shut the door and they had comparative privacy. "Off the record, I don't trust this Eilers guy. I know he's a friend of your parents, but he's shady."

"Awesome," Maiden said and chewed at her lip. "I kinda got that vibe from him, but Mom and Dad don't seem to see it."

"Maybe, maybe not," he said. "They did refuse his offer. They may be a bit soft-hearted, but they're not stupid."

"I certainly hope not," she said warily. "When I spoke with Eilers the other day he was cagey at first but very insistent that business was good, really good."

"Whether it is or not, it's going to take a while to pay off the money he's invested in the place," David replied. "That's what left him susceptible to a shark like Mercier. All he had to do was make the investors nervous, maybe fire them up about the money Eiler's dumped into a run-down shell of a building. *Their* money, not his."

"It wouldn't be too hard, would it?" She stared pensively through the windshield. "How are his other hotels doing?"

"Okay, as far as we checked, at least," he admitted with a shrug. "My interest doesn't go beyond the potential murder charge."

"It could be relevant though," Maiden suggested. "Eilers said that Mercier didn't start sniffing around until he bought this particular building and started refurbishing it. The building itself wasn't expensive, even if the renovations were, it's not *such* an outlandish project."

"How do you know that the building wasn't expensive?" he gave her a quietly amused look.

"I just do," she said modestly. "Do you think Eilers is the sort of person that would go so far as to kill a competitor?"

"Rather than have his family legacy and his life's work snatched away by some creep he'd hated for decades?" he asked bluntly. "Yeah, I think it's possible."

"Have you learned much else about Mercier?" she could only hope he'd actually tell her.

"A bit." He nodded. "He was a sleaze, to be perfectly frank. He had ties to some serious criminals, and I think the only reason he wasn't in prison himself is that he sold a few of them out to save his own neck."

"You mean, he testified against them to get himself out of trouble?" Maiden asked as the possibilities started to unfold. "Do you think that might be why he was killed?"

"It didn't look like a professional job." Was all he ventured.

"Well, what about the Highland Hounds?" she asked after the slightest pause. "Where do they fit in?"

"I don't know yet," he admitted. "I don't even know if there's a connection at all."

"Yes, you do," she grumbled before she could help it. "And what about Charles Brown?"

"*What* about Charles Brown?" David repeated, his eyes narrowed a fraction.

"He went off on his own to "sightsee" and ended up shot in the least scenic part of town," she said plainly. "Next thing you know his business partner falls out a window."

"How do you know all that?" he demanded quietly.

"Um..." Maiden realized too late that she'd talked too freely. "Look, I just happened to have heard about it. It doesn't matter how."

"You sexy little rat!" David whispered as he stared at her. "I can't believe you—I can't believe *both* of us! I was so caught up in the fake statement that you almost got away with it."

"Got away with what? I don't even know what you're talking about." She knew exactly what he was talking about.

"That night you were talking to Sean Dowling," he said as it all came together, "of course you weren't flirting with him, you were asking him about Brown's murder, weren't you?"

"Oh David, you're getting hysterical over nothing. Pivotal events in people's lives naturally arise in conversation. You've been around the block a few times, you *know* that's how people work." She kept her tone mellow and her gaze locked on a tree across the street. "The important thing to focus on in this situation is that I didn't cheat on you."

From the corner of her eye, she saw him lean forward and bury his face in his hands as he tried not to laugh out loud at her pitiful evasion technique. She was contemplating jumping out of the car and making a break for it when he sat back and pulled in a deep breath.

"I...really, *really* like you, Maiden," he said with a fond smile.

"Thanks." She stared down at the steering wheel and decided to keep pushing. "So, do you think any of the band members may be involved?"

"Anything's possible." He shifted slightly to face her more. "The initial checks we've run came back pretty clean. They're who and what they claim to be, a travelling folk band. Dowling and Brown only signed them on a couple of months ago."

"Anyone in the band complain about them?" She glanced at him as she rubbed her lower lip absently with her thumb.

"No one's walked up and handed me a motive, if that's what you mean," he replied even as his gaze fell to her mouth.

"You're cute when you're secretive," she said but gave up gracefully, she had her own lines of inquiry to follow. "Thanks for lunch."

"Yeah," he said dryly. "Maiden, leave it. I'll deal with these guys and find out why they tried to implicate you. I promise. Okay?"

"Thank you, David." She smiled at him.

"That's not agreeing to leave it alone," he said.

"And that's very perceptive of you," she acknowledged. "I won't lie to you, David...you really are cute when you're secretive."

"Maiden—" he began with a tolerant sigh when she interrupted.

"Did you know that the Old Chateau was supposedly built by some kind of pirate queen?" she asked brightly. "It's probably sitting on a secret cache of gold doubloons; wouldn't that be interesting?"

"I guess." He pinched the bridge of his nose. "Are you just going to dance around me until I give up?"

"Actually, I need to get back to work," she smiled ingenuously. "Busy."

He laughed and leaned forward, sliding his hand gently into her hair.

"You're the closest I'll ever get to dating myself." He grinned as he moved in to kiss her. "It's weird, but I like it."

Chapter Nineteen

Since it was still cold and starting to look like rain, Maiden drove David back to the police station before heading over to Eiler's Arms. On the way she thought about her parents.

She was deeply angry and bordering on resentful as she considered their behavior. Not only because they'd gone so far with considering Eilers' business proposal while deliberately keeping it from her and Von, but they'd also pressed her into trying to prove the man's innocence without telling her half of what they really knew.

She had to decide how best to deal with them now. Her favored options were to yell and scream and maybe throw the furniture around, or be petty and deliberately keep them outside of her investigation. She wasn't a brawler by nature, so she decided on the petty approach. It was safer anyway since she wasn't confident they wouldn't run to Eilers with everything she told them.

It was the first time in her life that she felt she couldn't trust her parents. All their sneaking around and the huge investment they'd considered without warning her and Vonny, it was so unlike them. Maiden shook her head and dragged her focus back to the case, murder was always a good distraction.

She arrived at Eiler's Arms and asked the bored receptionist if she could see Graham Harper. The girl obligingly set her magazine aside long enough to call his office. Fortunately he was in today and agreed to talk to her.

Maiden was directed down a cramped hallway in the corner and followed it to a pokey little hole that somehow hadn't been hit by Eilers' infamous transformative efforts. The walls hadn't been rendered, so the old stonework shone through in all its ancient beauty. She wondered why this part of the building had been spared but set that curiosity aside as she knocked on the door.

"Yes, come in," said a disinterested, rather nasal voice.

Maiden opened the door and peered inside. The small office was tidy and also bore no signs of redecorating. While it lacked the overdone hokey sailor theme, it was dank and dreary. The walls were the same dark gray stone and mortar that she saw in the hallway. There were a couple of lamps scattered around to provide light, and a small space heater jammed next to the desk was the only real refuge from the chill in the air.

She couldn't imagine spending hours trying to work in that room day after day, it was already depressing and she'd barely stepped inside. Her eyes flitted to the old, scratched up desk and then to the man who sat behind it. He stood and forced a tight smile of greeting.

Graham Harper was tall and startlingly thin. His long arms and legs were slender while his cheekbones were sharply defined. Overall, it appeared that there was little more than skin stretched over his bones. She wondered if he struggled with how cold the room was; she was already feeling it and that was through her jacket.

His pale brown hair was a mouse-colored haze over the top of his balding head. He watched her through thick, black-rimmed glasses as she walked further inside.

She recognized him easily, even without his 1970's leisure suit. He was the man she'd seen at the bar talking with Maddie Norris the night of the grand opening.

Maiden wasn't sure how much he knew about her efforts to clear his employer's name but, considering that he'd agreed to meet her straight away, he'd probably already been told to cooperate. She settled into one of two small chairs that sat in front of his decrepit desk and regarded him calmly as he resumed his own seat.

She considered how best to approach the interview. Usually she was polite and sympathetic until people talked to her; it was fairly effective but this situation was different. Graham would know what she was up to and had been ordered to play along. She needed to appear confident in her role but also encourage him to be forthcoming.

"Thank you for agreeing to talk to me, Mr. Harper," she said simply.

"It's no trouble, Miss Harlow." He fiddled with the pencil he was holding. "Fred mentioned that you're trying to help him."

That last statement was said cautiously. She could see that he was guarded and recalled that Eilers had accused the man of hating him. It again struck her as odd that Graham still chose to work for him, or that Eilers hadn't fired him.

"Have you worked for Mr. Eilers long?" She decided to ease into the topic.

"Years," he replied, a touch dryly, and gave her a curious look. "Are you on the payroll now? I haven't been informed of any new hires."

"No, I'm not." She shook her head. "I'm just gathering a bit of information at the moment. Eilers suggested that I speak with you. I found that strange, to be honest."

"And why is that?" He looked as if he had an inkling.

"I didn't get the impression that you two are on good terms," she replied.

"That's fair to say." He was still watching her shrewdly. "Are you a cop?"

"No," she said patiently. "Are *you* a cop?"

"No."

"That's interesting." She smiled wanly. "What did you think of Mr. Mercier? Had you met him?"

"Yes, I met him," he admitted, leaning back in his chair a bit. "If I'm honest, I thought he was a bit of a swindler…fitting that he was an old friend of Fred's."

"Do you believe they were actually friends?" she asked.

"That's what Fred claimed." He lifted a slim shoulder in an unconcerned shrug. "Of course, Fred isn't the most honest of men."

"Mm." She nodded once, hoping to get him a little more comfortable and perhaps talkative. "Businessmen do give off a certain vibe sometimes, don't they? I don't know him well enough to judge his honesty one way or the other though."

"Then why are you helping him?" He scowled.

"I haven't really decided if I am or not. Not yet." It was daring, but she needed Graham to open up a bit more or this would be a wasted trip. "I certainly won't lie for him, but I'll keep an open mind and see what happens. How's business, incidentally?"

"Lousy!" he said flatly. "The rooms aren't even half full despite his ridiculous publicity campaign."

"Yes, I've been hearing a lot about the hotel for a while now," she murmured. "Pretty high-profile stuff, good and bad. But you say the place still isn't busy?"

"Not enough," he said. "Not even close to enough."

"Interesting…I have reason to believe that Mr. Eilers' empire was in some danger," she mused, holding his gaze easily. "Is that true?"

"Of course it's true," he scoffed. "Eilers has as much business sense as a seven-year-old, and that's how he runs things. Straight into the ground!"

"How does he manage to have a chain of hotels across the country then?" she asked with genuine curiosity.

"Just barely, that's how." Graham rolled his eyes. "Look, Miss Harlow, I don't know what the old goat told you, but his so-called empire is on a knife's edge and has been for a while now. He jumps from one big idea to the next without seeing anything through. He's always looking for the next project, never happy to build up what he's already invested in."

"What do you mean?" she asked curiously.

"He likes restoring things. He has fun renovating old buildings," Graham explained. "Then the fool slaps the name Eiler's Arms on the front and moves on to find the next property. He doesn't take the time to build up the hotel itself or make sure it's profitable. He certainly never waits around for it to have a hope of paying for itself before he's off and spending again."

"Sounds…risky." She pulled a face. She was increasingly grateful that her parents hadn't bought in, but she was also mildly panicked that they'd even considered it. "Where does he find the money to keep buying new buildings?"

"Until recently, he's been selling off shares of the company to raise revenue." He shook his shiny head. "But you can only do that for so long before you run out of ammo, so to speak."

"Eilers claimed that Ulysses Mercier was trying to buy in." She noted the accountant's wry smirk. "And that he turned him away…what really happened?"

"Mercier turned up and started sniffing around. He did say something about 'acquiring an addition' to his existing portfolio," Graham intoned meaningfully and then smiled smugly. "It was a front. He was testing the waters, and the waters were shallow. Fred has effectively handed over control of his own company, a shark like Mercier smelled the blood in the water and went in for the kill."

"I'm assuming you offered your professional advice before it got to that point?" A corner of her mouth tilted upward.

"Repeatedly!" He gave her a grimly resigned look. "Fred hears what he wants and does what he wants, which is typically something stupid. I told him last year when he first found this place that he didn't have the capital to make it happen, not yet. I begged him to get his last three projects up and making the money they were capable of before he started on something new."

"He obviously didn't listen," she sighed in commiseration.

"No, he never does. And it wasn't as if he was in danger of losing the place to someone else." Graham threw up his hands in disgust. "I looked into it, this building has sat untouched for at least sixty years! One more wouldn't have hurt!"

"True, I've lived here most of my life and no one's ever touched the place," she mused. "He wouldn't even consent to buy the property but wait to refurbish it?"

"No, that would require patience, which would also require maturity," he muttered petulantly.

"So, when did Eilers realize that Mercier was looking to pull the rug out from under him?" she asked.

"When he got a phone call from some of the larger shareholders expressing concerns about his dwindling profits and large expenditures. Fred tried to placate them by detailing his new project, but even he couldn't explain it clearly." Graham ran a hand over his frizzy hair. "The original concept of this place was a British-styled pub. He gloated about the historic building he was able to snap up cheaply and the amazing transformation that would make it his greatest success to date."

"So what happened to the pub theme?" She quirked a brow.

"No idea. Maybe ask Maddie about that, she helped with the design phase," he suggested. "But the shareholders weren't happy to learn that he'd already invested hundreds of thousands into this old shell and didn't consult them. Fred, being Fred, got annoyed by their complaints and tried to start throwing his weight around."

"How'd that go over?" She almost chuckled despite finding less and less to laugh about.

"Not well," he practically sneered. "When he came to me after that phone call, he was finally nervous. I reminded him of what I'd told him over a year ago, the last time he sold more of his shares. He'd given away his power. He wasn't the majority stakeholder anymore. All I could do to help him at that point was to advise that there was a real risk of the shareholders turning against him if he kept being wasteful and started being belligerent."

"And?" she prompted.

"He grumbled and blustered that he was the head of the company. It was *his* company after all. But that's simply not true anymore, and I told him that," Graham said candidly. "That scared the old man more than he'd admit. He started shouting and had the audacity to blame *me!* Despite having ignored every bit of advice and doing exactly as he wanted. He stormed out and that's the last I heard about it until Mercier turned up dead in his office. I still don't understand why Fred hasn't been arrested yet."

"So, you believe he did it?" she asked as neutrally as she could.

"I hope he did," he said candidly. "The best result in this stupid situation would be to have both of those conniving old fossils out of the way."

"You've clearly given this some thought." She managed to not look startled by that ungenerous sentiment. "Were you here the night of the murder, by any chance?"

"Nope." Graham looked quite pleased with himself. "I was home having dinner with a friend, a very good friend that won't hesitate to swear to it."

"That's handy." She pushed to her feet. "Thank you for your time, Mr. Harper. I'll show myself out."

Maiden left Graham's dreary little dungeon and made her way back to the empty foyer. She glanced around and saw that the receptionist was staring down at her phone. She took advantage of the opportunity and slipped upstairs unnoticed.

She reached the second floor and started looking for Maddie Norris' office. Eilers had told her that it was right next to his and, considering that Eilers' office was probably still a crime scene, she doubted it would be hard to find.

It didn't take long to spot the door that was crisscrossed with police tape. Maiden smiled and tiptoed past, proud of herself for not giving in and trying to sneak a look inside as she went.

Maddie's door was ajar and she could hear papers shuffling quietly inside. Maiden peeked through the slightly open door and saw Maddie sitting at her desk frowning down at whatever she was reading.

She glanced around before making her presence known. It was a large office with a couple of windows and few pictures of tropical beaches on the dark blue walls. It was quite nice; all the furniture looked brand new and expensive. After Graham's dismal remarks about Eilers' financial situation, Maiden couldn't help wondering if such lavish touches were necessary in rooms that paying customers would probably never see.

She pushed those practical musings aside and knocked lightly. Maiden couldn't help noticing the cool wariness that crept into the other woman's gaze when she looked up at her. Maddie laid her papers aside and sat back in her chair a little.

"Miss Harlow." She put on a fake but cordial smile. "Do come in, I was wondering if you'd bother talking to me. I doubt I can help much, but I'm certainly happy to try."

"Good afternoon, Ms. Norris," Maiden said as she walked in and sat in front of the desk. "I'll try not to be a pest; I just had a few questions that I'm hoping you can clear up."

"Certainly." Maddie folded her hands and sat in a very businesslike pose. "What's troubling you?"

"What can you tell me about Graham Harper?" she asked mildly, aware that she'd seen them together at the grand opening party and curious what their relationship was.

"Mr. Harper?" Maddie frowned and then tilted her head to the side pensively. "He's all right, he does his work and keeps the books balanced. He and Mr. Eilers don't get along well but they put up with each other."

"Why is that?" Maiden asked.

"Polar opposites." Maddie finally smiled for real. "Mr. Harper is a numbers man, logical and mathematical through and through. Mr. Eilers is a dreamer and a sort of artist, in his way. He sees with his heart and that doesn't always match the numbers so he and Mr. Harper are forever clashing."

"So why does Graham stay?" Maiden asked. "Or why doesn't Eilers fire him? They can't actually enjoy the constant friction."

"They don't, but they've been this way for as long as I've known them," she said with an air of placid acceptance.

"Any theories?" Maiden asked quizzically. "You seem observant."

"I suspect that either Mr. Eilers knows he needs Mr. Harper's level head, and Mr. Harper is too afraid of change to look for something else, or," she gave a conceding nod, "Mr. Harper might have something on Mr. Eilers."

"Blackmail?" Maiden asked quietly.

"Possibly. I wouldn't put it past him," Maddie said with surprising ease, considering what she was suggesting. "It's sheer conjecture, of course, all of it. But those seem the most likely reasons to maintain a very fractious working relationship."

"Is that why Graham's office seems to be the only corner of the building that wasn't refurbished?" she asked

"Not entirely. Part of the deal when Mr. Eilers bought the Chateau was that at least twenty percent of the original structure had to be left exposed." Maddie explained. "The idea was to ensure that the history of the place was preserved while still allowing it to be functional again. But Mr. Eilers took more of a 'find the loophole' approach to it. He found the most out of the way parts of the place and left them in their unfinished state. And yes, he probably stuck Mr. Harper in that dank little room out of spite."

"Charming. So, do *you* get along well with Eilers?" she asked. "What's he actually like to work for?"

"Mr. Eilers is...really good to work for, until he's bad. When he's bad, he's a nightmare," Maddie said candidly. "We go through a lot of staff when he's in residence, and that makes my job harder. It's the constant hiring, training, correcting and then starting over with hiring again that wastes so much time."

"How does he drive out staff?" Maiden asked. "You're the manager, shouldn't you be the one that interacts with them?"

"Yes, in theory. But Mr. Eilers gets excited during these early days of a project, he's a little more hands on than he should be and expects more than is perhaps fair of a bunch of twenty-year-olds that don't view this hotel as their career." Maddie smiled wearily. "But he'll get tired of this place and move on...not that that will ease any of my problems."

"Why is that?"

"Well, right now things are difficult because the cash flow isn't where it needs to be yet, and until it is, things are a bit tight," she admitted. "I've tried to explain that to Mr. Eilers, but he just kept spending the money on advertising and the extravagant grand opening giveaways. He butts in enough to make things difficult and too expensive. And then he leaves me to make it work and gets angry whenever it doesn't."

"Sounds frustrating." Maiden gave a commiserating shake of her head and sought to press a bit further while Maddie was still miffed. "So, what happened to the original concept for this place? How did it go from a British-style pub to...this?"

Maddie's exasperated eyeroll said it all. She rubbed her temples and sighed deeply before resting her chin in her hand.

"Good question. That's another one I can only guess at," she exhaled slowly through her nose. "The concept art was great and getting the initial designs was expensive, but it would've been beautiful. Honestly, I blame Cooper Henderson."

"The local history buff?" Maiden frowned faintly over the slight to the friendly man. "Why? What'd he do?"

"Once he got into Mr. Eilers' head with his ridiculous pirate legends the vision for this place became more and more garbled." She ran a hand over her hair, looking like she wanted to tear some of it out. "Poor Mr. Eilers tried to take both ideas and mash them together. Obviously, it didn't really work. This place is certainly nothing like the atmospheric pub I'd signed on to manage, and now it's my job to try and make it successful."

"Yikes, I don't envy you that," Maiden chuckled.

"I'll make something happen," she said confidently. "I've worked with Mr. Eilers for a while. I know perfectly well that once he loses interest and moves on to his next project the money will dwindle and any profits we produce will be siphoned into his next "great" idea. But I'll still find a way to keep this silly place afloat, it's what I do."

"Is the hotel busy?" Maiden crossed her legs and drummed her fingers on her knee. "I've asked Graham and Eilers and got two very different answers."

"It's steady, but not quite as busy as we'd like," Maddie replied diplomatically. "It'll pick up, we have novelty value and the rates are reasonable. Our location is good and the food is all right. Mr. Eilers has racked up a lot of debt, but we're only in real danger if he follows his usual pattern and moves on too soon."

"What are your thoughts on the murder?" She deliberately changed the subject abruptly. It worked, Maddie was visibly thrown for a moment but soon settled.

"I really don't know much about it." She shook her head a little.

"Did you know about the attempted takeover?" Maiden asked.

"I do now, but I only caught wind of it when Mr. Eilers did." She clasped her hands together tightly. "I wasn't exactly flabbergasted; I knew he was on thin ice with his investors."

"What made you think that?" Maiden lifted her dark brows a fraction.

"Well, they started asking questions and wanting to see the books." She frowned gently. "Mr. Eilers tried to simply ignore the complaints until he realized that the danger was real and had arrived on his doorstep. The investors' concerns hadn't come out of nowhere, someone was already talking to them. That's when Ulysses turned up, and that's when the sudden concerns of the other shareholders made sense."

"What did you honestly think of Mercier?" Maiden watched her closely.

"I didn't really meet him," she replied mildly. "I know Mr. Eilers didn't like him, so maybe he was a bit of a snake. I can't see Mr. Eilers killing anyone though."

"Were you worried about a potential takeover?"

"Not deeply, no," Maddie admitted. "It might sound bad, but who owns the place didn't overly affect me. I'm here to manage the hotel and make it profitable, not to climb the corporate ladder. I have enough on my plate as it is."

"Hard to argue with that," Maiden smiled. "Were you here the night of the murder? Did you see anything strange?"

"I was here but I was downstairs in the kitchen," Maddie replied. "Its early days and I keep track of the inventory myself until I know the staff is trustworthy. Food is expensive and it's easy to let wastefulness creep in. I didn't know anything about the murder until Mr. Eilers came in white as a sheet and said Ulysses was dead in his office."

"And what did you think when you heard that?" Maiden asked impassively.

"I just hoped that he had an alibi," she said as she looked down at her hands somberly.

Chapter Twenty

After thanking Maddie for her time and insights, Maiden headed downstairs to the kitchen. It was all business in there, no cheesy decorations or vivid colors. Bare white walls, sterile lighting and stainless steel everywhere.

As Maiden walked through the long galley-style kitchen she noticed some of the appliances. The row of massive six-burner stoves and the four large refrigerators were a very high-end European brand. She'd looked at them herself when they'd upgraded the kitchen at Harlow House and quickly dismissed them as an option; they were staggeringly expensive.

A tiny frown creased her forehead as she looked around. There wasn't much staff to be seen, only a single chef was toiling away at one of the stoves. It was still close to lunchtime but the place was very quiet.

The man at the stove glanced over at her but said nothing as she walked past. Maiden kept her expression serene and confident as she continued on to the far side of the kitchen. He clearly wasn't terribly concerned and went back to the fish he was sautéing.

At the rear of the long kitchen she found two doors. One was marked with a large exit sign but the other, which sat near the end of the left side wall, was unmarked.

Pausing just long enough to make sure the chef was still preoccupied, Maiden opened the door and peered inside. It was a huge pantry and storage room. Rows of shelves full of canned goods and sacks of dry ingredients filled the space.

Maiden smiled and shook her head when she saw that the walls boasted the old stone and mortar in here as well. Eilers had indeed looked for the sneakiest ways to squeeze in the required twenty percent of the exposed original structure.

"Can I help you?"

Maiden glanced back sharply and saw a young man in a white uniform standing in the doorway. He was smiling politely but his eyes were watchful.

"Maybe," she put on her most confident expression. "I'm doing some work for Mr. Eilers; I'm just checking a few things on his behalf. My name is Maiden."

"Joe." He reached out and shook her hand. "You work here now?"

"No, not exactly. It's more of a freelance thing." She continued smoothly before he could give that too much thought. "Were you here Saturday night by any chance?"

"Yeah, I was." Joe replied.

"Did you happen to see anything or anyone acting strangely that night?" She held his gaze steadily. "Particularly around the time of the murder?"

"Not really." He shook his head, though he gave her a curious look at the question. "I was in and out of the kitchen all night so it's kind of a blur. I already talked to the police."

"I see. What about Maddie Norris?" she asked mildly. "She was here too, right?"

"Yeah," Joe said after a moment's thought. "Like I said, I was on the move a fair bit but I did see her a couple of times."

"Were you around when Mr. Eilers broke the news about the murder?" She stroked her chin thoughtfully.

"I was here in the pantry with Ms. Norris," he confirmed. "She asked for my help with some inventory; it was kind of a pain in the neck on a Saturday night. I was already pretty busy. But she's strict about stuff like that."

"Has the restaurant been busy?" she asked, knowing that it certainly hadn't been last night.

"It was on the weekend, yeah." Joe shrugged. "It's dropped off a bit but, hopefully come Friday night we'll get some traffic again."

"Did you ask her why she wanted to do inventory right then?"

"No, I didn't have to." He folded his arms over his chest. "One of the chefs is very careless when it comes to the food, even the really pricey stuff. He's kind of wasteful and she hates that. He was on that night and I think Ms. Norris was keeping an eye on him."

"All right, thank you." She turned back to the room. "That's all I have to ask you at the moment."

"Okay," he said slowly after a very uncertain pause. "Um, are you gonna be here for a while?"

"No, I won't." She still didn't look at him and pulled out her phone. "You can get back to work, I'll show myself out when I'm ready."

After giving him a minute, Maiden glanced over her shoulder and was pleased to see that Joe had finally walked away. She didn't blame him for being suspicious, she would've been too, but she did have permission to nose around. She peeked through the half open door and saw that the kitchen was empty now.

Maiden stepped out of the store room and went to the exit, she was curious about where it opened to and if Mercier, or his killer, might have used it to gain access that night.

She slipped outside and studied her new surroundings. The backlot was sparse and untidy. Bits of litter had blown around and gotten wedged in some of the clumps of scraggly weeds that had worked their way up through cracks in the asphalt. A few old crates had been dumped in a sloppy stack to the right of the door.

Several feet to her left were two large dumpsters that stank of discarded fish pieces and possibly spoiled milk. She wrinkled her nose and shifted her gaze.

Directly across from her was a long chain-link fence that lined the back edge of the property. A handful of cars, doubtless belonging to whatever staff was actually on site, were parked along it. On the other side of the fence was a large factory that had been transformed into a workshop and exhibition center that focused on making and selling glass jewelry and décor.

Maiden took a few steps out away from the building and looked it over. Much of the foundation had been patched up and covered, she tried not to cringe when she thought of the beautiful old stonework being blithely slathered with bright blue render.

She glanced to either side but there weren't too many people around. She spotted a few men outside the neighboring bakery carrying in boxes of ingredients and what looked like disposable takeaway containers.

Maiden waited a moment until they'd gone inside before walking along the rear wall, looking closely for anything that might be suspicious. She was nearing the far corner of the building and toying with investigating the alley when she glanced down and saw a pile of blue debris.

She looked up at the wall above it. Some of the external render had been chipped away along a mortar line. Someone was trying to get a closer look at the foundation.

She was leaning in to examine it more closely when she heard the back door fling open. Maiden jumped slightly and turned to see Cooper Henderson step outside and look around with a scowl. His expression quickly cleared when he saw her.

"Maiden?" he asked curiously as he approached. "One of the kitchen kids just came and told me someone was snooping around, was it you?"

"Yeah, I guess it was." She smiled. "I wouldn't have put it quite like that though."

"What are you up to, sweetie?" he asked patiently.

"Nothing bad, I promise." She held up her hands in an innocent gesture. "Eilers knows that I'm checking things out, so does Maddie Norris."

"That's fine then." He smiled, clearly happy to accept that vague claim. "So, what are you looking for?"

"Why do you ask?" She gave him a teasing look.

"I'm bored," he replied. "I'm also desperate to get a break from the badly re-recorded sea shanties. I wish that tone-deaf moron really did have fifteen men on his chest. You ever listen to the lyrics of *Yo Ho Ho and A Bottle of Rum*?"

"I've always meant to but it's hard to find the time." She grinned at him.

"It's not exactly lunchtime fare," he sighed and then hooked his thumbs in his pockets. "So what are you doing? I can help, or at least get in the way."

"All right," she allowed and pointed at the damaged render. "Maybe you can give me your opinion of this."

"Oh!" Cooper looked startled as he stepped in for a closer look. "That's...odd. You just found this now?"

"Right before you came outside," she said. "Any idea who might have done it or why?"

"No idea *who*." He folded his arms and studied the damage pensively. "But as to *why*, I have a few ideas about that."

"Do many people know the story of Claudia Arnaud?" she asked, fairly sure she knew where he was going.

"A few do, yes." He nodded. "But the later stories are more widespread; the rumors of prohibition-era gangsters and jewel thieves using this place as a hideout...I wonder if someone really believes it."

"Do *you* believe it?" she asked.

He considered that for a moment and then nodded again.

"Yeah, I do."

"The crooks that are said to have used the hidden cellar," she watched him closely, "how recent was that?"

"The last time I heard whispers about strange lights and funny noises in the night would have been..." he scratched his chin as he thought it over, "two or three years ago maybe."

"That recent?" Her eyes widened.

"It was only a rumor," he admitted. "It could have been teenagers getting drunk or something like that."

"So, someone may think there's really a treasure trove here under the Old Chateau, be it pirate or otherwise." She pursed her lips thoughtfully as she turned back to the defaced wall. "If so, they're probably looking for an entrance to the cellar."

"You see, this is why we need to preserve history!" Cooper exclaimed happily. "People really are interested in what came before them!"

Yeah, especially if it's worth a fortune and they can find it before anyone else, she thought to herself but opted not to disillusion him.

She pulled out her phone and took a few pictures before turning back to Cooper.

"I'll report this," she murmured and held his gaze sternly. "But I think it would be wise to keep it to ourselves beyond that. Agreed?"

"Sure, sweetie." He smiled and rubbed his hands together gleefully. "I don't want to scare off whoever's doing this...who knows, they might succeed!"

***

David sat at his desk and stared coldly at Braden Blair. He'd sent out the order to have him hauled in first thing that morning. Considering that he'd been told to remain available it took a lot longer than it should have to track him down.

Blair was a short man with sinewy arms, likely from years of beating his drums. He wore at least ten handwoven leather cords around his neck, each holding a different item. Several were stones and clay beads but there was also an old-fashioned key and what looked like a shark's tooth.

He removed his cap, revealing greasy hair and pulled absently at his big, scraggly beard. David gave him a moment to become uncomfortable as he maintained eye contact but let the silence stretch on.

"Um...how can I help you lads?" Braden finally asked as he flitted a worried look between David and Officer Smith, who stood impassively off to the side.

"You were seen acting in a suspicious manner in a hotel called Eilers' Arms last night," David said at last. "Why were you there?"

"Eilers' what?" Braden shook his head at him. "I've never heard of it, I've certainly never been there. Sorry, I'm just passing through, I don't know my way around the town very well."

"I am referring to a three-story, bright blue building that's been in the papers every day for two weeks," David continued stonily. "I don't believe for a second that you haven't heard of it. You may be passing through but you and your friends have been here for a while."

"That may be, Captain." Braden folded his arms over his chest. "But I've never been to this Eilers' whatever it is. I'll swear to that."

"For whatever that's worth," David replied sardonically and decided not to mention yet that he'd personally seen him enter the building. "You also lied in your previous statement, Mr. Blair."

"What?" Braden sat up straighter. "Never! I take Sean's death very seriously, Captain, I'd *never* lie to you about it."

"You very strongly and deliberately stated that Mr. Dowling was involved with a certain woman. We've since learned that she had almost nothing to do with him at all. Why the deception?"

"Oh, look, I really didn't know what they were to each other." He waved it away as though it were nothing. "I certainly never tried to deliberately say so one way or the other."

"Let me refresh your memory of what you did in fact say." David's eyes were like ice as he picked up a copy of his statement and started reading it aloud. "*'I looked through the doorway to the restaurant and saw Sean cozied up to some busty lass with dark hair. They were obviously very into each other, I half expected her to be there in the morning as well, if you know what I mean. Sean was bragging about this lass all evening, said her name was Maiden, but she didn't act innocent enough for a name like that.'*"

David lowered the page and just watched him coldly. Braden looked uncomfortable and a lot less confident than he had when he'd spouted his story. He shifted in his seat and looked away a lot.

David swiftly tamped down an anger that threatened to become violent as he watched the creep try to think of a way out of his lies.

He'd personally taken Braden's statement, he'd actually been forced to type out the details of what he'd claimed Maiden had done. Those words had haunted him and kept him awake and devastated all night. And now Braden was about to try and simply shrug it off.

"Listen, Captain," the man sighed wearily. "I was quite shocked when I said those things. I'd just seen my friend in a bloodied heap on the ground. I was deeply troubled and may have jumped to a conclusion or two. But I really was trying to help."

David looked at him for a long moment as he used every trick he knew to calm himself down. Now wasn't the time to dwell on what the lies had nearly cost him, it wasn't the time to hate himself for believing them; he could do that later.

"Giving false or exaggerated testimony is the opposite of helpful, Mr. Blair," he informed him. "You've wasted our time and caused needless strain on innocent people. You haven't heard the last of this, but for now you can get out of my office."

"I...certainly," Braden said quietly as he got to his feet and edged towards the door. "I apologize again, Captain."

***

Greg eyed the scruffy man irately as he opened the door and ushered him away from Captain McAlister. He'd escorted him down the hall and into the lobby when Braden stopped and turned to him.

"Listen lad," he said earnestly. "I swear that I said what I genuinely believed at the time. I'm not so sure now but Sean *had* mentioned meeting a woman that night. I must've misunderstood which one he meant."

"You shouldn't have assumed at all," Greg told him irately, still angry over what this jerk had put Maiden through. "It could have been either of them, they're sisters. As it is, *neither* of them would've been all over that guy!"

"Oh, sisters, of course!" Braden laughed at himself and smacked his forehead. "What an idiot I am! Sorry lad, I think I may have caused more harm than good. Never mind, hopefully no real damage was done."

"Yeah, *hopefully*," Greg muttered and pointed him to the door.

Chapter Twenty-One

Maiden arrived at the police station and found an infinitely more cheerful Nancy behind the desk. She glanced up at Maiden and smiled instantly.

"You can go straight through to the Captain's office, Miss Harlow," Nancy said nicely before she'd even crossed the foyer.

Maiden could only assume that David's improved mood had made life more pleasant for everyone. She inclined her head to Nancy and smiled to herself as she headed for his office. The door was slightly ajar so she peeked inside.

David was sitting on the front edge of his desk with his arms folded over his chest. He was staring out the window at the cloudy, dark gray sky. Maiden looked at him warily; he was obviously upset about something. She stepped quietly inside.

"What's wrong?" she asked as she closed the door softly behind her.

"Hmm?" He glanced over at her and forced a smile. "Oh, nothing. I was just thinking."

"Yeah?" She eased closer and smiled gently. "About anything in particular?"

He shook his head. She knew he was holding back but she'd also seen Braden Blair leaving the station as she drove in; it wasn't hard to guess what had gotten to him. And as much as he must blame Braden for lying about her, he probably felt even worse for believing him.

Rather than press him on it, she set her purse and jacket on the nearest chair and slid her arms around his shoulders. David's stoney expression finally softened, he uncrossed his arms and pulled her snugly against his chest. He cupped her cheek in his large hand and just looked at her for a moment.

Maiden was waiting for him to kiss her but he hugged her close instead, gently holding the back of her head. She slid him a curious look, as best she could with her chin resting on his shoulder anyway.

His hold was tight and his breathing was shallow, his whole body was tense. She hadn't seen him quite like this before and wasn't really sure how to make him feel better. She wondered if maybe a distraction would help.

"David?" she asked quietly.

"Yeah?" he murmured, burying his face in her hair.

"Um...what are you working on?" she finally asked.

"Why?" he asked slowly, cautiously.

"You just seem distracted." She touched her lips to his throat and felt goosebumps rise on his skin. "What are you up to?"

***

David was quickly shaking free from his wandering thoughts; he assumed that's what she was aiming for. The talk with Braden Blair had brought back bad memories that hadn't had time to fade yet. Seeing Maiden walk in had only reminded him of what he'd nearly thrown away.

But he pushed those niggles aside as Maiden nestled close and her soft breath warmed his skin. He finally remembered that she'd asked him a question.

"What am I distracted by?" He tried and failed not to smile as she continued her efforts. "Apart from three murders, you mean?"

"Yes, apart from those." She slid her hand into his hair. "What about the roof?"

"Did I even tell you about the roof?" he frowned a little.

"Yes, briefly." She nestled closer. "How bad is it?"

"Really bad." He flinched slightly. "It doesn't matter."

You actually bit me, he felt himself smile wider.

"Don't you have to get it fixed?" She arched her left eyebrow, he could hear it in her voice. "Preferably before winter, I would assume."

"I don't care about the stupid roof right now, if I'm honest." He spread his hands over her slender back.

"You're at work, David," she advised him between kisses. "You should really take that seriously."

"You're lecturing me about professionalism while biting my neck?" he asked wryly. "How is that reasonable?"

"That's not my problem, *I'm* not at work." She finally relented and raised her head so she could meet his gaze; she smiled warmly. "So, what do you say, Captain? Do you want to show me your quotes?"

He shut his eyes and smiled ruefully. "You're surprisingly cruel, but in a really good way."

"I know, it's fun, isn't it?" she ran her hands over his hair, smoothing it down where she'd mussed it. "So, do you have the quotes handy or what?"

"Yeah, I—probably." He sighed loudly and glanced back at his desk before reluctantly releasing her. "I put them somewhere."

"You don't have a file for maintenance?" she asked in mild surprise but smiled sweetly when he gave her a look. "That's cool, who needs it?"

David shook his head and shuffled through some papers. He was normally more organized, but the last several days had been far from normal. He glanced back at Maiden, she was watching him fondly, he felt himself relax a bit.

"I think I left them with Nancy," he said mildly and headed for the door.

He held it open for her and they both walked towards the ancient wrap-around desk that dominated the lobby. Nancy was seated on her throne, which was a wobbly-looking old chair, surveying her kingdom. The placid blonde glanced at them as they approached and smiled her quiet, knowing smile.

"Do you have those quotes I gave you the other day?" he asked as he leaned his elbow on the desk.

"Yes, sir." Nancy looked curious but didn't question him, she just pulled open a drawer and drew out a thick stack of papers. "Here you are."

"What's all that?" Maiden's big eyes widened briefly. "That can't be just for the roof."

"It isn't. The roof is one of many maintenance nightmares that everyone who ran the station before me was sweet enough to completely ignore," he grumbled as he dropped the papers on the desk. "They're extensive, unexpected and massively beyond the non-existent budget."

"Whoa." She stared at him. "No wonder you're stressed. Well, come on, how bad is the roof?"

He just handed her the report and the attached quote. As soon as she looked at the logo of the local roofing company a long, dark eyebrow rose sharply. She cleared her throat quietly as she flicked through the pages. David was instantly uneasy over her reaction, she wasn't impressed and he really didn't want to deal with anything getting worse.

"What is it?" he asked warily.

"Is there a reason you went with Russel's for your quote?" she asked politely.

"It's who they always use, apparently." He shrugged. "Why? No good?"

"Have you signed anything?" she asked rather than answer the question.

"You're scaring me, Harlow." He smiled weakly and shook his head. "No, I haven't accepted the quote yet."

"Good, don't." She released a relieved breath and pulled out her phone as she walked down the hall towards his office, still holding the papers. "Just let me make a phone call, I'll be right back."

David watched her until she disappeared through his door. A part of him was tempted to follow and see what she was up to, but he stayed put and just exchanged a look with Nancy.

"What happened to your neck?" She frowned at him.

"What?" He touched the side of his throat. "Oh...something bit me."

"Ah." Nancy smiled faintly. "Must have been a vicious mosquito to still be around at this time of year. You're still bleeding."

David glanced at his fingers and the smear of soft pink that was undeniably lipstick. He reluctantly met her amused gaze.

"Get back to work." He couldn't help laughing a little as he said it.

About five minutes later Maiden walked out smiling quietly. She glanced at David and handed him back the report.

"My roof guy will come by this afternoon to have a look," she said. "He'll get you a quote in a day or two."

"You have a 'roof guy'?" he asked with a faint frown.

"I have many guys for many things, David." She smirked at him. "My family's owned a business in this town for years. Why didn't you tell me you needed help when all this started?"

"I didn't realize I did," he admitted as he ran a hand through his hair. "What was I supposed to say? 'The bathroom floor is rotting out, want to come have a look?'"

"That's better than 'the bathroom floor is rotting out, and it's a road I have to walk alone'," she replied dryly.

David grinned down at the papers. Beside him Nancy shifted slightly and cleared her throat just loud enough to get his attention.

"It's not as if you have nothing else to do, sir," she pointed out. "If Miss Harlow has connections, it could be more efficient than trying to plow through everything on your own."

He flicked through a few more pages as he considered that, he was quiet long enough to betray that he didn't really want to ask for her help. Maiden draped her hands lightly on her hips and looked at him enquiringly.

"So are you going to show me your rotten floors?" she asked.

"I don't know," he said coyly. "This is all moving a bit fast for me."

"Just ride the wave, McAlister," she said with a smile and glanced at her watch. "And get on with it, please."

David held up his hands in surrender and motioned for her to follow as he walked down the hall. They stepped cautiously inside the ladies' room and stood silently for a long moment.

"It needs work," David said at last.

"I know," Maiden sighed. "I noticed the wear and tear when I threw up in here the other day."

David covered his face with his hands to hide his quietly touched smile. He then wrapped his arm around her and dropped a kiss on her temple.

"Why didn't you tell me about all of this?" she asked as she gestured to encompass the entire moldering building.

"I didn't want to burden you with all my problems. I kept thinking that it was almost under control and then something else would crop up," he said with a bewildered shake of his head. "And I wanted to give you something better than eating a sandwich in my office while I tried to untangle someone else's mess, especially for our first date. I wanted it to be really nice."

"It was." She smiled faintly.

"Yeah...it was," he murmured warmly.

When he leaned down and almost kissed her, she reached between them and pressed her fingers against his lips.

"Seriously, not in here," she said. "It's pretty nasty."

David laughed and obligingly led her out and back to his office, grabbing the pile of papers from Nancy's desk as they passed.

***

By the end of the afternoon, Maiden had looked through all the reports and failed inspections and sorted them by priority. She made a few more phone calls and arranged for some of her regular contractors to come and assess the station's various issues.

It wasn't all as bad as she'd braced for but there were some major works that needed to be done. She looked at the tidy and manageable piles of paper she'd arranged methodically on his desk and gave a satisfied nod. She glanced up to find David smiling at her.

"What?" she blinked at him.

"How can you be that hot," he began with genuine curiosity, "and still have time to know about replacing toilets and who to call to patch a roof?"

"It's all part of my intense sexual allure," she rolled her wrist in a tiny flourish.

"I'm serious," he laughed.

"So am I."

He held her gaze, still smiling faintly. Confident that she had his full attention, she asked the question that'd been on her mind for a while now.

"What made you regard Sean Dowling's death as suspicious?" she asked. He paused briefly at the sudden change of topic but otherwise took it in stride.

"He fell out of a window for no apparent reason," he said.

"But he was drunk and the windows are rickety and old," she reasoned. "You locked everything down pretty quick for what looked like a dumb accident that was readily reported."

"How do you know when it was reported?" he asked patiently.

"I went back the next day and spoke to a staff member, and Ewan Fraser," she confessed freely. "They told me that Arran Campbell heard the fall and called the police right away."

"And why did you go there?" his voice was a bit tight and he started drumming his fingers.

"Because someone lied about me and seriously damaged my reputation." She didn't flinch at his obvious stirrings of temper. "Incidentally, Ewan also flirted with me and got nowhere, in case it comes up later."

"That was a cheap shot." He held her gaze steadily.

"It was, I'm sorry." She let her eyes drift to her lap. "But you're getting mad at me and that puts me on edge."

"Slapping me in the face isn't the nicest way to deal with that," he said with remarkable patience.

"I'm *very* sorry." She glanced up at him and smiled again. "So, you were about to tell me about Sean's death?"

"What did you make of Fraser?" He grinned at her but deflected the question.

"Shifty," she said pensively. "Kind of sexy, but probably up to something."

"Has it occurred to you that you went and fluttered your big green eyes at him and your room was ransacked the next day?" he asked.

"Yes, it has." She nodded.

"You should've mentioned it when I sent officers over." He started drumming his fingers again.

"I was too busy being unfairly detained and harassed." She leaned back in her chair. "Somehow admitting that I'd spoken to one of the creeps that lied about me didn't feel wise. Besides, we were still fighting."

"We weren't fighting later that night," he reminded her with forced calm.

"True," she allowed, "but then you pinned me against the wall and I wasn't thinking of much beyond that. Then today I was too busy trying to find a turtleneck."

"Are you hitting on me?" He gave her a look.

"Typically, yeah," she said mildly. "Why? Am I getting to you?"

"Doc Jenkins concluded that Dowling had been beaten up before he died," he sighed and finally relented. "He had injuries that went beyond what he'd have sustained by the fall."

"Interesting," she mused and just waited, convinced that there was more to come.

"And…" He visibly debated how much he wanted to tell her. "When we examined his luggage, we found a rather expensive diamond necklace that had been sewn into the lining of his suitcase."

"Shady business."

"Yeah. We suspect he and Charles Brown were on someone else's payroll, and no, I don't know who that might be." He smiled faintly. "So, in light of that, is there anything else you want to tell me about Ewan Fraser?"

"He's nowhere near as sexy as you are." She gave him a wink.

"C'mon, Harlow," he chuckled.

"He got kind of weird when I mentioned Sean's death," she conceded. "Not necessarily in a suspicious way, he may have thought I was only being nosy."

"Which you were."

"Really?" She frowned at him and folded her arms over her chest. "Because *you* were the only one who's life was seriously impacted by the lie? I was just bored and happened to be in the area so I dropped in?"

"Sorry," he said quietly.

"Do you want me to tell you things when I find them out or not?" she demanded.

"*Very* sorry." He borrowed her tactic. "Please continue."

"He was flirty with me and one of the staff. I think he uses her to get special treatment but that's only a guess," she mused. "But he said he remembered me from the concert."

"Had you met him?" David quirked a brow.

"No." She shook her head and gestured towards her sweater. "But he was speaking mostly to my breasts at that point. To my knowledge they weren't introduced to him either, so he may have just seen me that night. I wasn't inclined to ask."

"Sounds like a real gentleman," David murmured.

"Yeah," she scoffed and waved it away. "Anyway, the reason I came here was to tell you about Eilers' Arms."

"You're scaring me again," he smiled weakly. "What about it?"

"I found evidence of tampering, well searching really, around the foundation." She stood when he scowled questioningly. "Someone's chipped away at the render, trying to find something underneath."

"What exactly?" he asked.

"Pirate treasure," she said simply.

"Pirate treasure?" he repeated.

"Mm-hmm." She pulled out her phone and opened up the picture. David watched as she walked around and perched on the edge of his desk.

"When did you take this?" He frowned as he took the phone and looked closer.

"Before I came here," she said and gestured at the photo again. "It looks like someone might be trying to find another way in."

"You think someone is trying to tunnel into Eilers' Arms through solid rock?" He glanced back up at her with a dubious smirk.

"Yes, David, that's exactly what I think," she replied sardonically and rolled her eyes. "They're not interested in solid rock; they're trying to find the secret cellar."

"What do they call it when really, really beautiful women go completely insane?" He leaned back in his chair and grinned at her. "I'm not judging, I'm just curious."

"I told you the Old Chateau was built by a pirate who hid her treasure there," she continued, politely ignoring it when he started laughing. "It's also rumored to have been used as a hideout for various criminals over the years, and fairly recently too."

"Where did you hear that?" he sniggered. "Did the man in the diving suit regale you with tales of adventure?"

"From Cooper Henderson." Her tolerant understanding was beginning to wane as his amusement persisted. "Did you speak to him at all?"

"Not personally." David did his best to hide his lingering smile when he noticed that she was getting peeved. "He wasn't there the night of the murder."

"That doesn't mean he has no useful information," she sniffed as she snatched her phone back and slid off the desk. "Never mind, I'll look into it myself. Just don't complain later that I never come to you."

David got quickly to his feet and grasped her arm when she started to walk away. He pulled her back gently and turned her around to face him. Sliding his hands around her waist, he pressed a kiss to her forehead.

"Maiden, honey." He kissed her again. "I'm listening, I promise."

She glanced away and took a deep breath. She was still a little annoyed, but she believed she was on the right track and that the police needed to know about it.

"Old houses often have cellars, David. They were a necessity when there was no refrigeration," she said quietly. "The Old Chateau sat unoccupied for a very long time and Cooper Henderson, who is also a member of the Golden Glen Historical Association, has suggested that the building had likely been put to 'unofficial' use."

She glanced up to see if he was still laughing. He wasn't and, as promised, he was listening, so she continued.

"If it's true, then it makes sense that the entrance is concealed," she said. "And even if it's not true, someone seems to think that it is. It's worth considering."

"Okay." He nodded. "We'll check it out, don't worry."

Chapter Twenty-Two

The following morning Maiden was sitting behind the desk at Harlow House. She was sipping her coffee and browsing through some catalogues that had been left there, presumably by Gloria.

They were mostly for upholstery and curtains, as well as a few sample books full of swatches. She noticed that they were all featuring vintage styles and the pages that had been marked were classic looks from the 20s and 30s.

She recalled the stores she'd seen her parents going to when she tailed them the other day and wondered why they would be shopping for curtains and furniture. There was even a book full of handmade rugs. Her eyes widened when it occurred to her that they might well be trying to help Fred Eilers with the décor of his hotel.

Maiden pressed a hand to her chest and let out a deep breath. It would take a lot more than throw rugs and wingback chairs to sort out Eilers' Arms. She hoped that Alfie and Gloria weren't getting that involved, even if they were just feeling guilty for not buying into Eilers' business.

She heard her mother's phone ring in the office. Maiden glanced over, idly toying with the soft, floaty green scarf she'd tied around her neck. She'd run out of time to buy new makeup yesterday and David's love-bites were still embarrassingly evident.

She was distracted from her blush-inducing bruises when she heard Gloria's loudly panicked voice. Most of it was incoherent as her mother's southern accent grew thick as molasses when she was excited or upset. Maiden stood and eased closer to the office in time to see Gloria run to the doorway with a look of fear.

"We'll be right there!" she shouted into the phone and then fumbled to hang up. "Maiden! We gotta go, baby!"

"Where to?" Maiden tried to stay rational even as Gloria charged towards her and thrust her purse into her hands.

"The hospital!" Gloria fretted as she hurried towards the door. "Fred's been poisoned!"

***

After a short and uncomfortably silent drive, Maiden barely managed to keep up with her mother as she charged down a hospital corridor to Fred Eilers' room. It occurred to Maiden that if he'd been poisoned he probably wouldn't be available to visitors yet but it was pointless to mention that to her mother.

As they neared the room that the nurse on duty had directed them to, they saw David and Sergeant Ramirez in the corridor talking quietly. David glanced up and frowned faintly when he saw them; under the circumstances Maiden didn't take it personally.

"What's going on?" he asked cautiously even as he subtly touched Maiden on the shoulder in lieu of a kiss.

"Mom says that Mr. Eilers was poisoned?" Maiden shrugged helplessly.

"Yeah, he was. The ambulance brought him in about twenty minutes ago." David shifted his warm brown gaze to Gloria. "Who told you about it?"

"Fred did." Gloria batted a thick set of false eyelashes at him.

"*Fred* did?!" Maiden and David demanded in unison.

"Could you please stop saying what I say when I'm working!" He gave Maiden a cranky look. "Save it for when I'm off duty."

"What?!" she asked incredulously. "I never do it on purpose!"

Behind them Sergeant Ramirez chuckled quietly, which effectively reminded them that they were in public. David took a deep breath and turned back to an anxious Gloria.

"What do you mean Fred called you?" he asked patiently. "Are you referring to Fred Eilers himself?"

"Yes, baby, how many people named Fred do you think I know?" she replied as if it were perfectly normal for someone to be poisoned and then stop to call a friend on the way to the hospital.

"Could you please elaborate on that?" David asked.

"I don't see how I can." Gloria shook her head, sending her blonde curls bouncing.

"Mom," Maiden interceded, getting progressively more confused as the nonsense piled up. "I believe the captain is trying to ask how the flippin' heck Fred Eilers called you to say he was poisoned after actually being poisoned. Most people would struggle to find the time."

"Maiden Vivienne Angelique Harlow!" Gloria huffed. "There's no need to use that tone with me, little missy!"

"Stop telling everyone my stupid name!" she whispered tightly and then cleared her throat and strove for dignity. "Was Eilers okay when he called you? What exactly did he say?"

"He sounded sick as a dog. Moanin' and groanin' that he was on his way to the hospital 'cause he'd been poisoned!" Gloria threw her hands up in exasperation. "Why are y'all askin' *me* about it? Ask Fred!"

Gloria pushed past, muttering irately in increasingly heavy southern as she marched into Eilers' room. Maiden turned to David and grasped him by the ends of his loose necktie.

"Do you have any spare poison for *me*?" she asked as she pulled him a bit closer. "I'm relatively small, it wouldn't take much."

"Like I'd let you off the hook that easy." He smiled and nudged her towards the door.

Maiden obligingly released him and entered the room. The first thing she noticed was her mother standing beside the bed. Fred Eilers was laying there looking washed-out and sweaty. He had an IV in his arm and a breathing tube in his nostrils. Gloria was looking him over critically.

Eilers groaned and clutched at his stomach as his eyes fluttered open. He glanced at the people gathered around, pausing only briefly on David, before fixing his attention on the lady at his side.

"Gloria," Eilers managed a smile as he looked up at her. "You came, thank goodness. Listen, if I don't make it—"

"Don't be silly, Fred." Gloria patted his hand. "You'll be fine now, doctors these days can work wonders. Now, tell me what happened."

Maiden tucked herself in a corner to listen and observe. She dared not ask too many questions with David there conducting his own investigation, but she had a feeling her mother might do most of the work for her. And she couldn't help noticing that David was also standing back and taking notes while Gloria got down to brass tacks.

"I was sitting in my office having coffee, right at 9:15am like I always do," Eilers wheezed. "The next thing I know I felt too sick to sit up at my desk and collapsed on the floor! If Maddie hadn't been there to call an ambulance, I don't know what would have happened."

"Who brought you the coffee?" Gloria frowned.

"Maddie handed it to me but she wouldn't have made it." He rubbed his face. "I can't believe this is happening. I think someone's out to get me."

"Now Fred, don't get into a panic," Gloria said soothingly.

"Don't panic!" he blurted angrily. "My life is at risk and the police have done nothing to protect me! A man died in my office and all they do is ask me insulting questions. What if the killer was really after *me* all along? It's a wonder I'm not dead! I ought to complain about the dangerously inept approach that's been taken!"

Maiden felt a flicker of annoyance but let it pass, she was pretty sure Eilers was all talk anyway. She glanced over at her mother, however, when the older lady bristled quite noticeably.

"You just hold on there, Fred!" Gloria planted her hands on her hips and narrowed her heavily painted eyes. "Don't you dare talk about my David like that!"

David, who'd more or less ignored Eilers' threats, glanced up sharply. Maiden eased closer and spoke under her breath.

"So, you're hers now? Nice," she murmured from the corner of her mouth. "Anything else you want to tell me?"

"I'm not entirely sure what's happened here." He grinned before carefully sobering his expression and walking towards Eilers' bed.

Your cute little backside just got southern belled, Maiden laughed to herself, *that's what's happened.*

"Mr. Eilers, no one is taking this matter lightly," David assured him.

"Oh look, I'm sorry, Captain." Eilers sighed and rubbed his eyes. "I just don't know what's going to happen next. I'm telling you I'm in danger!"

"Just sit tight, Mr. Eilers. We'll post an officer here overnight and I'll look into this matter personally," David said as he walked towards the door. "I'll let you know what we find."

Maiden frowned as she watched him slip outside without even sparing her a glance. She knew why he was avoiding her and he wasn't going to get away with it.

"I'll be right back, Mom." She glanced at her and Eilers and her scowl deepened. "Maybe you should call *Dad*, he's probably wondering where you are."

"Good idea, angel." Gloria pulled out her phone. "I'll do that right now."

"I wouldn't be surprised if Graham Harper was behind this!" Eilers hissed at Gloria as he sank back into his bed.

Maiden gave them both a look and then slipped out into the hall to find David. She quickly spotted him talking to a gray-haired man in a white coat. She waited until the doctor walked away and David started writing notes before she approached.

"So, what's going on?" she asked discreetly.

"Your guess is typically as good as mine," he said to his notepad as he continued to write.

"Yeah, it is," she said smugly and smiled teasingly when he glanced up and gave her a look. "Sorry. So, um, Eilers seems...pretty okay for a guy's that's been poisoned and rushed to the hospital."

"He does, funny that," he said mildly and started writing again.

"You're just scribbling nonsense to try and get out of talking to me," she said.

"Oh Harlow," he grinned and shook his head but still refused to look at her, "if we were alone right now, I'd find much better ways to avoid talking to you."

"Yeah, well, pity we're in one of the busiest places in town," she persevered rather than let him distract her with his flirting. "Have you got the toxicology report yet?"

"Not in the couple of minutes that he's been here, no," David chuckled. "I like your scarf, by the way, matches your eyes."

"You could use one yourself." She eyed the little mark she'd left on the side of his throat.

"No way. I'm desperately hoping that someone will notice so I can tell them how I got it." The dimple flashed in his left cheek.

"How was the roof inspection?" She refused to rise to the bait.

"Promising." David finally put his notebook away and faced her. "Your guy didn't shake his head and sigh as much as mine did."

"And yet you still tease me," she tsked. "Nice show of gratitude."

"Come by my office and I'll thank you properly." He looked her over appreciatively and gave her a wink. "See you around, gorgeous."

Maiden stood there and took a deep breath when he deliberately brushed against her as he walked past and made his way down the hall. He stopped long enough to say something to Ramirez; the man nodded and took up his post outside Eilers' door. She barely noticed; her eyes were on David.

He's still flirting to get around telling me stuff, she told herself as she watched him walk away, *it's a good thing I'm so patient and understanding.*

***

Maiden waited until Alfie turned up at the hospital before excusing herself. As she headed to her car she thought about what Eilers had said about Graham Harper. It seemed a stretch for a disgruntled accountant to resort to poisoning his boss, it's not like Eilers had been wasting Graham's personal funds. It warranted a quick check though; she decided to pay another visit to Eilers' Arms.

She wasn't surprised to see a couple of police cars sitting outside the garish hotel as she pulled into the parking lot. She avoided eye contact in hopes of no one noticing her and snitching to David. She slipped quickly into the foyer and headed towards the accountant's depressing hole-in-the-wall office.

"Maiden!"

She stopped and glanced over her shoulder to see Cooper walking over with a friendly wave. She smiled and turned to meet him.

"I thought it was you," he said cheerfully. "Fancy seeing you here again! Come and have coffee with me."

"Oh, I'd love to but I need to talk to Graham Harper." She smiled apologetically as she pointed towards the hall to his office.

"Come and have coffee with me," he repeated firmly and gave her a speaking look. He beckoned her towards the bar. "Right this way, fair damsel."

Hint taken, Maiden obligingly joined him in the empty room and watched him twiddle the knobs of the wondrous pipe organ that somehow spat out an excellent cappuccino. He set it in front of her and glanced at the doorway to make sure it was empty before propping himself on his elbows and meeting her gaze.

"Do you work for the cops?" he asked seriously.

"No, I'm dating the cops. Well, one of them," she conceded mildly. "Why? What's up?"

"They're crawling all over the place again, and I've heard that you're trying to help old man Eilers." He studied her questioningly.

"That's a favor to my parents, they're friends with him." She pulled her cup closer. "Not really a police thing. Do you know something helpful?"

"I might, but I don't know who to tell." He chewed at his lip for a moment and then rapped his knuckles on the bar as he came to a decision. "You like history; I'll tell you."

Maiden paused briefly but opted not to argue with his interesting reasoning. She just sipped her coffee and gestured for him to continue when he was ready.

"You know Eilers was rushed to the hospital this morning, right?" he asked, she just nodded. "Well, Graham was hanging around in the foyer before it all happened. I saw him walk over to reception and poke around in the drawers for a while, then he started looking through the guest register."

"Is that unusual?" she asked.

"Kind of, yes." He pulled a face. "I mean, he wasn't really doing anything, but why was he there? And when Maddie came downstairs, he ran back to his office. I lost track of him after that because she started shouting for help and saying an ambulance was on the way. It was chaos for about fifteen minutes."

"Any idea what he could have been looking for?" She narrowed her eyes pensively. "Or waiting for?"

"He could have just been looking to see how fully we were booked, trying to anticipate the earnings for the next week or something." Cooper looked her in the eye. "Or he could have been waiting to see if Eilers finished his coffee."

"Coffee?" she gripped her cup a little tighter, wondering how he knew about that.

"Yeah, Maddie said he drank half the cup and then keeled over, groaning like a harp seal," he said.

"Do harp seals—"

"It was likely his coffee that was poisoned, that's all I meant," he said tolerantly. "And Graham was off like a shot when he heard someone raise the alarm."

"Okay, back up," she said. "Did he hear what happened or did he run off the moment he realized someone was coming?"

"What difference does it make?" He gave her a quizzical look.

"If he heard that Eilers was poisoned and ran off in a panic, we have a reason to suspect he was involved or at least aware," she said. "If he ran just because someone was coming, he might have been up to something else entirely and simply didn't want to get caught."

"Too true." Cooper stroked his chin and then smiled at her. "Beautiful *and* deadly; I'm impressed."

"Thanks," she chuckled quietly. "So, which was it?"

"Oh, no idea," he said candidly. "But Graham's shady, I do know that."

"How?"

"He's always trying to learn things about people. Not nice things either, he isn't trying to build friendships. He's after *useful* things," Cooper said meaningfully. "Secrets, dirty laundry, stuff like that. He's tried it with just about everyone here, he even tried to get me."

"Oh?" she braced her chin on her fist.

"He was really interested in my stories and trying to buddy up to me when he first arrived here. I saw him floating around a lot of the staff, asking questions and trying to get people talking." Cooper pulled a distasteful face. "He kept fishing and started getting excited when I told him about the professional embarrassment this place was going to cause for me. He started talking about the value of a good reputation and how important it was to have discreet friends. But boy did the wind go out of his sails when I told him it was already common knowledge."

"You think he wanted something to blackmail you with?" Maiden asked carefully, recalling Maddie suggesting something similar.

"He's the kind of guy that collects favors and takes note of details that might come in handy later on." Cooper gave her a speaking look. "That's how he keeps his job here. Eilers hates him but can't fire him. I'm not exactly sure what Graham knows, but it's bad enough to keep the boss's hands tied."

"Have you checked the reception area for anything that might have interested him?" she asked.

"No," he explained patiently. "I thought he'd been waiting for someone to come running with news about Eilers, not snooping through the desk."

"Any point in having a look now?" she suggested.

"May as well." He nodded and led the way.

Maiden followed Cooper out into the foyer. He walked behind the boat-shaped desk and beckoned for her to join him. She walked around and watched as he went to the computer and opened up the bookings.

As he started scrolling through, she noted that it was a slightly different system to the one they used at Harlow House. Even so, it wasn't hard to figure out the basics.

For a start, they were nowhere near fully booked. As Cooper skipped ahead through the next few days, she could see that the situation wasn't much better.

It wasn't surprising, she'd been there several times and no part of the place had ever seemed busy. She wondered if it was the murder or the bad press about the ruined Chateau that was keeping people away. At the moment, however, she was more interested in what Graham

Harper might have been looking for that he didn't want anyone else to know about.

"Nothing that stands out?" she asked.

"Not really," Cooper said. "Not that I can see."

"All right, thanks for the heads up." She patted his shoulder and slipped out from behind the desk. "I'll go back to plan A."

Maiden glanced at the stairs to ensure there were no police officers to catch her. The coast was clear so she slipped down the hallway to Graham's office. Even though she and Cooper hadn't found any indication of what Graham had been doing at reception, she was intrigued by the blackmail angle.

Graham's door was slightly open. Hoping to catch him off guard, she stepped inside as she knocked loudly.

Graham looked up sharply and quickly shielded the papers he was looking at with his arms. He scowled when he saw her but Maiden smiled nicely.

"Good morning," she said.

"Is it really?" he replied sarcastically as he turned the pages over and shoved them under a ledger.

"Eilers is in hospital, isn't he?" she said mildly. "That's almost as incapacitating as being arrested for murder. That's what you said you were hoping for."

"You're twisting my words." He glared at her.

"No, I'm repeating the sentiments that you volunteered and pro- viding logical conjecture," she said as she sat in front of his desk without bothering to ask permission. "That being said, I'm sure this incident came as a shock."

"It certainly did." He took his thick glasses off and started cleaning them. "And I have no doubt that the old man will be accusing *me* of everything."

"The suggestion has been made," she allowed and gave him a curious look. "How long have you been blackmailing him?"

"What?!" He sat up stiff and straight as he pushed his glasses angrily into place. "Where did you get a crazy idea like that?"

"You've tipped your hand to a lot of people around here, Mr. Harper. You got a little overzealous in trying to harvest other people's secrets." She tented her fingers but kept smiling. "You'll find that makes you a tad unpopular. Besides, why else would Eilers keep you around and actually let you handle his money when you both obviously hate each other?"

Graham exhaled loudly and rolled his eyes. Maiden didn't back down, she was certain she was right and decided to up the pressure a bit.

"How well did you actually know Ulysses Mercier?" she asked mildly.

"You can leave right now, Miss Harlow," he said darkly. "I don't appreciate these insinuations and I'm considering telling the police that you're harassing me."

"That's fine, Mr. Harper," she replied as she pulled her phone out of her purse. "I happen to know the head of the police department fairly well, I can call him if you like so you can complain. After that maybe you can explain to him what you were doing behind the reception desk this morning, and why you ran for it when someone raised the alarm about Eilers."

"You think you're real smart, don't you?" he grumbled irately.

"I'm smart enough not to make enemies in the place I go to almost every day," she replied and gave him a direct look. "Are you the one that gave Mercier the details of Fred Eilers' financial problems?"

"Not as such, no," he said after a cautious pause. "He did come to see me and asked for some information. All I could tell him was that what he wanted was in Fred's office and I didn't have access to it. He thanked me and left."

"What did he ask for?" she murmured.

"Evidence of wastefulness, and any documentation that outlined exactly how much Fred spent on the renovations," he replied. "Fred kept all those numbers to himself and it's not hard to guess why. He'd spent way too much and he knew it, but he didn't want the investors to know it too."

"So, that could explain why Mercier was found dead in that same office," she mused. "Did you mention that to the police?"

"No I did not, and if you mention it, I'll deny it." He smiled nastily. "I had nothing to do with that man's death and I'm not going to get sucked in and left to take the blame."

"You really don't seem like the murdering type," she said mildly. "More the backstabbing-weasel type."

"You're too kind," he said sardonically.

"So, what alerted Mercier to the weakness in Eilers' empire anyway?" She forged ahead. "He seemed to have come here confident that there was an opportunity to chisel his way in."

"That, I honestly don't know." He shrugged. "Mercier walked through the front door a week or so before the grand opening and started asking about the business, the building, the mortgage. Stuff like that."

"Did he suspect that you and Eilers were at odds?" she sounded more curious than suspicious. "Is that why he came to you with such a bold request? Did he know you were manipulating Eilers?"

"All I ever did was make it very clear to Fred that there were distinct advantages to keeping me around," Graham sniffed. "Sometimes I have to remind him of that fact but that's all. It's just talk."

"So, you blackmail him to stop him from firing you?" Maiden reiterated.

"'Blackmail' is a misleading term," he protested. "All I did was point out two different options and let him choose. It's not as if I demanded payoffs, I simply informed him that I wouldn't keep his secrets for no good reason."

"Oh?" she quirked an enquiring brow.

"I have a talent for collecting secrets. And I keep them…most of the time." Graham smiled smugly.

"In exchange for things?" Her tone was only slightly dry.

"When the occasion calls for it." He said it as though it were perfectly reasonable. "Don't get the wrong idea about me, Miss Harlow. I'm not sending out nasty little notes with cut-and-pasted letters. If I know of something that I can use to my advantage, I'll do it. What's wrong with that?"

"It sounds risky," Maiden replied, opting to keep her opinions to herself as long as he was being so talkative. "Are there many others in your special archives?"

"Not really," he said. "No one you'd be likely to know anyway."

"What about Maddie Norris?" she asked.

"Mads?" He smiled wistfully. "No, that'd be a dream come true though. I'd love to find a way to twist her arm into just having coffee with me. She's cagey that woman, and she definitely has secrets, but I don't know what they are."

"Did you know her when she was married?" Maiden asked.

"No, that was years ago. I think she said his name was Dan or something." He shook his head. "The guy was a jerk though, she almost never talks about him. She did say that she married way too young and ended up having to start from scratch when it all fell apart."

"That's terrible," she said somberly.

"Yeah, but it happens," he replied. "She's a Detroit girl, raised to be tough. That's what she said, anyway."

Maiden considered that but her attention soon shifted back to Graham.

"Why were you hanging around the reception desk this morning?" she asked.

"Who said I was?" his eyes narrowed.

"That doesn't matter," she replied mildly. "Any particular reason why you were hanging around and then ran off when you did?"

"Yes, yes," he sighed and ran a hand over his head, tidying his combover. "I suspect that the head receptionist is letting certain people stay here at a reduced rate. They're either friends or relatives, I'm not sure yet. I was trying to find some more concrete information when I heard someone coming. I was afraid it was her, so I left."

"Why not take your suspicions to Maddie?" Maiden asked, knowing full well that he would have been looking for more 'useful' information. "Isn't she in charge of managing the staff?"

"I, um, didn't want to say anything until I was sure," he sounded as though the excuse had just occurred to him. "Why embarrass the poor girl needlessly?"

"Of course." Maiden glanced briefly heavenward as she got to her feet. "Thanks for your time, Mr. Harper."

"Certainly, always a delight," he said sarcastically but cleared his throat loudly when she reached the door. "By the way, if by some small chance it was Cooper Henderson that's been tattling like a school kid, he may have forgotten to mention that he had a very bitter fight with Mercier. I saw them arguing myself."

"Oh really?" She glanced back at him. "What about?"

"I wish I knew." He smiled unpleasantly. "I'd have already gone to him personally if I did."

Maiden said nothing as she walked out and made her way back down the dimly lit hall. After that distasteful discussion she decided the dismal dungeon-like atmosphere suited the shifty man perfectly.

She emerged into the foyer and looked around; it was empty. She peered into the bar but there was no sign of Cooper there either. Reminding herself that she couldn't put too much stock into anything that Graham told her, Maiden decided she could talk to Cooper about the alleged argument later.

She glanced down at her purse when her phone cheeped at her. She dug it out and grinned down at the message from David.

David

> Where are you? I've been alone in my office for half an hour, I thought you wanted some gratitude.

She bit her bottom lip to try and control her smile.

Maiden

> I thought you were busy?

David

> I'm willing to let myself be distracted.

Maiden

> I admire your dedication. Give me 10 minutes.

Chapter Twenty-Three

Maiden arrived at the police station assuring herself that she was actually there to tell him about Graham Harper's dodgy side-business. Anything else that might happen was purely coincidental.

She walked into the foyer and noticed that Nancy wasn't at the desk; that was kind of a relief as she felt her cheeks turning pink as she approached David's partially open door.

She glanced inside and frowned uncertainly when she saw his unoccupied desk. She walked in and set her purse on the nearest chair, she looked over sharply when she saw something looming in the corner of her eye. It was David, he must have heard her coming and tucked himself behind the door.

"Hey, Harlow." He smiled warmly as he stepped closer and wrapped his arms around her, lifting her against his chest. "What took you so long?"

She was too distracted by his firm hold to formulate an answer but he started kissing her which saved her the trouble. She entwined her arms around his neck and kissed him back.

He pushed the door shut with his foot and gently lowered her back onto her feet. His big hands slid up her back and pressed her close.

You are...tall...and much, much stronger than me. Even to herself she sounded like a besotted twit. She was just grateful that she hadn't blathered her observations aloud.

"I think you might actually like me a little." She smiled and nestled closer.

"I've only been thinking about you for the last four or five months. I can't believe you made me ask you to come over." He started carefully loosening the scarf around her neck. "Where were you anyway?"

"I was...um," she mumbled distractedly. "Oh yes! Was the file cabinet in Eilers' office open when you examined the room?"

"What?" His frown was in his voice. "I don't even know what a filing cabinet is right now."

"Sorry," she grinned and slid her hand over his clean-shaven jaw. "Don't worry about it, come here."

He obligingly lowered his head and kissed her deeply. Maiden let all her worries drift away and melted against him. After a few seconds, however, he broke the kiss and grasped her by the arms.

"Damn it, woman," he muttered under his breath and gave her a serious look. "Why did you ask that?"

"Hmm?" She'd wandered to a distant shore where time and space held no meaning, it took her a moment to find her way back. "Oh, forget it for now. It might not even matter, I'll think later."

"Maiden," he sighed. "Come on, why did you ask?"

"I think it's possible that Mercier was there that night trying to break into Eilers' files," she managed to scrape together enough common sense to reply.

"Why do you think that?" he asked cautiously but touched a kiss to her cheek.

"Graham Harper told me. Mercier asked him for some information that was kept in Eilers' office." She lifted her gaze to his. "He said he didn't tell you about it, and that he'd deny it if I did. He's a real creep, by the way, likes to find things to hold over other people's heads."

"How do you get mixed up in everything and manage to learn things that I don't?" He frowned down at her.

"I don't know, David," she sighed. "Do you really want to grumble about it *right now*?"

"No," he agreed and eased closer. "We've got maybe five more minutes before Nancy gets back from lunch and wanders down here to ask me something. Let's not waste it."

She grinned and sank her fingers into his thick hair as he kissed her again. A moment later she heard her phone ring. Her eyes cracked open and slid to her purse.

"Ignore it," David whispered and trailed his lips down to her throat, the good side.

"Good idea." She shut her eyes as he kissed her pale skin, and dismissed the concern that by tomorrow she'd look like she'd been strangled.

Her phone rang out, but then it immediately rang again. Her eyes opened when she felt David shift, he nuzzled his face against her ear and held her a little tighter.

"Just ignore it," he said again as he ran his big hand up and down her spine.

"I'll just put it on silent." She shivered against him and then somehow dredged up the self-control to reach over and fish her phone out of her purse.

She grumbled under her breath as she fumbled with it but then looked at the display and frowned uneasily.

"Oh, that's weird. It's Amelia Ferris, Tony's mom." She lifted her eyes to meet his gaze. "She almost never calls me...not unless something's wrong."

"Fine," he sighed tolerantly and started kissing her throat again. "But you can never get mad at me for taking a call at a bad time again."

"Yeah, that's gonna happen," she smirked and accepted the call. "Is that you Mrs. Ferris? Is everything okay?"

David was sliding his hands over her waist when her whole body tensed. He looked at her face and lifted his brows questioningly.

"Did you say someone's breaking into Tony's house?" she asked as she put it on speakerphone and met David's gaze. "Where are you?"

"In my apartment out back." Amelia sounded completely unflustered. "I just looked outside and saw some tall guy with a ski mask climbing in a window."

"Why are you calling *me*?" Maiden asked even as David released her and headed for the door.

"Vonny said you and the captain made up, I don't have *his* number," she said pragmatically. "You're with him aren't you?"

"Help is on the way, Mrs. Ferris," David said dryly. "Stay where you are and keep the doors locked."

"Thank you, honey," she chuckled and hung up.

***

They drove to one of Golden Glen's quaintest suburbs and parked outside Tony's ranch-style house. Unfortunately, they arrived in time to find only the aftermath of the break-in. Maiden knew they were too late when she saw Amelia walking out to meet them. Maiden's eyes flitted watchfully over the house as they headed towards her.

Tony had bought the place soon after he started working full-time, it particularly appealed to him because it already had a separate apartment built behind it. He loved his mother but had also hoped to get married someday, and having both a wife and his mom in the same house was never going to be a good idea. His forethought was especially justified as that wife could very possibly end up being Vonny.

It was a handsome red brick house. Tony was very proud of it; he kept the exterior clean and the lawn neatly mowed. Maiden was relieved to see that at least none of the street-facing windows appeared broken, hopefully the rest fared just as well.

"Are you okay, Mrs. Ferris?" Maiden touched her shoulder gently.

"Yes, sweetheart, I'm fine." She glanced back towards the house. "Whatever he was after, he didn't spend long looking for it."

"Did you see him leave?" David asked.

"I did." She nodded sagely and patted at her hair, she wore it in big, rolling waves and had long ago chosen to let the gray dapple its way through the dark, coarse strands. "He slipped out through the back door and skulked off around the far side of the house. He even left the door open, the neighbor's cat is probably in there already."

"Mr. Booties is better than a crook," Maiden pointed out.

"Not when he leaves scat on the kitchen floor." Amelia was unmoved.

"Did you notice if he was carrying anything when he left?" David strove to redirect the conversation. "The burglar, I mean. I can check out the cat's story later, if warranted."

"I didn't see anything...*on him!*" Her dark eyes widened and then narrowed on Maiden. "Did you fall down and hit your neck?"

"Oh!" Maiden gasped, remembering far too late that David had been fiddling with her scarf, she tugged it back into place even though it was pointless now. "I'm fine, Mrs. Ferris, thanks for your concern."

"Mm-hmm." A perfectly penciled brow arched knowingly, she slid her gaze to David and pointed a neon yellow acrylic nail at him. "Now

I'm no prude, but if you have any notions of heading further south, young man, she better have a couple of rings to pave the way."

A little part of Maiden died inside. She looked away and took a deep breath before she could collapse in mortification. She was vaguely aware of David pulling his notebook from his pocket.

"I'll take that under advisement, Mrs. Ferris. Thanks." He sounded calm, she had no idea if he *looked* calm as that would've risked eye contact. "Can we look inside the house now?"

"Yes, yes. Stop distracting me, please." She waved away their youthful nonsense and turned to lead the way.

"I told you not to answer the phone," David whispered to Maiden with a thoroughly amused chuckle before walking off after Amelia.

Maiden searched through the depths of her very being and found enough personal dignity to walk after them. She consoled herself that her parent's and Mrs. Ferris' old-fashioned watchfulness would always keep her feeling young if nothing else.

She forced her attention back to the burglary and what it might mean. Maiden doubted it was random; no more than the search of her own room had been.

By the time she'd reached the doorstep Amelia had just pulled out her spare key and slipped it in the lock.

"I called Tony too," she informed them as she gave it a twist and pushed the door open. "He's on his way."

"Let me go in first, just in case," David said as he stepped past and ran a careful and trained eye over the interior.

Maiden followed at a slight distance and looked the place over as well. It was an open plan layout that Tony usually kept very tidy. Today was no exception as far as the kitchen and dining area were concerned, it all looked completely undisturbed. But then her gaze swung to the corner that served as his living room. It was a mess.

The bookshelves had been emptied, their contents spilled onto the floor. The dinged-up but lovingly polished old credenza that he used as a liquor cabinet had also been searched and a couple of glasses were smashed in front of it.

Oddly, his watch was still sitting in the bowl on top where he left his wallet and keys when he was home. She stepped closer and noticed that there was even some cash still sitting in it too.

Maiden thought back to the search of her bedroom and recalled that nothing seemed to be missing there either. It was eerily similar to Charles Brown's murder, his car had also been searched but his valuables left behind.

These weren't random crimes and the person responsible wasn't after quick money. They were looking for something specific and, if the fate of Charles Brown was anything to go by, they were willing to kill for it. She was deeply grateful that Tony hadn't been home, and that Amelia was smart enough to stay locked in her apartment and call for help.

Maiden's uneasy thoughts were disrupted when she heard someone walk through the doorway behind them.

"What's going on in here?" Tony sounded the closest to furious that she'd ever witnessed from him.

"Hey, Tony." She glanced back at him and smiled kindly. "I'm sorry about this, but I don't think it's as bad as you might assume."

"Being robbed isn't that bad?" He gave her an unimpressed look, but his shoulders slumped when he saw the mess all over his floor. "Aw man, who would do this? This has always been such a quiet street."

"I don't know if anything was actually taken," Maiden assured him, giving him a quick hug as he walked closer. "It looks like my room did, everything's a mess but nothing's really missing."

"Are you absolutely sure you aren't missing anything?" David gave her a look.

"Nothing I've noticed, I looked around after breakfast and everything seemed to be there. I have a little bit of jewelry, and none of it was touched." She turned back to Tony and pointed to the bowl. "This wasn't random. Your money and watch are still here."

"Then what is it?" he grumbled and rubbed his forehead as though it ached.

Before she could answer, David's phone rang. He pulled it out and looked at the screen before answering.

"Hey Nancy, what's up?" he asked.

"Who the heck is Nancy?" Amelia gave Maiden an irate look.

"She's the receptionist at the police station, Mom." Tony put a discreet finger to his lips. "And she's very nice."

"Right," David sighed and shook his head. "Send Smith and Parker over. And then send Briggs and Spencer over to Tony Ferris' house, there's been a break-in here too."

"'Too'?" Maiden asked curiously as he hung up and turned to her.

"Yeah, Nancy just took a call from Harlow House." He kept his tone deliberately unrevealing. "Apparently Vonny's room has been searched as well. But everyone is safe."

He'd barely finished speaking when Tony's phone rang. He looked at it and then at them.

"It's Vonny," he said and started towards his bedroom. "I'll take this in the other room, she'll be pretty upset."

Maiden noticed Amelia roll her eyes but deliberately ignored it. She had no idea how well the two women got along now that Vonny was dating Amelia's son, and she certainly didn't want to get in the middle of it. She quickly returned to the most pressing problem.

Maiden thought about the various break-ins and what they all had in common. She set the matter of Charles Brown's car aside for the moment, that had been a murderous confrontation, it was different.

There had to be a relevant thread that tied this latest rash of searches together. It didn't take long to narrow it down to her, Tony and Von having all been at the Highland Hounds' concert and having spoken with Sean Dowling.

Maiden was more intrigued than frightened at this point, she wasn't even terribly angry anymore. Something was going on and it involved her and her friends; she wanted to know what it was. She sank into thought and started replaying the night of the concert. The sights, sounds and even the smells drifted back to her as she sifted through the sequence of events.

David had been surveying the carnage on the floor but turned when Tony emerged from his room.

"Well, Von's okay," he said. "She's just a bit shaken up."

David nodded and started to say something to Maiden when Amelia, who'd been watching her as she slipped into her memory, stopped him.

"Just wait a minute, honey," she whispered, her eyes were fixed on Maiden. "She's working on something."

Maiden was distantly aware of David and Tony watching her as she stared across the room without really seeing it. She folded her arms loosely and tapped her fingertips lightly on her sleeves.

"The concert ended...we went into the reception room and bought CDs. Stacey was there," she murmured aloud as she pictured the scene clearly in her mind. "I looked over at the band and Ewan was posing with a couple of women...that may have been when he spotted me...we gave up and went to the restaurant...Sean came in...and then—"

The CDs, she thought to herself. *Sean had left the room with them and was gone for a while.* She clutched the strap of her purse, knowing that her CD was still tucked inside it. She had been so distracted since the concert that she'd never bothered pulling it out and putting it away. She felt herself start to smile.

"Souvenirs…" she whispered. "Come to the next show as my guests…Hey, Tony."

"Yeah?" he replied cautiously when she seemed to awaken and shifted her gaze to him.

"See if your Highland Hounds CD was stolen," she said. "The one Sean Dowling took to have signed by the band."

Tony frowned at that but obligingly went to the shelf where all his other CDs had been rifled and spilled onto the floor. She flicked Vonny a text as he dug through and searched carefully. A few moments later he glanced back at her.

"I think it's gone," he said.

"So is Von's." She smiled down at her phone when her sister's reply came through, she glanced at David. "Well, that's interesting. We should head back."

"What?!" Amelia demanded indignantly. "You can't just do your crazy mind-jabber and then walk out. What's this CD business? I saw your face, Maiden. You know something about what's going on!"

"It's too soon to say, Mrs. Ferris." She smiled apologetically and gave her a quick peck on the cheek. "I'll have to think about it a bit more."

With that she grabbed David's hand and dragged him towards the door. David resisted long enough to assure Tony that the other officers would arrive soon and then followed her out.

Maiden almost ran to his car and climbed inside. David eyed her curiously as he sat behind the wheel. She looked anxiously back at the house as she put on her seatbelt.

"Are we going?" she asked expectantly.

"What's up, Harlow?" He arched a brow. "I thought I'd be having to drag *you* out of there."

"Just drive to the next block please," she said quietly and peered at Tony's house again. "Mrs. Ferris has eyes like a hawk and I guarantee she's watching us. She's also going to tell Mom about the hickeys for sure now."

"You're not a teenager." He grinned at her. "What's she going to do? Ground you?"

"No, she'll tease the heck out of me and start dropping enormous hints *again*," she sighed and shook her head. "Would you hurry up already!"

"Hurry up with what exactly?" He gave her a wry look.

"Drive to the next block!" She felt herself blush when she realized what she'd said. "Honestly! The stupid faux pas were supposed to stop once we were dating!"

David managed to start the car and pull away while also enjoying a hearty laugh at her expense. He obligingly crept down the street and pulled over again as soon as they were out of sight.

He leaned back and folded his arms over his chest, silently refusing to go any further. Maiden, who quickly recovered from her embarrassment as something more pivotal arose to get her attention, met his gaze and smiled faintly as she set her purse on her lap.

"Sean Dowling was some kind of crook, right?" she asked as she opened the bag and started digging around inside. "Which suggests that Charles Brown might've been too."

"Yes, it looks that way, but from what we've found they were small potatoes." David watched her. "They were likely moving merchandise for others, it would fit with the tour manager gig. They could move around and leave town quickly without raising many eyebrows."

"So they spent a lot of time in America?" she glanced at him.

"Yes. A lot more than the band did," he confirmed with a nod. "So, what are you getting at?"

"Sean was up to something," she obligingly explained. "He approached us the night of the concert and really made an effort to chat with us. Yeah, he flirted with me, but I wasn't interested, and it showed. For a total stranger to not take the hint and keep working the room isn't impossible, but it's weird all things considered. When the conversation was drying up he offered to get our CDs signed."

"Yeah, we know that," he said. "Why ask Tony and Vonny if theirs were missing? And why *are* they missing?"

"I suspect that Sean and Charles were here for something other than the show at the Addison," she said as she opened the case and set the disk aside. "I'm not sure why, but I think he slipped something into one of our CDs."

David watched as she carefully prized the case apart. Maiden smiled as she pulled out a folded piece of paper that had been tucked between the tray that held the disk and the glossy back inlay.

"What have we here?" she murmured to herself as she unfolded it.

"Well?" he prompted when she just stared down at it. "What is it?"

She glanced at him and smiled as she turned it for him to see. "A treasure map."

He scowled pensively as he took the paper and looked it over. Maiden leaned closer so she could still see it too. It was a crudely hand drawn sketch of a rectangular space filled with winding tunnels that ended in smaller rooms. One of them, the tiniest of all, was marked with an X.

"Weird," he pondered aloud. "I wonder what it leads to...and where it's located."

"No idea what it leads to but, as for where, there's only one place I can think of that links Ulysses Mercier to the Highland Hounds," she said in a pleased tone, David looked at her.

"The Old Chateau," he said.

"Specifically, Claudia Arnaud's secret cellar beneath it." Maiden couldn't help smiling in anticipation.

Chapter Twenty-Four

They arrived at Eilers' Arms and headed straight for the side alley that they'd snuck out of the other night. Maiden suspected that whoever was trying to locate the secret cellar was looking at the outside perimeter because it was a safer starting point than trying to sneak inside. It seemed unlikely that an outer entrance would've gone unnoticed when the render was applied to the walls, but it would be foolish not to at least take a quick look.

As they skirted down the side of the large building she noticed a few more places where the blue render had been scraped away. Each test site revealed only more unyielding stonework.

She and David approached the backlot watchfully; everything seemed peaceful and normal. When they were about to turn the corner, however, they heard a noise from behind the neighboring brewery. David grasped her arm and eased her back a step.

Maiden looked over but saw nothing except sturdy crates and empty kegs in the slowly growing shadows. He motioned for her to stay put and headed over to check it out.

She watched him for a few seconds as he peered closer and then stepped behind the building and out of sight. Maiden bit her lip and pondered what she ought to do.

It was possible that they'd heard a scuttling rat or something like that. The thought of rats always creeped her out but she hoped that's all it was. A part of her also wanted to be closer in case David needed help, not that she was sure she could do much. Either way, she was feeling a little too tucked away there in the alley all by herself.

She decided to wait closer to the kitchen door and maybe have a look around until David got back. Maiden rounded the corner and froze. Her gasp caught in her throat as she stared at a set of feet poking out from between the dumpsters.

"David!" her voice was barely a squeak as it struggled to escape a throat that was constricted with fear. She looked around frantically but didn't see him.

She turned back and took a steadying breath; she needed to check. It wasn't likely, but it was possible that whoever was lying there could still be alive and needed help. She willed her legs to start moving and crept close enough to peer around the first dumpster's edge.

It was Harris Clark, the Highland Hound's fiddler, he was lying on his stomach with his face turned towards her, there was a lot of blood on his head and on the ground underneath it. She gasped again, louder this time and found her voice.

"David!" she shouted as she stumbled back a few steps.

He ran back from behind the brewery and quickly spotted her. Before he could reach her, however, someone darted out from behind the second dumpster and grabbed her purse. He was dressed all in black and wore a ski mask that covered his entire face. The man gave her a hard push that knocked her to the ground and ran off. David was beside her a moment later and helped her to her feet.

"I'm okay," she said before he could ask and pointed off to the far corner of the hotel where the man had run to. "But he's got the CD!"

"Stay here," David said firmly and took off after him.

Maiden pulled in a deep breath and watched as David ducked around the corner. Her hip was a bit sore from where she landed but it was easy enough to ignore, particularly as she stared back at Harris Clark's prone form. A cursory glance at the bloodstain on the side of the dumpster made it clear that it was the murder weapon.

She wondered how long Harris had been there and what he'd been up to when he was killed. It couldn't have happened too long ago or someone from the kitchen would have found him already. Maiden wasn't the best at dealing with blood, her arms felt weak and tingly. She looked away and did her best to fill her lungs.

A moment later she heard dirt and gravel crunching underfoot and smiled with relief when she saw David walking back. He was safe and also holding her purse.

"You got it back," she said happily as he handed it to her. "Thank you!"

"He dumped it." David folded his arms and glanced around again. "I got there in time to see a black car with no plates drive off."

"The CD is gone," Maiden said as she took a quick look at the contents of her bag.

"I know, I already checked for it," he said. "Interesting that he knew where to find it."

"And that he was here waiting for us," she mused. "Or he was watching us outside of Tony's house and called someone who was here already."

"It's almost as if there's three or four of them involved," David said dryly.

"Well, three now," Maiden replied as she gestured towards Harris' body.

"Mm." David stepped away as he pulled out his phone. "I'll call this in."

Maiden waited until his back was turned before sidling over enough to see the section of wall she'd found damaged before. It looked the same, and the areas around it looked untouched. She'd been hoping that whoever had done it would have come back and tried again.

They know by now that this approach won't work. They know that they have to get inside...how do they plan to manage that? Maiden was frowning at the wall, silently begging it to tell her its secrets when David walked back.

"Okay, the team is on the way," he murmured. "And I've put out a call for the remaining members of the Highland Hounds to be brought in."

"Assuming they aren't on their way out of town right now." She rubbed her sore hip absently.

"Are you sure you're all right?" he asked as he touched her arm gently.

"Yeah, just a little shaken up," she said as she glanced down at the body again. "I'm glad to have my purse back though."

"It's just a shame that the map is gone," David sighed.

"It doesn't matter." Maiden assured him. "I've memorized it."

He gave her a smiling look and shook his head. He started studying the area and writing a few notes. When they heard sirens approaching he glanced up.

"You might as well go home for now," he said and ran the backs of his fingers down her cheek. "This is going to take up the rest of my evening, I'm sorry."

"I'll cope," she replied and then rolled her eyes. "Although, I'll have to deal with Vonny...and Mom and Dad. Seriously, any word on what happened to Eilers? I'm going to be pounced on the instant I walk through the door and I need something to distract from my throat."

"The amount of poison in his system was minimal, he'll recover." David said. "That's all I can give you. Feel free to try and tempt more out of me, but wait and do it tomorrow when I have more time."

"Very generous," she laughed and stepped back as she pulled out her phone. "I'll ask Von to come and get me."

***

The following morning Maiden had taken refuge in the office and basked in the peace and quiet. Much of the previous afternoon and evening had been spent listening to Vonny complain about her bedroom being broken into.

While acknowledging that she wasn't the only one to suffer such an indignity, the guy had smashed her bedside lamp—which she seemed to think was a priceless work of art with a bulb. Maiden knew for a fact that her sister had bought it for $10 off the clearance rack, but it was still worth complaining about for hours.

And as much as she'd dreaded listening to her parents being annoying about David's little displays of affection, the upside was that Gloria owned far heavier make-up than Maiden did. This she shared along with the sage advice to always leave a man guessing, not gasping.

Now as Maiden sat at the table in the office with a generous layer of concealer on her throat, she was able to think about the significance of yesterday's events. The attempt to poison Eilers was curious, mostly because he wasn't fed a lethal dose. The far more effective attack on Harris Clark was more disturbing.

It all seemed so haphazard, so seat-of-the-pants. Why leave Harris' body beside the dumpsters? They were sitting right there, why not hide him inside one? She suspected that they'd stumbled upon the crime almost immediately after it was committed.

So far they had four corpses on their hands and, with the exception of Charles Brown, they all seemed to have been killed without much forethought. His was the only murder that didn't feel improvised.

It appeared that his killer had gotten him to sit in the backseat and then shot him. The car was most likely searched after Brown was dead, unless he'd been somewhere else and caught the killer in the act. Could that have been why he was murdered? Maybe he surprised whoever was searching his car.

Maiden was again chilled to think what might have happened if she or her friends had been home when the break-ins occurred.

She sighed and touched the end of her pencil to her cheek as she studied the map she'd attempted to recreate. Drawing wasn't her specialty but her crude efforts actually did a decent job of recreating the original that had been stolen from her purse.

She stared down at the rectangular space and the narrow tunnels that wound through it. It didn't look like a typical root cellar, it looked like a cramped and twisty place that was used for storing ill-gotten goods, not turnips and potatoes.

"So..." she tapped the eraser on her chin, "how do we actually get in? This makes it look like there could be two entrances...I wonder."

A knock on the back door got her attention. She glanced up and turned the paper over before going to peek through the curtain. Her stomach did a happy little flip when she saw David smiling at her. She unlocked the door and pulled it open.

"Good morning." He leaned in and dropped a kiss on her lips.

Maiden blinked and felt herself smile shyly. She was still getting used to the casual displays of affection but he seemed to have transitioned seamlessly. She did have the presence of mind to invite him in and offer him a cup of coffee.

He settled into the chair beside hers and accepted the cup she set in front of him with a nod of thanks and a less than subtle look at the papers on the table. Maiden stacked her arms casually across the top page as he started to reach for it. David met her gaze and smiled.

"How did everything go yesterday?" she asked, happy enough to make him share a little information before giving him the map.

"It was interesting. Doc Jenkins confirmed the cause of death was trauma to the skull, it looks like he was bashed against the dumpster a few times. Not something that happens by accident," he murmured. "And the remaining three members of the Hounds are conspicuously missing. I have warrants out for all of them and the train and bus stations are being watched."

"What about the car they were driving?" She chewed at her lip.

"We're doing our best," he said. "There are a lot of black cars in this town. In any event, they won't get far. We've sent word to all the surrounding towns along with their pictures. We'll find them."

Maiden was satisfied with that for the moment. She obligingly turned over the page she'd been working on. She slid it towards him and rested her chin in her hand as he studied it for a moment.

"You're easily the coolest woman I know." He smiled at the carefully rendered drawing and sipped from his mug. "You make good coffee too."

"I didn't make it, Vonny did," she admitted.

"Good. It's actually terrible," he said without looking up.

"Nice," Maiden laughed but then gave him a wide-eyed, hopeful look. "Do you happen to have an original blueprint of the Old Chateau?"

He glanced up at her very patiently and quirked a dark brow. "No, of course I don't."

"Fine, do you have Cooper Henderson's phone number?" she asked with a long-suffering sigh.

David pulled his notebook from his pocket and flicked back a dozen or so pages. He scanned his notes and then held them out for her to see.

"Any particular reason why you want it?" he asked as she picked up her phone and started dialing.

"Of course there is," she said as though it were a foolish question and held a finger to her lips to shush him as it started to ring.

"It's a good thing you're hot, Harlow," he said but kept quiet when she started talking.

"Cooper? Is that you?" she asked eagerly. "It's Maiden. Yes, listen, do you know if the footprint of the hotel is larger than the original Chateau?...Where? Perfect. I'll come visit you later and explain, but don't mention this to *anyone* else. Promise? Okay, see you soon."

"You really do have many guys for many things, don't you?" David teased as she hung up.

"Looks like it." She smiled sweetly. "Don't worry, you'll be the only guy doing *your* job."

He had been about to take a sip of his coffee but quickly set it down as he struggled to hold in his startled laughter. She noticed he turned a very faint shade of red and mercifully veered the conversation back on course.

"We need to find the entrance to the old cellar. According to the map there are two ways in." She pointed them out on the drawing. "But I suspect no one's found them yet because they've been built over. If we find the areas that have been covered up, we stand a chance of finding our way in."

"So what did Cooper have to say about it?" he asked.

"He said he knows one part of the hotel that definitely isn't original." She met his gaze and held it. "The kitchen, which is very near to where we found Harris Clark's body."

"So, assuming this place is real, someone may have guessed that they need access to the kitchen to get to it," he mused as he studied the drawing again. "What about this other entrance? Where would that come out?"

"I'm not entirely sure," Maiden said slowly. "But I'm starting to think that Ulysses Mercier might have been looking for it too."

"Why?" He shifted his warm but watchful gaze back to her.

"I met him the night of the grand opening." She stared into space as she thought through the encounter. "He was looking at the walls around the staircase, knocking on them. When I asked why he made some dumb excuse. But now I wonder if he was looking for that other entrance."

"You could have mentioned this sooner," he said flatly.

"You could've accepted my invitation and been there yourself," she replied similarly. "Why was it that you refused, by the way? A leaky faucet or something equally harrowing? I remember it was something far too critical to wait for a single evening."

"It was nothing that flimsy, thank you." He grinned ruefully and rubbed his face with his hands. "Anyway, water under the bridge, right?"

She was laughing at him when they both heard the front door open. Maiden stood and went to the doorway that led to reception. She looked out into the foyer and stiffened when she saw Ewan Fraser walking cautiously towards the desk.

She glanced back long enough to give David a worried look and then forced her expression to calm. David was already on his feet and edging closer as she stepped out behind the desk and eyed the wary newcomer.

Chapter Twenty-Five

"**M**r. Fraser?" she said deliberately loud enough to alert David. "What brings you here? Tired of the Addison?"

Ewan winced and glanced around sharply as he motioned for her to keep her voice down. An instant later a charming smile graced his features. He came and stood on the other side of the desk, his smile widening as he looked at her admiringly.

"Hello again, beautiful lass." He rested his elbows on the desk, leaning towards her a little. "I was hoping you'd be in."

"Really?" She smiled a little, aware that David had tucked himself behind the door. "And why is that, Mr. Fraser?"

"Call me Ewan." His smile grew warmer. "I'm caught in a bit of a tricky situation, to be truthful. I'm hoping you'll help me. I was just wondering...do you happen to still have that CD from our concert the other night? The one Sean got us to sign for you?"

"Oh." She widened her eyes ingenuously as she pretended to think it over, apparently he wasn't aware of the theft last night. "Well, I haven't listened to it yet. I'll have to try and think where it could be."

"Take your time, lass." His smile was a bit strained as he glanced uncomfortably at the front door. "I need to have a quick look at it, that's all."

"That's a funny thing to ask," she mused. "You must have access to plenty of copies, what's so special about mine?"

"As I said, it's an odd predicament," he said with forced lightness and waved it away. "Trust me, beautiful, you're best off not knowing too much about it. In any case, if I can just have a quick peek I'll be on my way."

"What's the hurry, Fraser?"

Ewan's eyes flew to the connecting door when David's deep and distinctly displeased voice cut through the peaceful morning air. David stepped out from the office and eyed him coldly.

"Oh, McAlister, the Scottish captain. Lovely." Ewan's eyes widened and he eased back slightly. "I didn't realize you were working here, didn't mean to interrupt."

"I wouldn't exactly say I was 'working'," David murmured as he slid his arm around Maiden's waist and pulled her snugly against his side.

"Ah." Ewan edged away a bit further as his gaze flitted uneasily between them. "I wasn't aware the wind was blowing in that direction. Apologies for any offense."

"Why the interest in my CD, Mr. Fraser?" Maiden asked nicely, ignoring his hopeless attempt to sidle away.

"Oh nothing, lass. Nothing really." He tried to shrug it off. "Don't even worry yourself over it."

"You realize that we've been looking for you and your charming friends?" David muttered.

"Have you?" Ewan effected a surprised look. "I'm sorry, Captain, I had no idea."

"Step inside, Fraser." David's eyes were as cold as his tone.

Ewan walked around the desk and into the office rather sheepishly. David pointed him towards a chair and stood alert and watchful as he settled into it.

Maiden smoothly snapped up the map, folded it a few times, and tucked it into her pocket.

"Well?" David prompted. "What have you got to say for yourself?"

Ewan lowered his gaze to his hands, which were loosely clasped on the table, and said nothing. Maiden came and sat opposite him. When the silence stretched on she felt her curiosity rise.

"You were the one that searched my room," she said, it wasn't a question. "You followed me after we spoke at the Addison. Are you also the one that searched Von's room? And broke into Tony's house?"

"No!" He looked up sharply. "I had nothing to do with any of it!"

"You definitely searched my room," she continued with no real trace of anger. "But you couldn't take the CD because I still had it on me."

Ewan just shook his head and kept his mouth resolutely shut.

"Which one of you actually killed Sean Dowling?" David spoke up. "You probably all had a hand in beating him up, but who actually finished him off?"

Ewan shut his eyes and sighed softly, he looked resigned.

"It wasn't that straightforward," he said quietly. "And I never touched Sean. I wasn't involved that deep in any of it."

"Except for following me home and breaking into my apartment," Maiden pulled a face.

"I saw an opportunity to maybe find the CD before the others did," he said by way of apology. "I knew I'd never get a look in once they had it."

"What do you think Sean hid inside?" she asked.

"I have no idea," he said. "I think Braden and Arran know, but they won't say a word to us."

"It's not 'us' anymore. Harris Clark is dead and you can save us all a lot of time by not pretending that you didn't know that already,"

David told him plainly. "What makes you think the other two know more about Sean's business?"

"They got his phone and read through all his messages," Ewan mumbled down at his hands.

"Right." David pulled out his notebook and pen. "Start at the beginning."

Ewan seemed to accept the hopelessness of his situation. He took a deep breath and shut his eyes briefly before facing David again.

"Well...none of us were happy with how Sean and Charles were running the tour. They'd sometimes send us to far-flung places to perform in front of small audiences. There wasn't as much money being made and we were all starting to feel the pinch." Ewan sat back a little and folded his arms over his chest. "We'd started discussing firing them and getting a better management team, but that's not the easiest prospect mid-tour so we weren't rushing into it. And then one day Braden decided to slip into Sean's room and have a look around. He found a lot of money hidden in his luggage. He didn't tell us at first, but he started following Sean and Charles around to find out where the money was coming from."

"And did he find out?" David asked.

"To a point. At first he suspected they were skimming profits and pocketing more than they were due. But as Braden followed them he realized they were doing side jobs; pickups and deliveries," Ewan explained. "That made Braden mad enough to tell the rest of us. He said we were being bankrupted so Sean and Charles would have an excuse to go to these random places for their own benefit."

"That would be annoying," David conceded. "So, what did you decide to do about it?"

"We just wanted what we were owed." Ewan held his hands up to ward off any misconceptions. "But Sean was acting strangely about this town in particular, so was Charles, but it was Sean that booked the hotels and such. He had us get here a week before the show and that's unusual, it also wastes money and the money wasn't exactly pouring in. We guessed that the lads were onto something big this time, and we wanted a piece of it."

"What does 'acting strangely' mean exactly?" Maiden asked.

"Furtive. Disappearing and coming back without any explanation. And then Charles said he was going out to meet someone and ended up getting himself shot." Ewan exhaled slowly. "That threw a scare into me, to be honest. Braden and Arrin weren't so fainthearted though."

"Are you claiming that none of you had anything to do with Charles Brown's murder?" David asked skeptically.

"We certainly did *not*!" Ewan said emphatically. "That came out of nowhere as far as I'm concerned. I honestly suspected Sean at first but it shook him up pretty badly; he was very cautious after that."

"More than you'd expect considering that his business partner was killed?" Maiden stroked her thumb thoughtfully along her jaw.

"Yes, lass." Ewan inclined his head. "He was in a state, sure, he would be. But he was frightened, not sad."

"Who was Brown supposed to be meeting?" David asked.

"He never said. And meanwhile, Braden was putting the pieces together but he was keeping a lot of it to himself. Then one night he told us we needed to get Sean drunk and keep him busy, so we did." Ewan shrugged and ran a hand through his long hair. "Braden took the opportunity to swipe his phone and read enough of his messages to know that he and Charles had been doing a big job for a big client, but Braden didn't tell us who it was."

"Do you expect anyone to believe that?" Maiden asked candidly.

"Not really, no," Ewan acknowledged.

"What's this big client's name then?" David asked.

"Dugan, James Dugan," Ewan admitted quietly.

The effect was immediate, on David at least. He pulled in a deep breath and released it in a hiss. Maiden turned to him with an inquiring look but he just shook his head. She pulled a face and thumbed through the pages of her memory. She knew she'd read the name in the newspaper but she mustn't have taken particular notice of it. Nothing was coming to her straight away.

She had to push deeper to recall who he was. She was sure she knew the name, and as she thought harder she started to recall that he was bad news. Maybe he'd been involved in some shady dealings? And then it came to her.

She'd read about the arrest of James Dugan in the Golden Glen Gazette about two years ago. It had been big news locally because the man had allegedly had ties to their quaint little town. But after he'd been arrested, the fervor died down and she'd forgotten about it.

Dugan had been in trouble with the law many times and in many places, but on this occasion he was arrested on several counts of grand larceny and embezzlement. Maiden searched her memory further and caught snatches of the article, Dugan had been arrested in Stanton, the city where David had worked as a detective for ten years before moving to Golden Glen. His immediate and strong reaction started to make sense.

The article said that Dugan had evaded the police for years until an unnamed accomplice sold him out.

An unnamed accomplice...about two years ago.

"Oh!" Her eyes were wide as she turned to David with a look of sudden understanding. "Dugan...yeah, okay."

He gave her a meaningful look and subtly tapped a finger against his lips. She nodded and fell silent even though her mind was racing.

David had told her that Ulysses Mercier was crooked and had only been running free because he'd turned on some former associates, could one of them have been the infamous James Dugan?

If that was about two years ago, it would also have coincided with the last time Cooper had heard that the Old Chateau was being covertly used. Months later, Eilers bought and refurbished the Old Chateau and then, seemingly out of nowhere, Mercier turned up and tried to drive Eilers out of his own company.

If Dugan was the link between Mercier and the Hounds' managers, what did it mean? Could Dugan have wanted revenge on Mercier for turning against him? Perhaps he found out that Mercier was closing in on the Chateau and sent Sean and Charles to get there first. Perhaps he told them to stop Mercier more permanently. But now they were all dead.

Could Mercier have killed Charles Brown? It was possible, if what Ewan was saying was true, Mercier seemed to have the strongest motive. He was also reputedly a heartless narcissist looking to gain a fortune, perhaps he wouldn't balk at murdering a rival.

Of course, it was also possible that Sean could have had a falling out with Brown and then killed him. Perhaps he got greedy and wanted to run the whole operation himself. Ewan thought Sean had been pretty shaken up by the murder, but maybe that was because he was guilty.

The theories were rapidly springing to life in Maiden's mind, until David distracted her when he spoke again.

"What led up to Sean Dowling's murder?" he asked.

"The concert that night. We had no reason to stay here any longer, we were supposed to move on to the next town." Ewan fidgeted and shifted in his seat. "But then Sean came and got us to sign some CDs for 'friends of his'. He'd never done that before and any strange behavior immediately caught our notice."

"And what did you do about it?" David asked as he jotted a few notes.

"Nothing, we were stuck in front of a fairly substantial lineup of fans. Typical that the snake would do his slithering the one time we were too busy to watch him. All I know is that he turned down the hall towards the stairs, not back to the bar. He had to have gone to his room, and he was there too long; we knew something was up. When he finally went back, Braden snuck away and checked on what he was doing. He saw him hovering around Miss Harlow and her friends and watched him hand the CDs over."

"Why lie about Maiden?" David cut in with barely concealed anger.

"To be honest," Ewan shifted uncomfortably, "Braden did that to throw you lot off the scent of the other lass. He said the other girl was smiling at Sean and seemed *really* friendly, he'd most likely slipped something to her planning to get it back later."

"What did he say about Maiden?" he pressed.

"Uh...nothing worth repeating in front of the lady." Ewan's gaze drifted briefly over Maiden's face and full bust before he smiled faintly at her. "Let's just say he thought it was unlikely."

"Very astute." David said dryly. "So, he claimed that Maiden and Dowling were all over each other to stop us investigating Vonny?"

"That was the idea." Ewan nodded. "It was only intended to buy some time. But then the numpty couldn't find the other lass. Sean mentioned that he'd met a girl whose family ran an inn or something in town, but he didn't say which one. We got him drunk that night and he started talking about staying behind while we went on to the next gig. He claimed he'd met a girl and wanted a bit more time to...well, yeah. But we knew it was a coverup for whatever he was really doing here."

"And then you beat him to death and threw him out a window?" David asked coolly.

"No! I swear to you that's not what happened!" Ewan sat up straighter and shook his head vehemently. "We helped Sean upstairs to his room and Braden finally came out with everything. He told Sean that we knew what he and Charles had been up to and he needed to give us a cut since we'd certainly played a part in their little game."

"That obviously didn't go well," Maiden said.

"No, lass, it didn't." Ewan shook his head. "Sean denied everything and said we were imagining things. He said he didn't need a bunch of mediocre musicians whining about their bookings and told us we weren't good enough to pull in a bigger audience. Well, we all got a bit angry at that point. We'd had a lot more success before he and Charles took over managing us.

"Braden threw the first punch and then Harris joined in; he was a hot-tempered fool. Sean didn't stand much chance against two of them. He took some nasty blows and then fell and hit his head on the bedside table."

"So, you're claiming his death was an accident?" David asked impassively.

"Not really." Ewan pulled a face. "The idiots weren't thinking clearly and I doubt they'd have backed off either way. They were too drunk and stupid to consider the consequences. But I didn't touch him, neither did Arran. He's too smart for that."

"How did Sean end up in the alley?" Maiden asked.

"That was Arran's ingenious idea," Ewan said sarcastically as he rolled his eyes. "'We'll make it look like an accident', he said. 'Get the money and get out of town'. Well and good until you lot started sniffing around too much."

"Who broke into Vonny's room?" Maiden asked curiously.

"I did," he finally admitted. "Once Braden said that you and the other lass were sisters, I realized that I'd found the right house but searched the wrong room. Stacey recognized the man with you as a local postal worker. But she told Arran about it; he tracked him down and searched his house."

"Why didn't you turn the others in?" David tapped his pen on the page he'd been writing on. "If you claim to be innocent, despite knowing what they were up to, why shield them?"

"At first it was because they're my friends. And I felt like the money was owing to us." He sighed heavily and scratched his jaw. "But then things started getting really serious, and really nasty. Arran and Braden in particular. They took charge and started calling the shots, keeping information to themselves, not saying where they were going or what they were doing. It was all getting a bit sinister, so I just stayed quiet and left them to it."

"Uh-huh." David sounded as unconvinced as he looked. "So what happened to Harris Clark?"

"Well, after Sean died, Arran took his phone and wouldn't let anyone but Braden see what any of the messages said. I took exception to that but kept my mouth shut. Harris didn't." Ewan rubbed his eyes. "He started complaining a lot. Braden told him to back off or we'd say that *he* was the one that killed Sean. Harris was furious but he did shut up. That little victory gave Arran and Braden the confidence to be even more heavy handed. It became pretty obvious that there wouldn't be an even split of whatever was found."

"So, you started looking on your own?" Maiden surmised.

"I hadn't really planned to," he said. "But when you came back to the theater, I started to wonder if we hadn't gotten the wrong impression after all, so I took a chance. Sorry, love."

"You still haven't explained the murder of Harris Clark," David murmured, glancing up from his notes.

"Harris wasn't willing to sit in the backseat and wait for them to toss him some scraps; he was in it up to his neck and wanted a full share." Ewan wet his lips and clasped his hands together tightly. "They must've got tired of dealing with him. He'd followed them to that crazy blue hotel; I went along but hung back. Braden was poking around at the walls, I don't know what he was trying to do, but Harris charged in. They started arguing and...Braden threw him against the dumpster pretty hard, a couple of times. When I saw him drag his body behind it, I knew he'd lost whatever mind he had left, so I ran."

"Where was Arran?" David asked watchfully.

"Not sure." Ewan shook his head. "But Braden got a phone call when Harris and I turned up, it was probably him."

Maiden and David exchanged a look but neither mentioned aloud that Arran had probably just finished the break-in at Tony's and was telling Braden that Maiden had the map in her purse.

"What about Ulysses Mercier?" David flicked Ewan a quick look.

"What's that?" Ewan almost laughed. "It sounds like a brand of lager."

"It *was* a notoriously unscrupulous businessman," David said mildly. "You're claiming not to know him?"

"I'm telling you for a fact that I've never heard of anyone by that name," Ewan said without hesitation. "Why ask? What's he got to do with Sean?"

"Who's to say?" David replied enigmatically. "Anything to add before I take you into custody?"

"Is that necessary?" He winced. "I'll cooperate in any way I can. I'll happily testify against Braden and Arran...better than waiting for them to come after me as well."

"That'll help, I'm sure," David said as he gestured for him to stand. "But you're too deeply involved to ignore."

"Lovely." He pulled a face but didn't argue as he pushed to his feet.

Chapter Twenty-Six

Maiden rode along to the police station and waited while David had Ewan locked up. The man wasn't thrilled but even he had to realize that he was safer there than outside waiting for his remaining bandmates to pick him off.

They drove to Eilers' Arms and went inside looking for Cooper. Maiden went straight to the doorway of the bar and spotted him standing behind the counter doing a crossword puzzle. Cooper glanced up and smiled as they approached.

"Maiden, finally!" He closed his book and chucked it under the bar. He squinted inquiringly at David. "Is this the cop you're dating?"

"Captain McAlister," David said. "Head of the Golden Glen police department."

"Well, you snagged yourself quite an impressive catch," he replied.

"I certainly think I did," Maiden chuckled.

"I was talking to him." Cooper gave her a wink. "So why'd you ask me about the size of the Chateau?"

"Are many of the internal walls here original?" she asked rather than explain outright.

"Yeah, some of them. These ones are." He gestured to indicate the entire bar, "So is the restaurant and some of the downstairs conference rooms. And all of Graham's office, of course."

"What about the main staircase?" Maiden pressed. "Was that walled in before the renovations?"

"No, it would have been when it was originally built, but half of that wall had collapsed." He shook his head. "Eilers replaced it."

"So, in theory, it's an empty space under there?" David asked.

"It's not really a theory," Cooper said patiently. "It's a walled in staircase. We probably should have used it for storage or something, it's a shame to have that space being wasted."

"Cooper." Maiden hopped onto the stool in front of him and held his gaze intently. "Do you have a blueprint or floorplan of the Old Chateau?"

"Yeah." He rubbed his chin and then a hopeful glint lit his eyes. "Do you actually want to see it? No one ever does!"

"Yes please right now if you don't mind!" It all issued forth in one crowded, eager sentence.

"Great! I'll be right back!" Cooper hurried out from behind the bar and disappeared into the foyer.

David glanced at Maiden and smiled. She was twisting her legs back and forth on the velour stool as she tapped her fingertips excitedly on the top of the bar.

"You having fun, baby?" he asked fondly.

"It's exciting!" she whispered happily. "Don't you want to see the secret cellar?"

"Honestly, all I want right now is to give you a very thorough tour of the backseat of my car," he said candidly and then grinned at her barely muffled laughter. "But a secret cellar will have to do, assuming it exists."

Before she could hope to form a reply, Cooper hurried back in with a long piece of rolled up paper. He resumed his spot behind the bar and unrolled it in front of them. David helped him pin down the corners with salt and pepper shakers while Maiden silently pulled her map out of her pocket.

"What's that?" Cooper asked as she unfolded it and laid it across the blueprint.

"A map," she murmured as she looked the plan over carefully. "Possibly a very important map."

The Old Chateau was hardly tiny, but the new hotel that had been built on its rotting bones was definitely larger. She looked at the original rendering of the staircase. The scale wasn't exact, but it looked feasible that if the first entrance was under the staircase, the other might well be in the new kitchen.

She glanced up to find Cooper studying the map closely. He met her gaze and lifted his brows a fraction.

"Is that what I really, really hope it is?" he asked seriously.

"Might be." She nodded once.

"Under the stairs, you think?" He didn't look away and scarcely blinked.

"Yeah, that's my guess," she said. "I'd like to check it out but Eilers is still in hospital..."

"No, he's not, he was released this morning. He's here somewhere." Cooper glanced around furtively, as if expecting the man in question to leap out of one of the artificial palm trees tucked around the room. "I'll go see if I can get permission."

He slipped out of the room once more but this time Maiden and David, after grabbing the map, followed as far as the foyer. They went to the staircase and started looking it over. There was certainly enough room for a secret door under the highly polished steps.

Maiden was running a hand over the dark blue paint but glanced up when they heard footsteps. Cooper walked in from the long hallway that led to the kitchen. He was carrying a large flashlight and a hammer and had a very intent look on his face.

"What's this?" Maiden asked cautiously as he handed David the flashlight and gripped the hammer tightly.

"Permission," Cooper said with a wink. He then stood beside her, studying the wall closely. "So, just start anywhere, you think?"

"We can't take liberties with someone else's property," David said firmly, holding up a hand to stop him.

"Of course not." Cooper met his gaze even as he swung the hammer out and punched it clear through the wall. "Oops."

Maiden put a hand over her mouth to hide her smile while Cooper flailed the hammer around needlessly as he pulled it free, widening the hole in the process. Maiden deliberately avoided looking at David as she pulled out her phone and switched on the flashlight.

"Let's just have a look at the damage," she said, ignoring David's exasperated muttering behind her. "Oh, interesting."

"What is it?" Cooper crowded in beside her.

"It's a room...," Maiden eased back to let him have a better look, "but it's empty."

"We'll see." Cooper pulled a face and smashed out a larger hole.

"You both need to stop and ask Eilers for permission!" David said a bit louder.

"I haven't touched anything!" Maiden protested, giving him a dismayed look.

"I'll apologize to the old man if we're wrong," Cooper said placatingly. "And I'll patch the wall, relax."

"You'll apologize to the old man for what?" Eilers demanded as he descended the stairs and eyed them all suspiciously; Maddie was hovering uncertainly behind him.

David muttered under his breath and Cooper winced. Maiden, however, smiled brightly up at him and motioned for him to join them.

"Mr. Eilers! Hurry up!" she said eagerly. "We may have found something that gives someone else a better motive than yours!"

She noticed but chose to ignore David's attempt to swallow his amusement at her audacious response to getting caught. She kept smiling as Eilers clambered down the rest of the stairs and scowled furiously.

"What happened to my wall?" Eilers demanded.

"Accident," Cooper said immediately.

"It was not." Maiden rolled her eyes and draped her hands on her hips. "Mr. Eilers, I said I'd look into things and try to help you."

David started to laugh but pressed his lips together and glanced away when she shot him a warning glare.

"And in doing so," she continued with a long-suffering sigh, "I think we may have found out why Mercier was suddenly so interested in your company. But we need more information, can we please keep looking?"

"Well since you're halfway through doing it anyway," he grumbled. "Go ahead, but you'd better find something good."

"Thanks." Cooper grinned and started smashing away at the drywall again.

Everyone stood back and watched as Cooper opened up a hole big enough to step through. He got his flashlight back from David and followed Maiden as she climbed through without waiting.

She swept her phone-light around the tight little nook, revealing the dark stones of the original structure. The area was lit up much brighter as Cooper joined her with his larger light.

At first glance there appeared to be nothing. The floor was solid and the wall was intact, not so much as a crack in any of the stones. Maiden was starting to wonder if she'd got it wrong when she noticed a subtle difference in part of the wall.

"Hey, Cooper." She knelt before the wall and beckoned him over. "Could you shine the light over here please?"

"Sure, sweetie," he said as he did so. "What have you found?"

"Do you see how the mortar around these stones is thinner than the rest?" she ran a fingertip along one of the narrow lines, "The color is slightly different too."

"It is," Cooper breathed as he studied the wall. "You think they hid the entrance by walling it up?"

"I hope so." She gave him a smiling look. "Otherwise we ruined a perfectly good wall for nothing."

"I'm sure it's fine." He patted her shoulder reassuringly as he stood. "I'll get more tools; wait for me."

When Cooper slipped back out into the foyer, David ducked inside and crouched next to her. Maiden glanced over at him and winked. He smiled very briefly before edging closer and lowering his voice.

"What are you going to do if this turns out to be a dead end?" he whispered.

"Try somewhere else." She shrugged. "But I think this will work."

They both glanced back when they heard Eilers' indistinct grumbling. Maiden smiled faintly as Cooper waved the irritable man away and hurried back inside with an old metal toolbox.

"Now, I need…aha!" he whispered to himself as he dug through. "Hammer and chisel. All right, let's see what we can find."

Cooper knelt before the suspicious bit of wall and began chipping away. The mortar crumbled easily under his chisel, it was barely more than a shallow façade. With remarkably little effort the stones started to shift.

Maiden bit her lip and held her breath for a moment as she and David helped to pull the stones away and stack them off to the side. Within minutes they found themselves kneeling in front of a narrow doorway with an old stone staircase behind it.

"Claudia Arnaud's secret cellar!" Cooper whispered ecstatically. "It does exist! I knew it!"

"Let's not get ahead of ourselves," David cautioned as he stood and took Cooper's flashlight. "Stay close and keep quiet until we know what we're dealing with."

David walked carefully through the doorway, shining the light over the stairs and down a narrow hallway beyond them. Maiden pulled the map out of her pocket and handed it to him; she didn't need it personally and knew they'd soon be confronted with two different paths.

The one to their left would lead to the room that had been marked with an X. She glanced around as they made their way cautiously through the narrow passage. The walls were damp and the air was cold and dank. It all looked positively ancient but she was increasingly certain that someone had been there comparatively recently.

They turned left and soon came to another two hallways. Maiden was already heading towards the first when David glanced up from the map and pulled a face.

"Wait up, Harlow," he said seriously as he grasped her arm and hauled her back gently. "Keep in mind that there are murderers on the loose and potentially another secret entrance to this place."

She compromised by grabbing his hand and dragging him behind her as she wove through the chilly tunnel. There was only one room at the end of the passage, the one that was marked on the map.

Maiden, David and Cooper stepped inside and looked around at a very empty room. David cleared his throat; the sound reverberated throughout the disappointingly bare space. Cooper edged forward and started slowly sweeping his flashlight around.

"Let's not panic. Nobody goes to the trouble of sealing off a secret cellar if it's empty," he said patiently.

"You've obviously known more people that have secret cellars than I have," David murmured under his breath.

Maiden ignored them both and shifted her attention to the floor. Pirates buried their treasure, maybe other crooks did too. The floor looked like it was made of some kind of flagstone, she kicked away the dirt and debris that was scattered over it. There were gaps between the stones in the center that hadn't been completely filled like the ones closer to the walls.

"I wonder..." Maiden chewed at her bottom lip and tapped her foot on the center-most slab of rock. "Does this spot sound a little more hollow underneath?"

"Not really," David said with a tiny shake of his head.

"Can we check anyway?" she asked hopefully.

Cooper pulled the chisel from his pocket and wedged it between two of the stones. It took a bit of prying before it finally lifted but he and David were able to slide their fingers beneath and lift the flat stone out of the way.

They all gasped when they saw the lid of a large metal box nestled in the dirt beneath. David glanced up at Maiden briefly before turning back to the box. He and Cooper used their hands to clear away the dirt from around the edges. He then started feeling around for any sort of a latch.

"I know I'm a child," Maiden whispered as she bounced on her heels, "but I really hope it's full of gold coins and cutlasses and pe-glegs!"

David lifted the lid and laid it aside. Cooper aimed his light at the contents. There was no sign of ancient treasure, or ancient anything. She frowned and stopped bouncing. So much for pirate myths.

"Poop," Maiden grumbled. "It's just cash and guns."

"There's some jewelry too," Cooper offered helpfully, pointing to what looked like a diamond bracelet. "It's still swag of some description."

"This is actually huge," David breathed.

He patted down every pocket until he found a pair of surgical gloves in the depths of his jacket that looked like they'd been there for a while. Maiden silently acknowledged that some aspects of dating a cop were going to be weird.

David pulled on the gloves and carefully dug beneath a few bundles of money and pulled out a disappointingly modern document holder.

"James Dugan embezzled a huge amount of money from an insurance company that he'd been ostensibly consulting for," he explained. "The team that investigated him never found the missing money and couldn't make the charges stick."

"Then why was he arrested?" Maiden asked.

"They caught him out on some lesser charges thanks to an anonymous informant. He still didn't get anywhere near the sentencing he deserves," he said as he peeked inside and smiled faintly. "Bingo. Maybe we can do something about that now."

"So, if Ulysses Mercier was the informant, that means he worked with Dugan," Maiden said. "And he possibly would have known that the money and the evidence was hidden here."

"And that's why he got so hotted up about taking over the hotel!" Cooper snapped his fingers and smiled. "He never cared about the company, he wanted full access to the Old Chateau! But who killed him?"

"Hard to say." David shook his head slightly and pulled out his phone.

"It could've been Sean Dowling." Maiden pulled a face even as she said it. "If he was working for Dugan, that's probably who sent him the original map. But I don't know...it doesn't feel right."

"We'll worry about that once we catch the last two members of the Highland Hounds," David said. "They knew about Dugan, and his stash down here, they might know more about what exactly happened to Mercier."

Maiden grunted with little enthusiasm, David gave her a look and a wink. Cooper was lost in his own thoughts. He scratched his chin thoughtfully.

"The Highland Hounds, you say? A couple of Scottish guys did come by a week or so ago," he said as he thought back. "They asked about the building's history, so I told them the pirate story...but they didn't ask about a basement or anything like Maiden did."

"Maybe because they already knew it existed. They may have just wanted a clue about what they could find here," Maiden suggested.

"I'll ask when I find them." David shrugged calmly. "Let's go, I'll call this in."

"Aren't we going to check out the rest of the cellar?" Cooper asked with a tinge of whining in his tone.

"The police will," David said wryly. "And no sulking, I didn't have to let you come this far. This is serious business but relax, the cellar will still be here after the case is wrapped up."

"Well..." he almost stamped his foot as he looked around for some excuse to linger, "you aren't going to leave this stuff unguarded, are you? Can I at least stay until you come back?"

"No," David said.

"Come on!" Cooper frowned and threw up his hands in exasperation. "I've been studying this place for twenty years and this is the first time I've set foot in the secret cellar! Can I have five more minutes to just look at it?"

"I'll wait with him," Maiden laughed softly. "You won't be long anyway, will you?"

"Fine." David rolled his eyes and then fixed them both with a stern look. "Three minutes and touch *nothing*."

***

David stepped back into the brighter light and fresher air of the foyer. He was already dialing the station and proceeded to tell Nancy to send over a team of officers and forensics. He glanced up to see Eilers and Maddie still hovering.

"Did you find anything?" the man asked dubiously.

"Potentially, yes," David allowed. "Your cooperation earlier is appreciated, Mr. Eilers, and officially noted."

"What does that mean?" Eilers frowned.

"It means you're not under arrest, for now." David said in a cautioning tone. "But I don't appreciate the time you wasted with that coffee stunt. Don't try to trick me again, it won't work out well for you."

Maddie gasped at the suggestion and turned to a slightly reddened Eilers. He slid his gaze away and straightened his tie.

"I don't know what you're talking about," he said stubbornly. "But I'm certainly glad to go on cooperating however I can."

"Glad to hear it, Mr. Eilers." David smiled faintly and was heading back towards the cellar when they heard rapid footsteps.

"Ms. Norris!"

"Joe?" Maddie frowned at the young kitchen hand as he ran down the hallway towards them. "What's going on?"

"I don't know!" He skidded to a halt in front of them and pointed back in the direction he'd come from. "I just went into the pantry and there's a big hole knocked in the rear wall!"

David's heart started pounding. The other entrance; Maiden had said it was probably somewhere in the kitchen. And there were only two people that would be likely to have found it. He ran back into the cellar.

Chapter Twenty-Seven

"Hey Cooper," Maiden said when they were alone, "can I ask you something?"

"Sure, sweetie." He said as he looked around the old room in quiet awe.

"Graham told me that you had a pretty bad fight with Ulysses Mercier...is that true?"

"I've never had a *good* fight." He set his flashlight off to the side, letting it shine straight up at the ceiling.

"What was it about?" She quirked a brow when he knelt beside the box again. "Remember not to touch anything."

"I know, I know," he sighed and then a slow smile spread over his face as he looked at the two guns laying on top of the money. "This is like 1920's mobster stuff; do you know much about guns?"

"Point and shoot." She shrugged. "Do you?"

"Only the really old stuff," he admitted. "I wish these were muskets or something. What were we talking about? Oh yeah, the Mercier thing. After I realized how stupid I'd been about helping Eilers buy this place I tried to sort of right the wrong a bit. Tipped off the other history nuts about Eilers' loopholes. That's what led to all the complaints and newspaper articles."

"Okay, I guess I understand that," she murmured. "What's it got to do with Mercier?"

"He found out about it, or just suspected it and claimed to know for a fact." Cooper hovered a finger over the handle of one of the guns. "Said he'd go straight to Eilers if I didn't help him get into his office."

"What did you do?" Maiden eased back slightly as his fascinated gaze remained on the guns.

"Do?" He glanced up at her and blinked. "Nothing, I told him to do his own dirty work. Really, being fired for working against Eilers might have actually improved my reputation a little."

"Graham said you were bitterly angry," she said as neutrally as she could.

"Pardon me for using the f-word," he gave her a patient look, "but Graham Harper is a *fibber*. I don't get bitterly angry, Maiden."

"Yeah, I found it unlikely," she said with a smile.

Cooper winked at her and turned back to the box of loot. Maiden watched him for a moment but then a wisp of a memory floated up to the surface. It was something about the hotel's grand opening party; she had a sinking feeling that she'd made a dangerous assumption.

A moment later she heard footsteps approaching. Maiden assumed it was David until she heard accompanying whispers. Whispers with a very distinct accent. Her stomach sank and her heart pounded, it was Braden and Arran, it had to be.

She looked at Cooper and put her finger to her lips, he just nodded. She reached into the box and grabbed one of the old guns, then she turned to the doorway and waited.

Braden and Arran turned the corner and stopped in their tracks when they saw them. Maiden held up her phone and swept the light over them, they both carried heavy flashlights. She noticed the look they exchanged between them and the way Braden tighten his grip on the heavy steel handle.

"So, you finally found the door," she said in what she hoped sounded like a confident voice, she wasn't sure where David was or when he'd get back.

Braden and Arran looked haggard, desperate and deeply annoyed to find that someone had beaten them to the treasure. They all glanced briefly at the box in the floor. Braden edged closer but Maiden pointed the old gun at him. He and Arran both stopped when their lights glinted off the cold metal.

"Now what are you planning to do with that, lass?" Braden's smile was arrogantly confident.

"Stop you from committing yet another murder," she replied.

"Do you even know how to use it?" he chuckled.

She held his gaze steadily as she cocked it and trained it at his chest. "Yeah."

"Let's just relax, shall we?" Arran said soothingly as he held up his free hand. His voice was rich and smooth and terrifying. "There's no need to be frightened, Miss Harlow. We only want the box, we don't want any more trouble."

"I doubt that," she replied stonily. "You've already killed two friends, why would you spare any witnesses?"

"That's not true," Arran insisted. "We haven't hurt anyone."

"That's a relief," she said sardonically. "Out of curiosity, were you planning to pick up where Sean left off or try to blackmail his boss?"

"You know a fair bit about our business, it seems," Arran said coolly.

"So do the police," she said. Both men smiled smugly.

"I don't think so, lass. But nice try." Braden sounded amused. "We're a couple of steps ahead of them."

"You're not," Cooper said as he grabbed the other gun. "The head of the local force was with us when we found this; he's sending for backup right now."

"How petrifying," Arran mocked. "We'd better hurry then."

"Too late for that, *lads*," Maiden retorted. "You can't go around killing people and then just walk away."

"We haven't killed anyone," Arran said

"We'll see what the police think about that." Maiden glared at him.

"No, lass. We won't," Braden said grimly. "We've come a bit too far for that."

He and Arran exchanged a look and a brief nod before turning off their flashlights. Maiden tensed as almost all the light was extinguished in an instant. She saw both men lunge towards her. She pulled the trigger.

***

David was almost back at the secret chamber when the light spilling from the doorway vanished and a gunshot rang out. He ran harder as he heard panicked and angry shouts. All he could think was that Maiden was in there, and someone had fired a shot.

"Police! Don't move!" David barked out as he drew his gun and peered into the darkness.

A moment later another light flicked on as Cooper pointed a large flashlight at the scene. The light revealed Braden Blair lying still on the ground next to Arran, who was clutching his shoulder and groaning in pain. David glanced from them to Maiden.

She was taking deep breaths as she stood holding a gun. She glanced at David and smiled weakly.

"Hey," she said quietly. "Did you call for backup?"

"Yeah, I did. What happened?" He asked carefully as he stepped inside.

"Oh, Braden and Arran surprised us and charged at me," she said shakily. "I sort of...shot him."

"And then I clocked the other guy." Cooper held up the gun he was holding. "I didn't want to shoot and risk hitting Maiden in the dark."

"Right, good thinking." David glanced at him briefly and then back at Maiden. "Are you okay?"

She nodded jerkily and looked down at the gun she was holding. She lifted her big eyes back to his.

"I hope you didn't need any fingerprints off these," she said apologetically.

"We'll manage." He almost smiled but was still too tense to let it fully emerge.

Arran's pained groan dragged his mind back to the matter at hand. He flicked him a glance as he walked over and gently reclaimed the gun from Maiden.

"Nice of you to join us at last, Campbell," he said dryly. "Don't worry, plenty of help is on the way."

***

Soon thereafter the hotel felt full of police. The two remaining members of the Highland Hounds were taken into custody and both entrances to the cellar were placed under guard.

As thrilled as Maiden had been to find the secret treasure trove, she was equally happy to leave it now. She was grateful to be alive and safe and more than a little rattled at having actually shot someone.

She was deeply relieved that she hadn't killed him, even in self-defense, it wasn't something she wanted stuck in her mind forever.

Maiden, David and Cooper emerged from the doorway under the stairs and walked a bit numbly into the foyer. She knew David was upset about her close call; she saw the way his eyes kept darting to her as if he was afraid she'd explode if he left her on her own again.

She smiled faintly at him but her expression sobered when she saw Eilers and Maddie standing nearby. She looked at Maddie and thought what a normal and lovely person she seemed to be. Then she thought about what had just happened, how she herself had just been driven to shoot someone, something she never thought she'd ever be capable of doing.

Circumstances. Sometimes that made all the difference. The difference between life and death. She felt goosebumps raise up over her entire body.

She glanced over as Eilers rubbed his hands together and gave David an eager look. David looked tolerant but hardly obliging.

"So is that everything settled now?" he asked hopefully. "You arrested the killers?"

"Some of them," Maiden said uneasily, her eyes were still on Maddie. "Hey, Maddie."

"Yes?" She turned to her.

"You said you were in the kitchen the night Mercier was killed, right?" Maiden watched her closely.

"Yes, I was." She frowned warily and shook her head. "So?"

"Anybody see you?"

David looked at Maiden sharply, but she kept her gaze fixed on the manager. Maddie had paled slightly; she was silent for just a moment too long before she answered.

"Joe was with me." She cleared her throat quietly. "We were doing some inventory checks in the pantry."

"He didn't see you the whole evening," Maiden replied. "He was really busy, but he was there when Mr. Eilers came and told you he'd found the body."

"What are you getting at?" Maddie scowled and rested her hands on her hips. "I was downstairs working that night. You have no reason to be questioning me like this, I don't care who your parents are, I won't be harassed or insulted!"

"You had a bad marriage, didn't you?" Maiden continued softly. "That must have been so difficult for you...What was your ex-husband's name?"

"Dan Norris," Maddie replied after a slight pause.

"He treated you badly, didn't he?" She smiled gently.

"Why are you asking me that?" Her tone was guarded and she was getting visibly upset.

"I'm trying to understand you better," Maiden admitted; beside her David just looked between them but didn't interfere. "I think you're carrying a lot of old scars around."

"Maybe I am," Maddie admitted. "So are a lot of people. So what?"

"What was your first husband's name?" Her voice was relentlessly calm. Eilers was frowning and started to speak up but Maiden held up a hand to stop him.

"I didn't—" Maddie's eyes widened and she shook her head even as she stepped back a few paces.

"You did," Maiden interrupted. "Marriage and divorce certificates are considered part of the public record, by the way. It's not as hard as you might think to access the information."

It was a partial bluff, the records were surprisingly accessible but she hadn't looked them up. The quietly horrified expression on Maddie's face confirmed her suspicions though. David arched a brow but said nothing as he also took in Maddie's reaction.

Eilers looked confused as he turned to Maddie and Cooper was trying to watch everyone as he started piecing it together too.

"I saw you the night of the grand opening, just after the dust up between Eilers and Mercier. I saw you staring at someone through the doorway. I wrongly assumed that it was Eilers, but it wasn't. You were looking at Mercier," she said. Maddie shook her head but Maiden persisted. "When we spoke in your office, I noticed how professional you were with the men you worked with, even if you'd known them for years."

"So what?" Maddie said in exasperation. "What's so terrible about it?"

"You say 'Mr. Eilers' and 'Mr. Harper'." Maiden smiled faintly. "But when we talked about Mercier, you called him 'Ulysses'. You did know him and you had a very different relationship with him. I saw the expression on your face when you looked at him that night. You saw your ex-husband, the man that probably treated you like dirt, barging in and causing trouble. That must have been infuriating."

"No!" Maddie gasped. "I didn't even know him!"

"Yes, you did." Maiden nodded. "Mercier was married three times. He was a cruel and selfish man that liked to win and threw people away when he was done with them. Isn't that true, Mr. Eilers?"

"Yeah, it's true," Eilers said slowly. "But I don't know who his wives were...Maddie?"

Maddie shifted her weight from one foot to the other and shook her head. David folded his arms over his chest and regarded her watchfully.

"I can find out in a matter of minutes, Ms. Norris," he said. "Do you want to just tell me yourself?"

Maddie stared down at her hands, they were shaking. She squeezed her eyes shut and hugged herself.

"I was twenty-two when we got married," she said quietly. "He was almost forty. He'd been married once already and dropped her when he saw something he liked better. I didn't know that at the time, of course. I found out a lot of things when it was too late. He used me for a couple of years and then walked away. But he was smart and I was young and naïve; I had to start again from scratch."

"That would have been so hard," Maiden said gently. "Did he recognize you straight away?"

"No," Maddie scoffed and folded her arms in disgust. "I was a redhead back then, and he never paid much attention to anything he didn't care about. He certainly never cared about me."

"What happened that night, Maddie?" She tried to keep her tone steady and understanding.

"I heard noises coming from Mr. Eilers office next door. I found Ulysses digging through the filing cabinet," she murmured. "I told him to leave it alone and get out or I'd call the police. That's when he recognized me. He laughed; he thought it was so funny. He told me that he was going to take everything from Mr. Eilers, the building, the business...everything."

"So, what did you say?" David asked.

"That he'd better get out or I really would call the police." Maddie gave a humorless laugh. "He just started gloating like he'd already won and said he'd make sure I was the first employee to go. I got really mad; he'd ruined me once before, he wasn't going to do it again."

"Did you kill him?" David asked gently.

"Not on purpose." Maddie's eyes filled with tears. "Like I said, I was really mad. I told him he was a pathetic old man that had to steal from others because he wasn't good enough to build anything of his own. He started getting angry but I didn't care, he was a horrible man and I was tired of cowering away from him. I told him exactly what I thought of him and how disgusting he was, how terrible he'd been in bed. Everything."

Maddie was staring off at nothing in particular, her eyes were distant and her voice was numb. Maiden and David exchanged a look. David eased slightly closer but they both stilled when Maddie started talking again.

"He used to hit me sometimes, apparently he thought he still could." She sniffled. "He shoved me really hard and I fell near the fireplace. He was still coming at me...I grabbed the poker...yeah. After that I panicked, I knew no one would believe that I was trying to protect myself. No one ever believed me when we were married. So I wiped my fingerprints off the poker and slipped outside. I went to the kitchen and pretended that's where I'd been the whole time."

"Sounds like self-defense to me. I understand, Maddie, I just shot someone for similar reasons." Maiden smiled. "Don't assume that no one will listen now."

Maddie put a hand to her face, she shook as she started to quietly cry. David approached and touched a hand to her shoulder.

"Come on," he said nicely enough. "We'll take you to the station and you can tell your story. I promise we'll listen. Do you have a lawyer?"

"Yes, she does."

They all glanced at Eilers; he was watching Maddie with a kind expression.

"I'll call mine right now," he said as he pulled out his phone. "And I'll go with her to the station."

"Thank you, Mr. Eilers." Maddie shook her head uncertainly. "But—"

"You could have told me from the start, Maddie." He smiled faintly. "I would've always helped you. I know what Ulysses was and I believe every word you've said. Let's go, we'll see what we can do."

"I'll arrange someone to take her in," David whispered to Maiden. "I'll be right back."

Maiden watched somberly as David led Maddie outside with Eilers hovering close behind. A part of her had hated exposing the poor woman but there was still a chance that Eilers could have been blamed for the killing.

"You're a smart little cookie, aren't you?" Cooper stood beside her and gave her a nudge with his elbow.

"Hmm? Oh." Maiden smiled a little and shook her head. "I just noticed a few things, that's all."

"Yeah right!" he chuckled. "Poor old Mads. When did you figure out it was her?"

"About three minutes ago," Maiden admitted. "Something about her had me wondering for a while but it wasn't until I really felt the motivation of self-defense that I started to look at Mercier's death differently. It wasn't murder at all."

"Well, you did good." Cooper gave her an approving nod. "You caught three killers and found an ancient pirate's refuge. You'll make the Golden Glen Historical Association's monthly newsletter for this."

"Please, I can't handle that level of publicity." She grinned. "Just tell them the police sorted it all out."

"History demands the truth be told, Maiden." He winked and sauntered away. "I'll see you again sometime, sweetie."

Maiden smiled as he disappeared back into the bar. She hoped he was exaggerating but assured herself that not that many people were likely to read their newsletter anyway. Hopefully.

David walked back in a moment later and pulled her back into the hidden room under the stairs without a word. He dragged her into his arms and hugged her tightly and wordlessly for a long moment.

"Everything okay?" she asked gently as she slid her arms around his neck.

"You're having a few too many close calls, baby," he said very quietly.

"This one wasn't really my fault," she pointed out as he loosened his hold enough for her to lean back a bit and look up at him.

"*Most of them* haven't been your fault," he sighed warily. "That doesn't make it any easier to deal with."

She decided a strategic change of subject was in order.

"Who do you think killed Charles Brown?" she asked, locking her clear gaze on his.

David tried valiantly not to smile. Her eyes widened furiously as she started to realize that he knew more than he'd shared with her.

"Who do *you* think did it?" he asked mildly and wrapped his arms more fully around her when she tried to push him away. "Come on, let's hear your theory."

"You know who did it!" She scowled at him. "How long have you known?!"

"It doesn't matter." He stroked her hair soothingly. "Look, you don't have to tell me your guess if you're afraid you're wrong."

"Stop petting me, I'm not a cat!" She knew she sounded sulky. "Mercier killed him."

"How do you figure that?" David's smile grew and his hold on her tightened.

"I just do," she sniffed, still annoyed that he'd held back so much. "How did you work it out?"

"We found the murder weapon in Mercier's hotel room the day after he was killed," he admitted. "It looks like Mercier caught Brown snooping around the hotel and confronted him. He might've known that he and Dowling were on Dugan's payroll, and that there was only one reason they'd be in Golden Glen."

"So you think Mercier lured him to the Eastern Quarter and killed him?" Maiden chewed thoughtfully at her lip. "He may have met him outside, forced him to get in the backseat and then shot him. When he didn't find the map he went back to prowling around the hotel himself."

"That's what the available evidence suggests," he said modestly.

"You suck." She eyed him with a begrudging smirk.

"And you love it," David grinned and kissed her.

Chapter Twenty-Eight

Maiden had opted to take a taxi home and walked into Harlow House with a deep sense of gratitude. She was still alive, still had a wonderful boyfriend and there were no more killers on the loose. None that she felt responsible for catching at least.

She climbed the stairs to the family apartment and stood for a long moment in front of the door. There was still one more mystery to be solved and she was ready to get it done and over with. She took a deep breath and opened the door.

As she stepped inside her eyes zeroed in on her target. Gloria was in the kitchen drinking a glass of water. Maiden met her welcoming smile with a look of steely determination.

"Hey, angel." A look of worry dimmed Gloria's countenance. "Everything okay? You and David didn't fight again, did you?"

"No, Mom, nothing like that." She shook her head and gestured towards the kitchen table. "We need to talk."

"Okay," Gloria said uneasily as she came and settled into her usual chair. "What's happened?"

"We caught Mercier's killer," she told her.

"Was it Fred?" Gloria whispered, her eyes were wide and anxious.

"No!" Maiden said irately. "Did you actually think it was him all this time?!"

"No, no, no!" Gloria said a little too vehemently. "I'm just on edge that's all. So who did it?"

"The hotel manager, who also happened to be one of Mercier's ex-wives," Maiden sighed.

"So, who poisoned Fred?" Gloria's fearful expression was reborn.

"He did," Maiden replied flatly.

"What?" her soft brown eyes widened.

"I think the nutbar spiked his own coffee to try and convince the police that he was another victim so they wouldn't suspect him." Maiden rolled her eyes.

"Oh, does David know that?" She chewed at her lip.

"I didn't ask him, but yeah, I'm sure he does." Maiden shrugged. "There was too little poison in his system to be a real threat and he was very conveniently not alone when he took it. He was released pretty quick and went straight back to work."

"Oh." Gloria frowned faintly and stared off into the distance as she took that in. "That's...disappointin'."

Maiden looked at her mother and couldn't help seeing the truth of her words. Gloria's mouth was set in a displeased line and her forehead was creased as the ripe, sweet fruit of whatever hopes she may have nurtured shriveled into raisins of disillusionment. It was too much, it needed to stop.

"Mama," Maiden said after a moment.

"Yes, angel?"

"You love Dad, don't you?" she asked quietly.

"Of course I do!" Gloria sounded surprised at the question.

"Are you and Fred Eilers...having some kind of a thing?" She felt terrible for asking and couldn't even face her as she said it, but she had to know.

"Maiden, look at me." Gloria's kind smile was in her voice.

Maiden reluctantly turned to her and lifted her eyebrows questioningly. Gloria held her face gently between her hands.

"No, not ever," she said solemnly. "Harlows don't cheat, Maiden baby. Never forget that."

"No...we don't." Maiden smiled back and felt a lot of the pain and fear finally let go. An instant later she fixed her with an unyielding stare. "So what the heck *have* you been doing? Just tell me already!"

Gloria glanced heavenward as she released her daughter and sat back. She nodded and pushed to her feet.

"All right, I suppose this is as good a time as any." She walked back into the kitchen and pulled out a bottle of wine and four glasses. "Alfie! Vonny! Come and join us."

A moment later Von's bedroom door opened and she peered out. Maiden met her gaze and motioned for her to walk over. They both glanced towards the master suite as Alfie emerged and looked out at them.

"What's going on?" Vonny asked uneasily as she sat beside Maiden.

"We need to talk about somethin'," Gloria murmured and turned to her husband. "I think it's time, honey."

"Oh, okay." Alfie looked the situation over and inclined his head.

Gloria waited until Alfie came and sat at the head of the table and then took up her usual seat to his left. She motioned for him to speak when he slid her a questioning look. He cleared his throat loudly and turned to their daughters.

"So," Alfie folded his hands and sat up as tall as he could, which still left him the shortest of everyone assembled, "you've noticed that Gloria and I have been acting strangely...what you don't know is that we've been sneaking out and meeting with our accountant."

"And your lawyer," Maiden said. "And every boutique in town that carries fabric swatches."

"How'd you know that?" Gloria demanded with widened eyes.

"She just happens to know!" Vonny's cranky voice rose high enough to stop the topic from shifting. "It doesn't matter! Tell us what's going on right now or I'll throw this table out the window!"

"Please," Maiden tacked on politely.

"Fine. Honestly, you women get hysterical over nothing," Alfie sighed tolerantly but hurried to continue when Vonny half-stood and grasped the edge of the table. "We've also been talking to Bella, and we've come to an arrangement. She's agreed to invest in a new project that we've been considering since her wedding."

"You've been scheming for a couple of weeks with Aunt Bella and it's *still* a secret?" Maiden blinked at them.

"Ha! Nice one!" Alfie chuckled and snapped his fingers.

"What's the project?" Vonny looked less confused but more worried now.

"Riley Manor," Gloria said calmly. "We've bought it."

The room fell so deathly silent that Maiden was sure she heard one of the kittens fart. She and Vonny looked at each other and then back at their parents.

"You did what?" Maiden asked.

"We negotiated a very good price and, with Bella agreeing to bankroll the project," Gloria stacked her hands behind her glass, "we now own a mansion. What do you think?"

"What are you going to do with an old mansion?" Vonny breathed.

"*We*, all of us, are going to refurbish it and turn it into the most spectacular destination getaway in the state!" Gloria said enthusiastically. "This is a family endeavor, sweet babies. It's all of us. We didn't say anything before because we didn't want to get your hopes up and have it all fall through. Aren't you excited?"

"I guess so, but where did all of this come from?" Maiden shook her head slightly.

"It's something we kind of talked about since we first saw it, just before Bella's wedding," Alfie said. "What had started as a bit of chat over coffee in the mornings and before bed at night gradually gained momentum. We started thinking about how the place could be refurbished while preserving its heritage, and how to make it financially viable."

"Fred's offer to buy into his hotel sort of gave us the push we needed to really do somethin'," Gloria admitted. "We know Fred's pig-headed and immature when it comes to business. We weren't about to throw away the family's hard-earned money on a man that would spend it without thinkin' on the first thing that sparked his interest."

"Well, that's a relief," Maiden said cautiously. She couldn't help feeling a little worried that they may have done exactly that themselves.

"I called Bella and started the discussion. She was interested and certainly has the money to invest and help us get started. So, we set the wheels in motion," Gloria explained. "Harlow House is in a very good position financially, thanks in no small part to you girls and your knowhow. We've seen what you can do, and we think that we're all ready for a bigger challenge."

"It would be pretty cool to restore that old place." Vonny chewed at her thumbnail. "It's a great setting for weddings, but we could host anything there."

"Yeah, we really could," Maiden whispered to herself and then slid her parents a look. "Is that why you were talking about hiring staff to run the inn?"

"Yes." Alfie nodded. "As you would've noticed at Bella's wedding, the place needs a lot of work, it's going to take up a lot of our attention. But we can't neglect Harlow House, this is still our bread and butter."

"I suppose if we restored the ground floor a little better, it could be used for events fairly soon," Maiden mused. "I didn't take a close look at all the rooms, hopefully they won't be in too bad a shape."

"We've walked through the place." Gloria held up a hand and winced slightly. "There's a lot to be done."

"But that helped us to cut the price down quite a bit." Alfie chuckled and rubbed his hands together gleefully.

"Now, let's be clear from the start." Gloria interceded. "This is about family. We want you girls to have an equal share in all of it. We built Harlow House together, now we'll build Harlow *Manor* together too."

"Harlow Manor." Maiden smiled a little. "I like the sound of that."

Gloria looked absolutely giddy as she hopped up and ran to their room. As she started pulling out reams of magazines and bags of fabric samples they all started talking excitedly about what they ought to do first.

Maiden was reeling from the news. She'd gone from fearing her parents' marriage was on the rocks and their business was in the balance to owning a stake in a gorgeous, though dilapidated, mansion. Added to that was the capture of a few killers and a stroll through a historical marvel built by a French pirate; all things considered it had been a good day.

"Well," Gloria grinned, "we gotta celebrate! Go call David and Tony and have them come over for dinner, this will end up affectin' them too."

Maiden and Vonny both blushed slightly at that optimistic assumption but went to their rooms to do as she requested. Maiden could hear her mother rattling pots and pans as she got ready to cook up a feast. She smiled and shut her bedroom door.

Ruffian, never one to be left out of a secret, pushed through the cat-door and stared up at her with his big blue eyes. Maiden smiled at the kitten as she pulled out her phone and called David.

"Don't look at me like that," she murmured to the tiny cat. "You probably knew about this the whole time."

Ruffian yawned contritely and then ignored her as he hopped up on her bed and curled up. David answered as she was reaching over to ruffle his fur.

"Hey, I said I'd call *you*." His teasing smile was in his voice.

"I know, you'll get over it eventually," she laughed softly. "Can you come to my place for dinner tonight? It's important."

"Um..." he hesitated for a timeless moment.

"'Um' what, McAlister?" She quirked her left eyebrow. "Were you planning to work until midnight?"

"I'll be there in an hour." She could hear the grin in his voice.

"Thanks, David!" She bounced up and down. "I have something exciting and terrifying to tell you!"

"I'll be there in *half* an hour," he said wryly.

THANK YOU!

I can't express how much I appreciate everyone who takes the time to read my books. I've been a writer for as long as I can remember, and being able to share my stories with others is one of my very favorite things.

The inspiration for the various aspects of this book came, as they often do, from my memories and experiences. The Highland Hounds are a nod to a Scottish folk band that I was fortunate enough to see live a few times when they were touring Michigan. The Addison Theater is a fond wink to a quirky little establishment in a town called Ann Arbor. I have happy memories of both and, to my knowledge, they were never mixed up in any murders.

The Maiden Harlow series was my first foray into publishing any of my work. At the time I'm writing this, I'm five books in and loving the journey. I have a soft spot for cozy mysteries and these books take me to places that I love to be. I hope they do the same for you!

If you have enjoyed your time in Golden Glen, it would mean so much to me if you would please leave a review. Publishing is a tough business, particularly for indies like myself, and your reviews really do make a difference.

Thank you again, I hope you enjoyed Maiden's latest adventure!

Warm regards,

Camille

JOIN THE FUN!

Sign up to my mailing list to get your **free** copy of Blood and Money – A Maiden Harlow Mystery Prequel! It's a fun and twisty mini-mystery that's only available to subscribers!

My newsletters are geared towards book news, writing insights and sneak peeks of new content. If you're interested in hearing from me now and again as well as the **free** eBook, head over to my website, **www.camillesharpbooks.com**, where you can sign up!

ALSO BY CAMILLE SHARP

ABOUT CAMILLE SHARP

I've been writing for as long as I can remember, but my serious storytelling began in my teens. I dabble in mystery, fantasy and speculative fiction.

I write from many perspectives – heroine, hero, side characters and sometimes even villains. I like to write about heroines that are smart, sexy and basically kind. All the things I want to be if I ever decide to grow up.

While I weave romance into most of my books, I love to explore other relationships as well. Friendships and the various bonds within families are deeply important and I draw on my personal history for a lot of it.

I firmly believe that books are vital, that our imaginations need to be protected and cultivated, and that boredom has the potential to breed creativity.

One of the most useful lessons I've learned along the way is that if you're in a situation where you can't really conquer or surrender, stories give you the option to **escape**. Even if only for a few hours. I hope I can help transport you someplace you'd like to be.

Camille

www.ingramcontent.com/pod-product-compliance
Lightning Source LLC
Chambersburg PA
CBHW030555170726
48283CB00002B/341